Praise

S. W.

'Rich, intelligent and dark in equal measure, leaving you wrung out with terror. Historical fiction at its most sumptuous'

RORY CLEMENTS

'S. W. Perry is one of the best'

THE TIMES

'Wonderful! Beautiful writing'

GILES KRISTIAN

'A rattling good read'

WILLIAM RYAN

'Dramatic and colourful'

SUNDAY TIMES

'No one is better than S. W. Perry at leading us through the squalid streets of London in the sixteenth century'

ANDREW SWANSTON

'The writing is of such a quality, the characters so engaging and the setting so persuasive… S. W. Perry's ingeniously plotted novels have become my favourite historical crime series'

S. G. MACLEAN

'A compassionate story, skilfully told'

DAILY EXPRESS

Also by S. W. Perry

The Jackdaw series

The Angel's Mark
The Serpent's Mark
The Saracen's Mark
The Heretic's Mark
The Rebel's Mark
The Sinner's Mark

S.W. PERRY

BERLIN DUET

Published in hardback in Great Britain in 2024 by
Corvus, an imprint of Atlantic Books Ltd

10 9 8 7 6 5 4 3 2 1

A CIP catalogue record for this book is available from the British Library.

Hardback ISBN: 978 1 80546 061 9
Trade Paperback ISBN: 978 1 80546 257 6
E-book ISBN: 978 1 80546 062 6

Printed and bound by CPI (UK) Ltd, Croydon CR0 4YY

Corvus
An imprint of Atlantic Books Ltd
Ormond House
26–27 Boswell Street
London
WC1N 3JZ

www.atlantic-books.co.uk

For Jane

BERLIN DUET

PART ONE

Running out of time

One

11 November 1942
Languedoc-Roussillon, Vichy France

Dismounting half a mile short of the rendezvous, Harry Taverner began to wheel his bicycle up the track that led into the hills above the village. The late autumn sky was bright and clear and as the path steepened, the view offered itself to him. Ahead, the Corbières rose in folds of arid scrub, dotted with olive trees and rocky defiles. To his right was the sea, flecked with white foam; at his back, the snow-capped Pyrénées. An almost perfect world, he thought. Certainly too perfect to be at war.

To ease the climb and to calm his nerves he sang the jaunty '*Paris Sera Toujours Paris*' that had been popular before the city fell. And because there was no one to hear him, he sang the lyrics softly but in English – his own little act of defiance against an imagined chorus of marching jackboots. 'Paris will always be Paris… despite the deep darkness, its brilliance cannot be darkened… Paris will always be Paris!'

His destination was a dilapidated *capitelle*, a shepherd's shelter of dry stone with a missing roof. From there you could look down to the village, which lay in a narrow col between this hill and the one to the north, where a ruined castle stood.

Harry had rejected the castle as a rendezvous because it was favoured by courting couples – which he and Anna Cantrell had long ago assured each other they were most definitely *not*. Not in Paris. Not in Berlin. Not in Vienna. Not now, not ever. The world could wait until it turned to dust and nobody bothered with love any more, because Harry Taverner and Anna Cantrell had a war to win. Besides, the gendarmes in Narbonne were in the habit of raiding the place, searching for contraband wine the village hadn't already sent to Paris for German consumption.

By the time Harry reached the crest he was sweating heavily inside his coat. He propped the cycle against the crumbling stone wall of the *capitelle* and glanced at his watch. He was half an hour early.

Dipping into his pannier pack, he retrieved a canvas binocular case and an apple. Squatting down amongst the clumps of wild thyme, he set the apple between his feet. With his hands free he removed the Air Ministry field glasses from their stowage, put them to his eyes and adjusted the focus. Then he began to study the scene in the col below – to pass the time as much as for security – breaking off every now and then for a bite of the apple.

Harry Taverner had taken the coastal road north from Perpignan in slow time because a speeding cyclist drew attention anywhere. Once it wouldn't have mattered: since the fall of France, two and a half years before, the Germans had left the *Zone Libre*, the unoccupied sector run by the puppet government in Vichy, pretty much to its own devices. And while the gendarmerie was happy to do the Nazis' dirty work for them, Harry was confident his name was not to be found on any list in the Gestapo's headquarters on the Avenue Foch in Paris.

But, three days ago, everything had changed. An Allied army had landed in French North Africa. Now the Germans had responded by invading Vichy France. Since crossing the Spanish border, Harry had passed a steady stream of frightened people heading south. Whenever his gaze met theirs, he saw the same taut expressions, the same anxious eyes he'd seen in 1940 when France had fallen. Some travelled on foot, others in donkey carts, on horseback, or even in motorcars, though God alone knew where they'd found the petrol. He'd seen men in the suits they wore to Sunday Mass, feigning cheerfulness for the sake of nervous wives and children. He'd seen the elderly hiding their fear behind a brittle stoicism, while they wondered if they'd live long enough to see home again.

It must be like this after an earthquake, he thought.

If any of them had wondered why a young man on a bicycle was heading in the opposite direction, they were too preoccupied to call out and enquire. They must surely have recognized him as a foreigner. Tall, long-limbed and with a grace that bordered on the balletic, a loose fringe of flaxen hair habitually falling over the right temple at inappropriate moments but otherwise cut high around the ears and nape, Harry had no need to call out in his well-modulated voice, 'I say, old chap, what a *dreadfully* rum do', to identify his Anglo-Saxon origins. He might as well have carried a tag tied to his lapel that read: *If found, please return to the green and pleasant shires of England.*

He even had a dimple in the centre of his otherwise strong chin – put there, so his mother told him when he was ten, to remind him that God gives blemishes just as He gives perfections: to see what people's characters will make of them. At prep school, being by nature a solitary boy with an imagination, he'd told his classmates it was a scar inflicted in Australia by Ned Kelly's outlaws, who'd shot him with a pearl-handled revolver. They had believed him without question, until the maths master, Mr

Foreman, on learning of his preposterous claim, had slippered Harry into confession and repentance. It had been his first lesson in the art of the covert: even a single crack in your cover makes it no cover at all.

Like many an English prep-school teacher of that era, Mr Foreman could have taught the Nazis a thing or two, Harry reckoned with a wry smile. But to give him his due, were it not for his appetite for punishing schoolboy sins, Harry might never have perfected the skill of lying through his teeth while maintaining a straight face.

Take as evidence his presence there today. Although his French was good, it was nowhere near good enough to support the *Carte d'Identité de Français* he carried. To help him out, the forgers in London had included amongst the thirteen digits on its front cover that recorded his civil status (sex, place and date of birth) two that also identified him as foreign-born. On the inside page, the box recording his place of birth stated *Île de Guernesey*.

The island of Guernsey – British but occupied – with a centuries-long connection with France, would account for the English-accented French. And if all else failed, as a last resort, he carried in the pack strapped to the pannier of his cycle a rolled-up dark blue blouse. It bore the insignia of an RAF wireless operator/air-gunner. If the Vichy police caught him and sent him to Paris for the Gestapo to gnaw over, he'd claim to be a downed flier. With a bit of luck, he'd end up in a Stalag.

The alternative didn't bear thinking about.

In London's ideal world, Harry would never have been their pick for Anna Cantrell's case officer. Certainly not as her courier. The Secret Intelligence Service, MI6, would have picked a native-born Frenchman, or a Spaniard antithetical to the fascists. But

Anna was *his*. Anna Cantrell – *la photojournaliste Américaine* – was his star.

Harry had recruited her in Berlin before the war. Born to an American mother and an English father, her US passport was her protection. It gave her the freedom to live unmolested in Vichy France, because Pétain's regime had not yet declared war on America. But that protection had vanished two days ago, when the first German Panzer rolled across Vichy's border.

It was time for Anna to get out. And Harry was on his way to deliver the news in person.

'What about a radio?' Anna had once suggested to him over a cognac in an almost empty bar in Port Leucate. Harry had almost had a coronary on the spot. 'Out of the question!' he'd told her in a harsh whisper. Wireless sets were as precious as gold dust. Most were earmarked for the networks in the occupied zone. Besides, the Gestapo monitored the ether for suspicious transmissions. And they weren't listening to Tommy Handley on *It's That Man Again*. They could triangulate the approximate location of a sender in minutes.

And so Harry had appointed himself to the post of His Britannic Majesty's secret ambassador to the court of Queen Anna. With a little help from the British consulate in neutral Spain, and favourable-minded officials of the Spanish Ministry of the Interior, he had rented a house in Portbou on the Spanish side of the border, from which he could make his stately embassies northwards on his black-framed Motobécane, returning with Anna's secret state papers rolled up in the piston of his bicycle pump.

Observing the village through his binoculars, Harry once again saw how it lay astride a single road that sliced inland from the coast, splitting the terracotta-roofed houses into two opposing ranks that faced each other across the cobbles like Napoleonic regiments awaiting the order to fire their muskets.

At the foot of the village the street parted around a small island where a café stood, and an old plane tree that in summer provided shade for the customers sitting at their tables. Although hidden from him now, Harry knew that beside the café door the Vichy authorities had plastered a poster of a joyful-looking, sun-kissed teenager with a pickaxe over one shoulder: *Français! Allez travailler en Allemagne*, invited the slogan. *Frenchmen! Go to work in Germany*. It mentioned nothing about becoming a slave labourer.

His gaze took in the simple stone houses. It lingered on their arched entrances, checking for doors cracked open just enough to give a view of the street. They were all firmly shut. He lifted the binoculars to the shuttered windows behind the little iron balconies on the upper floors. If anyone was peering through the slats, they were invisible to him. Then down again to the main street. No suspicious black Peugeots parked there. No unfamiliar men in overcoats taking far too much trouble over doing nothing. No one sitting outside the café pretending to read yesterday's *Le Matin*. Just one old woman in widow's black, making her arthritic way towards the boulangerie, rolling like a buoy in a high sea as she went.

Despite the stillness the adrenaline went on surging through Harry's body, making his fingers tingle as he held the binoculars. He'd crossed the border a dozen times this year alone, but the tension now was just as acidic as the very first time. He preferred it that way. Complacency came in only one flavour: fatal.

Moving his gaze to the top of the village, Harry picked out the house Anna rented. It was grander than the others: a neat little villa in the belle époque style – a comfortable bolt-hole for

Anna, her two children and her mother, Marion. He imagined Anna in the basement she had converted to a darkroom, bent over her trays of fixer and developer as she brought her pictures to life. He had witnessed for himself her enchantment as the ghostly images emerged from the glistening white paper, speaking to them as if she were bumping into old friends she hadn't seen for a long time. And she was good, to Harry's mind, a real artist. She'd told him once that she'd studied under the Austrian art-photographer Rudolf Koppitz in Vienna.

As Harry watched from the hill, the front door of the house opened and into the picture stepped a woman in a dark coat. She turned her back to him and appeared to study the street. Was she, too, confirming the absence of black motor cars and men with unfamiliar faces? As elegantly as a dancer, she turned in his direction and began to walk out of the village, in the direction of the hillside.

Harry leaned into the eyepieces of the binoculars, keeping the woman centred in the field of view, just in case it was not Anna but a lure meant to bring him out of his vantage point and into clear sight of anyone hiding in the old castle across the valley.

At first she was too distant, her movements too often interrupted by the terrain and the intervening houses for him to make out much detail. But he knew it was her, if only by the way she walked: purposefully, a woman with little time for indecision or prevarication. Within moments he could see her face clearly, and then he was grinning widely.

Every time he saw her, he was reminded of Greer Garson: he could make out a pair of finely arched eyebrows drawn slightly together as she faced the wind, the long straight nose, the full but compact mouth. He could see the glint of the sun in the four tortoiseshell buttons set in a square on her wide-collared, blue woollen coat, nipped at the waist. And the trousers she wore instead of stockings, because no one in their right mind would risk valuable silk walking up a dusty, rock-strewn hillside. And the sturdy walking shoes that today hid a pair of delicate ankles. The wind was playing havoc with her hair. She wore it pulled back from the hairline, curled around the ears and curtained across the nape of her neck. But even the Tramontane wind and the effort of toiling up the slope between the clumps of thyme couldn't diminish her elegance.

You're still safe, he heard himself say. You're still mine – even though we both pretend there's a border between us to be patrolled, protected and defended. Maybe when peace comes we can lift the barriers. We can stop pretending we inhabit different lands.

Rising from his hiding place, Harry waited for her to approach, the binoculars trailing from his left hand.

When she saw him, she called out in that soft American accent: 'Well, upon my soul, if it isn't the wandering knight. How's the quest going? Look, you've even brought your trusty steed.' She nodded towards his bicycle while she set down the photographer's bag that she carried over one shoulder, her excuse to the village for their secret rendezvous in the hills.

'There's quite a Tramontane blowing today,' Harry said.

It was their all-clear sign. On meeting, he would mention the state of the wind. She would answer, 'Nothing in comparison to last week.' Then he would know she was not compromised – no policemen or Gestapo hiding behind the curtains of the rented house. If he didn't mention the wind at all, Anna would know that it was he who had been compromised. The only drawback was her mischievous habit of teasing him mercilessly. It was a trait she'd inherited from Marion.

Her mother was a woman who had yet to meet an authority she wouldn't attempt to defy.

'You're telling me, honey,' Anna said, leaning close and giving him a kiss on the left cheek that lasted a fraction too long to be considered entirely chaste. 'I swear the dust has scoured away most of my lipstick.'

Harry rolled his eyes to heaven. He repeated the sentence, this time with more deliberation in his voice. 'There's... quite... a... Tramontane... blowing today.'

'Whatever you say, Harry,' she replied, grinning at his barely concealed exasperation. '*The wind's nothing in comparison to last week*. Happy now?'

'There *is* a point to all this, Anna,' he said. 'I have to know you're not under duress.'

She laughed brightly. 'Harry, try spending just about *forever* in this wilderness with a seven-year-old, a five-year-old and an addled mother. Then you'll know what duress is. The whole place has gone downhill. The bread that used to be so scrummy now tastes like compounded dust mixed with birdseed. What little meat the charcutier in Leucate sells is mostly all fat. And all the decent wine has gone to Paris for the Nazis to drink. Apart from that, everything's just hunky-dory.'

'How's Marion coping?'

'Well, the good news is that my mother has discovered it's about as hard to find cocaine around here as everything else. If there was turkey, it would be cold. So that's a blessing.'

'I'm relieved to hear it.'

'Next time, though, I could do with more warning. What's up?'

'That's the whole point of me coming, Anna. There can't *be* a next time.'

She placed one palm against her breast and tilted her head to the heavens, adopting the exaggerated pose of an abandoned woman in a silent movie, while she mouthed, 'Oh, don't say it! Abandoned and alone! What to do?'

'It's no laughing matter,' Harry said, confirming it by refusing to smile. 'Have you heard the news of the landings in Algeria and Morocco?'

Suddenly serious, Anna nodded. 'Monsieur Bechard told me. He listens to Radio Londres. He said he heard about it on *Les Français parlent aux Français.*'

'Well, it's true.'

'Madame Soulier says they'll be pushed back into the sea within a week. But I think she got that from Radio Vichy.'

'She's wrong. They won't.'

'If you've come all this way to warn me the Germans have responded by invading Vichy, you've wasted your shoe leather. It's all round the village. Besides, I didn't think the traffic on the coast road was for market day in Perpignan.'

'Then you know you must leave. It's too risky for you to stay here now.'

'Leave? Are you crazy – with two children and a recovering addict in tow?'

Harry knew how stubborn she could be – Marion's influence again. It scared him. 'Anna, be reasonable,' he urged. 'Everything's changed. You're in grave danger.'

She shrugged. 'So what? I've been in danger before. Vienna... Berlin... Paris... this girl should have her own page in the *Baedeker Guide to Danger*.'

It was true, and he had always admired her courage. But this was different. 'The Germans could be here before nightfall,' he said. 'What if your husband comes looking for you?'

That knocked the confidence out of her. He could tell by the way her eyes narrowed.

'Ivo? Why would Ivo come here?' she asked, her voice taut.

'For the children.'

She stared at Harry, then shook her head in a sudden display of anger. 'No!'

'Can you be sure?'

'Sure enough. He's in some smart office in Berlin, strutting around in his uniform, quaffing Riesling and sucking up to Joseph Goebbels.'

'But he has friends. He could find out where you are.'

Anna gave a dismissive toss of her head. The wind caught her hair, blowing it across her face. She pushed it out of her eyes with one gloved hand. 'I have my US passport back now. Marion has hers. We'll be fine.'

'It doesn't work like that,' Harry said brutally. 'Vichy might not have declared war on America, but Hitler *has*. The Germans will put you all in an internment camp. I can't let that happen.'

She gave him a cold look. 'What do you mean *can't*?'

'I have the network to think about. You know exactly what you signed up for, Anna.'

There was silence while she considered the implication of what he'd said, silence save for the moaning of the wind. Then, 'You don't get to tell me where I go, Harry Taverner. You're not my husband. And even if you were, I still wouldn't listen to you.'

Harry counted off a beat or two, allowing her anger to lose itself in the emptiness of the hillside. 'Even if you're not afraid for yourself, think of the consequences if you stay,' he said. 'You'll put everyone in danger, every courier we've recruited, everyone who's sheltered an airman for so much as a night while we sent them down the line. You know what the Boche will do to them if they break you.'

Anna sighed. 'Okay. Okay. You know us Cantrells. No time for borders. We cross every last one we can find, if only for the excitement of what we'll discover on the other side. How do we get across this one?'

Harry glanced at the pannier bag on his bike. 'Emergency visas to allow you to enter Spain, arranged through the US consulate in Madrid. I've had them for a while. Just in case we ever needed to get you out in a hurry.'

Anna raised her hands in surrender. 'What do you do for an encore, Harry Taverner – pull rabbits out of a top hat?'

'Something like that.'

'Are they real, these visas?'

'As real as they need to be.'

'And where would we go, once we're in Spain?'

'That's your decision. America, if you want. Or England. The BOAC service between Lisbon and Bristol still operates.'

'You've planned it all, haven't you?'

'Sorry. It's my job.'

Anna thought about what he'd said, staring at her feet and the dust devils swirling around her boots. 'It can't be Britain. You know Marion hates the English with a passion.'

Harry laughed as he imitated her mother's nasal way of speaking: a Fifth Avenue drawl with hints of Lower East Side speakeasy and a distant *shtetl* no living relation of Marion's had known – contrived originally to infuriate her staid parents. 'You Englishmen! Good for nothing. You're all either goddamn nancy boys or communists. Or both. That's when you're not screwing over the Irish.'

Anna looked up, trying not to grin. 'She doesn't mean *you,* obviously.'

'Obviously. Even so, you can't allow your mother's loathing for your father to put you and the children in danger. She can stay in Lisbon, paint her pictures and sell them outside the Café Brasileira, for all I care. But you can't let her keep you all *here*. Not now.'

'What if she refuses to go? You know Dr Braudel's proposed marriage—'

'To Marion?'

'Well, it certainly wasn't to me.'

'Your mother is Jewish,' Harry said. 'And even though your father wasn't, to my gentile understanding – not to mention the Nazi race laws – that means you are, too.'

Anna looked at him as if he was an idiot, which in her presence he sometimes seriously believed he was.

'Thanks for reminding me, Harry,' she said, her face impassive. 'I really had forgotten.'

He scrabbled for the words to make amends, sensing the spreading blush in his cheeks. 'Look... what I meant to say was... just because you wrote "Roman Catholic" in the marriage register to please your husband, that's not going to save you. You know as well as I do what's been happening: the arrests, the deportations. There's a transportation camp down the road at Rivesaltes, for heaven's sake, where they send Jews to Germany and only God knows where.' He looked at her, hard. 'If the reports are true, the Nazis have started murdering them in an industrial fashion. And when they get here, an American passport isn't going to save you, Marion' – a pause for the *coup de grâce* – '*or* the children.'

Some people show their fear through anger, others through bluster. Some vent it through laughter, or a flat refusal to even admit the danger. At that moment Anna Cantrell was displaying none of those responses. But Harry knew that she was afraid. And it worried him, because in the six years he'd known her, he had never seen her truly afraid of anything.

After an age she said, 'When do we go?'

He felt like the worst bastard on earth. 'Now. It must be now.'

'Are you shitting me, Harry?'

'If Spain shuts the border when the Germans arrive, not even your emergency visas will get you through. It would mean a trek across the Pyrénées. It's November.'

The fight went out of her in a gust of breath. She looked around at the hills, as though to give herself a last memory of them. Then she said in a matter-of-fact voice, 'I'll go tell them to pack. How much can we take?'

'Only what you can carry.'

'Harry—!'

'We can take the border crossing at the Col de Belitres. Bär can pedal the bike. Antje's small, she can sit on the pannier rack. If your mother needs a break from the walking, Bär can dismount. He and I can hold a handlebar each while Marion takes a rest on the saddle. Do you think she'll manage the steep places?'

'She's fifty-three, but she walks in these hills to paint. She'll make it.'

'She'll have to. We can't allow her to slow us down.'

'Just when I've got her clean,' Anna said, with a roll of her eyes. 'If we could find her a line of cocaine, she'd be up the Pico de Aneto like a racer. She'd beat us to Madrid by a week.'

For a moment Harry thought she might be serious. He knew she enjoyed being provocative, forcing the observer to look beyond her surface beauty. Or maybe, like her mother, she just enjoyed shocking people.

'Are you coming down to the house?' she asked brightly, squaring her shoulders in acceptance of this new reality. 'The children are eager to see you, and they'll take the news better if it comes from you.'

He said he would. And, just when Anna turned to lead the way, she saw them: a pair of black Citroëns crawling like scarabs up the Rue du Pla.

Harry heard her appalled whisper even above the wind. Or had he simply borrowed her voice for the thoughts in his own head?

'Oh, Jesus! He's found us.'

Anna wondered if she'd been shot. She couldn't think why else she would be lying on the hillside, the breath gone from her lungs, a stabbing pain in her chest and dark shapes waving before her eyes. Perhaps Harry had been shot too, because his weight was pressing her down into the dirt. Then she realized that it was his body that had felled her, his arms that were pinning hers, his breath that was loud in her ears. She could smell the coarse Spanish soap he used on his skin, like old motor oil.

'Christ, Harry! You're hurting me.'

'Keep your voice down. This wind will carry sound down into the village.'

'Okay. *Okay*. Just get off me.'

Rolling away, Harry raised the binoculars to his eyes.

Freed from the pressure of him, Anna lifted her head. The breath came back into her lungs in a rush, harsh and dry. 'What can you see?'

'Vichy police,' Harry said. 'They've stopped directly outside your house.'

'It's him,' Anna replied, the awful certainty twisting her mouth into a slash. 'I just know it is.'

'I can see two other men with them. They're in German uniform.' Harry paused. Then: '*Shit*—'

'Let me see,' Anna snapped.

In transferring the binoculars Harry must have nudged the focus wheel, because when Anna looked through the eyepieces, she saw nothing but a blur. She was looking at the world through a film of watery soup, struggling to sharpen the image because her hands were shaking. When the image finally snapped into perfect clarity, it took what seemed like an age to drag the house into the centre of the view.

They were Vichy police, just as Harry had said – she could tell by their midnight-blue tunics and their peaked, pillbox hats. One of them was hammering on the front door. Anna had the ludicrous urge to shout out to Bär and Antje inside the house, urge them not be frightened because the gendarmes had only come to check if Mama's American passport was still valid, or ask her if she knew anything about Monsieur Chastain's wayward son, Auguste, hording petrol in the castle on the opposite hill. But then, as the door began to open, two more men, this time wearing the grey-green tunics of the German *Kriminalpolizei* – the Kripo – pushed past to take centre stage.

'Sweet Christ and all his angels,' she said, the words torn from her as though someone had ripped a dressing off a still-open wound. 'I was right: he *has* found us.'

Anna was halfway to her feet, but Harry had already guessed what she might do and was even faster. Again, she felt him slam into her, knocking her back down – if it hadn't been for her woollen coat she would have shredded her knees on the track.

As he tried to roll her onto her back she lashed out, raking his face with her nails. We're making angry love, she thought. We're admitting everything we've denied. We're trying to kill each other.

It was only when he didn't flinch that she realized she was still wearing gloves.

'Do you want to get us both shot?' he said, his voice an angry growl in her ear.

'I'm going down there,' she spat at him. 'I don't care what he does to me. It's the children—'

And that was when he hit her. Not designed to hurt. Not in anger. Just to concentrate her mind. A jab to the solar plexus that even the coat did little to soften. Preventative medicine, because he couldn't risk the lives of all his other agents for one deranged mother on a mission that could only end in their capture.

The breath went out of her again. Her head swam. When she opened her eyes he was lying beside her, the scent of the crushed thyme beneath her head reminding her of the *Schwenkbraten* they served in the restaurant around the corner from her old apartment in Berlin – even though her attention was otherwise wholly concentrated on the barrel of the Webley revolver he'd pulled from his pannier and was now pressing into her jaw.

'You're not going to shoot me, Harry Taverner,' she said, fighting for air because her lungs seemed to have forgotten their purpose.

'I won't have a choice. There are more lives at stake than just yours.'

'It's not in you. You've got a conscience.'

'I'll find a way to live with it.'

She stared into his face, not wanting to believe what she could see written there. He was so close to her that she could see he had a tiny stye in one eye. But there was a resolution there that frightened her.

For the first time since they'd met, she realized that this otherwise polite, uncomplicated, decent man would kill her if he had to.

They lay together in the shelter of the scrub while Harry observed the scene below through his binoculars.

'Who's that with him, the one who looks like a crooked accountant out on bail?'

'Manis Möller, his old boss from Berlin. Please, Harry. I *have* to see what happens.'

Reluctantly, he handed her the field glasses.

The door of the neat little villa, where they have all lived since leaving Paris, is still open. First to emerge are the two gendarmes. Then comes Möller, the crooked accountant. Behind him, young Bär – seven years old but showing he is the man of the family because his back is as upright as that of a Prussian guardsman. And trailing Bär, attached to him as if she were his teddy, is little Antje. Their faces almost make Anna choke right there on the hillside.

He's told them he's bringing them to *me*, she thinks. That's why they don't resist. He's promised we're all going to meet in Narbonne, or Paris, or wherever he's come from. Everything is going to be just fine and dandy. When Christmas comes, it will be the best we've ever known. Ivo has lied to them, just as he always did.

But no sign yet of Marion.

From her vantage point in the hills, Anna feels as if she is watching a silent movie, like the ones her father, Rex, used to shoot in Hollywood, before Marion took her back to Europe. She half expects to hear a piano burst into a suitably dramatic accompanying score.

On the screen, the actors are playing their roles as directed. Anna can almost hear the soft whirring as Rex turns the handle of his hand-cranked camera.

The gendarmes are opening the doors of one of the sedans. Bär and Antje are invited to enter. The car doors close on them. From her director's chair, Anna can see only the top of Bär's head as he turns to comfort his sister.

The villain of the show, the star everyone has come to watch, is matinée-idol-smart in his Kripo uniform. Tall, blond, chiselled, he pauses before entering his limousine. Then, as if he's remembered he still has some autographs to sign, he turns on his heel and marches back into the house. And because this is a silent movie the gunshot must be imagined, though Anna is sure a faint *clack* reaches her after its heroic struggle against the wind. A moment later, the star emerges, smoothly holsters his pistol, joins the crooked accountant in the lead car, and, with exquisite symmetry, the two vehicles execute identical three-point turns, and depart.

Cut! shouts the director. That was fabulous, everyone. Especially Marion. A perfect performance. Oscar-winning, without a doubt.

Marion?

Marion?

Can somebody please check on Marion? She seems not to be moving.

Two

9 November 1989, 8 p.m.
Berlin. The Western Sector

On the night the Berlin Wall came down Harry Taverner was standing before the Brandenburg Gate, his polished ox-blood brogues gleaming in the glare of the sodium streetlamps and the TV spotlights, his undiminished hair as white as any concert maestro's. He cut a smart, regimental figure, his back straight despite his years, his shoulders braced as though he'd forgotten to take the coat-hanger out of his recently dry-cleaned green Loden overcoat.

Around him, free Berlin was transforming herself from a sober European capital into a veritable carnival. At the checkpoints along the concrete curtain that divided the city, thousands of West Berliners were gathering in the chill November night air to welcome the *Ossis* – the East Berliners – across when, as was imminently expected, the Central Committee on the other side threw in the towel and ordered the barriers raised.

But Harry Taverner did not share their joy that night: he was in the grip of troubled memories, a confusion he could only describe as a sudden attack of temporal vertigo. It was as if time itself was sliding any which way but forward, twisting, coiling into an impossible knot, making him think that he was living in the wrong city, in the wrong year, perhaps even in the wrong life.

And he was late.

Needing an anchor to stop himself drifting, he read for perhaps the twentieth time since he had left his apartment the message written on a small rectangle of battered pasteboard. He held it between the fingers of his leather officer's gloves, turning it over and scrutinizing it yet again before returning the card to his coat pocket. Then he began to push his way through the crowd, back and forth along this section of the Wall, his mind becoming ever more perturbed.

Occasionally he glanced up at the East German border guards standing atop the parapet. They had been his enemy, once. Tonight, they were observing the growing crowd of happy people below with self-conscious discomfort, their power leaching away with each friendly wave from the West. Leather-coated Stasi policemen with notebooks edged amongst them. Harry supposed they were there to pass on the Politburo's latest contradictory orders, or just to take down the names of the guards whose officially stern faces were in danger of committing the decadent Western sin of grinning.

Being this close to the Wall and its vivid, invasive weeds of graffiti meant Harry had lost sight of the Brandenburg Gate. This only added to his growing agitation. Pushing his way back through the throng, he found a suitable spot that allowed him a glimpse of the monumental stone pillars topped by the goddess Victoria in her chariot. She was an old friend to him. He had seen her noble and imposing. He had seen her blackened and defeated. He had stood in her shadow and, quite unwittingly, let Anna Cantrell run rings around his professional skill.

The night was cold, but in Berlin Harry had known far colder ones. He recalled the winter of '46, when fifty-three refugees arriving from Poland had died of hypothermia on the train that was supposed to be carrying them to a new life in the city. Anna had been away in Frankfurt then; he'd been trying to forget her. But that night he'd had a dream in which he saw her face, whitened with frost, and he'd woken in a terror, convinced she'd been on that train.

Time looped another of its coils around him, pulling him even further back, just as his mind had been doing from the moment he'd picked up that little scrap of pasteboard in his apartment, less than an hour ago.

He saw himself standing before his tutor at Oxford, on his way to a double first in History. He smelled burned tobacco in the bowl of a pipe, and old tweed cloth. The day's edition of the *Daily Express* lay nearby on an occasional table, pinned down by a half-full sherry glass in case it made a bid for freedom. If he tilted his head a little, he could make out the date on the masthead: Monday, 6 August 1934.

THE HORROR OF THE UKRAINE screamed the banner headline, lest the stark pictures taken by a tourist had somehow failed to tell the full story. *STARVED MEN AND HORSES DEAD ON THE ROADSIDE – LEFT FOODLESS BY MOSCOW'S SWOOP ON CROPS.*

'Am I right in thinking your people were refugees, young Taverner?' his tutor is asking in the refined nasal tones of the English academic.

'Actually, my father is in shipping insurance, sir.'

'No, I mean your *old* people.'

'Oh, French Huguenots. Came over in the early sixteen hundreds, or so we're led to believe.'

'And it's reached my ears you've been spending rather a lot of time in the Ashmolean. An interest in German art, I hear.'

Harry nods. 'But to be honest, sir, I'm having a little difficulty squaring my admiration for Dürer and the younger Holbein with the present rise of Herr Hitler.'

'You're not the only one, Mr Taverner,' his tutor replies, striking a match and holding the flame to the bowl of his pipe. Then, as if Dürer and Holbein had somehow made a personal recommendation, he says casually, 'Perhaps you might care to meet some friends of mine in London. Government friends. Nothing too formal. Just a friendly chat.'

And now the memories began to spill into Harry's head in a torrent: jumbled, competing, utterly disconcerting and discordant – like one of those dreadful avant-garde compositions he liked to call 'squeaky door music'. He could no longer tell the difference between the past and the present.

'I have to get across,' he muttered in German to no one in particular when the frustration became too great to bear. 'I'll be late. I *can't* be late.'

Feeling a tug at his sleeve, he turned his head. A girl in a white sweater was standing at his side. She looked worried, and it took him a moment to realize her concern was for him. She was much younger than his daughter, Elly – hardly out of her teens – but her eyes had Elly's compassion for helpless cases. Taking a deep drag on her cigarette, she exhaled the smoke over his shoulder. 'Are you okay?' she asked. 'You look lost.'

'I should be at the Hotel Adlon,' Harry told her with relief, as if he'd found amongst the babel someone who spoke a language he could understand. 'I *must* be at the Adlon.'

The girl laughed brightly. 'The *Adlon*? That was on the other side, wasn't it? Didn't they pull it down a few years ago?'

By way of compensation, she offered him the glowing stub of her cigarette.

Harry refused with a confused shake of his head. He hadn't smoked for years. Or had he only now made himself a promise to quit? He could no longer be sure. He checked his watch. He was running out of time. Or was he running out of lives?

'I have to get across,' he said plaintively.

From close by, a male voice called out, 'Don't be daft. There hasn't been a crossing point here since the *Ossis* shut it in the sixties.'

Looking for the voice, Harry saw an officer of the *Schutzpolizei* watching him. Desperate now, he reached into his coat pocket and drew out the pasteboard card again. He handed it to the policeman as if it were his identity card, which, in a way, it was.

The officer took it from him and by the light from his torch read the lines of copperplate script. Then he shone the beam into Harry Taverner's face.

Harry didn't shield his eyes. He just stood there, as if waiting for the firing squad. As if he knew time had run out.

The officer was a kind man. He had a grandfather in an old-folks home in Hamburg, a survivor of Stalingrad. He knew the signs: he could spot an old warrior in distress where others might not. He lowered the beam of the torch.

'Is this you?' he asked, 'You're Captain Taverner?'

'Well, yes,' Harry said. 'That *was* me, once. Now I'm just the old fellow who sits each morning at his regular seat at the Café Kranzler, eating their excellent *Bauernomelett* and reading his *Die Welt*.'

As if to be quite sure this elderly, seemingly harmless gentleman wasn't playing a prank on him, the officer read the words on the card again. And as he did so, he began to understand that this little card was of immense value to its owner, and that he should hold it with great care, because he was glimpsing in the faded print the tiniest sliver of an entire lifetime.

THE HOTEL ADLON IS PLEASED TO WELCOME

Captain H Taverner

TABLE 12, 21.00 HRS

Dress: white tie
Dancing to the music of the Joe Bund Orchestra
9th November 1938

And underneath, written in a hand which – had the policeman been a richer, more travelled man – he might have guessed was that of a maître d'hôtel now long dead, was the addendum:

And guest.

*

The bedside phone rang with a trill that Elly Taverner didn't recognize. She groped in the darkness, momentarily unsure of where she was. Then her fingers touched cold plastic. Lifting the handset to her ear, her wrist brushed against the small bottle of mineral water she'd taken from the minibar – hotel air conditioning always made her thirsty. She heard it hit the floor and roll under the bed. Had she screwed the top tight before turning out the light? Or was the liquid now soaking the hotel room's gaudy carpet?

'Bugger!' she muttered.

The amber digits on the electric alarm clock told her she'd only been asleep for twenty minutes. It was one in the morning. She felt like shit.

'Elly? Elly, is that you?' said a male voice she instantly recognized from the British embassy in Bonn.

'Sorry, Mike. I wasn't calling *you* a bugger.' She held the phone at arm's length for a moment while she stifled a yawn. 'If you've rung to tell me they've opened the crossing points, you've wasted the Foreign Office's money. I was with the *Bundesministerium* till gone midnight. It's like Cup Final day here.'

'I'm not calling about that, Elly. It's about your father.'

Elly came out of sleep's last grasp as if she'd been slapped. 'Oh, God! What's happened?'

'He's alright,' Mike's voice assured her. 'Seems he's had a bit of a wobble.'

'Not *another* one,' Elly lamented to the darkened hotel room as much as to Mike. 'Where is he?'

'Safe back in his apartment, apparently.'

'Are you sure he's alright? Honestly?'

'I'm told he's fine, but he got himself into a spot of bother at the Brandenburg Gate. The *Schupo* took him for his own safety. They checked him out with the Foreign Ministry. Turns out he's still on their computer, so they called the embassy.'

'What sort of bother are we talking about?'

'Nothing serious. He wasn't dancing naked down the Ku'damm or anything like that.'

I should have stayed at his place, Elly scolded herself. I should have been a dutiful daughter and told Admin to go to hell when they announced they'd found me a bed in a cheap cathouse because Berlin is suddenly home to every journalist in the world. But what thirty-eight-year-old woman wants to doss down in her elderly father's apartment when the action is all down at Checkpoint Charlie?

'I'll go straight over,' she told Mike.

'My mum was like that at the end,' Mike said. 'Three a.m. phone calls wanting to know why I wasn't there to take her to the Co-op.'

Even down the scratchy line Elly could hear him gulp at his own crassness.

'Shit! I'm really sorry, Elly. I didn't mean—'

'Forget it, Mike. I know what you mean. Thanks for letting me know. If they call back, I'm on my way.'

Replacing the receiver, Elly Taverner threw back the cheap nylon sheet. Swinging her legs over the side of the bed, her toes landed squarely in a wet patch from the spilled water. She groaned, anticipating the snotty letter to the embassy complaining about how its staff treat their host nation's hotel rooms like rock guitarists on tour. She fumbled for the wall switch. The light came on like an explosion, as bright as the arc lamps the television crews were using down by the Wall. Half-blinded, she went to the bathroom to fix her make-up; the last thing she wanted was to give Harry a heart attack on top of what she called his RLDs – his recent little difficulties.

In reception, the Turkish night manager was asleep behind his Formica counter. Leaning over, Elly filched a sheet of hotel notepaper. With one of the three pens she carried in her bag on the presumption that a British, B3-grade third secretary, cultural, should never be without the means of taking down her ambassador's every *bon mot* for future reference, she left a note for her colleague in room five: *Sorry, Derek. Dad's had a turn. Might miss breakfast.* Then she went out through the rear entrance into the car park.

As Elly drove across the city the streetlights and the bright shop windows bloomed in the wing mirrors of the embassy motor pool Opel. But even tuning the radio to the late-night music show on RIAS 2 couldn't soothe the dread mounting in her. What if Mike had been downplaying things? What if it was really bad this time? She forced herself to concentrate on her driving.

Elly felt more than just a daughter's concern for a father's health. There was a professional bond between them too. Harry had once been what she was now: *declared* – an intelligence agent of an allied power, disclosed to the West German Foreign Ministry. That was why Harry's name had still been in the Foreign Ministry files. She wondered if she should call her mother once she'd taken stock of Harry's condition. Glancing at the dashboard clock, she saw it would be seven in the evening in New York – Mum would be charming a client somewhere. Even in her seventies, her mother was still the driving force behind Galerie Louisa Vogel, the international antiques business she'd built while Elly was still a child. She and Harry were like the proverbial passing ships, though Elly knew the marriage was bombproof. When they met up, they were like twenty-year-olds falling in love all over again, which was sometimes a little more than Elly could comfortably take. She decided to wait until she'd assessed the situation. Do what you've been taught to do when facing a crisis, she told herself. *Nothing*. Sit on your hands for a minute or two. Don't go off at half-cock.

The apartment block was one of the few old buildings in Berlin the Allies hadn't flattened. It stood at one end of a cobbled street. At the other, a small but jubilant crowd lined the Wall, lit by the streetlamps as if they were actors on a stage. Standing shoulder to shoulder with the East German guards on the parapet were *Ossi* civilians, mostly young. If she lifted her gaze to the rounded concrete rim she could imagine they were enjoying a pool party, daring each other to jump in fully clothed. She remembered what Louisa had said in her last call from New York: *It's all over the news here. On every channel. I never thought we'd see the bastard thing come down in your lifetime, darling, let alone mine.*

Elly found a parking space. It was residents only and there was an empty *Landespolizei* vehicle parked two cars down. But she took the space anyway, feeling a slight sense of guilt at the immunity the car's CD plates gave her. She wondered if the police car was there because of Harry or because of what was happening at the Wall. Locking the Opel, she glanced with loathing at the monstrous barrier at the end of the street. She thought of those who'd tried to cross it and failed, shot down in cold blood by the guards. Tonight was their night, the final vindication of their courage.

Pushing through the tall wooden doors of the apartment block, she decided against the ancient lift waiting on the far side of the courtyard and took the wide stone staircase instead, two steps at a time.

The entrance to Harry's apartment was ajar. The lights were on inside. Standing in the hall she could hear an old woman's voice lamenting that the *Ossis* would eat the West out of house and home by Christmas, now that the Wall was open. Elly guessed it was Frau Hedemann from downstairs, come to lend succour to her favourite Englishman despite the hour. Only Harry had the power to prize Frau Hedemann from her god-awful puce sofa and the rented black and white television she'd installed for President Kennedy's visit in 1963. 'Why do I need colour,' she would often say to Elly, 'when I have such brightness upstairs.' She was referring, of course, to Harry's smile.

From the lounge came the muted soundtrack of a TV news commentary. Dropping her raincoat onto the art deco chrome coat stand, Elly took a deep breath and called out, 'Daddy, it's me. Is everything alright?'

Of course it isn't, you stupid girl, she told herself. If it was, you wouldn't be here at almost two in the morning.

But when she entered the lounge, there was old Harry sitting on his Biedermeier sofa in his best dress shirt and black trousers, as comfortable and content as if he'd just come back from the opera. Frau Hedemann hovered nearby with an empty soup bowl, while a young female *Landespolizei* officer with her cap under one arm basked in her father's warming smile.

'Daddy, what *have* you been up to?' Elly asked, kissing him on the forehead as he raised his face to hers. 'You haven't been arrested, have you? Mummy is going to have a fit when she finds out.'

'Hello, Puffin,' Harry said wearily.

Elly winced. He'd coined the nickname during a family holiday on Anglesey. She'd been six.

'Fräulein Taverner?' asked the *Landespolizei* office. She was barely twenty, with blue eyes and tight pale skin from working too many night shifts.

'Guilty as charged, Officer,' Elly said pleasantly.

'My superiors told me you were on the way. I understand you're with the British embassy in Bonn,' the officer said in good English, putting her cap back on for extra authority. 'May I pass Herr Taverner into your care?'

'Yes, of course you may. He hasn't caused a diplomatic incident, has he? I wouldn't put it past him.'

The officer smiled. 'We just wanted to ensure Herr Taverner was with someone until you arrived. He's been telling me what Berlin was like when he first came here, before I was born. Before my parents were born, actually.'

Elly rested one hand on her father's shoulder. 'He does that a lot, given half the chance. If he's bored you silly with his awful anecdotes, I apologize unreservedly on behalf of Her Majesty's government.'

The young woman laughed as she shook her head. 'Not at all. We ended up watching the news on the television. And Frau Hedemann makes excellent *Buttermilchsuppe.*'

Frau Hedemann gave a wan smile, as though she'd been accused of ratting to the authorities.

Buttoning her green jacket, the officer made a short formal bow first to Harry, then to Elly. '*Charmant,*' she said on her way out. '*Sehr charmant.*'

'Yes, he can be. Very,' Elly called after her. 'By the way, sorry about the parking.'

When Frau Hedemann, too, had left, Elly turned down the volume on the TV and sat beside her father. She took his hand in hers, smoothing the skin as if to make it young again, as if to rub away the invisible poison she knew would take him away from her long before either of them were ready for it.

'What on earth have you been up to, Daddy?'

'I've been a bit silly, Puffin,' he said distantly, staring at a small brown card she had just noticed lying on the Bauhaus walnut coffee table that Louisa had bought him as a present for his sixtieth. 'I thought I had an appointment somewhere, but it turns out I was wrong.'

Elly leaned forward over his left knee and retrieved the card. It looked like something you might find in a museum case. She read the words that the *Schupo* officer had read several hours earlier at the Brandenburg Gate:

Captain H Taverner… Table 12… Dress: white tie… 9th November 1938.

When she read the date, she put her arms around him. She could barely speak because her throat seemed to have suddenly tied itself into a knot. 'Oh, *Daddy*.'

When he looked at her, she could see his eyes – usually so bright and clear – were moist.

'Face it, Puffin,' he said, patting her knee. 'Your father's losing his marbles.'

'Don't be silly. It's alright to get a little confused sometimes. At the embassy, I'm like that by Thursday lunchtimes, to be honest.'

'I can imagine. After tonight, it's going to get worse. In a good way, I hope.'

'Reunification?'

'Gorbachev has cut the GDR adrift... Honecker has gone... the *Ossis* have had enough of the Wall shutting them in... In Poland and Czecho they're staring down Moscow and not flinching... Who knows what's going to happen now?'

'Maybe it's time to go back home,' Elly suggested. 'Make Stoke Gabriel into a proper home for the two of you. God knows, you both deserve it.'

A sudden anger appeared to flare in him, though she knew it was directed at himself, not her. 'I'll not force Louisa into being a nursemaid. Besides, *this* is my home. I've survived everything that Hitler, Stalin, Khrushchev and all those other desiccated ghouls could throw my way – not to mention Her Majesty's Foreign and Commonwealth Office. I won't leave now.' He jabbed a finger at the television. 'Look there. See who's turning out tonight, on both sides of the Wall? Mostly they're young. They've had a generation and more to cleanse the old poison out of their national blood. They're the future. They – the whole damned continent – need to know that the nation which helped liberate them – the UK – is ready to stand with them now, to encourage them, to help lead them into whatever comes next.' He gave Elly an apologetic look. 'Sorry about the speech, Puffin. But you know what I think of that lot back in Westminster. If Harry Taverner is destined to go ga-ga, he'll damn well do it where his heart is.'

As Elly returned the card to the table, she noticed the photos in their silver frames standing to attention like guardsmen on the sideboard. Each one was as familiar to her as her own memories: Harry and Mummy at Bayreuth for the Wagner… Mummy at the opening of her very first antiques gallery, proudly pointing at the shop sign that read *Galerie Louisa Vogel*… Harry and Mummy at the house in Devon, taken the winter the pipes burst and the ceiling of Elly's bedroom fell in and they'd all had to spend Christmas in a hotel in Totnes. And Harry and Mummy on their wedding day, photographed in the Allied sector of 1950s Berlin; Daddy looking as if he'd just stepped out of the Royal enclosure at Ascot, his beaming face a decade smoother than its forty-one years, Louisa an angel in Dresden lace, thirty-six but looking twenty because of all the bliss bubbling away inside her…

'Daddy—?' she said, as the thought struck her.

'What, Puffin?'

'You met Mummy during the occupation, didn't you? This invitation – 1938 is positively *eons* before that.'

'I'm tired, darling,' Harry said, kissing her on the cheek. 'This turn of mine has knocked me back a little. If you want to stay, the spare room is made up.' He stood and went out into the hallway to his bedroom.

'Let me get you a scotch to settle you down,' Elly called, playing along with his evasion.

'That would be nice, Puffin.'

Taking a decanter from the drinks cabinet, Elly poured out a good measure of her father's favourite whisky. She knew there was ice in the fridge. On the TV she saw the boxy Trabant cars streaming through Checkpoint Charlie, the faces inside turning to the waiting cameras with the sort of expressions she imagined released prisoners might wear if they'd served a lengthy sentence for a crime they hadn't committed. It seemed to her an injustice to switch off the set.

When she took the tumbler to Harry's door there he was, sitting on the bed, still in his shirt, trousers and socks, his polished dress shoes neatly positioned by the bedside table.

'Thank you, darling,' he said, as she handed him the glass. 'You're a trouper. Sorry to be such a bother.'

It was then that she saw the battered leather portfolio case unzipped on the bed behind him. It was the sort of case an artist might carry their work in. The flap was thrown back to reveal a sheaf of paintings and photographs.

'What have you got there, Daddy – a case full of memories?' Elly asked gently.

'Something like that, darling,' Harry said.

When he looked up at her, Elly's heart almost broke. She could tell he was wondering how long the lucidity would last, how much time he had left before the next RLD came along to mess up his world. Yet it wasn't fear she could see in his eyes: it was as if he'd come to a difficult decision, one he'd been battling with for more years than he might care to admit.

Harry reached for the portfolio case and drew out a photograph. It was a ten-by-twelve black and white print. She knew the size because as a child she'd dabbled with photography herself, before she'd discovered ponies. It wasn't a snapshot. It wasn't a holiday photo. It wasn't even a formal composition, like the ones on the sideboard in Harry's lounge. It was a landscape: a panoramic view of a hillside looking down across a lagoon to the sea beyond. An art photo, because even in monochrome the chiaroscuro was striking. The sun on the hillside, the sparkle of the lagoon and the sea, seemed to jump out of the picture and raise the temperature of the room even as she leaned across to look at it. When her father turned the photo over Elly could see, written on the reverse in now faded blue ink, an inscription:

Mussel beds at Leucate lagoon. Rolleiflex Standard. B1 film. June 1942.

And in the bottom right-hand corner: *To Harry. Now that it's all over and we're free. From Anna.*

Elly felt as though a secret door had just been cracked open a fraction. But was she prepared to peek through? Did she even have the right?

'Who's Anna, Daddy? Some *affaire d'amour* from your past we don't know about?' she asked, though she intuitively knew the answer to her question was to be found on that little piece of card: *And guest.*

'Oh, just someone I knew once,' Harry said.

In the light from the bedside lamp, his white hair seemed to have regained its youthful colour, though Elly could see a furrow or two of pink scalp. Was he thinking about the woman who presumably had shot the photograph, the guest he had taken dancing at the Hotel Adlon exactly fifty-one years ago this very night? Had he loved her? And had this Anna – of whom until tonight she had never heard so much as a single mention – loved him back?

Of course she had, Elly decided. Everyone loved Harry. She, Elly, loved him. Mummy loved him. The Service loved him; he was a legend to them. Even Mike in Bonn, whose call had woken her just a few hours ago, knew Harry's reputation, and if he didn't exactly love him, he loved to hear the stories. The

West Germans loved him. Frau Hedemann loved him enough to serve him soup at two in the morning. Impressionable young *Landespolizei* officers loved him at first meeting. *Charmant… Sehr charmant.*

Don't press him any further, she told herself. Leave him with his memories; who knows how much longer he'll have them? Leaning over, Elly kissed him on the forehead.

But as she turned to go, Harry took her wrist. 'Stay a while, Puffin,' he said, clearly oblivious to the hour. 'It's time you knew.'

As Elly sat down beside him, Harry reached for the portfolio case again. This time he pulled out not a photo but a painting, unframed and unbacked. It was a watercolour, painted *en plein air*, an outdoor scene set on a public terrace, with a fountain and people in what Elly took to be Edwardian dress. Harry studied it at arm's length, as if he was testing his eyesight. Or maybe he was looking at something Elly would never be able to see.

'If you're really going to understand Anna,' he said, in a voice that now seemed to come from somewhere inside the painting rather than the apartment around her, 'first you need to know about Marion.'

Three

Bethesda Terrace, Central Park, New York
Watercolour on card. Marion Bauer. 1915

If a scrawny, tubercular Serb student named Gavrilo Princip hadn't emptied his revolver into Archduke Ferdinand's open-topped limousine at the north end of Sarajevo's Latin Bridge on a hot summer day in 1914, Marion Bauer's life, like millions of others, would have turned out very differently.

For a start, she would never have met Rex Cantrell. Anna, their daughter, would have remained unconceived: a what-if, a never-person, doomed to be discarded like trillions of other unborn souls in fate's waste basket. Because Rex Cantrell might never have come to America in the first place.

In 1914, Rex was one of an emergent fraternity of artist-technicians: a cameraman, employed by Hepworth Studios in leafy Walton-on-Thames, a brief journey by steam locomotive from London. There, he filmed short silent documentaries – *actualities* – of everyday English life, viewable for tuppence a ticket in establishments like the Electric Theatre, the Picturedome and the Bioscope.

Until his dying day, Rex lamented that he had not been there in Sarajevo to film the Archduke's assassination. 'Would 'ave given my right arm to see that, an' no mistake,' he would tell the young Anna with a wink, the echo of his origins – the son of a Limehouse stevedore and a Stepney parlourmaid – still audible in his voice. It was a joke father and daughter shared: Rex was left-handed. He had adapted the crank handle of his 35 mm movie camera to suit.

That was Rex all over, Anna would say, when she was old enough to understand about such things. Everything about him was transactional. Where Marion would sing her to sleep with lullabies of Old Austria, Rex would close her eyelids with ditties of his own invention: '*A little bit of this... for a little bit of the other. Don't tell the rozzers... and don't tell your mother...*'

And because Anna had been far too young to comprehend the implications of the lyrics, she entered their shared conspiracy – father and daughter together against the world – with innocent, giggling delight. In later years she often said that if Rex hadn't been a cameraman, he could have been a vaudevillian. Or a con artist – which was exactly what Marion would later say he was.

Why did Rex come to America when other fellows of his age – mid-twenties, and with all the possibilities and excitements of life still ahead of them – were answering the recruiting sergeant's call? That question was easily answered. Public opinion, over its morning newspaper and toast and marmalade, might well have been harrumphing that the war would be over by Christmas, but Rex had sniffed the wind. And Rex could smell a hurricane coming. While everyone else was singing patriotic songs in the music halls and refusing to buy from shops with German-sounding names, Rex decided he couldn't give a monkey's how far it was to Tipperary: all *he* was concerned about was putting a safe distance between himself and the possibility of getting his noddle blown off.

And there was another reason why Rex Cantrell suddenly upped sticks and took a train to Liverpool, where he purchased a third-class ticket aboard the RMS *Olympic*, bound for New York: on page five of the *London Evening News,* dated Tuesday, 3 November 1914, the relevant passage from the notebook of one Albert Lavender, a constable of the City of London Police, read to the panel at Lambeth Magistrates Court, revealed all. It described in prosaic but brutal terms an encounter in the gentlemen's toilets at Waterloo railway station between Reginald 'Rex' Cantrell, and a corporal of the Royal Scots Fusiliers.

Acquitted on a technicality, Rex packed a small valise, returned to his landlady the keys of a shared lodging room on Tooley Street, and hurried north to the great seaport on the Mersey.

A little bit of this... for a little bit of the other...

Within two years of their marriage, Marion Bauer – born to a well-off Jewish couple who'd emigrated from Austria – was lamenting that while it might be hard for her to forgive Princip for the crime of firing the shot that started the Great War, it would be even harder to absolve him of being the cause of Rex Cantrell's visit to the offices of the White Star Shipping Line on James's Street, Liverpool.

'Excuse me. Do you mind? You're in my light.'

It is a little after eleven on a warm spring Saturday morning and a young woman in a blue velvet jacket and a pleated skirt that reaches to her ankles is at her easel on Bethesda Terrace in Central Park. Far beyond the skyline of Fifth Avenue, British and Australian fighting men are landing at Gallipoli, and the first vile yellow clouds of chlorine gas are spewing from the German trenches in the Ypres Salient. But here the air smells of cherry blossom or horse dung, depending upon where you are standing. The citizens of New York are taking their ease. The sky is dimpled with creamy white clouds.

'*Ho contraire*, miss,' replies the man to whom the woman has spoken. 'I think you'll find it's you oo's in *my* light.'

Rex Cantrell stops screwing his hand-cranked cine camera to its tall wooden tripod and, as a gentleman should, tips his cap to her, at first simply out of courtesy, but then – as he takes in her beauty – from astonishment.

'What's that contraption you're fiddling with?' Marion asks. 'It looks to me like a coffee-bean grinder on stilts.'

Marion knows very well what it is, is already a fan of the cinema and saw Charlie Chaplin in *Tillie's Punctured Romance* at the Audubon in Harlem only the previous week. But she's not going to let the handsome devil off that easily, and besides, she's rather attracted to the accent.

'It's the magic eye, *made-moiselle*,' Rex tells her conspiratorially, indulging his habit of seeding his sentences with a smattering of strained French, the better to appeal to gullible New Worlders. He tugs the lapels of his jacket together, so that she won't detect his failure to take his shirt to the laundry on West 81st as often as he ought to. 'Take a peep in here,' he adds, nodding at the side-mounted viewfinder, 'an' you'll see the world as you've never seen it before.'

'It's still in my light. Would you mind moving it, please.'

'I shall, if you let me see your painting in return.'

'It's not finished.'

'No work of art ever truly is,' he answers with a knowing grin. He can't take his eyes off her.

At this stage in his life, Rex Cantrell's appetites are not solely confined to corporals of the Fusiliers.

To the surprise of both parties, the blossoming romance was met with approval. While the Bauers attended synagogue they were not observant. The notion of their daughter having a *goy* – a gentile – for a suitor did not offend them. Papa Wolfgang considered himself a man of the world. Tolerant. Liberal. Forward-thinking. He admired those American states that had already enfranchised women. He supported suffragists everywhere.

'Marion's a fine girl,' he said to Rex one evening at the Knickerbocker Club, slapping him on the knee while they enjoyed Old Forester on the rocks and Havana cigars – his treat. 'Though why she insists on speaking like a Bronx bar tender is beyond us. We sent her to Hunter College, you know. I think she does it just to upset us.'

'To my ears, sir, she's a proper songbird,' Rex assured him. 'I'm privileged for her to merely glance my way an' let me bask in her trillin'. An' if that was all she ever did, I'd be content never to look at another woman for the rest of my days.'

Papa Wolfgang nodded sagely. 'Just between the two of us, man to man,' he said, 'I used to cut a swathe or two across the dance floor in my youth. Didn't much care if the girl wasn't to be found in the women's gallery at temple. More interested in the gleam in her eye.'

Relieved, Rex turned the conversation to politics. He had already taken the precaution of checking Papa Wolfgang's affiliation – Democrat. 'I do hope Woodrow Wilson gets a second term,' he said.

'We need a fellow like him to keep us out of this wretched war in Europe,' Papa Wolfgang replied, his Austrian-accented English giving weight to his words. Then a thought occurred to him. 'How come you're not back home in uniform? You look fit enough to me.'

Rex, who had spent most of his salary from his new employer, Czibor Global Studios, on a new suit to impress, replied with all the manly honesty he could muster. 'Because, sir, I ain't – I aren't – a man who takes much to the idea of the kingly h-houses of Europe' – he took so much care not to drop the *h* in 'houses' that he doubled it – 'slaughterin' their people over lines drawn up harbitrarily on the map, just so they can stay sittin' on their golden thrones.'

'Quite right, old man,' Papa Wolfgang said admiringly. 'The old world is dying. Thank God there's an ocean between us. You're not a socialist, are you?'

'Lord above! No, sir,' replied Rex ardently. 'I came here to make my way in the world of the silver screen.'

'Isn't that a little risky? Oil or mining would be wiser,' Papa Wolfgang suggested. He knew a thing or two about investing: he was a partner in Bauer Manhattan Mercantile and Savings, the New York branch of the family bank in Vienna.

Rex sensed the opportunity and took it. 'How much do you think *Tess of the Storm Country* cost to make?'

'Can't say I've given it a thought.'

'Ten thousand dollars.'

'Is that so?'

'It's grossed almost three million.'

Papa Wolfgang whistled appreciatively, took a sip of his bourbon. 'That Mary Pickford, she's a honey, ain't she?'

Rex gave Papa Wolfgang his best smile. 'Not as lovely as your Marion, sir, if I might make so bold. Not by a country mile.'

'D'you think you could fix it?'

'Fix what, sir?'

'A meeting – with Mary Pickford?'

Rex leaned closer over the occasional table and glanced at the bottle of Old Forester waiting uncapped by his now empty glass. He gave Papa Wolfgang a conspiratorial wink. 'I can try.'

The wedding was discreet but stylish. It even merited a line or two in *Sunday World*, though Cantrell was spelt with a single *l*. The bride broke every male heart in the room. Her mother, Freda, flirtatious in the extreme, was equally admired. In her youth, it was rumoured, she had been the spark for several disagreements, some of them physical, between the gentlemen patrons of Delmonico's. Rex – looking handsome in his morning suit – now understood where his new bride got her chutzpah. The suit, however, was not his. Rex had borrowed it without permission from the costume department of his employer.

A honeymoon in Vermont. Marion, though precocious, had no gauge against which to judge her new husband's performance on the wedding night. Otherwise, she might have detected a certain *réticence,* a hint of Rex's mind being at times elsewhere. But all seemed as well as two young innocents – one real, the other not quite so – could possibly have hoped for.

Until their return to New York.

László Czibor, owner and president of Czibor Global Studios – a somewhat overblown name for a single-storey wooden storehouse in the Bedford Park district of the Bronx – was a mad, very short Hungarian. Rakish in a bow tie and an immaculate Schulz Brothers suit, he wore a scar under his left eye, which gave his narrow face a dangerous but romantic aspect. A duelling scar, he liked to claim, even if you hadn't asked. In truth it was the result of a childhood tantrum, during which he managed to disfigure himself with his mother's pastry cutter. László and tantrums had been close companions ever since.

Just then he was delivering the latest one in his high, Slav, sing-song voice. And to be fair, Rex Cantrell thought that this time his employer had just cause.

The studio looked to Rex as though a German shell had missed its target in France, skipped across the ocean and landed right there in the Bronx. The result was a devastation of broken scenery and smashed mercury vapour lights.

'Is those crazy bastards at TransAmerica Pictures!' László was screaming, his face puce with rage. 'Is them! I *know* is them! I smell it. Look what they do. I fucking kill them with my bare hands.'

But Rex barely heard him. He was too busy kneeling beside his beloved camera, talking soothingly to it as if it were a mortally wounded comrade. It lay beside its overturned tripod, a miniature alien from *The War of the Worlds* felled by an earthly germ. Only, in this case, two shots from a revolver had done the trick instead.

'And that is why we, along with a whole lot of other film makers, are here in California,' Rex would explain to Anna years later, when she was old enough to understand. 'Out of reach of those East Coast gangsters that some of the bigger studios paid to rough up the competition. Besides, in Hollywood we had the space and the scenery – any place on earth we wanted. One day we could be in the Wild West, the next in Robin Hood's merry England. The deserts of ancient Egypt? No problem. We had the best lighting of all – the sun. God's own beneficence smilin' down upon us. Papa Wolfgang even chipped in for our train tickets and temp'rary accommodation – a cool hundred dollars to see us started.' Then he had given his daughter a long, theatrical wink. 'Of course, I never told Uncle László that. It was his company, so he bankrolled the move. But I mean, who ever heard of your old man turning down free money? It'll be a secret between you an' me. You can keep a secret, Anna, my poppet, can't you?'

'Yes, Papa,' Anna had replied proudly, wriggling her toes in the red Mary Janes he'd bought her for her birthday.

'That's my girl. Always make sure there's nothing in the shot that's going to trip you up later. What the audience don't see, they can't complain about.'

Anna's earliest memories were of her infant fingers kneading the warm wickerwork of her baby carriage as she mewled happily beneath her parasol; the crispness of dry, desert air; and later the creamy scent of leather seats and the *put-put-put-put* sound of the engine as she rode in Uncle László's Studebaker, and the smell of wild brickellbush and greasepaint.

The first words she learned after 'Mama' and Papa' were 'Action!' and 'Cut!'

Before she was old enough to know it, Anna had become the unofficial mascot of the Hollywood Studio Club Building Campaign, chairman *Mrs* Cecil B. DeMille, whose name was clearly visible on the photograph of its leading ladies in their crinolines, posing before the board on which their fundraising efforts were tallied. The club raised money to provide safe lodgings for the increasing number of young women coming west to try their luck in the movies. And what true gentleman could leave his pocketbook unopened in the presence of a beautiful and determined campaigner as Marion, especially with an eighteen-month-old angel on her hip?

For Marion, there was more to it than just the satisfaction of doing good works. Doors opened. Invitations proffered. Contacts made. But Anna was a grown woman before she learned that Uncle László had suggested Marion join the campaign – and bring her infant daughter with her – solely to give him access to the very girls Mrs DeMille and her campaigners were trying to protect.

On shooting days, Rex and Marion would tuck their daughter into the dickie seat of László's tourer and head either for the studio – a glass-roofed converted warehouse on Mission Road – or to the Hollywood hills. If shooting was to be outdoors, they were accompanied by however many rented trucks needed to carry the props, actors and extras for the day's filming. The procession would wind its way up San Fernando Boulevard like migrant fruit pickers, until the clapboard houses fell away behind, and the mosquito grass and sagebrush took over. Because László could barely see over the dash, Rex would rise from the passenger seat, brace himself against the top of the windshield and call out the potholes, as if he were the harpooneer in the bow of a whaling ship. And everyone would sing, because only God in His heaven knew what artistic miracles the mad Hungarian and his English cameraman were going to conjure out of the bright California sunshine that day.

László's rendition of '*O Sole Mio*', delivered to the hills, the gophers and the jackrabbits in a surprisingly good tenor, was almost a match for the great Caruso, Rex would insist, before belting out 'Any Old Iron?' in his best impersonation of Harry Champion. Then everyone would join in, and for a while – a very short while – Rex could imagine himself back in his East End boozer. But all were agreed that the best audience anyone could have for a song was little Anna, because when Marion sang 'Pretty Baby' to her, her face would light up like a stage lamp.

'Everybody loves a baby... that's why I'm in love with you... Pretty baby...'

For Anna, those early days were a cavalcade of fascination. When she wasn't dozing in the shade of her perambulator's parasol, a succession of extraordinary faces beamed their *oooh*s and *aahh*s into her cosy world: beautiful courtesans with pompadours and beauty spots, savage Sioux warriors, a Charles the First with his head still attached to his body, gauchos, cowboys, beautiful but impoverished young mothers up from the country and about to be evicted into the snow, wicked landlords, moustachioed villains taking time out from tying virgins to rail tracks, and handsome riverboat cardsharps in velvet frockcoats and raffish gamblers' hats.

While tiny László bellowed direction through a bullhorn and Rex cranked the handle of his camera, Marion would sit beside the baby carriage at her easel, painting.

Looking at her mother's watercolours many years later, Anna was surprised to note that not so much as a single member of that day's shoot's itinerant cast ever appeared in any of them.

When filming was done, Rex was always the last one back to the open-topped tourer, usually because he was working his Cockney charm on the actors. 'Sorry, one an' all. I'll be late for me own funeral,' was his standard apology as he climbed up on the running board.

It was usually on the way home that Uncle László would invite Marion to appear in his movies. 'You have most perfect face, my dear,' he would say in his Hungarian gypsy voice, the one that everyone knew was phoney but didn't dare say so out loud. 'Is face made by God for camera to capture. Is face of goddess. The great László make you look lovelier than Aphrodite, with new panchromatic film we got now. We all make fortune together, yes?'

Marion's reply was always the same: 'First we got to get you some shoe lifts, so you can see over the top of the camera tripod.' Then she would kiss him very loudly on the forehead, leaving behind a stigmata of eye-blindingly red lipstick.

Uncle László took the jibe in good spirit. And there was no doubting that Marion had the looks for what he proposed. But

Rex never showed the slightest objection to his employer's barely veiled moves on Marion. And she, herself, was developing a little of Freda Bauer's fabled flirtatiousness as an antidote.

Marion was also beginning to realize that if her husband had any interest in her at all, it was as an adornment to boost his image at Hollywood parties. It would be sixteen years before she confessed to her daughter that, after Anna's birth, he'd refused to come anywhere near her in the bedroom.

Anna was four when Rex showed her how to create the world she somehow knew she had always wanted to look out upon.

'Do you want to see what I can see, Puddle?' he asked her one day, during a break in filming.

Anna was standing in the shade of a fan palm, holding her mother's hand while Marion chatted to one of the women extras.

'Why do you have to call her that, Rex?' Marion snapped, turning her head.

'What do you want me to call her? Pile? Heap? She's a tiny kid. They do that sort of thing.'

'How do you know? You never changed a diaper in your life. Besides, she's always been a clean sort of girl. You only use that name 'cause you know it riles me.'

Rex gave her a cold smile. 'The only time you got proper riled, my girl, is when they passed the Eighteenth Amendment and brought in prohibition.'

'*Bastard*,' said Marion under her breath, her anger as hot as a Santa Anna wind. The extra found a sudden need to be elsewhere.

Taking Anna by the hand, Rex led her into the sunlight, and towards the boxy camera standing on its tripod. The three rotating lenses looked to her like the eyes of some strange monster. Rex turned the peak of his cloth cap back to front and lifted her up so that she was looking into his face. 'Can you squint, Puddle?' he asked.

For the rest of her life, Anna would remember that close-up of his blue eyes and the suntanned oval of his face, as brown as the leather football the actors played with when they were off set.

'What's squimp?' she asked.

'*Squint*,' Rex said, closing one eye and arching the eyebrow of the other. 'Like *this*.'

Try as she might, Anna couldn't do it. The notion of disappointing this large, handsome man who smelled of the sun and hair oil brought her almost to tears.

'Here, let me try,' Rex said, slipping two fingers over her left eye as he positioned her at the eyepiece of the camera's side-mounted viewfinder box. 'Look through there. Tell me what you see.'

What Anna saw was extraordinary and prosaic at the same time: a Sioux chieftain in full feathered war bonnet in conversation over a shared cigarette with a horse-soldier of General Custer's Seventh Cavalry. She squealed in amazement and delight. She could see the sheen on the vanes of the feathers, the smudges of dirt on the white gloves of the cavalryman. It was like looking into another world, catching a dream in a little box.

The rest of the day's filming took an hour longer than Uncle László expected because Anna kept insisting on another 'squimp' through the viewfinder.

On the way home, Rex announced to Marion that from now on he would call their daughter Squimp. It pleased Marion no more than Puddle. All Anna imbibed at the time was the growing harshness in their voices when they thought she couldn't hear, or later, when they'd given up caring.

Though she sensed the growing gulf between her parents, and it disturbed her, there was recompense: hot days in the hills and trips to Venice Beach and the ocean, where Anna would frolic in her striped, knee-length swimming costume and cloche hat. And a growing wish for a companion who wasn't an adult.

'Mama, I want a sister. *Please* can I have a sister?'

Anna is seven. Even at that age, the beauty lies in her face like a bud waiting for the spring sunshine. Marion, on the other hand, is visibly fraying from eight years' marriage to Rex Cantrell.

'I'll put up with a brother if I must, but I'd really prefer a sister. It's so unfair. All the girls at school have sisters.'

Marion draws on yet another of the Lucky Strikes she smokes through a polished maplewood holder while she considers an appropriate reply.

'Yeah, good luck with that, honey,' she drawls out of the corner of her mouth. 'The day handsome young actors get to give birth is the day you get a sister. Sorry. You want a kitten instead?'

Anna thinks a kitten would be even more fun than a sister. She doesn't ask again. But before her mother can fulfil even that offer, her world ends.

The dark angel that brought catastrophe with him was not a handsome young actor but a forty-year-old Sicilian immigrant waiter at the Montmartre on Hollywood Boulevard named Bruno Maniscolo. He was a gentle, contemplative soul with mournful eyes and the face of Michelangelo's David gone to seed. Rex fell in love with him as he skilfully filleted *sole meunière* at the Cantrells' table.

Until that moment the evening was going swimmingly. It was Anna's eighth birthday. They had all gone to the Montmartre for a good time. Dressed in her best tulle frock with the Peter Pan collar, Anna could almost imagine herself grown up, while her mother looked the equal of any of the stars who regularly dined there. Rex had put on a rented tux. The dance floor was heaving. Vince Rose and his orchestra was on top form.

From their table, Anna watched entranced as adult bodies stamped, spun, writhed and entwined to the Charleston, the Black Bottom and the Shimmy. And if that became too much and her attention needed a *remise en bouche* – a phrase she'd learned from Rex, who'd told her it was something to do with making your mouth feel good – why, right there at the adjacent table were Lillian Gish and D. W. Griffith, surrounded by a doting bodyguard of smooth young men in Brooks Brothers suits.

A girl's birthday could simply not be better, Anna was thinking – until the waiter made a slight bow to Rex and his eyes lingered on her father as though he was waiting for a tip. Then he turned and glided away with a theatrical flourish. To Anna's surprise, Rex watched him go, his whole body seeming to expand and contract as if he was sighing.

'*What?*' hissed Marion, fiddling with the napkin in her lap. 'Am I so disgusting to you now that you prefer to make mooncalf eyes at a goddamn waiter in public?'

Rex turned his head back towards his wife. 'Not now, old gal,' he replied with an easy smile, his teeth a white scar in his brown face. 'Not the place, is it?'

For once the blush on Marion's face wasn't down to the Prohibition-defying hip flask in her bronze leather clutch purse. It was humiliation.

'Best hurry up and eat your damned fish, Rex,' Marion said coldly. 'Valentino might be in later. Maybe you'd like to sit on his lap and lick his ear like a damn Chihuahua. Would that make you happy?'

Although Anna couldn't begin to comprehend why her mother was inviting her father to do such a ludicrous thing, the anger in Marion's voice was not lost on her. But even at eight, she was learning that what her mother said, and what was in her heart, weren't always the same thing. The proof – and she could see it now – was the unmistakable look of pain in Marion's eyes.

Rex's reply was spoken so softly that Anna barely heard it over the hubbub. But hear it she did.

'More than living with a sour bitch who pops nerve pills when she doesn't get the attention she thinks is her due.'

The venom in her parents' voices made Anna shrink back into her seat. Her fingers gripped the hem of the blue and white tablecloth. Apparently, they had forgotten she was there. She felt scared, yet detached, as if she were observing two actors playing a scene.

And in that moment was the genesis of her later skill as a photojournalist: the ability to make herself almost invisible while she framed the shot, captured the catastrophe unfolding around others, as she observed with professional detachment from an almost safe distance.

Rex laid down his fish knife, the sole barely touched. He pulled the napkin from his collar and rose in as stately a manner as he could contrive in the circumstances, dabbing at the corner of his mouth as he did so. 'It's Squimp's birthday. Or 'ave you forgotten?' he said calmly. 'Look after your daughter. I need some fresh air.' And with that, he strode off into the crowd.

'Why are you and Papa arguing, Mama?' Anna asked.

Marion was staring at her food, her whole body as rigid as if she'd just been electrocuted. 'We weren't arguing, darling. We were just rehearsing a scene Papa's going to shoot with Julia Faye tomorrow.'

'Then why has he gone away? It's my birthday.'

'You heard what he said. He's just gone out for a breath of air.'

'But he's left his fish.'

'That's not all he's left, honey,' Marion said icily. Then the electric-chair current cut out and she regained the use of her limbs, lifting one hand to wave to a friend passing by the table as if nothing had happened.

Anna caught only one glimpse of her father until he returned, bringing with him a frostiness that made birthdays a time of conflicted emotion for her for years after. And that was of Rex standing languidly at the edge of the band, talking to the waiter who'd served them.

Perhaps, she reasoned, he was apologizing for leaving his fish to go cold.

'It's a meeting of the Society of Cinematographers,' announced Rex, as he buttoned his tuxedo. It was two weeks to the night after the ruin of Anna's birthday and they were in the kitchen of their little rented clapboard house in Hollywood. Anna was doing her homework at the table.

'And I'm the queen of Sheba,' growled Marion, giving him a haughty profile, as if she was ready for a close-up. 'Where's it happening?'

'The Villa Fiorentina.'

She let out a brittle snort of laughter tinged with hurt pride. 'So, you're not even paying me the courtesy of hiding it now. That's real sweet of you.'

The Villa Fiorentina was the worst-kept secret in Hollywood. A mock Venetian palazzo on Lake Shore Avenue surrounded by cypress trees, it had statues lining the driveway, terracotta tiles on the roof, stuccoed walls, tennis courts and clipped lawns tended by Mexican gardeners in crisply pressed white shorts. The owner was the bachelor scion of a railroad magnate. He had a penchant for interesting male company and threw fashion parades around the pool – the latest fabulous cocktail dresses from all the top designers, not one of them ever modelled by a woman.

'You don't think by now the police know what goes on there?' Marion asked caustically.

'They don't care, love – so long as the charity cheques to the station welfare fund keep arrivin'.'

'You could at least bring me back a goddamn frock.'

'You'd only spill wine on it,' Rex said cruelly, as he closed the kitchen door behind him.

Marion stalked off to her bedroom while Anna attempted to resume her homework. She heard the front door close and waited for the sudden splutter of the Model T Ford that Rex had recently purchased.

Instead, she heard what she assumed was a taxi pull up at the kerb. A voice carried to the open window. A throaty, male voice, rich with what Anna took to be an Italian accent. The taxi door slammed. The car drove away.

Silence reigned, for two glorious hours.

Anna was just about to get ready for bed when Marion walked back into the kitchen. She was wearing her wool-velour coat with the opossum fur trim and reeked of what Anna had long since learned to identify as bootleg rum. In one hand she held a tin of Dr Miles' Effervescent Tablets. *Guaranteed effective in the treatment of female nervous irritability and other hysterical conditions* proclaimed the slogan in the front.

'Put on your shoes, honey,' she said to Anna in a faintly slurred but determined voice. 'We're going out.'

'It's late, Mama. It's past my bedtime.'

Marion laid a hand gently under her daughter's chin, lifting her head to meet her somewhat unsteady gaze. 'Honey,' she said, 'it's never too late to see the truth about what kind of man your mother married, God save her poor deluded soul.' Then, removing her hand and wagging a finger at Anna in warning, she added, 'Let me give you some advice, sweetie. If you ever have the notion to paint the Bethesda Fountain in Central Park, padlock your ankles to something immovable and throw away the key.'

It was a miracle they reached the Villa Fiorentina alive. For a start, Marion fell over on the pavement trying to crank the Ford. Then there was a tense hiatus while Anna, being small, had to search under the chassis to recover the starting handle. Only anger and humiliation kept her mother sober enough to get the car to its destination.

Anna had no idea what was happening, or why they were careening down Broadway, almost taking a wheel off on the kerb. Her nose started to run. She began to weep.

'Don't know what you're crying for, honey,' Marion said brutally, taking her eyes off the road, which only added to Anna's misery. 'You're not the one married to the rat.'

Streetlights and brilliantly illuminated shop fronts sped by. At the junction of Broadway and West 2nd Street, Marion took the corner against the raised semaphore arm of the traffic lights. The sound of blaring horns would echo in Anna's ears for days. 'Mama, I want to go home,' she whimpered pitifully, as the Ford swerved to avoid flattening a cat.

By the time they reached Lake Shore Avenue, Anna had mastered her tears, though the sleeve of her sailor dress was sodden from her snotty crying.

Marion managed to park the Ford against the pavement without tearing out the nearside tyres.

'Please let me stay here,' Anna begged. If the Ford had survived this far, she reckoned, it must be the best place to shelter from whatever further calamity her mother had in mind.

But Marion was having none of it. She climbed out of the Ford, crossed over to Anna's side, opened the door and hauled her daughter out. 'I'm not risking him sweet-talking you with that phoney English charm,' she snapped. 'You've got eyes in your head, haven't you?'

'Yes, Mama.'

'Good. Because tonight I want you to use them. I'm not taking the blame for any of this crap later, understand?'

And although Anna nodded, she didn't really understand. All she knew was that somehow everything certain in her life was losing its outline, like a photo that had been overexposed. The thought of seeing her father was meant to make her feel good. It always had. But this felt as if she was being led to the scene of some terrible accident that had befallen him.

The night smelled of desert lavender as they crossed the street. The clean, crisp air made everything bright and sharp: the imposing stone pillars at the entrance to the plot, the lamps along the curving drive, the unmoving stars in the night sky.

As she drew close, Anna could see that the upper drive was full of cars, backed up in front of the villa's floodlit façade. Men in dark uniforms milled about. Anna assumed they must be chauffeurs. As Marion pulled her by the hand she heard her mother mutter, 'Never realized there were so many pansies in this goddamn town.'

The young Anna peered around, wide-eyed, but she couldn't see a flowerbed anywhere. She wondered if her mother was hallucinating from the rum and the effervescent tablets she'd been taking.

A dozen paces, no more, past the pillars and they came up against the first of the parked cars.

Marion stopped dead, causing Anna's shoes to scuff on the asphalt drive. 'Holy crap,' her mother said. 'They're not chauffeurs. They're police.'

And Villa Fiorentina appeared to Anna to explode. The night was suddenly filled with brilliant white light and the *whoosh-pop* of photographers' magnesium flashlights going off, followed by the yelling of reporters assembled around the grand entrance.

Marion couldn't have planned their arrival better if she'd tried; no leading lady ever stepped onto a stage with such timing. No one stopped her as she led Anna forward: all attention was fixed on the procession of well-dressed men being led out of the villa to the waiting cars.

Each one came out handcuffed to a policeman. Some shielded their faces with their free hands; others dropped their heads like penitents on their way to a scourging. Still others stared around in terrified dejection as they considered the imminent collapse of their lives and reputations.

Only two men left the Villa Fiorentina with their heads held high. The first was the railroad heir. Once a talented college quarterback and built for the part, he emerged magisterially in a sequined, mermaid-hem ballgown in maroon silk that he'd had tailored to fit. The policemen by his side returned his wide, confident grin with malevolence. Anna couldn't take her eyes off him – until Rex came out.

She had never seen her father looking so upright, so proud, so damn-you-all-to-hell. He was wearing the jacket of his tux unbuttoned over his bare chest. *Silly Papa!* she wanted to shout.

You forgot to put on your shirt when you went out! She couldn't imagine why he was being arrested for going to a party. She wondered if Uncle László had somehow got him into trouble. *He hasn't done anything naughty*, she wanted to yell. *He's my daddy.*

Marion beat her to it. She put two fingers in her mouth and whistled. 'Hey! Cantrell, you Limey bastard! We're over here. You got anything to say to your daughter – before they put you in the slammer?'

As their eyes met, Anna noticed her father's chin give the merest hint of a wobble. She knew that was what her own face did when she cried, and for a moment she was horrified that he was going to do the same. But all Rex did was circle the thumb and forefinger of his free hand, lift them to one eye and squimp at her, as if readying himself to start filming.

And he smiled.

Although she had no idea what crime he'd committed, at that moment Anna thought him the most guiltless, bravest father that had ever lived.

After the carnival had passed by, Marion lifted her eyes to the dark California night and let out a bitter sigh. 'That's all I ever was for him – a beard.'

For years to come, Anna was often troubled by the thought that one day she might wake up, look in the mirror, and find herself hirsute, like a bearded lady in the circus.

The Berlin apartment. 1989

On the bedside table the second hand of the travelling clock went on softly sounding the beat, even though Harry Taverner had lapsed into silence. Elly heard the distant clanking of the old Weimar-era lift as someone came home late from the celebrations down at the Wall. She waited for Harry to find himself in the present. It took a while. He'd run a marathon and needed time to recover.

'It was the same people who'd smashed up László's New York studio,' he said at length, as if confiding to her a great secret. 'They'd paid another police precinct to raid the Villa Fiorentina and tipped off the newspapers about it – there were a few actors signed to the competition there that night: they had morality clauses in their contracts, so it was a headache for their studios.'

'What happened to Rex and the others who were arrested?' Elly asked.

'They were lucky. The charges were serious: lewd and lascivious behaviour and outraging public decency, contrary to the California penal code. Rex could have ended up serving fourteen years in San Quentin. He could even have been chemically castrated. They did that to thousands of gay men back then. But the railway heir's lawyers got the charges dropped. Money changed hands, probably. It usually did in those sorts of circumstances.'

'What an awful experience for Anna,' Elly said. 'And for Marion, too, I suppose – a marriage based on a lie, public humiliation. Did it ruin Rex's career?'

Harry shook his head, a lock of white hair falling across his brow. 'It wasn't getting arrested that did for Rex. After the war, he ended up on a Hollywood blacklist, probably because someone thought László, being Hungarian, was a secret communist.'

'What happened to him?'

'When Bruno Maniscolo went back home to Sicily, Rex went with him. They ran a *pensione* together, in Palermo.'

'And Anna?'

'The very next day Marion took her back to New York.'

'Did she ever see her father again?'

'Alive, only once – twelve years later, in New York. The next time was at his funeral, in Palermo. He died of a heart attack. In 1951, if my memory serves me. Bruno died a few months later.'

'At least Rex found his soul mate, then.'

Harry looked into his tumbler and Elly could see by the lift in his cheek that he was smiling. He continued: 'Anna told me that when Rex was buried there was a delay at the graveside; the body hadn't arrived from the mortuary. The priest was getting impatient. A brightly painted lorry drew up and Anna thought Bruno had arranged some sort of traditional Sicilian send-off. But it was just a local farmer bringing in his vegetables – the hearse turned up half an hour later.'

Elly shook her head in incredulity. 'Then Rex was right: he *was* late for his own funeral, just like he'd always said.'

'Anna could laugh about that night later, but not for a long time. It broke her heart.'

'So, what happened next?'

'Are you sure you're not too tired to hear, Puffin?'

'Are you kidding? I'm hooked. It's better than sleeping in that awful hotel. I'm more worried about you.'

'The Bauers took Marion back in, for a while at least,' Harry said. 'But by that time their broadmindedness had narrowed somewhat. Wolfgang had his position in New York society to think of. He decided Marion needed a while to reflect on things, until the scandal had died down – somewhere where she could relearn the old-world conventions she'd apparently forgotten in California.'

Harry set his glass down on the bedside table and pulled another sheet from the portfolio case. He laid it carefully on the quilt between them.

Elly could see that this time it wasn't a photo or a painting, but a curled and yellowing advertising flyer. Turning it towards her, she saw a sleek ocean liner ploughing bravely through the waves, smoke streaming from rakish funnels. She read the copy.

SAIL IN LUXURY TO EUROPE

The HAMBURG-AMERICA LINE offers the discerning traveller a PALACE AFLOAT. Regular sailings from Pier 86 New York via Southampton, aboard our new steam turbine liner, *DEUTSCHLAND.*

Make the crossing in the highest degree of comfort and convenience.

FIRST-CLASS staterooms.

Second- and third-class cabins also available.

'Wolfgang stumped up for a second-class cabin with no port-hole, and the train fare from Hamburg to Vienna, plus a small stipend – just enough to get them settled,' Harry said, with just the trace of laughter in his voice. 'He loved his daughter as well as any father might. But he wasn't going to have his generosity taken for a reward. Not after California. Anna told me she'd cried nonstop all the way across the Atlantic at the thought of leaving Rex behind. I think that might have been a slight exaggeration, but I can't be sure. What could she have done? She was eight. And Marion was more than just a mother: she was a minor force of nature. Besides, no divorce court would have awarded custody to Rex. Not with his record.'

'So, they went to Vienna.'

'Spring, 1925,' Harry said, taking a pull from his whisky. 'I don't think Wolfgang's relatives back in the old country had the faintest idea what they were in for.'

'You mean with Marion?'

'I mean with them both.'

Four

Destitute in Vienna.
Picture taken by Anna Cantrell. Leica D camera.
Agfa monochrome film. February 1934

He was one amongst thousands in the city that day, but the misery in his eyes was unique to him alone. He had chosen a spot close enough to the tram stop to be seen but not to inconvenience, because in Vienna being a victim of the Great Depression was no excuse for bad manners. His face was deeply furrowed, gaunt with hunger and despair. He could have been thirty or eighty; it was impossible for Anna to tell. He squatted on a damp wooden board in a clear patch of pavement between mounds of melting, filthy snow. The placard across his chest read: *Ein ehrlicher Arbeiter. Bitte helf mir – An honest worker. Please help me.* No one, save Anna, paid him attention. With a third of the population out of work, many Viennese had found their stomachs settled better if the desperate were allowed to become ghosts, wraiths you couldn't see in daylight.

'I don't have much to give you,' Anna said in the faultless German she'd learned during her nine years studying in Vienna. 'I need to take the tram, you see.' She laid the coins on the board beside him. Her breath misted in the cold air as she fished in her bag for the roll she'd bought at Meinl's. 'But I've got *this.*

It's freshly made and the chicken's good. Would you allow me to take your photograph? If you say no, it doesn't matter. You can still have it.'

The shoulders of his dirty trench coat gave a heave. It could have been acquiescence, or the first signs of pneumonia; suffering had made him unreadable. Anna gave him the roll. He held it in his almost blackened fingers and tore at it with his teeth like an animal. While he ate, she put down her bag, swung the camera case across her body and drew out the Leica Model C that Rex had bought her for her sixteenth birthday.

She felt bad about asking for the shot. But it would go down well in the exhibition tomorrow, and surely that was a good thing: a few people might be moved enough not to turn away the next time they met someone like him on the street.

She heard a bell jangle and a brief shriek of brakes. The D-line *Elektrische* was approaching. She looked at the tramp again. He glanced up from the *Schnitzelsemmel* she'd given him and, seeing the hesitation in her face, nodded.

Anna waited until he'd devoured the roll – mere seconds – then fired off a salvo of shots. Returning the camera to its case, she picked up her bag just as the tramcar came to rest at the Schwarzenbergplatz stop, the doors neatly aligned with twin paths cleared through the slush banked up against the kerb. The destination board on the front read *Sudbahnhoff, Belvedere.*

'Thank you,' she said to the man in the snow. 'I'm sorry—'

But his head was down and he seemed to have forgotten her presence.

Hurrying to the tram stop, she caught the fusty smell of damp wool from the overcoated office clerk ahead of her in the queue. Anna followed him aboard and found a vacant seat, settling herself between a plump matron guarding a wicker basket on her knees and a nun who looked old enough to remember Franz Joseph before he became emperor. She had no sooner sat down than the trilbies and fedoras began to turn in her direction.

Anna knew she'd inherited her mother's looks, along with a measure of Marion's sassiness. But she was almost eighteen now and she wasn't going to apologize to anyone for it. Besides, in her own mind, whenever she looked in a mirror, all she saw staring back at her was someone with the looks of a surprised Afghan hound. Too angular. Too haughty. Eyebrows so arched they looked as if they were about to spring off her face at any moment.

Then there was her hair – the bane of her life. Marion called the colour 'polished chestnut', as if she was a piece of furniture. She'd been made to wear it in a pixie cut ever since she began attending classes at the Institute for Applied Graphic Arts. But it had always had a rebellious curl to it, and now she was letting it grow longer. Every night she prayed that one day soon the Afghan hound might miraculously transmute into Myrna Loy or Katharine Hepburn. Strange, she thought, catching a glimpse of the destitute man through the window, how we decide what's worth looking at and what isn't.

The driver released the brake lever and with a lurch the tram resumed its journey towards Prinz Eugen Strasse and the Belvedere. Anna bought a ticket from the uniformed *schaffner* and glanced again at her watch. Home in under twenty minutes, she reckoned. Whether her mother would be there to meet her was another matter. It was more than likely that Marion had forgotten about tomorrow entirely. These days her memory was like a slab of Gouda cheese: full of holes. The exhibition had cost Anna every ounce of goodwill she had so diligently hoarded. All those favours called in. All those closed doors knocked upon. All that unabashed pleading – just to secure a tiny corner of the art gallery at the Belvedere orangery in which to display for one day only, admission free, her and her mother's collection of paintings and photographs: *Vienna: Through the Eyes of Two Women.*

Anna knew how ridiculously fortunate she was to be able to present her work. It wasn't as if the city didn't have more pressing things to occupy its mind. The headline in the spread newspaper that at that very moment blocked her view down the car demanded a crackdown on communist agitators; the poster stuck to the wall of the tramcar explained in strident tones that ruling by decree was the only way Chancellor Dollfuss could protect Austrian democracy from both socialism and the Nazis. *Save Austria – join the Fatherland Front!* it proclaimed.

Anna closed her eyes and made a mental list of who to call, who might have time to spare to help her transport the paintings and mounted photos from the apartment on the Karolinengasse to the Belvedere – student friends she could rely upon not to put their feet through the canvases. Soon she had a vision in her mind: the exhibition staged successfully, money and cheques in the cash box, Marion's only visible presence her erratic signature on the paintings. If she had learned anything in the almost ten years they had been in Vienna, it was how to remain optimistic.

At her stop, Anna alighted and looked back down the boundary of the Belvedere palace towards the city. The streetlamps were coming on, gilding the elegant buildings along the Ringstrasse with pearls of light. Spotlights illuminated the zigzag mosaic roof and the great spire of St Stephen's cathedral.

One day soon, she thought, in a sunset such as this, I'll take the shot: Vienna, with the setting sun painting one side gold, and the approaching night hiding the other half in darkness. The trick will be to capture the chiaroscuro in black and white.

But then Vienna was all about playing tricks: a refined dowager duchess with a side-line in delinquency. A pearl with more grit in it than most cared to admit.

Anna had fallen in love with the city almost the moment they arrived. Even though it had become an imperial capital bereft of an empire, its grandeur was unlike anything she had seen before. And there had been an edge to it that, even then, at eight years old, she could almost taste. The cafés to which Marion took her could be grand and, as she now realized, louche at the same time. The waiters with their white napkins draped over their arms possessed an air of superiority not even the heads of the great studios in Hollywood could match, and Anna had seen most of *them* up close. She loved the bustle of the *Naschmarkt*, listening to the competing voices of shoppers and stallholders alike: sing-song Austrian German; Hungarian – real country Hungarian, not like Uncle Lászlő's phoney Greenwich Village version; and Yiddish, the authentic sound of the *shtetl* that made her mother smile even though she'd been born in Manhattan.

She loved the shops in the Graben just as much, with their elegant mannequins draped in furs and their shiny black store signs with polished gilt lettering above the windows.

Then there was the annual Opera Ball.

'Mama, please, *please* can we go?' Anna had asked when she turned ten. In her head she was seeing handsome counts in glittering dress uniform and beautiful women in ballgowns that rustled and billowed like silk sails in a gale. 'I promise I'd be on my best behaviour.'

'Are you kidding me, honey?' Marion replied. 'I'd have to sell you to a white slaver – twice – just to afford a seat in the ladies restroom.'

As a consolation, Marion had taken her for a ride around the city in a horse-drawn fiacre. Happier than she had ever been – despite missing Rex dreadfully – Anna had imagined herself a Hapsburg princess out for a jaunt around her hunting estate.

And then the Great Depression had struck.

Almost overnight, millions were out of work.

'Are we going to starve, too, Mama?' thirteen-year-old Anna had asked her mother as they passed a group of defeated, hungry-looking men searching for scraps in the Stadtpark's wastebins.

'Not while this broad can still lift a paintbrush,' Marion replied fiercely.

In fact, good though her mother's watercolours were, they didn't sell well. Few Viennese had the cash to spare. But while Marion had to cut back on nights at the Café Central, starving was never on the horizon. Papa Wolfgang's stipend kept them afloat, though it had been trimmed considerably: Bauer Manhattan Mercantile and Savings was no more immune than any other bank to the economic crisis.

On Anna's sixteenth birthday, Rex had reached across the Atlantic to spark a dreadful row between mother and daughter. He'd sent one hundred dollars – a small fortune – through Cooks, so that Anna could purchase the very Leica camera that now nestled in its leather case on her knees. She could have bought a better one with the money, but she'd settled on a used Model C and given what she saved to the local soup kitchen.

In his letter, Rex had sworn her to secrecy: he'd known Marion would try to appropriate the money. And indeed, when Marion saw the camera, she'd demanded to know how Anna had managed to afford it.

Anna had found it impossible to lie convincingly.

Marion then demanded she pawn the Leica.

'I need it for my classes at the institute, if I'm ever to become a real photographer,' Anna had protested.

In the end, she'd handed her mother the pittance she'd saved from a part-time job in a milliner's shop on the Argentinierstrasse, and kept the Leica.

It was the first time she'd had the courage to confront her mother's unpredictable temper.

Anna had stood up for herself again, only a fortnight ago. 'I'd like my name on these,' she'd told Marion in the living room of their apartment, as they chose the photographs for the exhibition together.

'Of course, honey,' Marion said, pinching her cheek as if she were eight again. 'I'm not a glory thief. You know that.'

In the silence that had followed, Anna had swallowed hard. 'I mean, I want them credited to Anna Cantrell.'

The eruption had been titanic. No ocean was wide enough to free her mother from that English pansy. No hell was fiery enough for a deceiving husband who had humiliated her so. But then Marion had always been a woman of absolutes.

Again, Anna had stood her ground. 'I'll be Anna Bauer whenever you want me to be, Mama,' she had said boldly, holding the Leica across her chest like a shield. 'But when I'm taking pictures, *then* I'm Anna Cantrell.'

Turning her back on the panorama before her, Anna hurried down the street towards the apartment. It was empty, just as she had feared. The stack of paintings and photos lay where she had left them that morning, waiting to be curated into a proper order for hanging in the Belvedere orangery tomorrow.

Sighing, she threw her coat on the sofa. Unlike many apartments in the block, this one boasted its own bathroom. By placing thick cardboard over the window and a red-painted bulb in the ceiling light, it made a tolerable darkroom. Anna made a contact print from the film she'd shot at the tram stop, choosing the best frame for the portable enlarger she had been allowed to borrow from the institute for the exhibition. When it was printed to her satisfaction, she took it into the lounge.

The apartment was too silent for her taste, and too cold, so she wound up the gramophone. Singing along to Ethel Waters' 'Heatwave', Anna went about the task of mounting the photograph of the destitute man.

She was pleased with it. She was wise enough not to think she'd caught anything noble in his suffering. A heart of stone would spot the raw hopelessness in his stare. If there was truth in the picture, it was in his eyes – not in the art of taking it.

Anna then turned her attention to her mother's paintings, curating them into what she considered would be an appropriate order of hanging. She knew she was taking a gamble: Marion could turn up in a moment and breezily overthrow everything she'd done.

It was almost eight when she picked up the phone and began calling around. She started with the Café Nihlisimus, down by the Karlsplatz. Marion often enjoyed a boozy evening there with her friends from the Association of Women Artists.

'Ah, the beautiful Fräulein Anna,' oiled Herr Wendell, the manager, down the phone when she identified herself. 'I am sure tomorrow will be a great triumph – at the Belvedere – no?'

'No. I mean yes. At least I hope so. Is my mother there, please, Herr Wendell?'

'Regretfully, Fräulein, I must inform you that she is not.'

'Has she been in today?'

'Indeed, she has. Her favourite table was occupied. She was most put out. My ears still wear the bruises.'

'When did she leave?'

'About an hour ago.' Herr Wendell's voice suddenly dropped an octave or two, becoming more intimate than Anna cared for. 'May I ask, Fräulein Anna, have you perhaps considered posing for Herr Professor Koppitz? I'm sure the results would be most… agreeable.'

Holding the phone, Anna blushed. Professor Koppitz was renowned for his artistic photos of naked men and women. He was also her tutor at the institute.

'That would be most improper, Herr Wendell,' she said, her jaw tightening. 'Professor Koppitz has his own models. He is also a gentleman. Now, did my mother give any hint as to where she was going?'

There was a hint of disappointment in Herr Wendell's voice. 'I believe I did hear the Red Panther mentioned, Fräulein.'

Oh God, Anna mouthed at the ceiling. The exhibition only hours away, and Marion has decided to squeeze in a visit to Sodom and Gomorrah.

The Red Panther was a basement nightclub down by the river, a dimly lit cavern of scarlet velour, gold-painted Grecian pillars and a pyramid of cocktail glasses over which cascaded a fountain of fake Slovak champagne pumped by a hidden electric motor. The clientele was an argumentative mix of nationalists, social democrats from the bourgeoisie, poets, avant-garde artists, cross-dressers and communists. The only thing they had in common was a taste for the passable American jazz. Marion had found it within a week of their arrival in Vienna and loved it. Now she was a well-known habituée.

It was almost ten when Anna descended the stairs beneath the brilliant neon outline of a springing feline. She pushed at the snarling panther's face that formed the brass doorknob and entered. She felt like an imposter, being woefully underdressed – beneath her overcoat she still had on the plain dress she'd worn to her classes at the institute. Her only concession to Viennese nightlife was a little hastily applied make-up.

Behind the coat-check counter sat a young woman barely older than herself. She wore the alabaster face of the recently deceased and a severe Joan of Arc haircut. She was reading Schopenhauer by the light of an art deco lamp in the shape of Aphrodite reclining in a giant seashell. Anna endured a long stare of scrutiny – head to toe and back again – and knew she would be the least interesting person the girl would see all night. From beyond a heavy crimson curtain came a thumping version of Johnny Marvin's 'Crazy Words, Crazy Tune' and the murmur of voices.

'Are you sure you're in the right place, sweetheart?' the coat-check girl said, laying aside the book.

'I'm looking for my mother,' Anna replied, promising herself she would never again utter those words upon entering a nightclub.

'Your mother – in *here*?'

'She's a regular. Marion Bauer, the artist. I need to speak to her.'

The woman's eyes widened. 'You're the American's kid?'

Anna winced. 'I was at classes. I haven't really had time to change,' she said lamely.

'Yeah, I can see it now – in your face,' the woman said, her stern features breaking into a friendly smile. 'I'm Ilsa.' She put out a spidery hand for Anna to shake.

Black nail polish, Anna noted. How rebellious does a girl have to be to wear black nail polish in the city of Klimt?

'Is she here?'

'She came in with a couple of friends, just after we opened. I haven't seen her leave,' Ilsa said, pointing to the curtain. 'She must still be inside.'

'I'm not intending to stay. I just need to speak to her. I think she's forgotten something important. Is there a charge?'

'No, not for women. Here, let me take that,' said Ilsa, gesturing at Anna's overcoat. When she saw the simple floral dress Anna was wearing, and the lace-up Oxfords on her feet, she frowned.

'I *know,*' Anna said defensively. 'I wasn't expecting to go out. I was in a hurry.'

'Oh, you look fine, sweetie,' the coat-check girl said. 'Just be careful in there. There are some men who like to pay extra for the virginal-secretary look. They might think you're, you know, dressed that way for a reason.'

The club had been open barely an hour, but it was already crowded. The air was heavy with the smell of perfumed sweat, hazy with cigarette and cigar smoke. The parquet dance floor thrummed like the skin of a drum. A rotating mirror ball fired bullets of lights over the heads of the dancers. Stockinged legs kicked and twisted; suited arms flailed; organza-sheathed elbows scythed; and torsos jerked, writhed and convulsed to the energetic efforts of the band.

Anna began to make her way through the throng. She passed a table where three young men in pinstripe suits that looked too big for them were sitting. Each had a women perched on their lap. The men had shiny faces, eager eyes and oiled hair parted down the centre. The women looked about as animated as if they'd stopped for a rest on a park bench on their way home from the dentist.

At the next table sat a group of shaven-headed men in baggy work jackets. They seemed engaged in an intense discussion, punctuated with expansive hand gestures. Communists, Anna decided, without any evidence – probably plotting a proletarian uprising that would blaze and die by the time they left, drunk, and having changed nothing.

The next table was a throne to a large, balding man with jowls like a lifebelt. The woman he was with wore an ill-fitting satin gown and her lipstick was overdone, as bright as the neon sign over the club's door. Anna observed her leaning forward on her elbows to hear what her escort was saying, smiling and nodding just a little too readily. Anna guessed both woman and dress were rented. She pictured a home in Floridsdorf, a husband out of work – or maimed in the Great War – and a clutch of children to feed. She wondered if the husband knew where she was.

Still there was no sign of Marion. Anna pressed on into the club, feeling as out of place as she had on her first day at *Volksschule*. But despite what Ilsa the coat-check girl had said, no one seemed to pay her much attention as she manoeuvred around the dance floor in her search.

Having made a reconnaissance of the tables, without success, she turned her attention to the booths that lined the walls. With mounting embarrassment, she encountered a series of tableaux that frankly bordered on the pornographic. It came as a blessed relief when, on visiting the fifth booth, she saw her mother and two female friends sitting on the velour-covered settle behind the booth's table.

Marion was in fake gold lamé, her two companions in severe black satin and looking like the victims of a famine. The three wise monkeys, she thought uncharitably: See-no-evil…

Hear-no-evil… Forget-you-have-an-exhibition-at-the-Schloss-Belvedere-tomorrow-evil.

'My darling daughter!' Marion cried as she caught sight of her. 'What the Sam Hill are *you* doing here? No homework from Prof Koppitz tonight?' She checked the two bottles in the ice bucket beside the table, pulled out the one that was still half-full, filled her own glass and pushed it across the table towards her daughter. 'Here – have some champagne, darling,' she said, with a gesture to her friends to make room.

Her mother appeared worryingly animated. Her movements were spiky, exaggerated, barely under control. Her skin gleamed. The pupils of her eyes were as large as pennies. She seemed in need of a handkerchief: she was having difficulty stopping herself sneezing.

Anna took a gulp of champagne, telling herself she deserved at least *some* reward for the night's efforts. Then, as she put the glass down, she noticed a mirrored plate lying on the table. It was smeared with traces of white powder. Three paper straws and an open silver-handled clasp knife lay close by.

Oh God, she thought, it's worse than I dared fear – she's back on the cocaine.

What came out of her mouth was rather more prosaic. 'Mother, it's almost ten o'clock.'

The pupils of Marion's eyes swam alarmingly. 'Is it *really*, honey? Doesn't fun fly when you're having time?'

'You've forgotten, haven't you? About tomorrow.'

'Tomorrow?'

Anna noticed her mother's cigarette case and lighter on the table. What the hell, she thought, as she leaned across and helped herself. It's been a long day and now it's about to get longer. 'The exhibition – at the Belvedere.'

'Is that tomorrow?'

'Oh, for God's sake—' Anna knew she was sounding like the worst kind of fussy puritan, but this was beyond the endurance of a saint. 'The gas was off, the fridge was empty,' she went on. 'I've collated the paintings and the photos. The only thing I haven't done is carry them to the Belvedere orangery on my back, because I'm not a bloody beast of burden!'

'Calm down, darling. You're beginning to sound like your father,' Marion cooed, topping up her friends' glasses and returning the now empty bottle to its companion in the chrome bucket. 'Girls, you must have met my little Anna—'

The two women with Marion turned their languid gaze in Anna's direction. She'd seen them before at the Café Nihlisimus. One, she knew, had studied at the Academy of Fine Arts with Egon Schiele; the other was reputed to have been one of Hanna Gluck's lovers.

'Mother, I'm not little. I'm almost eighteen.'

'To me, darling, you'll always be my itty-little-bitty mite,' Marion said, pinching her thumb and index finger together to indicate something tiny and blowing her a kiss. She patted the space the women had made on the settle. 'You've come all this way to make sure I'm not getting into trouble. Stay a while. We'll order some more bubbles and see if we can't find you a nice young boy to dance with.'

'A nice young boy – in here?'

'Don't blow your wig, honey,' Marion soothed. 'We're just having fun. Don't spoil it.'

Acutely conscious of her mother's worldly friends – all cadaverous black satin and studied ennui – Anna relented and sat down.

Marion hailed a passing waiter for another bottle and a fourth glass. 'While we wait for the ammunition to arrive,' she said, 'let me tell you girls about how well Anna's doing at the institute. Professor Koppitz thinks she's his best student in years.'

Anna wished there was a bottomless pit below the Red Panther that would gape and swallow her. She looked hard at her mother. 'He's never said anything of the sort,' she mumbled, looking down and seeing her reflection in the mirror plate on the table. The traces of cocaine on the glass made her flushed cheeks look like those of a red squirrel.

There was nothing she could do, she decided, other than endure.

'She gets all her talent from her mother, of course,' Marion said. 'That Limey bastard taught her nothing.'

It wasn't true, and Anna suspected her mother knew it. But all she could do was cringe while Marion went through the same old excruciating lament: Rex the fraud, Rex the liar, Rex the pervert. *Rex this, Rex that, Rex damned twenty ways to hell and back.*

Anna was forced to admit that this all-consuming bitterness hadn't dented her mother's beauty. She was still liquid and elegant in her movements. As she spoke, she held her cigarette as though she were conducting 'Dido's Lament', ordering exquisitely slow beats of suffering from the orchestra. Only when Anna looked deep into her mother's eyes, at her saucer-sized pupils, did the hurt in them show itself, as raw as it had ever been. All the wild parties, the men, the drink, the lines of cocaine – a habit her mother thought she didn't know about – an improvised antidote to pain, making herself someone other than the sap who had fallen for Rex Cantrell's smile.

When the refreshment arrived, Marion refilled everyone's glass and raised hers in a toast. Anna sank deeper into her seat, expecting to be the subject.

'Here's to Herr Hitler – Germany's funny little new chancellor,' Marion said instead. 'May his ass grow itchy and his arms too short to scratch it.'

Marion's two companions laughed as they echoed, 'To Herr Hitler!'

'That's not funny, Mama,' Anna said pointedly. 'Don't you read the papers?'

'Of course I read the papers, darling. But the best way to deal with angry little men is to laugh very loudly at them. They don't like it. You'll learn that soon enough.'

'Aren't you concerned about what's going on in Germany?' Anna asked. She knew she was being too serious for her mother's liking, but she didn't care. 'It's happening here in Austria, too, if you bother to look around. I heard someone on the tram this morning complaining about *Judenkunst* – *Jew* art. You're Jewish. And that makes *me* Jewish.'

'Honey, we're *American*,' Marion said laboriously. 'Well, you're American *and* English, but we can't all be perfect, can we? Anyway, all that unpleasantness will soon blow over. The way that silly little man keeps shouting at everybody – who's going to put up with that for long? Someone's bound to take a pot shot at him, for sure.' She waved in the direction of the dance floor, where Anna could see two men dancing together. Both wore sequined ballgowns and Carmen Miranda headdresses. They waved back.

Anna had a memory of that night at the Villa Fiorentina: the hatred in the faces of the policemen when the railroad heir was led out.

'Let's not speak of tiresome things,' she heard Marion say. 'We came here to enjoy ourselves.'

'I thought you disapproved of the sort of places Papa frequented,' Anna said, looking around.

'No, sweetie. It was your papa I disapproved of.' Marion turned her face to the friend on her right. 'Say, how would *you* like it if you thought you'd purchased an expensive mink from Bloomingdale's, only to find they'd sent you a bag of dirty old rags?'

The woman laughed loudly and for too long for Anna's taste.

'I think we should go home, Mama. *Please*,' Anna said, standing up. 'How are we going to put on a proper exhibition tomorrow if one of us is as high as a kite? Influential people will be there. I wrote all the invitations myself, remember?'

'All in good time, darling. Sit down. You look like you've had a hard day at the institute. You deserve a little *gemütlichkeit*.'

If her mother's friends hadn't been there, Anna would have stood her ground. She would have insisted. But at that moment she couldn't think of anything more embarrassing than attempting to drag a doped-up woman out of a nightclub. Reluctantly, she retook her place on the settle. I'll give it until eleven, she thought. Then, if she still won't come, I'll tell her I've just realized I forgot to turn off the gas in the apartment.

The band had just started to play 'Let's Do It, Let's Fall In Love' when she heard the first scream. It came from a distance, somewhere by the entrance, barely heard above the music. Anna looked up. The crowd heaved and parted like the bow-wave of a ship. The dancers stopped dancing. The band faltered. The music trailed away, leaving only the saxophonist to blow a dying, uncertain coda.

'Oh, Christ,' murmured one of Marion's friends, taking a nervous gulp of champagne. 'Nazi brownshirts!'

But as soon as she saw them, Anna knew her mother's friend was mistaken. For a start, the dozen or so men standing in an angry phalanx in the centre of the club weren't wearing brown: they sported a motley collection of makeshift uniforms, while some had no uniform at all. At first, Anna couldn't take them seriously. What did it say about the ruling party, the *Vaterländisce Front* – Chancellor Dollfuss's Fatherland Front – if it couldn't dress its volunteer paramilitary militia in proper outfits? Several of them didn't even look healthy enough to be described as martial: skinny, underfed boys and older, overweight men. But then she saw they were all armed with clubs, hammers, knives and brass knuckledusters. One even had a revolver. And these *Heimwehr* boys were clearly spoiling for a fight.

For an instant, Anna thought she was dreaming. I'm on Uncle László's backlot, and these are all actors. If I look to my left, I'll see Rex bent to his movie camera. Then the fear cut in.

'Where's the red sewer trash?' the one with the gun shouted. He had sunken eyes and pimples, but his expression was killer-cold.

'Where are the trade unionists and the Marxists?' another cried.

From the safety of the crowd, someone called back, 'Troublemakers! Fuck off back to your friends in Germany, why don't you?'

The man with the gun glowered as he moved the weapon back and forth. Dancers dived out of his aim. Women screamed. Men grovelled to get out of the line of fire. 'Strike tomorrow, and we'll search you out and hang every last one of you from the Floridsdorf bridge!' the gunman shouted.

'Into the Danube with concrete boots would be better,' shouted one of his companions, grinning triumphantly at the effect a single firearm could have on a crowd. 'Let them try to organize a collective of the fishes.' He waved a length of lead pipe in the face of the nearest nightclubber – a lanky man in a grey moleskin suit who promptly hid himself behind his dance partner.

'Someone should telephone the police,' Anna heard a woman say loudly.

'Even if they bothered to come, whose side do you think they'd be on?' came the reply. 'That's something else we seem to have learned from Germany.'

But not everyone was cowed. A lone male voice called out, a worker's voice, harsh and defiant. Unafraid. 'If you've come for a fight, we'll gladly give you pigs the hiding of a lifetime.'

This brought a growl of agreement from the men Anna had assumed were communists.

The gunman's eyes fell contemptuously upon the two men in glittering ballgowns Marion had waved to earlier. 'What with – handbags?'

'Where are the National Socialists?' the ruffian with the lead pipe shouted.

'Heil Hitler!' came the angry reply from the pinstriped young men in baggy suits Anna had seen on her way in.

Whether they were really Nazis or just being facetious, it didn't matter. The words were enough. A beer bottle sailed through the air. Anna had the fleeting impression it had been launched from the communist table. It was well aimed, exploding right amongst the three men. The women they were with screamed, diving off their laps to escape the flying glass and the spray of *Mohrenbräu*.

It was the only signal the *Heimwehr* men needed. Their attack was as fierce as wildfire and just as indiscriminate. No one close by was safe from their flailing fists and their weapons.

Some of the clientele fought back bravely. Anna saw a woman in a silver strapless cocktail dress floor one overweight *Heimwehr* man with a chair. But the paramilitaries were practised street-thugs, well-schooled in sudden violence.

While Marion and her friends ducked below the table for shelter, Anna looked down the length of the Red Panther. At the far end, a knot of frightened people jammed the exit, spilling out into the coat-check area and falling over on the stairs as they tried to escape. To her left, one of the two men in the sequined dresses took a *Heimwehr* fist square in the face. Bloodied, he staggered backwards into the pyramid of glasses that Anna had passed when she'd arrived, scattering them like shrapnel. The electric pump underneath went on spraying the fake champagne like a broken fire hydrant, until one of the militiamen kicked it over. Even then it went on hosing the edge of the dance floor, where now, instead of dancers, there was a mass of brawling, scrapping, biting and punching bodies. The band formed a corral around their precious instruments, fending off attackers with their music stands.

Anna had seen a lot of violence in her young life – but all of it fake, observed through Rex's viewfinder: Sioux massacres, Revolutionary beheadings, Wild West gunfights. At the end of the scene, all the casualties had climbed to their feet, brushed themselves off and gone for a refreshing drink at the commissary wagon. The reality was something else entirely, and it scared her beyond measure. And yet she could not hide from it. Even self-preservation didn't seem enough to overcome her need to observe, to frame, to record. She was quite unaware of Marion tugging at her sleeve to pull her down under the table.

And then – as if God had decided He needed to intervene in this human insanity by cracking a celestial bullwhip – there came three gunshots. Deliberate, evenly paced, slow enough to be taken as a signal.

The noise, confined in this velveteen cavern, was deafening, and the fight stopped as suddenly as it had begun. Anna caught the sharp rasp of gun-smoke in her nostrils as her ears rang.

And then she saw him.

He was standing in the centre of the now empty dance floor, legs braced heroically, one foot set purposefully behind the other, as though he was about to plant a flag at the summit of a conquered peak. He held one arm aloft, aimed at the ceiling, a still-smoking pistol in his hand.

Where had he come from? He hadn't been amongst the motley gang that had started the confrontation. I would have noticed a man like that, Anna thought. *Anyone* would notice a man like him.

He was young, twenty-four at the most, she reckoned. He wore his fair hair swept tightly back from his forehead. It made him look like an Olympic swimmer who'd just climbed out of the pool after winning gold. His eyes were piercing blue, his gaze demanding an attention that surprised her, given his relative youth. His uniform, unlike the others, was smartly pressed, fitting his athletic form like a sheath. He was broad at the shoulder, slim at the waist, so different from his companions that he could have sprung from an entirely separate species. Even his chin was tilted slightly upwards, as though he was searching out some distant, impossible goal. She imagined a Siegfried, a Tristan, a Galahad, pausing temporarily in the Red Panther before continuing upon whatever noble quest consumed his heart. Anna didn't know whether to swoon or laugh out loud. If he speaks, she told herself, it will be with a squeaky Mickey Mouse voice, because no one can be that perfect.

But when he did speak it was in formal German, his voice surprisingly gentle and pleasingly melodic. But it carried. Lord, how it carried – straight into her marrow. 'Enough! Let there be order. What manner of people have we become? We are all

Austrians here, are we not? People who believe in order and decorum.'

His gaze swept the crowd, challenging anyone to disagree with him. No one did. Whether that was because of some innate authority – unusual in one so young – or the pistol he bore, Anna couldn't be sure.

There was a sudden flash of dazzling light, and she wondered if someone had fired at him. But no sound came, he did not flinch, and Anna caught the smoky tang of a photographer's magnesium flash.

The *Heimwehr* men rallied around their hero, bloodied, flushed with excitement. They looked to Anna like schoolboys after an invigorating time on the sports field.

The newcomer holstered his pistol and calmly ordered his men out of the club. Then, to Anna's astonishment, he went around the cellar checking who needed help, who might need a taxi called to take them home or to hospital. He consoled tearful women. He soothed angry men, bringing them down from violence with the good-fellowship of well-matched competitors. He assured the manager there would be compensation, a formal apology from the Fatherland Front. He was just one man. Even if he did have a pistol, a determined rush could have easily overwhelmed him. But no one seemed inclined to do it.

Looking past him, Anna saw the coat-check girl kneeling beside one of the sequinned-dress men. He was younger than she'd first realized, and was sitting propped against the wall, his Carmen Miranda headdress clutched to his chest like a precious childhood toy animal.

Memories of the Villa Fiorentina surged into Anna's mind: her father's smile as he was led away by police… the look of proud defiance on the face of the railroad heir… Anger she'd repressed for ten years came with them, a hard rage against the uncaring impact that blunt and brutish force had upon those caught up in its passing. Its impetus made her stand and go over to see if she could help.

She stayed with the boy in the dress until his partner returned – his friend now wore a man's jacket to hide a great rent in his bodice. Anna was consoling them both when she felt a presence behind her. She turned, and there he was: the man with the gun.

'Are you in need of assistance, Fräulein?' he asked.

She stared at him, more than a little in awe. And perhaps it was the shock of the fight, or the fact that her innermost thoughts still came to her in the language of her birth, she answered him in English. 'No. No, we're all fine, thank you.'

His eyebrows – as straight as if they'd been drawn with a ruler – lifted a little. 'I can only ask that you forgive this dreadful failure of discipline,' he answered in clipped English tones with only a hint of an Austrian accent. 'Those men were not members of my squad, I assure you. I will make a report. They will be called to account.' He looked around, then shook his head and sighed. 'Here we are, the heirs to Mozart and Haydn – yet a respectable young woman like you must think us all barbarians.'

'No, of course not,' Anna said, desperately afraid of getting tongue-tied. 'I can see it wasn't your fault at all. I mean… what could be?'

Not quite knowing what to do with her hands, she began to smooth the front of her very ordinary floral print dress. And then she remembered what the coat-check girl had told her: *There are some men who like to pay extra for the virginal-secretary look… they might think you're, you know, dressed that way for a reason…*

Colouring as crimson as the club's decor, Anna prayed once again for the earth to swallow her.

In the taxi back to Karolinengasse, with Marion snoring loudly on her shoulder, Anna became aware of an odd fluttering sensation in her stomach. She couldn't place exactly when it had started, but it seemed to have been there for some time. It must be hunger, she thought. Or a reaction to the violence. Or perhaps it was just the thought of tomorrow's exhibition and the fact that she'd had a long and very trying day.

It was still there the next morning. But Anna was far too occupied with the exhibition at the Belvedere to pay it much attention. Or to see the brief item in that day's edition of *Die Presse.* Most of the front page was given up to the expected general strike, but on page three her attention would have been drawn by a flash-photo of a familiar young man in uniform striking a heroic pose. *Lone* Heimwehr *hero ends fight between Red Thugs and Nazis* screamed the headline.

It would be years before Anna learned the truth about that night. That the young man had known exactly what the *Heimwehr* had planned for the Red Panther. He had followed them to the club, accompanied by a reporter and a cameraman. Party manifestoes, convictions, grand ideals, all these things meant nothing to him.

What was important to Ivo Wolff was hitching himself to the cause that would serve him best. His charm was always in direct proportion to his self-interest. He did nothing – raised no flag, swore no oath, took no vow – unless it was expressly to his advantage.

Five

To Anna's relief, the exhibition attracted a steady, though modest, procession of visitors to their little enclave in the Moderne Galerie.

At eleven the next morning, Professor Koppitz came by. He was unlike any academic Anna had ever encountered before. He wore a permanently intense expression, and his hair swept back from his lined forehead as though he were standing behind the propeller of an aeroplane. At fifty, he was still as athletic and striking as when he'd been his own model for artistic photographs composed in the pictorialist style, celebrations of the naked human form – or as Marion preferred to call them, 'French postcards'.

'This is new, Fräulein, is it not?' Koppitz asked, peering at the photo of the man she'd taken the day before, at the tram stop.

'Yes, Herr Professor. Brand new.'

After a few moments' close inspection, he said, 'Is this a political work?'

'No, Herr Professor.'

'Well, it should be. Everything today is political. Art cannot, should not, remain apart from it.'

'It's just a memory. I wanted other people to see what I saw, so that he wouldn't be forgotten.'

'He's a vagrant, correct?'

'No, Herr Professor,' Anna said firmly, pointing to the message on the board the man wore across his chest. 'He's an honest worker, who needs help.'

'And you decided to steal from him.'

'I didn't steal from him,' Anna protested, colouring.

'You appropriated his image. I presume you wish to sell it, otherwise why would it be here? What is that if it's not stealing?'

'But I gave him a *Schnitzelsemmel* in payment.' Even to her own ears, it sounded lame.

'Then you have learned something important, my dear.'

'Have I, Herr Professor?'

'Indeed, you have, Fräulein,' Koppitz said, waving a cautionary finger at her. 'You have learned that one cannot photograph suffering without there being an exchange.' He paused, looking at her intently. She always found his direct stares rather unsettling: it seemed to her a little inappropriate to look too deeply into the eyes of a man you'd seen naked, even if it was only in a photograph. 'As you take, so you must give a little something of yourself in return,' Koppitz went on. 'And if your talent is what I believe it to be, there may well come a time when you discover your account is empty. I advise you to take care, Fräulein. For the artist, the cost of his labour is not counted solely in time and material.'

As if lending gravity to his warning, Anna heard a rumble of thunder from somewhere across the city. Odd, she thought. A storm wasn't forecast.

'I'll bear that in mind, Herr Professor,' she said. And then she blushed, because she'd realized the earlier image in her mind – of an athletic, naked man – wasn't Professor Koppitz at all, but the young *Heimwehr* officer from last night.

After the professor had gone the thunder continued sporadically. The flow of visitors to the exhibition slowed to a trickle, then stopped completely. But by that time, Anna had learned that a very different type of storm to the one she'd imagined had come to Vienna.

At dawn that day, almost two hundred kilometres away, in the city of Linz, the government's *Heimwehr* troopers had raided a building owned by the Social Democratic Workers' Party, searching for hidden weapons. The *Schutzbund,* the Party's paramilitaries, had fired back. Within hours, the violence had spread across Austria.

The distant storm Anna thought she'd heard had been the thunder of government artillery.

It was a brutal audition for the role of war reporter – one Anna wouldn't repeat for a decade. Not yet eighteen, she was at once terrified and captivated.

Her very first battle was mastering the shaking of her hands when she raised the camera.

At the institute, classes were suspended. The lecturers with known socialist or communist leanings were summarily dismissed. Anna was free to go looking for subjects for her camera, ignoring Marion's increasingly hysterical protests.

She labelled the photographs she shot over the next seventy-two hours, 'The February War'. That was the title Austria had given the uprising, though in Vienna it lasted barely two days. The socialists were quickly overwhelmed, and harsh reprisals followed: brutal police interrogations, mass arrests, even executions.

Whenever the *Heimwehr*, the police or the soldiers challenged her, Anna shouted '*Journalisten!*', accentuating her American accent. It made her feel more adult. It also made her feel safer.

Anna swiftly became something of a mascot for the foreign correspondents who'd flocked to the city. Even the grandest would acknowledge her, if only to ask which bars were still open. Dorothy Thompson, who wrote for the *Saturday Evening Post*, soon knew her face. But her favourite was a young Englishman who'd come down from Cambridge the year before and was in Vienna helping the socialists. He'd introduced himself to her as Kim Philby.

The day after the *Schutzbund* surrendered in Vienna, Anna found herself at the western end of the Floridsdorf bridge. The grey afternoon light washed the colour from the residential buildings on the far side. The tram wires were down, cut by gunfire. A government field-gun and its crew had taken up position on the city side, the weapon's barrel trained on the Born-Hof across the river, though not a single shot had come from there since yesterday. An elderly flower-seller was offering snowdrops to the correspondents gathered nearby. Anna had just captured the scene with her Leica when she heard someone calling her name.

'Fräulein Bauer! What a surprise to encounter you here, of all places.'

In stark contrast to the *Heimwehr* artillery crew, the young man calling her name looked the least dangerous person in Vienna. His face was pinched from the chill, but it was pleasant enough. Almost handsome, if a little too earnest. He wore a battered leather jacket and coarse, worker's trousers.

The questioning look Anna gave him in reply brought a hint of disappointment to his eager spaniel eyes.

'Lukamir Vogel—?' he said with a trace of uncertainty, as if it might be open to debate. 'You'll have seen me, perhaps, at the institute? I'm taking graphic design. Everyone calls me Luka.'

The graphic design department was on her floor, but Anna had only the vaguest recollection of him. She smiled and nodded vigorously, to save his feelings. 'Of course! Luka. Yes – silly of me. I remember now. Golly! How are you?'

They shook hands. Anna could sense the nervousness in his grip.

'I'm well, thank you, Fräulein Anna – considering the circumstances. And you?'

'Yes, very well. Thank you for asking.'

He seemed unsure what to say next. She could see that conversation didn't come easily to him. His tongue flicked across his lower lip.

He must have a dry mouth, she thought. How sweet.

'So, what are you doing here?' he managed at length.

Anna tapped the Leica slung from her shoulder. 'Oh, just taking a few photos.'

'Isn't that a rather dangerous occupation?'

Anna nodded towards the correspondents grouped around the field-gun. 'Not if you keep in with the right people.'

'Are you going to send your pictures to the newspapers?' he asked.

'I hadn't really thought about it.'

'Don't bother,' he said, suddenly sounding a little snappy. 'What would be the point? Dollfuss has the press all sown up. They'd only tell one side of the story.'

'You're right,' she replied. 'And anyway, I'd probably get thrown out of the faculty. I suppose I could give them to the foreign newspapers, ask them to publish them under a *nom de guerre*.'

'Don't do that, they might find out and deport you.' Luka looked as though that would disappoint him immensely. 'If you want to see the real truth about all this, why don't you come with me, now?'

'Come where?'

'Across the bridge, to Floridsdorf.' Luka Vogel pointed to the far bank and a building scarred by shell splinters. 'My sister and our parents live right there – in the Born-Hof. You can see for yourself what it's like on the other side. Then you'll know what Dollfuss and his gangsters are really doing to the people.'

Anna looked at the government field-gun, its barrel pointing menacingly at the very place Luka was indicating. The truce seemed to be holding, she reasoned. And what kind of war reporter would she be if she didn't take the opportunity?

'Okay,' she said, smiling. 'Lead the way.'

The Born-Hof was a five-storey art deco layer cake of concrete with communal balconies that ran the entire length of the building. Raised in the early twenties, it had been one of the very first of the city's *Gemeindehäuser* – municipal apartment blocks built for ordinary workers. Or so Luka told her proudly as they approached. In honour of this, he said, it bore the name of a famous Austrian trade-unionist. 'And look how those fascists have defiled it.'

Anna could see that one corner of the building had taken a direct hit in the shelling of the past two days, perhaps by the very field-gun she had seen earlier. The hole was large enough to drive a truck through, and the shot had gutted the interior. The rest of the building seemed undamaged, though there were plenty of broken windows.

'Was anyone hurt?' Anna asked.

'Mercifully, no.' Luka pointed to the gaping hole surrounded by scorched rubble. 'That was the library the tram-workers' union paid for. Now look at it. They think even books need shooting.'

Barely constrained outrage gave his face a strength Anna hadn't noticed before. It made him look older. Attractive. Noble, if she were honest.

He caught her looking at him and began to blush.

Hurriedly turning her gaze away, Anna inspected the damage. The interior of the room was soot-blackened. The air still stank of burnt paper. She took some pictures, though the light was terrible.

'We had to form a human chain to carry water from the river, or else the whole place could have burned down,' Luka said.

Luka steered her towards a wide stairwell gleaming with freshly scrubbed white gloss paint. The handrail she gripped was made of polished wood, not cheaper cast iron; the doors to the apartments she passed boasted brass handles and knockers. This was a block whose tenants took pride in order and cleanliness. But there were also signs of spirited independence: posters on the wall emblazoned with slogans calling for workers to resist the Fatherland Front and the illegitimate authority of Chancellor Dollfuss.

The stairway was busy, mostly with women coming and going. As she climbed, Anna caught snatches of conversation: fathers laid off without unemployment pay; husbands arrested and returned bloodied and bruised; sons going missing. Most of the women recognized Luka. When he encountered any who didn't, he answered their challenges with a single word: *Freundschaft* – friendship. Anna guessed it must be a password, protection against informers.

'The government accused us of hiding weapons here, for the *Schutzbund*,' he told her. 'We said it was nonsense. They shelled us anyway.'

The Vogel family's apartment was on the fifth floor. As Anna emerged from the stairwell onto the communal walkway she turned to look out over the city. Thin trails of smoke still rose over the Karl-Marx-Hof, where the worst of the government bombardment had taken place.

Vienna no longer looked majestic to her. It looked ugly and cruel.

Frau Vogel was a sparrow of a woman with dark crinkly hair subdued beneath a proletarian headscarf. Though slight, there were skeins of muscle and tendon visible on her arms. She wore an apron and kept it on even after they'd shaken hands. She was a woman quite unlike Marion: unafraid of hard work and dirty hands. Anna could easily picture her toiling in a foundry or at the city gasworks.

The apartment, though modest, was spotless. The housing department had thoughtfully given the rooms rounded corners instead of sharp edges to make them easier to clean, and Luka's mother had scrubbed the place cleaner than a hospital. The faint smell of domestic ammonia seemed at odds with the chintzy furnishings.

'You should have warned me you were bringing home a friend,' she told Luka sternly as she fussed over Anna in a way that reminded her of Grandma Bauer, back in New York. 'I have so very little to offer you, my dear. We haven't dared go to the market for fear of the bullets. What must you think of us?'

Anna assured her she wasn't hungry. Frau Vogel insisted. If one couldn't rely on a decent welcome in a fraternity like the Born-Hof, where could one expect it? 'You'll probably want to keep your coat on,' she said. 'Those swine out there have cut the heating off.'

Luka made polite conversation about the institute until his mother returned with spicy Liptauer cheese and coffee on a tray.

'Mama, tell Fräulein Bauer about what's happened to Papa,' Luka said, as his mother poured coffee from a battered stainless-steel pot.

'Your nice young lady friend doesn't want to hear about our tribulations, Luka. I'm sure she has more interesting things to occupy her.'

Anna assured Frau Vogel that there was nothing she would prefer more.

Frau Vogel set the coffee pot back on the tray. 'Does this look to you, Fräulein, like a sewer, or a home for vermin?' she asked primly.

'No, of course not,' Anna said. 'It's very neat and tidy. Very orderly.'

'But they call us red troublemakers – sewer trash.' She leaned closer across the table. Anna could see a resentful hardness in her gaze. 'My husband is a foreman with the railway company, Fräulein. At least, he *was*. Now he's arrested and his pay is stopped. And for what?'

If Frau Vogel thought Anna might have an explanation, she didn't seem inclined to wait for it.

'They say he was carrying messages to the *Schutzbund* fighters at the Karl-Marx-Hof,' she continued. 'That's nonsense. He wasn't anywhere near there. They arrested him for belonging to the union, for wanting justice – that's all. We can't even complain to the courts – our men are lucky not to get beaten to death before they get anywhere near a judge. Do they think we don't know what's going on?'

'I'm so sorry, Frau Vogel,' Anna said, surprised by the woman's sudden vehemence. 'It must be dreadful for you. But I'm sure they'll soon realize your husband is an innocent man.'

Anna sipped her coffee while her host continued her lament:

the Social Democrat Party leadership were all cowards... Dollfuss and the Fatherland Front were all gangsters... the only official body offering help to the poor workers was the Catholic church, and only then because the priests wanted their children so they could indoctrinate them... Austria should invite Herr Hitler to sort things out...

Anna waited for Frau Vogel to draw breath, but she seemed to have no need of it. She only stopped when the front door opened and a pretty girl of about sixteen entered, two loaves of black bread clutched in her arms.

'This is my sister, Louisa,' Luka informed her. 'Lulu, meet Fräulein Bauer, from the institute.'

Louisa balanced one loaf on the other and reached out to shake Anna's hand. She had a friendly, confident smile, and the pageboy cut of her blonde hair suited her oval face. Anna guessed she was the stronger-willed of the Vogel progeny.

'I'm very pleased to meet you, Louisa,' Anna said. 'I didn't know Luka had a sister.'

'You must be the American girl Luka told me about,' the girl said. 'I can hear your accent.'

Luka Vogel turned a deep scarlet.

'Part American, part English,' Anna said, trying not to add to his humiliation by laughing. She turned back to Frau Vogel. 'Do you think I might be permitted to take a few photographs of the inside of the apartment, perhaps with you and your children? I'll give them to one of the foreign correspondents, to show that the municipal blocks aren't full of machine-gun nests, as the government claims.'

'If it will help to counter the lies,' said Frau Vogel, sounding pleased. She got up and began to tidy the little collection of knick-knacks and family photographs on the sideboard.

'That's quite unnecessary, Frau Vogel,' Anna assured her. 'Your apartment is wonderful – a credit to you. But for the picture to work properly, it needs to look like a home.'

But there was no stopping Luka's mother. Only when she was content did she compose herself on the small, threadbare sofa, her birdlike head tilted defiantly against the onslaught of the reactionary capitalist bourgeoisie and their field-guns. Luka and Louisa sat either side of her, looking uncomfortably self-conscious.

Anna took a few shots, though she didn't think they'd amount to much. Then she thanked Frau Vogel for her hospitality, expressed the hope that Herr Vogel would soon be restored to the family, and made for the door.

'I'll escort you to the bridge,' said Luka.

On the small landing outside the apartment, Frau Vogel extended a hand for Anna to shake. It was calloused and red, an old woman's hand, though Luka's mother couldn't have been very much older than Marion.

'Be careful, Fräulein,' she warned, with what was very nearly a wink.

'Please don't worry about me, Frau Vogel. The *Heimwehr* at the bridge know me.'

'Oh, no, my dear,' said Frau Vogel, a look of kindly concern softening her face. She nodded at Anna's camera case. 'I meant for you to be careful on the way down – when you pass the third floor.'

'Why, has the shelling damaged it?' Anna asked.

Frau Vogel laughed. 'Heavens, no, my dear. It's your camera.'

'My camera?'

'Indeed. It looks like a very expensive camera to me – and the third floor is where all the Jews live.'

Anna said nothing until she was almost at the Floridsdorf end of the bridge. Only when Luka turned to her to say goodbye did she see the misery and embarrassment in his normally gentle eyes.

'Please, Anna… I don't know what to say. She's from the country. She's traditional. Sometimes they say things without thinking. I'm sure she didn't mean it.'

'Tell me, Luka, do *you* think there are too many Jews on the third floor of the Born-Hof?'

He looked appalled. 'No, of course not.'

'You do realize that *I'm* Jewish?'

'Someone at the institute told me, when I asked about you. I'm *so* sorry.' He looked almost as though he wished the *Heimwehr*'s last shot had been fired directly at him.

Anna relented. 'Trust me, Luka. I'm the last person to blame someone for their mother's behaviour.'

She watched the relief flood into his eyes.

'Would you like to come with me to the Nestroy-Kino tomorrow evening?' he asked in a rush. 'They're showing *King Kong*, with Fay Wray.'

The offer took her by surprise. But he seemed pleasant company and was a good-looking boy. Besides, he appeared genuinely upset by his mother's words, and she knew what *that* felt like.

'I suppose so,' she said, before she'd had a chance to think it over.

He gave her the time and place, then made a courteous bow from the shoulders. He must have thought it made him look sophisticated, though to Anna it was the return of his youthful awkwardness.

She said, 'Well, goodbye, then,' and set off across the bridge. She didn't look back.

When she arrived at the Karolinengasse flat it was dark. The lights were off: Marion wasn't at home. That was the least surprising event of the entire day. But she'd left a note on the kitchen table:

> Beuschel *in the fridge – also eggs.*

And, scrawled as a hurried addendum:

> *Prof. Koppitz phoned. You're invited to his studio to watch him at work. Tomorrow at noon. Better excuse than etchings! Keep yourself unsullied, darling. But put on fresh undies just in case.*

The professor's studio was in the Margareten district, a fifteen-minute walk from Karolinengasse, in a street of smart turn-of-the-century townhouses. Promptly at twelve on the appointed day, Anna paused before its smart black-gloss front door.

She blushed when she thought of the note her mother had left her. Professor Koppitz might have won an international reputation for his photos of the naked human form, but he'd never suggested Anna pose for him. He'd always behaved in a manner that was nothing other than professional. Besides, he ran the studio with his wife, also an accomplished photographer.

But this was Vienna. All sorts of goings-on occurred behind its elegant façade. What if Marion was right? What if the Herr Professor and his wife had some sort of photographic *ménage à trois* in mind? How would she respond? She couldn't cause a scene. She knew how helpful the professor could be to her professional future.

A maid opened the door and showed Anna through to the parlour, where three other students from her class were already listening intently to the professor. Two were boys she knew well. The other was a sour-looking girl named Gustl Faas. She had plump cheeks and an ungenerous mouth and had made her dislike of Anna plain from the first day of their course – Anna wasn't Austrian. Anna was foreign. Mostly, Anna suspected, it was because she was a Jew. True to form, Gustl didn't join the two boys when they acknowledged Anna's arrival.

Koppitz was leaning casually against the fireplace, one hand in the pocket of his midnight-blue morning suit; the other – a cigar between the fingers – emphasizing his words with airy flourishes.

'Ah, Fräulein Bauer, I'm so pleased you could join us,' he said, smiling. 'We were discussing originality of composition.'

'It's Cantrell, actually, Herr Professor – not Bauer,' Anna said, with a boldness that surprised her. 'For my work, I'd like to be known as Anna Cantrell, not Anna Bauer.'

Koppitz nodded approvingly. 'Ah, yes, I noticed the name on the photographs you exhibited at the Moderne Galerie. I assumed you had chosen a pseudonym.'

'Cantrell is my father's name.'

'Is he here, in Vienna?'

'I wish he was, but no, he's in Hollywood. He's a movie cameraman.'

Gustl gave a little squeal of delight. 'You never *told* us that. Does he know Clark Gable?'

'Probably,' Anna said nonchalantly.

The girl gasped. 'Clark's so handsome, don't you think? You must tell us *everything*.' She beamed at Anna as if they were best friends, her fingers working with excitement.

Anna tried hard not to wallow in satisfaction.

'I think we should go through to the studio,' Koppitz said, unaccustomed to having his students' attention drawn away from him. 'My wife has set up everything for the session. Please refrain from asking questions until I signal that I have completed my work. Until then, I shall require absolute silence. It goes without saying, I hope, that distracting the model in any way will not be tolerated.'

The studio was at the back of the house, with windows looking out over a small private garden. It had a high ceiling and walls draped with white cloth. A coal stove sat in a whitewashed chimney breast to provide heat. Nearby, a screen provided cover for models to change their clothes, or in the case of the professor's celebrated *Bewegungsstudien* – motion studies – disrobe entirely. A trio of arc lamps on tripods blazed and hummed, flooding the studio with light and making Anna squint.

In the centre of the floor stood a fake Roman couch, like a chaise longue. At a table set against one wall, the professor's wife was checking a collection of cameras and lenses.

But Anna saw none of this, even though her eyes had recovered from the glare before she'd taken more than two steps into the room. Professor Koppitz was saying something about shutter speeds and how the light could alter the external appearance of human musculature, but she wasn't listening. Her attention was seized by the figure reclining on the couch.

The model was stark naked. And even before Professor Koppitz had taken a single artful shot Anna could see he was perfection: a dying Adonis, waiting for Aphrodite to come and staunch his fatal wounds.

If the other students struggled not to gawp or giggle, Anna suffered no such conflict. She was too busy staring at him. Not at his body – though it would have taken a dose of ether for her not to appreciate *that* – but at his face.

'Oh, my,' she gasped. 'What are you doing here?'

But the young *Heimwehr* officer, whom she'd last seen at the Red Panther, was taking his present incarnation far too professionally to answer her.

The Berlin apartment. 1989

Elly Taverner was beyond tiredness. She knew she couldn't leave until her father had finished his story, even if it took until dawn. His voice had become hypnotic, as if this was one of his compelling bedtime stories that had so entranced her as a child. Only this time there were the photographs to prove it was no invented fairy tale.

She looked again at the interior shot of Frau Vogel's apartment in the Born-Hof, a rather stiff little trio sitting on a sofa staring self-consciously into the camera lens. One of them she recognized.

'So, this is Mummy at sixteen,' she said, touching the image of Frau Vogel's daughter as reverently as if she were touching a plaster saint in a shrine. 'Louisa Vogel – before she knew there was a handsome Englishman named Taverner on the loose.'

'Yes, Puffin,' Harry said, with a gentle smile. 'That's her. That's our Louisa.'

'She looks so young.'

'Sixteen-year-olds did back then.'

'I remember her telling me about her mother and father. They were killed during the war, in a bombing raid.'

'Yes, I'm afraid they were.'

Elly frowned. 'But I don't recall Mummy ever speaking of a brother. I'm sure I'd have remembered a name like Luka.'

Harry sank the last of his whisky, placing the tumbler on the bedside table before he answered. 'She prefers not to, darling. She has her reasons.'

Elly's eyebrows arched just a little. 'Ah, a family secret. Are we talking skeletons in closets?'

'No. Nothing like that,' Harry said. 'I'll get to Luka in time, don't worry.'

Elly turned her attention to the photograph of the naked young man. Lifting it from the quilt, she fanned her cheek with her free hand, theatrically. 'Well, I don't quite know where to look with this one,' she said. 'Calling him a magnificent specimen doesn't come close. What was he doing posing in the buff for Professor Koppitz?'

'He was doing what most Austrians were doing at the time: whatever they needed, as long as it made them a few schillings. His name was Ivo Wolff.'

Elly nodded appreciatively. 'Well, we already know he's set Anna's heart aflutter. But yes, he does look somewhat wolverine.' She paused, only now registering the tension in Harry's voice when he'd spoken the name. 'Am I to assume Anna ought to be a little afraid of this particular big bad wolf?'

'Yes,' Harry said. 'Ivo Wolff was a very bad man. A very bad man indeed. Or at least, that's what he was to become.'

Elly thought for a moment. 'Nineteen thirties Austria… are we talking about what I think we're talking about?'

'I fear we are,' Harry said.

'Oh,' exclaimed Elly, dropping the photo as if it were suddenly burning her fingers. 'Oh, dear.'

'In the pantheon of Nazi monsters, I suppose he'd barely make the top thousand,' Harry continued. 'But in his own limited way he was about as bad a man as any woman would want to encounter.' He tapped the image. 'Apart from this, there is only one other surviving photograph of him in existence – so far as we know.'

'Do you have it?' Elly said, glancing at the portfolio case. Now she was imagining Ivo Wolff not naked, but wearing an immaculate black SS uniform complete with silver *Totenkopf* death's head emblems on the lapels.

Harry reached for the empty whisky tumbler on the bedside table. 'You know what they say, Puffin – in any successful interrogation, the inquisitor must always give up a little in return.'

Elly stood up. 'I'll get you a refill while you dig out the photo.'

'I can't do that, darling,' said Harry.

'You don't have it?'

'It's probably in Moscow, in the KGB archives in Lubyanka Square. It was taken here in Berlin, at the Brandenburg Gate. There are only two people in the shot – if you discount the crowd in the background. One of them is Ivo Wolff.'

'Don't tell me,' Elly said. 'The other is Heinrich Himmler.'

Handing his daughter the whisky tumbler, Harry Taverner shook his head.

'No, darling. The other man in the photograph is me.'

Six

While Anna Cantrell might have met her future husband during a nightclub fight and seen him stark naked even before the first date, her love affair with Ivo Wolff began as conventionally as any other in Vienna that spring of 1934.

Professor Koppitz declared the shoot complete. Ivo took himself behind the screen to dress.

Why he felt the need for modesty when putting *on* his clothes never occurred to Anna: she was too busy trying to recover her composure.

'I do believe I recognize you, Fräulein,' Ivo said to her, when he emerged from behind the screen, as if from a chrysalis. He was wearing high-waisted Oxfords and a white cotton shirt. Anna could almost smell the jealousy oozing from Gustl Faas.

'I see you came without your pistol today,' she said, trying to affect a nonchalance beyond her years. 'Do your friends in the *Heimwehr* know what you do for a side-line?'

He looked at her intently, as if he wasn't sure about her German pronunciation.

'I'm joking,' she said, feeling the heat rising in her cheeks.

'You're the American girl, from the Red Panther.'

'Yes, I am. Well, I'm part American, part English.'

'Excellent,' he said. 'Modern and yet traditional.'

For one dreadful moment, Anna thought he was about to click his heels in the Prussian manner.

Instead, he suggested supper at the Rathauskeller.

Later, sitting opposite from each other across a crisp white tablecloth whose creases looked sharp enough to draw blood, Anna said, 'This is a little crazy, don't you think?'

Ivo looked around at the vaulted cavern that could have been designed by a Byzantine sultan. 'Maybe a little ostentatious, yes. But the *Tafelspitz* is superb.'

'I meant dining with a stranger you've already seen naked.'

He laughed, which served only to energize the corps de ballet that was already dancing in her stomach.

'At least you know I have nothing to hide,' he said, summoning the waiter with a confidence that Anna couldn't imagine any of the boys at the institute matching.

And then she heard Marion's voice in her head. *Keep yourself unsullied, darling. But put on fresh undies just in case.*

'Are you alright?' Ivo asked, leaning forward, concern clear on his face. 'You've suddenly gone very red.'

Anna fanned her cheeks. 'No… no… I'm fine. It's just very hot in here.'

They were halfway through a bottle of excellent red wine before she realized she was supposed to be sitting beside Luka Vogel at the Nestroy-Kino, watching *King Kong* making mooncalf eyes at Fay Wray on the top of the Empire State Building.

'Honestly, Luka, I'm so, *so* sorry,' Anna said, when she bumped into him in the corridor at the institute three days later.

'I waited until the last moment,' he said, trying to look dignified rather than hurt, and failing miserably. 'But you didn't come.'

He had changed his hairstyle, she noticed. He'd over-oiled his hair, combing his teenage locks sideways and back from his forehead like Fred Astaire. Rather than sophisticated, it just made him look even younger.

To make herself feel less guilty, she said, 'Professor Koppitz invited some of the photography students to watch him work. I didn't have your mother's telephone number, otherwise I would have called – honestly.'

It was only half a lie, she told herself. Not really a lie at all. Just half the truth.

'It doesn't matter,' he said, now apparently wanting to absolve her of blame – which only made Anna feel worse. 'Anyway, the lines are still down to the Born-Hof.'

'Well, there you are—'

'Perhaps next week?'

'Oh, Luka – I'm really busy with classes at the moment, and my mother doesn't like me going out while all this political nonsense is going on…'

That he had got the message was clear by the hurt in his eyes.

'That's quite alright,' he said, doing his best to appear untroubled. 'I understand. I really do.'

And indeed, he did – far better than Anna herself. Because, on her way home from a fruitless search for news of her father, Louisa Vogel had seen Anna and Ivo walking towards the Rathauskeller together, and looking more relaxed than any couple out on their first date had any right to.

There were walks down sun-dappled paths through the Wienerwald, and a bicycle trip to Grinzing to see Mahler's grave: Ivo had introduced her to the great man's music. There were pastries at Demel's and rides on the aeroplane carousel in the Prater Park. In the Stadtpark, Anna and Ivo chased each other around the Schubert Memorial as if they were children. At an outdoor *Heuriger*, over glasses of cold, crisp Grüner Veltliner, he spoke to her of his family, while a rotund man in plus-fours and waistcoat played Strauss on an accordion.

'You'll love my mother,' he assured her. 'She's everything that's fine and noble about Austrian motherhood.'

'Good for her,' Anna replied. 'My mother's a train wreck.'

Ivo threw back his head to laugh. 'A train wreck! That's very good.'

He could have said anything, because Anna's attention was firmly on the tendons in his neck, taut as bracing wires.

Herr Wolff senior was Ivo's hero – a patriot who'd lost an eye in the Great War and now ran his own motorcycle garage in Graz. 'My father was proud to fight in the Imperial German army,' Ivo said. 'But he was betrayed. They all were. All his comrades. All the millions who died. All betrayed. They were never defeated, you know. The French, the British, the Americans… they never actually forced them to surrender on the battlefield.'

'But they still lost,' Anna said, suddenly a little uncertain in the face of such fervour.

'There was an armistice. They were stabbed in the back by Bolshevik bankers and communists.'

Anna wondered if she ought to tell him that her Grandpa Wolfgang was a banker, that he paid the rent on the Karolinengasse apartment and provided the stipend that allowed Marion to paint and frequent the Café Nihlisimus and the Red Panther even when her canvases weren't selling. But she didn't. She didn't want to spoil the occasion. The wine was good, the company even better. And his eyes! As she gazed into them, she fortified herself with the knowledge that Grandpa Wolfgang couldn't be held responsible for betraying Ivo's father, or anyone else for that matter, because to her certain knowledge he had never been either a Bolshevik or a communist.

In a boat on the Danube, Ivo told her of his dreams for the future. They weren't dreams for himself, he assured her. His own future was already mapped out: inheriting his father's garage business, hopefully turning it into an Austria-wide concern – perhaps even expanding into Germany. Rather, his dreams were for all mankind: men and women together, prospering in a brave new world where science had defeated want, and honourable men ran things for the benefit of all who were prepared to put a shoulder to the wheel.

When Anna took him home for a meal – at the third attempt, because Marion forgot the first two – her mother was entranced.

'Great. He's perfect,' Marion declared after Ivo had departed to catch the tram home. By perfect, she meant everything that Rex Cantrell wasn't. 'He's not English and he's not a goddamn—'

'Please, Mama,' Anna interrupted. 'I know Rex hurt you, but he *is* my father. I can't bear to listen to you speak about him like that.'

For the first time Anna could remember, her mother backed down.

'Yeah, well...' Marion said, with a shrug. 'I'm happy for you, sweetie.'

'You approve?'

'Of course I approve,' Marion said, opening her arms wide to demand an embrace. 'Okay, he might not be a banker, but who the hell cares what's in the larder when the wallpaper's so fetching? And I guess you've already seen what he keeps under the stairs—'

Anna's face turned crimson. 'Mama!'

'Just promise me something—'

Anna waited, cringing inside, for her mother to make the demand. She was certain she knew what it would be: don't give yourself to him before he's proposed… if he does, stand up for yourself in the marriage… make sure you please him in bed… don't let yourself go as you get older… She'd read lots of advice like that in *Modenschau* magazine.

'Don't let him make you give up your American citizenship.'

Later, Anna would regard that as the last piece of rational advice that her mother ever gave her. At the time, she didn't mention it to Ivo. She was young enough to think that, once ignited, love will burn forever.

Summer came and the days grew hot. Ivo took her home to Graz to meet his parents. The closer the train got to its destination, the more nervous Anna became. Emerging from the station's classical portico, she took the opportunity offered by a temporary absence of taxis to rush back inside and refresh her face from the public spigot in the ladies' restroom.

She needn't have worried. Herr Wolff senior turned out to be a grizzled version of the son. He was charming, with a sharp smile and a piratical patch worn over his missing left eye. When he took her for a ride in the sidecar of his motorcycle, it terrified her half to death but gave her an appetite for speed that was never to leave her. Throughout her stay, Frau Wolff, a jolly woman with greying plaits, hovered in the background as if she were in domestic service, waiting for her husband to call her forward. But when they were alone, she made Anna feel more than welcome. 'Ivo is every inch the equal of his father,' she told Anna proudly. 'And you are very beautiful. You will make fine babies together for the Fatherland.'

Anna smiled politely. Frau Vogel was a traditionalist, she told herself, a woman steeped in conservative country ways. They said that sort of thing. On balance, she reckoned, being told to procreate for the Fatherland was better than stumbling across the remains of a line of cocaine in the bathroom.

'They were enchanted by you,' Ivo assured her, on the journey back.

'I do hope so,' Anna told him, though she'd gained the distinct impression the Wolffs considered an Anglo-American daughter-in-law brought up in Hollywood as a somewhat exotic addition to the family.

For Anna, those early summer days in Vienna were the happiest in her young life so far. The only cloud in the sky was Ivo's continuing support of the Fatherland Front. There were still street fights between the government's paramilitaries and members of the Austrian Nazi Party and the communists. She was frightened he'd get hurt. But he brushed off her fears with a grin. 'I'm like one of those knights in a Wagner opera,' he told her, 'and you're a beautiful river goddess whose spell keeps me safe from all harm.'

They made love for the first time on the banks of the Dechantlacke, the dappled June sunshine turning their flesh into gleaming snakeskin beneath the close canopy of trees.

Afterwards, Ivo uttered the words Anna had been longing to hear.

'I've decided to resign from the *Heimwehr*.'

The wedding took place at the Catholic Antoniuskirche in Graz, in late July 1934, two months after Anna's eighteenth birthday. Marion almost missed the train. She had decamped temporarily to the home of a surrealist painter, a third-rate Salvador Dali, where, presumably, her wristwatch had melted, time becoming even more fluid for her than usual.

Before the ceremony, Anna pulled her mother aside.

'What is it, honey? I thought you already knew all about the birds and the bees.'

'Don't be silly, Mama. It's not that. It's about religion. He wants me to sign "Roman Catholic" in the register.'

Marion's make-up made scowling difficult, but she attempted a small one. 'You're a Jew!'

'But we've never been observant,' Anna protested. 'Not even in New York.'

'Honey, it's not like washing a cheap vest too often. It doesn't fade out.'

'He's trying to protect me,' Anna explained. 'Some of his family – some of the people he knows – aren't too friendly towards Jews. I don't have to actually convert or anything.'

Marion thought about this for a moment, then said, 'We still get to celebrate Rosh Hashanah together every new year?'

'Try and stop me.'

The scowl turned into a grin. 'Then, hell, I'd be happy to write "Druid" or "Zoroastrian" if it meant I got to have a guy like that keeping my sheets warm.'

'Mama!'

At the marriage feast, Herr Wolff senior seemed much taken with Anna's mother, and she with him. Even the excitement of the occasion couldn't stifle Anna's discomfort. Frau Wolff – despite her earlier comments about babies and the Fatherland – was a woman as round, warm and generous as the *Knödel* served for dessert. She dismissed her husband's over-familiarity with the sort of weary laugh a farmer's wife might keep for recalcitrant cattle, patting Anna's knee under the table.

'Men!' she lamented. 'They see a beautiful woman and they're like sparrows after a crumb: peck... peck... peck... Don't you agree, my dear?'

Marion's wedding gift was a fox-fur stole from the Gerngross store in Vienna. Rex, from the safety of Culver City, sent a congratulatory telegram and a money order for $100 via Western Union.

They honeymooned in a guesthouse on the idyllic shores of the Zeller See, the snow-capped Austrian Alps reflected in the dark waters of the lake. Anna had a dreadful premonition: that her mother would suddenly appear and suck up the joy like a sponge.

She didn't – but that didn't stop the outside world intruding.

On the third morning, while breakfasting with Ivo on the terrace in the clean mountain air, Anna became aware of a sudden commotion inside the house. It seemed to coincide with the answering of a telephone.

Then the owner appeared. He removed his apron, laid it on a nearby table and struck a stiff, solemn pose. 'That was my sister, in Vienna,' he announced, as if sisters were the approved channel for disseminating news of national importance. 'Herr Chancellor Dollfuss has been assassinated – murdered by the Nazis.'

'If you ask me, the little rat had it coming,' Ivo said later, as they lay together in bed.

Anna was drawing coils on his left bicep with a fingertip. Through the floor, she could hear an official-sounding voice, thin as a whistle, issuing from the radio set in the lounge. She could picture the other guests clustered around it, listening intently to the announcer as he described the events of the day: the attempted Nazi coup, the warning from Prime Minister

Mussolini in Rome that Italian troops would defend Austrian sovereignty if Herr Hitler sent German troops across the border, the defeat and capture of the plotters…

'But to be gunned down in his own chancellery, denied even the last rites. That's awful,' Anna said.

'You can't just dissolve parliament and rule by decree,' Ivo mused. 'You can't shut down every group that opposes you and expect nothing to happen.'

'You don't agree with it, surely?'

His reply surprised her.

'There should have been a trial first,' he said, a distinct note of bitterness in his voice.

'Thank God you left the *Heimwehr*,' she said, clutching Ivo's arm. 'You could have been caught up in this awfulness.'

He reached over to the bedside table for his cigarettes. Lighting one, he lay back on the pillow, inhaling the smoke with a slow, deliberate pull. The fingers of his free hand began to play in her hair. 'I don't ever plan to hitch my wagon to doomed causes,' he said.

Anna laughed. 'It's a bit late to say that. You've married me, and I come with Marion attached. If that's not a doomed cause, I don't know what is.' She reached for his cigarette. 'Share?' she asked.

The question seemed to catch him by surprise. As if his mind had been elsewhere. As if he'd only just realized that he was sharing the bed with her.

The question of where to live had been settled long before the wedding: Anna had her studies at the institute to complete, and she couldn't possibly move in with Ivo, who shared a room in a lodging house in Rossau. And although he'd recently landed a junior sales clerk position in the Vienna offices of Steyr-Daimler-Puch, the automobile manufacturer, his salary was dependent upon commission. As Grandpa Wolfgang paid for the rent on the Karolinengasse apartment, it seemed logical for them to live there, with Marion.

No one baulked at the idea: newlyweds living with parents or in-laws was as common as fleas on a dog. Anna even entertained the thought that Ivo might prove a moderating influence on her mother. And so it proved, for a while at least.

Two days after they returned to Vienna, Anna went to the hotel where Dorothy Thompson, the American journalist she'd met during the fighting, was staying. Thompson had offered to look at some of her photographs.

'A honeymoon by the Zeller See, eh?' Thompson said with a grin, over coffee and *cremeschnitte* in the hotel lobby. She chewed the custard pastry with her strong, square jaw and continued: 'How perfectly lovely. I spent mine caravanning in England. Is he very handsome?'

'Yes, he is,' Anna laughed, blushing. She wondered how long it would take to become as confident and worldly as this already famous woman.

'You're lucky I'm still in town,' Thompson said. 'I'm going back to Germany tomorrow.'

'I read your interview with Herr Hitler, in *Cosmopolitan*. I thought it was very good,' Anna said, hoping a compliment wasn't too obvious a way to begin a sales pitch. From her bag, she pulled out an envelope filled with a selection of her favourite photos.

'If you want an example of the worst kind of little man, the German Führer is it,' Thompson said with a grin, sounding just like Marion. 'I got the impression he's built not of bones, but of gelatinous self-regard. He'll amount to nothing, you mark my words. He'll be—' She broke off as she looked at the spread of Anna's photographs. 'Say, these are real good. You've got a talent, young lady. I can see a hint of Cartier-Bresson here.'

'I was hoping you might consider helping me get my work published,' Anna said, trying to suppress her delight in case Thompson thought her gauche.

'I wouldn't hold your breath here, or in Germany. They only want shots that show gleaming modernity – anything that flatters the Party. They don't like the truth being shown. But if you can leave these with me, I'll send them to some of the folks I work with in America. Is it a deal?'

'It's a deal!' said Anna, now quite unable to smother the grin breaking out across her face.

When Anna returned to the Karolinengasse apartment, Ivo was there. He was in a foul mood.

'What's the matter?' she asked, taking off her coat. 'Is it work? Oh, God, they haven't laid you off, have they?'

Ivo went silently into the bedroom and began taking off his suit. From a distance, Anna watched him, something that usually gave her indescribable pleasure. But today, it seemed as if a fissure had opened in his usual carapace of calm authority. Through it, she thought she could see the fleeting shadow of an angry child. And, yes, a hint of spite.

'Ivo – speak to me,' she urged, suddenly a little frightened.

He pulled his vest over his head and threw it over the bed rail. His body stiffened, accentuating the muscles, reminding her of the photos Professor Koppitz had taken of him – she kept a print in the drawer of her bedside table.

'It's nothing,' he said. 'Just an argument at work. They're such fools, these people. They don't know what they've done. But there'll be a reckoning.'

'Don't let it get you down, darling,' Anna called to him. 'You'll be running the Vienna sales office before they know what's happened. Then you'll be able to make *their* day miserable. Just promise me you won't flirt with the typists.'

He gave her a tight smile and blew a kiss. It didn't reassure her.

While he showered, she went into the kitchen to prepare the evening meal. Lying on the table was a copy of that day's newspaper, presumably cast aside when Ivo had come home. She glanced at the front page.

Thirteen Nazis hanged for Dollfuss assassination. Condemned men give Heil Hitler salutes as they die.

And being young, newly married and wildly in love, she didn't immediately make the connection between the newspaper headline and Ivo's anger. A bad day at work, he'd said. And for Anna – then – that was good enough.

In late August, two envelopes bearing US postmarks arrived at the apartment within a week of each other.

When the postman delivered the first, Anna hurriedly tore it open, assuming it contained a letter from Rex. It didn't. Instead, it was a note from Dorothy Thompson, explaining she'd been deported from Germany for insulting Herr Hitler and his cronies once too often. Now back in America, she'd shown Anna's photos to a few people who might be interested in them.

Anna, not wanting to risk proving a jinx, told no one.

When the second letter arrived, it had Anna dancing around the apartment with excitement, even though she'd experienced her first bout of morning sickness that very day. It was from the picture editor at the *Chicago Tribune*. The paper had used one of Anna's photographs from the 'February War' in a story about the parlous state of European politics.

Please feel free to submit material to us again, the letter said. *We have pleasure in enclosing a cheque for the standard fee of ten dollars.*

That night, eager to tell Ivo the good news, Anna rushed into the hall the moment she heard his key turn in the lock. 'Isn't it wonderful?' she gushed. 'I'm on my way.'

He followed her into the lounge, saying nothing until she'd poured him a glass of schnapps. She raised her own in a toast. 'Here's to me,' she said. 'Here's to *us*.'

'It's good for a wife to have a hobby,' he told her, downing the spirit. 'Idle hours are unproductive.'

Anna stared at him. 'A hobby? Is that what you think it is?'

'It would be better if you joined one of the political clubs. Start doing something worthwhile. The future won't build itself you know.'

Marion was out, but Anna knew what she'd have said. Marion would have told him to fuck off.

But she was eighteen – every morning, after Ivo left for work, she would open the drawer of the bedside table to steal a glance at the photo Professor Koppitz had taken of him.

So she held her tongue and went back to the kitchen.

'You see – my idle hours haven't been *that* unproductive,' Anna told Ivo when her pregnancy was confirmed.

His embrace was spontaneous and warm. That comforted her, because she'd noticed a recent change in his demeanour. It wasn't that he was becoming distant – he often carried himself with a military flintiness, especially in public. But now he was frequently severe indoors too, as if there was a higher call on his attention than mere domesticity. She wondered if he'd rejoined the *Heimwehr*.

But at that moment, Anna was content simply to take pleasure from the closeness of his body and his smile – sincere, but lips still closed tight.

Their first child, a boy, was born the following spring, May 1935. They named him Bernhardt after Ivo's father. Anna suggested Rex for a middle name. Ivo approved. It had a regal connotation, and he much admired the former kaiser, whom he said had been betrayed by the same bankers and Bolsheviks who'd cost Herr Wolff senior his eye and a victory medal. 'They should have all been hanged for what they put the people through: hyper-inflation, hunger, humiliation on the world stage,' he stormed.

'Shush, Ivo – you'll make him cry,' Anna said, rocking the infant in her arms. 'Don't let him see you looking so angry.'

To the family, the boy was known as Bär – German for 'bear' – because, to the delight of Ivo's mother, if not exactly to Anna, he weighed in at four kilos.

The birth achieved another miracle: a distinct – though inevitably temporary – improvement in Marion's behaviour. For a while at least she became an exemplary grandmother. She doted on Bär, though Anna suspected that might be partly because she saw the child as living proof that Rex Cantrell's malign influence had been successfully bred out of the Bauer bloodline.

'They're sending me to the Berlin office for a week or two,' Ivo told Anna in September. Although his mouth smiled, the rest of his body seemed unusually tense, as if he were challenging her to object. 'I can't turn it down. Sorry.'

'Well, at least you'll get some sleep,' Anna said, rocking Bär's cradle. 'Is it a promotion?'

'No, but it will get me known amongst the German directors.'

'If they invite you to Berlin's equivalent of the Red Panther, please stay out of trouble,' she said, only half joking. 'I've read the papers. It sounds as if you can't walk the streets without running into a fight. Worse than here.'

'I promise,' Ivo said, laughing. 'Best behaviour. No shooting my pistol into the ceiling. Those days are all over.'

'And bring me back something nice,' Anna said, smiling.

'I promise that, too. You have my word.'

In the event, he brought her back a box of Stollwerck chocolates – and a gaunt, dead-eyed man with a greasy manner that reminded her of a con artist trying to fleece a war-widow of her pension. A man Ivo introduced as Manis Möller. A man in a baggy blue serge suit and a gaudy, knitted tie – held in place with a swastika tiepin.

Seven

Marion had exchanged the third-rate surrealist painter for an assistant manager at the Galerie Felix Bezner, a new establishment in the museum quarter that dealt mainly in Austrian expressionism. She had gone out with him the evening Ivo brought Manis Möller home, so there was enough goulash to go around.

Anna was in the kitchen ladling the stew into the bowls when Ivo came in, searching for a corkscrew.

'Who on earth *is* he?' she whispered.

'I met him in Berlin. I didn't think you'd mind.'

Anna wiped her hands on her apron and frowned. 'Where's he going to sleep? We don't have any room here. There's Bär to think of.'

'Don't worry, Manis won't be sleeping here.'

'Well, where then? He doesn't look to me like the sort who's going to book himself a suite at the Hotel Sacher.'

'He'll sleep at the police barracks.'

Anna's jaw dropped. 'You've brought me chocolates – and a Nazi *policeman*? Have you lost your senses, Ivo?'

'Why are you getting upset? I don't see the problem.'

'Oh, let me think about that for a moment,' Anna said, closing her eyes to feign deep deliberation. Then she snapped her fingers and opened them again, very wide. 'Perhaps because they're a bunch of brutal thugs?'

'You're talking of things you know nothing about,' he said, a harshness in his voice she'd never heard before.

'Well, if that's not enough, then how about because the Party's banned here in Austria, and you can go to prison for being a member? Is that enough of a reason for you?'

Ivo gave a dismissive little laugh, which only served to irritate Anna further. 'Manis is from the Kripo, the Berlin criminal police. He's been sent here in a liaison capacity. They're not going to arrest him.'

'He looks to me as if he should be under investigation himself,' Anna said, in a whisper. She took off her apron, picked up the tray with the steaming bowls of goulash on it, and marched past her husband.

Möller was already sitting at the table. She forced a smile. He might well be a policeman, but that didn't mean she shouldn't count the cutlery when he'd gone.

As Ivo poured the wine, Möller spoke up: 'Ivo was more than correct in everything he told me about you, Frau Wolff. Enchanting. Absolutely enchanting.'

Her new name still didn't fit Anna comfortably, even after a year and more of marriage and the birth of a child. Whenever she heard it spoken, she couldn't stop herself thinking of Ivo's mother. It made her hesitate before answering. But Möller appeared to expect a response. What did he want her to do: curtsy... blush... simper?

He's Ivo's friend, she reminded herself. Be nice to him. Just because he's wearing a Nazi Party tiepin doesn't mean he *has* to be a creep, does it?

As she took her place at the table, Ivo said, 'You can call her Anna, she won't mind.'

That really made her wince, though she just about managed to keep her composure. Why was Ivo speaking about her as if she were his pet dog? She fussed with her spoon to stifle a sudden flare of anger.

As they ate, Ivo told her about his trip to Berlin, how Chancellor Hitler's Nazi Party had brought pride back to the city, how they'd cleaned it up, how fine it looked with the swastika flags hanging from government buildings...

'But what about all these stories of Jewish shops being attacked?' protested Anna, who frequently bought the foreign edition of the *New York Herald Tribune* from the newsstand on the Schwarzenbergplatz.

It was Möller who answered her, not Ivo: 'Oh, that's mere overblown nonsense, Anna,' he said. 'Just a few people getting rightly upset over profiteering. It's mostly made up by the international press, to make us look bad.'

Möller dabbed at his mouth with his napkin. Anna noticed he had a small mole under one corner of his bottom lip that sprouted little bristles his razor hadn't reached. She had to stop herself laughing. She had seen a science fiction movie at the Burg-Kino a week earlier, and now she imagined that Möller's body was nothing but the mole's appendage, and that what was really controlling him was that little ball of hardened, hairy, alien tissue.

It occurred to her as she ate just how few of Ivo's friends she had actually met. Had he kept them from her deliberately, knowing her opinion of the *Heimwehr*? Were they all like Manis Möller? Suddenly, her memories of their courtship made it seem to her unnaturally closed, as if she'd been inducted into a secret order, and was only now – after successfully passing the indoctrination ceremony – being permitted to meet the other members.

'And how long do you plan to stay in Vienna, Herr Möller?' she said, hoping *liaison* was something one could achieve in a day or two, certainly less than a week.

'That rather depends on Chancellor Hitler,' Möller said, casting a sly glance at Ivo.

'What's it got to do with him?' Anna asked. 'This is Austria, not Germany.'

Ivo patted her knee under the table. If they'd been alone, she might have wanted his hand to linger. But in this company, it seemed belittling.

'What Manis means is that it won't be long before Herr Hitler will be the one deciding police policy here,' Ivo explained.

'But our policemen swear their oath to Chancellor Schuschnigg and the citizens of Austria,' she pointed out reasonably. 'Not to Herr Hitler in Berlin.'

'It is the Führer's firm conviction that Austria is as much a limb of the German Reich as a man's right arm is of his body,' Möller said ponderously. 'After all, he was born here.'

'If you say so, Herr Möller,' Anna replied. To her shame – and only because she didn't want to cause an argument with her husband's new friend over the dinner table – she added a lie. 'I don't really know about these things. I'm honestly not that political.'

'There are plenty of people I know who feel the same way as Manis does,' Ivo said, cutting off her line of retreat. 'You can't stop the will of the people just by issuing decrees. Dollfuss learned that the hard way.'

To her surprise – and, yes, her consternation – Anna suddenly found herself wishing her mother was home. Marion would know what to say. She'd know how to bring the conversation back to the frivolous. Marion would put Manis Möller in his place with a single barbed retort, or a gush of overdone flattery. Even Ivo wouldn't dare stand up to her. *Where are you when I need you, Mama? Come back and make me feels less outnumbered.*

It was thinking of Marion that gave her the courage to look Möller directly in the face and say, 'How exactly does your Herr Hitler plan to convince those who don't feel that way? Will he march his stormtroopers across our border, for a little friendly persuasion? I hear he employs them very effectively on those who disagree with him.'

The colour drained from Ivo's face as if someone had pulled a plug. He slammed his fist down on the table, making his wineglass jump almost enough for it to topple. 'That's enough, Anna!' he said. 'I won't have my good friend challenged in such a manner at my own dinner table. It's embarrassing.'

She stared at him. He'd never raised his voice to her before. Part of her wanted to cry. The other part wanted to stab him in the back of the hand with her fork.

What was she was meant to say in reply? To remain silent was to accept he had power over her. She thought of Rex, and how he'd smiled in the face of overwhelming force when he'd marched out of the Villa Fiorentina with his head held high. She thought of Marion – exasperating, yes, but with a wayward, indomitable spirit.

Taking a deep breath for courage, she stabbed a lump of goulash meat with her fork and raised it to her lips. And just before she put it into her mouth, she waved it slowly around, very delicately, as if it were a paintbrush, and she was Marion at her easel, considering with the utmost care quite where on the canvas it should go. Then she said, 'But it's not actually *your* dinner table, is it, Ivo darling?'

In the bedroom, Bär began to cry.

Ivo seemed unable to speak.

Manis Möller wiped his lips with the napkin once again.

Anna swallowed the chunk of goulash and laid down her fork. 'Well,' she said, turning her head towards the bedroom, 'there's one Austrian who's not impressed by talk of unification. If you'll both excuse me, my son needs his mother.'

Möller left the apartment at eleven. Marion still hadn't returned. Anna assumed she wouldn't see her now until at least tomorrow. It was a pattern she was used to. Bär had settled again, so she thought she'd better emerge from the bedroom to say goodbye to Ivo's friend.

'Ivo, you have a very forthright wife,' Möller said at the front door, speaking across Anna as if she wasn't there.

'I'm sorry for the embarrassment,' Ivo said, without looking at her.

It wasn't the implied criticism that made Anna's anger begin to boil again, it was Ivo's expression of submissiveness. It just didn't seem right to her that a man as striking as her husband should seem to grovel to someone who looked as though he should be in the dock for embezzling the petty cash.

'There's no cause for embarrassment, my dear fellow,' Möller replied, with a greasy smile. 'The best of our womenfolk should be fearless. The Party has little use for those who duck at the first sound of gunfire.'

'Look out for a blue light on the front of the tram,' Anna said loudly. 'It means it's the last service. After that, you'll have to walk.'

She went back into the lounge and put 'Tiger Rag' on the gramophone to make herself feel better. She was studying the record sleeve when she sensed Ivo behind her. She turned.

His face looked stiff and immobile, as if he'd had a jab of novocaine for a tooth extraction.

'That was quite unnecessary,' he said.

'He's a fucking creep,' said Anna, who seldom swore. Her sudden vehemence surprised her. She wondered if somehow Marion was exercising a mesmeric influence on her from a distance. Or perhaps she'd just realized she'd grown up. Either way, it felt good. Powerful. 'I don't know why you brought him back without asking me. What did he mean by "our womenfolk"?'

Ivo went to the sideboard, took out a bottle of schnapps and poured himself a large shot. He didn't ask her if she wanted one.

'I have something to tell you,' he said casually.

Not *ask*, she noted. Not *put past you*. Just *tell*.

'Really?'

Ivo downed the schnapps in one gulp. 'I'm going to apply for a place with the police department.'

'The police?' Anna said, hardly believing what she'd heard. 'In Berlin?'

'No. Here, in Vienna.'

For a while she just studied him, a puzzled look on her face. Then she said, '*You?* A policeman?'

'Why not? I've done that sort of thing before.'

'Breaking up fights in nightclubs? That's not being a policeman. Besides, you already have a job.'

Ivo turned his eyes to the ceiling and gave a scornful laugh. 'Yes, selling motor cars.'

'What's wrong with that? It's an income. There's plenty in Vienna who'd be grateful for one of those.'

'It's frivolous,' he said, which she thought was rather pompous of him. 'Selling motor cars isn't going to help make us a stronger, better nation. It won't help protect us from the bankers and the deviant troublemakers who do their bidding, will it?'

Anna was confused now. Ivo had never once expressed a desire to be a policeman in all the time she'd known him.

'But I thought you planned to take over control of your father's motorcycle garage one day.'

'I could be waiting for ever,' he said resentfully, as if longevity were an injustice. 'He's fit. Healthy – apart from having only one eye. He could live for another twenty years at least. Maybe thirty. He's not the sort of man to retire. He's not one of those fellows who'd rather spend his time shooting boar in the company of his old comrades from the war. I can't wait that long. I need to do something constructive.'

'How do you know the police would take you?'

He seemed to think her question risible. 'Why wouldn't they? I've served with the *Heimwehr*. I know how to use a pistol. I'm good in a fight. They'd snap me up.'

Suddenly, the image of Frau Vogel in her Born-Hof worker's apartment jumped into Anna's mind. She could hear her bemoaning her husband's fate at the hands of the police: *Our men are lucky not to get beaten to death before they get anywhere near a judge... Do they think we don't know what's going on?*

Surely Ivo didn't want to join an organization like that. But then, he *had* joined the *Heimwehr*, even if he'd later come to reject its behaviour.

Or had he left for another reason altogether?

Anna put another record on the gramophone. She set the volume control so that it wouldn't wake Bär, but not so low that it couldn't mask the silence while she wondered how to reply.

'I'm really not sure, Ivo,' she said at length. 'I think you should reconsider.'

'What's the matter – don't you approve of maintaining law and order? God knows, this city could do with it.'

'Does this all stem from your trip to Berlin, Ivo? Has your friend Manis Möller put you up to this?'

'It was Manis who suggested it, yes.'

Anna frowned. 'How did you meet him? You haven't told me.'

'At a march.'

Now she wished that the Boswell Sisters were singing '42nd Street' loud enough to drown out the warning voice yelling inside her head.

And never mind about Bär, because any moment now it's going to be me waking up and starting to howl, not him.

'You went to a *march* – in Berlin?'

'I didn't *go* to it. It passed by me,' Ivo said defensively.

'And who exactly was marching? Let me guess—'

'Manis was helping keep the crowd in order. We got talking, that's all.'

'Talking about *what*?'

'About how they've really got a grip on things there. They've shut down all the vice dens, and the places where the transvestites go about parading themselves in their filthy outfits…'

Anna suddenly remembered the boy at the Red Panther, lying in his bloodied sequined dress amongst the shattered glass.

'Why do you care what other people do in nightclubs?' she asked. 'If you disapprove so much, don't visit them.'

There was a sharpness to his reply that Anna didn't much care for.

'That's just the sort of nonsense I'd expect to hear from your mother's airy-fairy arty friends – people who'd rather splash paint about in meaningless doodles than do a proper day's work for the general benefit of the Fatherland. Am I supposed to applaud your mother for taking drugs in places like that? Do you think I don't know what she gets up to?'

Anna felt herself beginning to blush. It wasn't anger, she realized – it was more akin to fear. Not fear that he might lash out and hurt her, but fear that she was listening to a voice she didn't recognize, coming from a man she hadn't met before.

'Where's all this anger coming from, Ivo?' she asked, trying to keep her hands from shaking. 'Are you telling me that you want to join the police so that you can arrest my mother's friends, and beat up boys who've done you no harm other than to offend your sense of propriety? What ever happened to "the heirs to Mozart and Haydn – you must think us all barbarians"?'

He gave her a blank look. 'I don't know what you mean.'

'It's what you said to me at the club, the night we first met. There was a fight – remember? The one you broke up by firing a pistol into the ceiling.'

Ivo's voice began to harden, like that of an agitator at a demonstration. '*Somebody* has to get a grip of this nation! It needs men of courage. Men with a clear vision of how to sweep all the shit out of the stables before it's too late! Before we all drown in a tide of degeneracy!'

Turning his back on her, he stomped to the gramophone and swept the arm off the disc. The music died with an agonized screech.

'And we'll have no more of this disgusting Negro noise, either!'

'I like it,' Anna objected, standing her ground. 'And if you ever bothered to take an interest in the things I enjoy, you'd know the Boswell sisters are white.'

'It's jazz,' Ivo responded contemptuously, close to shouting now. 'And that makes it Negro music.'

From his cot in the bedroom, Bär began to wail again.

In the Karlsplatz the leaves were turning, edged with the first scatterings of autumnal gold and crimson. A pale, mid-morning sun burnished the great green dome of the church. From the Kärntner Ring came the goose-honk of motorcar horns and the rumble of tram wheels.

The park was the safest place in which to read the latest letter from Rex. Anna had learned that years ago, when Marion had caught her at home, halfway through an account of his experiences filming *The Jazz Singer*. Now Rex wrote to her care of the delicatessen on the corner of Argentinierstrasse, where Herr Szilárd, the Hungarian owner, kept them for her to collect. When she had composed a reply she would place it in an envelope – taking care not to seal it because the counter clerk would want to check she wasn't sending precious currency out of the country – and carry it to the post office. If she had saved enough money from her part-time job at a photography shop on the Sudtiroler Platz – four hours a week while Marion looked after Bär – she would ask for a *Par avion* stamp and send it by Zeppelin mail.

Another useful function of the Karlsplatz was that it required Anna to control her emotions. She missed her father dreadfully. No matter how good the news in his letters, imagining his voice always brought her close to tears. Reading them in a public space forced her to make an art out of feigning composure.

So when she heard a male voice calling her name, she looked up with barely a hint of dampness in her eyes.

'Fräulein Anna? Yes, it is! It's *you*.'

Gazing down at her was the smiling face of Luka Vogel.

For a moment she barely recognized him. He had filled out, grown up. The once over-oiled fair hair, styled like Fred Astaire's, now really suited him. He still had the same leanness of face, but the highly strung boy she remembered had been somehow transformed into a good-looking young man with a confident manner. Beside him stood his sister. She, too, had changed, from a schoolgirl into a beauty.

'Luka! Goodness… what a surprise! I haven't seen you for – what, it must be over a year? And… and…' Anna tried to recall his sister's name and failed.

'You remember Louisa, my little sister,' Luka said, coming to her aid.

'Yes, of course I do.'

Luka put his arm around his sister's shoulders. 'And you remember Fräulein Anna, don't you, Lulu? She came to take some photographs at the Born-Hof.'

The young woman held Anna's gaze a little too long for comfort. 'Yes, I remember her well, Luka,' she said primly. 'The last time I saw her, she was going into the Rathauskeller with a gentleman.' She glanced at Bär, sleeping in his pram. 'I presume it was a most satisfactory meal, Fräulein.'

Ouch, thought Anna. Cruel, but deserved.

'I heard somewhere you'd married,' Luka said. 'That's wonderful. And a baby, so soon. How lovely.' His pleasure seemed genuine enough. He'd clearly long since got over the hurt of being stood up.

'Are you still attending the institute?' Anna asked. 'I had to leave, when I fell pregnant. They insisted.'

'I've just completed my course,' Luka said. 'Now I'm off to Berlin, to further my studies. It's all a bit parochial here, don't you think?'

'Berlin? Are you sure?'

'Oh, I know what you mean: the way they don't like socialists there any more. The form I had to fill out for the University of the Arts even wanted to know what my political allegiances were.'

He laughed. 'I didn't tell them my father was a member of the Social Democratic Workers' Party and got himself arrested. I just wrote "anything that promotes *Heimat* – the art of the nation, its history and its glorious culture." They loved it. They said I had exactly the right attitude.'

Anna smiled. 'I'm sure you'll prosper. My husband went there a short while ago. I hear there are a lot of flags everywhere. And marching. Is your mother well? And your father – safely restored to you?'

'Those bastards in the government beat him up before they let him go. But he's fine now. Back at work.'

'Well, make sure you take care in Berlin, Luka, won't you?'

Luka tapped his nose. 'Don't worry. I've learned my lesson. Keep out of politics, that's my motto now. Father's been active in the workers' movement all his adult life and look where it got him.' He pulled his scarf a little tighter around his throat. 'No, all I'm interested in is studying graphic design, and they seem to be very modern in Germany. Very forward-thinking.'

'Then I shall wish you the very best of good fortune, Luka,' Anna said.

'Goodbye, Frau—' He hesitated, unsure of what to call her.

'It's Wolff, now,' Anna said. 'With two *f*s.'

Luka Vogel squinted at her, as though the sun had made her features indistinct, and he couldn't be sure if he still recognized her.

'But you're still Anna Cantrell – when you take your pictures?'

The question hurt her like a paper cut. She could no longer be sure.

Luka must have noticed something in her eyes because he said, 'Actually, we're on our way to the Café Ludwig. Would you care to join us? A farewell *Wiener melange*, perhaps.'

'Oh, I'd only be intruding,' Anna said. 'And there's Bär, here—'

But Luka would accept no refusal. 'Nonsense! It would be a pleasure. Who knows when we might meet again?' He turned to his sister. 'You don't mind, do you, Lulu?'

'If it's your wish, Luka,' Louisa Vogel said. She made no attempt to hide her lack of interest in his proposition.

'Then it's agreed,' he said confidently. 'The Ludwig it is. It's not far.'

Anna folded the letter from her father, returned it to its envelope and put the envelope back in her handbag. Then she said, 'On one condition – that it's my treat. I think I owe you that at the very least, after my rudeness at the Nestroy-Kino.'

Luka smiled and Anna was forced to admit that he really had grown up. 'Oh, I'd forgotten all about that,' he said. 'That was ages ago. Professor Koppitz kept you late, I seem to recall.'

As Anna released the brake on Bär's pram, she smiled briefly at how Luka had managed to forget all about being stood up but still remembered her excuse. But as they walked together out of the Karlsplatz towards the Café Ludwig, she found the thought of different company, and an excuse not to hurry back to the apartment, surprisingly pleasurable.

With a baby and an unreliable mother, Anna found it hard to pursue her photography. But she tried, if only to keep her mind off the state of her marriage. Mostly it was everyday stuff: families enjoying themselves in Prater Park… artistic shots of the city's grand buildings… boaters on the Danube. The pictures were never going to win awards, she knew that; but practising her skill was satisfying. When she showed Ivo the better ones, hoping for his approval, he seemed indifferent. The only art that interested him was to be found on the strident posters for the Fatherland Front.

'The cretinous, myopic, self-serving bastards,' Ivo shouted one morning when the mail arrived, as he hurled both letter and opened envelope onto the floor like a toddler in a tantrum.

Even Marion flinched. Anna started to bounce Bär on her hip to distract his attention.

'The police – they've turned you down?' she said cautiously, fearful of pouring petrol on the fire.

'Manis told me it was bound to be a foregone conclusion.'

Anna felt inclined to suggest that perhaps the Vienna police department didn't much care for a candidate having a Nazi for a sponsor. But she wisely kept her thoughts to herself.

'Perhaps they have a quota for the year,' she said, trying to make things better. 'Or maybe they haven't been given the money for more officers. I'm sure it will be something like that.'

She handed Bär to Marion, went over to Ivo and embraced him. Despite the change that had come over him since he'd returned from Berlin, despite his new hair-trigger temper, despite *everything*, she still loved him. The child in him had become more visible to her. Sometimes she even pitied him.

He let her hold on to him for a moment, as motionless in her grasp as a mouse caught by a cat. Then, to her surprise, he pushed her away.

'I'm going down to the Franz Joseph quay,' he said, the rejection letter apparently forgotten. 'I've agreed to go rowing with Manis.'

In October, the *Neues Volksblatt* ran a sequence of photographs that Anna had taken of Vienna in the autumn. The next month, through a friend of Marion's, she got an exclusive shot into the

Wiener Zeitung, of the Austrian women's fencing team in training for the following year's Berlin Olympic Games. Through contacts she had made via Dorothy Thompson, the same picture was taken by the *Milwaukee Journal Sentinel*, whose many readers of German and Austrian descent were interested in the goings-on back in their homeland.

Marion had traded in the assistant manager at the Galerie Felix Bezner for a young waiter from the Café Landtmann, who read Goethe and Schiller in the living room with his shirt unbuttoned to the waist. Ivo didn't approve. And if she were to be honest, neither did Anna. But Bär seemed entranced by him, and anyway, Marion – through Grandpa Wolfgang – still paid the rent.

On Christmas Eve, 1935, Anna and Ivo took Bär to the Christmas market outside the Rathaus. While their son gazed in wonder at the decorations and the lights, they ate roasted chestnuts served piping hot from a brazier. In the new year, they went ice skating, while Marion pushed her grandson in his pram around the Stadtpark. Anna began to entertain the possibility that her life was ordering itself as neatly as she could dare hope.

And then came the moment its course was changed forever.

'Hey, kids, attention on deck!' Marion yelled from the hall, waving the letter the postman had handed her only a few moments before with the words, 'It's for you, Frau Bauer – from America. Is it, perhaps, Herr Roosevelt, wanting you to paint his portrait to hang in the White House?'

It was no such thing, of course. But it was an invitation.

'It's from Grandpa Wolfgang,' Marion said, as Ivo and Anna gathered around her. 'He and Grandma Freda want to see their new great-grandson. He's going to arrange tickets for us all to take a vacation with them, in Maine. Isn't that just the best news ever?'

And indeed it was. Because as far as Anna was concerned, there wasn't a wall Marion or Grandpa Wolfgang could build around the Bauer summer home in Maine that would stop her from seizing a few days alone with Rex.

'Where are we sailing from?' she asked.

'Oh, no leaky old tugboat for the Bauers, honey,' Marion replied. She held aloft the letter in much the same way that Neville Chamberlain was to, less than three years later, when he returned from Munich proclaiming *Peace for our time*. 'We're going in style,' she announced. 'Grandpa Wolfgang's bought us all tickets to go by Zeppelin, no less. Aboard the *Hindenburg*.'

Eight

The Hindenburg airship at the Zeppelin landing ground, Frankfurt.
Picture taken by Anna Cantrell. Leica Model C with wide angle lens.
Agfa monochrome film. 17 May 1936

'I'm lost for words. It's just… extraordinary. I've never seen anything like it before.'

Anna lowered the camera, letting it hang by its strap. She stared at the vast silver torpedo that rested with almost impossible lightness on the earth in front of her.

She had seen photographs of the *Hindenburg* in the newspapers, but nothing could have prepared her for its sheer size. As large as an ocean liner, its taut fabric gleamed in the sunshine. It almost seemed alive. The only thing that unsettled Anna were the giant swastikas emblazoned on the fins.

She heard her mother's voice behind her, remonstrating with the clerk. She turned. Marion was standing on the plate of the weighing machine, the last of the fifty passengers to do so.

'This damned contraption is way wrong, honey,' Marion said loudly, tapping the glass cover over the pointer. 'I've never been more than one-fifteen pounds in my life.' She still refused to use kilos, even after almost twelve years in Europe.

'I assure you, madam,' the clerk said, 'the machine is calibrated perfectly. It is a requirement.'

'Calibrated, my ass,' Marion hissed.

The weighing clerk gave her a Teutonic nod of the head, very correct, exquisitely polite. Then he said, 'And perhaps, madam, therein lies the problem.'

Marion glared at him, turned her back on the insult as haughtily as she could manage, and joined the rest of the family. 'Jeez,' she said, fishing in her bag and pulling out a pack of Ecksteins and a lighter. 'I need a cigarette.'

An attendant, the words *Deutsche Zeppelin-Reederei* embroidered on his uniform, spotted her at once and came over. 'I'm afraid no smoking is allowed, madam. There is a smoking room aboard. Once you are airborne, the purser will announce when it is open.'

'So, when does the bar open?' Marion sighed petulantly as she put the pack and the lighter back in her bag. 'I'm as parched as the goddamned Gobi Desert.'

'That, too, will be announced – once you are safely aloft.'

'Safely?' Marion queried. 'You mean there's doubt?'

The attendant smiled reassuringly. He was used to nervous passengers. 'The *Hindenburg* is safer than any steamship in service, I can assure you of that, madam. On *this* Atlantic crossing, the only ice you will be in danger of hitting will be that in your cocktail glass.' He indicated the rest of the passengers climbing into the airship's silver hull. 'Now, if you please—'

Anna pulled the camera strap over her neck and put the Leica back in her travelling bag. Then she took back Bär's bassinette from Ivo. 'Come along, Mama,' she said to Marion. 'Let's not spoil Grandpa Wolfgang's present before we get to enjoy it.'

Their cases were waiting for them in one of the two cabins on A Deck that her grandfather had reserved. Anna looked around, impressed. There wasn't much space, barely more than what one might find in a railroad sleeper car. But everything was very modern and clean, in a freshly painted light blue. There were two bunk beds, the upper reached by a little aluminium ladder; a call bell for service, should they feel the need to summon a waiter; even a little plastic sink with running water. She caught a faint whiff of acetate-doped fabric and motor oil. They were in the belly of the ship; Anna could imagine, above the ceiling, the vast hydrogen-filled lift bags that would carry this monster into the skies as if it weighed less than a breath.

'The restrooms are on B deck,' the steward advised. 'And also, a shower room, for your convenience.'

'Where's the window?' Ivo asked.

'There is no window in the cabin, sir, as we're in the centre of the ship. But the lounge, the dining room and the reading room all have access to a promenade with fine panoramic windows. I'm sure you'll find the view breathtaking – when we're not in cloud.'

'How long will we be aloft?' Anna asked.

'If the winds are as forecast, around seventy-six hours. That's Germany to America in one day less than it took the SS *Normandie* just to cross the Atlantic alone when she won the Blue Riband last year,' said the steward proudly.

Anna hung up her three dresses in the tiny canvas-sided wardrobe and slid her suitcase under the bottom bunk. When the purser's voice announced over the loudspeakers that it was time to depart, they fetched Marion from the cabin next door and hurried to the nearest promenade, where the other passengers were gathering. The wide windows there were angled outwards from a long counter that ran the length of the compartment, so that people could lean forward for a better view. She placed Bär's bassinet on the shelf between her and Ivo, Marion to her left. There was a carnival mood of anticipation.

The ship began to move slowly along the ground. Outside, Anna could see scores of ground staff hauling the monster forward by mooring ropes. Suddenly the *Hindenburg* seemed to tremble, as if eager to be unleashed. The groundsmen let go of the ropes and sprang backwards. At once, the ship rose quickly into the air. Anna felt her stomach drop. One or two of the more nervous passengers grabbed at the shelf in front of them for support. A deepening rumble went through the ship as the engines came to life.

Ivo positively glowed with pride. 'Isn't it wonderful?' he said. 'Didn't I tell you this was how the future would be, when I took you boating on the Danube? We're entering a whole new world of modernity, made possible by German science.'

Anna nodded. She remembered the moment well. Newly in love, she'd been entranced by his dreams, by his certainty at the prospect of progress making a better world for them to live in. Though now, as she watched the ground crew become tiny ants, and the great Frankfurt Zeppelin hangar shrink to the size of a matchbox, she couldn't recall him ever mentioning that it was specifically *German* science that would achieve it all.

Thirty-five hours after leaving Frankfurt, the *Hindenburg* was far out over the Atlantic Ocean. It was night. From the windows, the Azores could be easily picked out in the moonlight, three thousand feet below. Supper had been served in the spacious red-carpeted dining room – a starter of beef broth with marrow dumplings, followed by a choice of Rhine salmon or roast gosling, with pears Condé to finish. Now the passengers had decamped to the bar, the smoking room and the lounge, where the ship's pianist was playing requests on the specially made lightweight aluminium piano. Anna couldn't help noticing the framed picture of Adolf Hitler hanging on the wall behind him.

A stewardess was keeping watch over Bär and the other young passengers while their parents chatted over their martinis, Manhattans and Bronx Sidecars. Marion was on her third LZ129 – orange juice and gin served in a frosted glass and named after the airship's tail number.

Anna was returning from the ladies' restroom on B deck when she noticed Ivo standing on the starboard promenade. He was deep in conversation with a passenger in a smart lounge suit. She recognized him from dinner: a Berliner who ran a successful agricultural feed business, or so he'd bragged. He'd assumed her photography was some sort of hobby, to keep the little lady occupied at home. She'd taken an instant dislike to him.

Both men were lounging by the windows, their backs to her, looking out at the islands passing below. They were oblivious to her approach, and because of the throbbing of the engines Anna was almost upon them before she heard what her husband's newfound friend was saying.

'… quite correct, Herr Wolff. She is indeed a triumph – proof, if we ever needed it, that we were wise to put our faith and our future in the Führer's hands. It's a crying shame, though, to waste all this technological effort in order to provide luxury and speed for Jew bankers visiting their friends on Wall Street.'

Anna froze. What manner of conversation had she interrupted? In Vienna, she had grown almost accustomed to overhearing such comments. They were becoming worryingly commonplace. But how would Ivo reply? Would he protest on her behalf? Would he quickly change the subject so as not to cause an argument?

She couldn't comprehend why they hadn't heard her sudden intake of breath.

The one thing she had never expected Ivo to do was *laugh.*

The little cabin trembled like a bird held captive in the hand as the *Hindenburg* sailed on through the air currents of the night. Anna was only half aware of the vast airship around her. Its aluminium carcass creaked. Its motors grumbled their endless, droning fugue to modernity. She heard Ivo cough and realized he was still awake.

'Ivo—'

'Go to sleep.'

'That man you were talking to, tonight—'

'Which man? I spoke to several.'

'The one I saw you with on the starboard promenade, after we'd eaten.'

'Oh, him,' Ivo said, leaning over the edge of his bunk and looking down at her. 'Just a fellow from Berlin. Eisner, I think his name was. What about him?'

'Was he an interesting conversationalist? Did you become friends?'

'He's alright, I suppose. Why do you ask?'

'I just wondered.'

There were so many questions she really wanted to ask him in the privacy of their cabin suspended high above the dark ocean. Was this Eisner a Nazi Party member, like his other friend, the odious Manis Möller? Why had he laughed at Eisner's bigotry, when any normal husband would have taken offence? Had Ivo brought something back from his trip to Berlin other than just a desire to join the police force? And what had he really been seeing when his eyes had lingered – as she had seen them linger more than once that evening – on the piano in the lounge? The pianist, or the framed photograph of Adolf Hitler on the bulkhead behind him?

And then she recalled how, just before their wedding, he'd asked her to write *Roman Catholic* in the official register.

Safer all round, he'd said. That way, none of the less enlightened will give you a hard time.

The dim glow from the nightlight over the door gave a blue, sepulchral sheen to the metal frame of Anna's bunk, to the little sink, and to the stepladder rising to the bunk directly above hers where Ivo lay snoring gently.

I'm in the belly of a great whale at the bottom of the ocean, she thought. I'm in a funeral parlour. I'm on the moon.

I'm in a marriage with a man I no longer trust.

The passengers had gathered on the promenades on either side of the ship, everyone leaning over the sloping glass of the observation windows to get a view of New York harbour and the skyscrapers of Manhattan.

'Say, look – isn't that a giant gorilla I can see, on top of the Empire State?' someone called out. Laughter rippled down the line.

The *Hindenburg* made a long, slow turn so that everyone could get a sight of the Statue of Liberty and Ellis Island. An American woman standing near Anna said to her husband, 'Look, that's where Grandmother arrived from Estonia. Right there. Isn't that wonderful? "Give me your tired, your poor, your huddled masses yearning to breathe free." Brings a tear to the eye, when you think on it, don't it?'

To Ivo's right, the man named Eisner was observing the view. Anna heard him say softly, in German, 'Why would you dilute your nation's blood by leaving an open wound for the germs to enter?'

She glanced at Ivo, waiting for his reaction. But he said nothing, watching the view unfold like any other tourist.

For a while, as they approached the landing field at Lakehurst, Anna felt relief that this time Ivo hadn't responded. Perhaps that laugh he'd given Eisner on the promenade as they watched the Azores drift by below had been nothing more sinister than embarrassment. Perhaps he had been too polite to give reproach. Perhaps his suggestion about the entry in the marriage register really had been made only to protect her.

But as Anna gazed out at the breathtaking view below, she couldn't help wondering how confident of their own immunity Herr Eisner, or Manis Möller for that matter, had to be to spew such bile in the presence of strangers. Or how complicit a husband might be if he just stood there and said nothing.

The brownstone on West 76th Street hadn't changed in twenty years. It was still the dark, chintzy shrine to the Tyrol that Anna remembered from her childhood, with heavy, rustic furniture and Wolfgang's scattered collection of stuffed birds in bell jars that you stumbled across in places you least expected to encounter them. Only her grandparents had changed, though by how much it was hard to judge; they had already seemed impossibly old when she was six.

But they made an enormous fuss over her. And they loved Ivo. To them, he was living proof that the old country hadn't lost its mettle. And he, in turn, was charm personified, which went some way towards convincing Anna that she'd got it all wrong, that Ivo had never signed up to the anti-Semitism of Möller, Eisner and their fellow travellers in Berlin.

In the meantime, she waited for the phone call that would despatch her on her very first mission behind enemy lines.

They had planned it with utmost care: such a dangerous mission could not be left to chance. In the letters Anna and Rex had exchanged via Herr Szilárd's delicatessen in Vienna, her father had acquainted her with their respective roles as spy-runner and agent. One week to the day after the *Hindenburg* landed, Rex would telephone the house on West 76th Street, having first checked with the operator that the number hadn't changed in the years since he and Marion had courted. Then he would call, claiming to be a friend of Dorothy Thompson's who wished to speak to Anna about publishing her photographs. He would affect an American accent in case the receiver was lifted not by the Bauers' maid, Marjorie, but by Wolfgang or Freda, or – in the worst of all possible worlds – Marion herself. For a cover name, he would announce himself as Howell Bell – an inversion of the Bell and Howell camera brand name, and a sign of just how much Rex was enjoying himself.

True to his promise, he made the call on the allotted day promptly at ten o'clock, according to the Bauers' forbidding grandfather clock in the hallway – Anna had always thought it looked like an upended coffin with a white, round, dead-looking face staring out of it.

It almost went horribly wrong from the very first moment.

'May I speak to Miss Anna Cantrell, please?' the voice on the line said.

'I'm afraid you've called an incorrect number,' Marjorie countered. 'This is the Bauer household.' And with that, she replaced the receiver in its cradle, cutting off the call.

The phone rang again, almost immediately.

'I'm most dreadfully sorry,' the caller said. 'I wish to speak to Miss Anna Bauer – or Mrs Wolff, as I believe she's now known.'

When Anna took the receiver from the maid, it required every ounce of her determination not to burst into tears with expectation. 'Hello? Anna Cantrell speaking.'

'Ah, Miss Cantrell. It's Howell Bell here.'

Anna just about managed to say, 'Why, Mr Bell, how delightful to talk to you,' without choking on her emotions.

They had agreed Rex would stay in character, just in case Marion picked up another extension.

'I've received your photographs, and I must say, they're very good. Is it OK if we use print number two? It'll be the agreed size and the agreed price. Is that acceptable?'

'That would be wonderful, Mr Bell,' Anna said, gripping the receiver so hard she wondered later how the Bakelite hadn't cracked under the pressure.

'Goodbye, then, Miss Cantrell.'

'Goodbye, Mr Bell.'

Print number two was their code for the Museum of Modern Art, prints one and three being Penn Station and Bethesda Fountain in Central Park respectively. The agreed size meant tomorrow. The agreed price meant two o'clock in the afternoon. Thus, the date, place and time of the rendezvous could be easily amended just by altering the numbers.

Anna had to lock herself in the bathroom for fifteen minutes to compose herself.

'I have to go and see someone tomorrow about publishing my photographs,' she told the family when she returned to the salon. 'Grandma, could you look after Bär for a few hours?'

Freda said she could think of nothing better. Wolfgang promised to take Ivo to his club. Even Marion was fooled, though she couldn't stop herself saying, 'Don't you even think of hopping on a Greyhound for Los Angeles, honey. If you do, I'll be sailing home without you.'

The Museum of Modern Art occupied several rented rooms on one of the upper floors of a building on West 53rd Street. Anna stepped into the elevator car and reached for the correct button. Her hands were shaking. That didn't surprise her – her whole body was quivering. Thankful that she was alone, she let the car whisk her skywards.

Rex was standing in front of a work by Max Beckmann, his head tilted slightly as he studied distorted bodies that looked as though they'd been frozen at the height of some strange paroxysm. It was the sort of art that Ivo had recently begun to call 'degenerate'.

When he heard her soft, 'Papa!' he turned, and for a moment she was back in her pram, beneath the parasol, the air warm from the desert sun, and the face leaning in over hers was one huge smile – the only face she wanted to see.

When at last they had released each other from their embrace and Anna had come back from the restroom with her make-up restored, he took her by taxi to an English Chophouse on West 36th.

'I still can't believe it,' Rex said as they settled into their seats, facing one another over the starched white tablecloth. 'Just look at my little girl.'

'Not so little any more, Papa.'

He shook his head slowly in wonder. 'I've thought of you so, *so* often over these past twelve years. But you've grown up to be even more beautiful than I could ever have imagined.'

Anna touched his hand. 'You'd say that even if I looked like Bela Lugosi in his Dracula cape.'

'And you're getting your pictures published. That's tickety-boo, that is.'

Anna grinned. She hadn't heard the phrase since she was eight. 'Not *that* tickety-boo, Papa. I'm not going to be famous any time soon.'

'It'll come. Don't worry.'

The waiter brought the wine that Rex had ordered even before they'd reached their table. They raised a glass to each other. Anna nearly began to cry again at the thought of the years together that had been stolen from her. Who was the thief, she wondered? Rex? Marion? Or did life itself sometimes just rob you without compunction?

While they waited for their food orders to arrive, Rex demanded to know all about the journey. 'I saw the pictures in the paper, the day after you arrived. It's really something, that airship, ain't it? Before you know it, we'll all be sailing the skies in whole fleets of them. Shame about the swastikas, though.' He smiled ruefully at her. 'You know, I worry about you, being in Europe now – all the things you hear.'

Anna sipped her wine and smiled to reassure him. 'Mother's sure it will all blow over. After all, Berlin is hosting the Olympic Games in August. People are saying Herr Hitler will be forced to tone things down a bit. He'll have to start behaving himself.'

'And this handsome young Austrian husband of yours – I thought you might bring him today. And where's this new grandson your old dad's been busting his braces to see?'

She felt a sudden pang of guilt. She could have brought Ivo and Bär; she could have contrived some deceit that would have fooled Marion. But the truth was she'd never for a moment considered it. After so many years apart, she wanted Rex all to herself.

'What's wrong?' he asked perceptively.

'Ivo,' she said bluntly.

'Is he cheating on you? Is he a cad?'

She let slip a laugh of embarrassment. 'No. At least, I don't think so.'

Rex looked concerned. 'Does he beat you? Is he a brute?'

'No. Not physically. It's just that I'm not sure of him any more. He's changed.'

Rex laughed. 'I'm the last person on earth to give you marriage advice, darling. Or to criticize you for falling for a pretty face and marrying in haste.'

'I was so sure, at the start,' Anna said.

It seemed strange to be confessing her doubts about the man she slept with to a father who'd last seen her when she was eight. But it was so easy to do.

'When we first met,' she continued, 'he was so idealistic. I listened to his dreams for the future, and I couldn't help being excited by them. Then he went to Berlin. Now those dreams have a hard edge to them. He's become intolerant of… I don't know… it's as if everyone who isn't on his wavelength must be an enemy. He has friends who are Nazis. He talks about Austria becoming part of Germany.' Anna felt her eyes begin to moisten. 'Papa, I don't know what to do.'

'That's simple. Stay here, in America. Don't go back.'

'You mean *leave* him?'

'If he's making you unhappy.'

'But he's the father of my child. And I still care for him, I really do. I can try to make it work, I know I can. Besides, Mama won't stay in America.'

Rex gave her a sheepish look. 'You can lay the blame for that squarely upon your old man's shoulders, I'm afraid.'

'That's not true, Papa,' Anna said, with a sheepish grin. 'We've only been with Grandpa and Grandma Bauer a week, and Marion's already getting scrappy round the edges. She needs me with her in Vienna.'

'How is she?'

Anna shrugged. 'She's Marion. What more do you need to know?'

'Is she well?'

'That rather depends on what you mean by "well". She has… issues.'

'She always did. Mostly with me.'

Rex's smile faded. For the first time ever, Anna could see guilt and sadness in his eyes. 'I should have been more honest with her,' he said. 'But you must understand that I didn't know myself then. I believed that I was someone else. I tried very hard to *be* that someone else. But you can only be honest about something if you know what the truth of that something is. Anyway, that's the way I looks at it.'

Anna lifted her father's hand and kissed the back of it. 'Oh, you're alright, Papa – you're strong, you've got Bruno. But Marion – well, she might come across as a fighter, but underneath… Let's just say that if I wasn't there to keep an eye on her, I'd worry.'

The food arrived, but there was still so much to catch up on. So infrequently did they lift their forks to their mouths, that the waiter came over to check if there was something amiss.

When dessert came, Rex said, 'I have to go back to Los Angeles in two days. We're shooting a new movie.'

'Oh,' said Anna. 'I'd hoped we might see more of each other.'

'So did I.'

'Can't you delay, just for a while?'

Rex shook his head. 'Cameramen don't get to tell studio bosses they have more important things to do – not if they want to keep working.'

'I understand,' Anna said, as bravely as she could.

Rex leaned closer to her. 'But I'd really like to see my grandson before I go.' He glanced left and right, conspiratorially, taking in the wood-panelled restaurant and the other diners. 'If two super-spies can arrange *this*,' he said, 'then surely we can contrive that.'

Anna considered the possibilities. There had to be a way. 'Perhaps we could meet somewhere near Grandpa Wolfgang's house,' she suggested.

Rex looked horrified. 'If I'm found within five blocks of there, Marion will call out the vice squad, the Immigration Service, the IRS and very likely the FBI. It'll have to be somewhere else.'

Anna suddenly clapped her hands with delight: she'd just thought of the perfect place. 'I know the very spot,' she said. 'Just as long as it doesn't bring back uncomfortable memories for you.'

Rex's eyes held hers. He knew exactly what his daughter was thinking. The old smile returned, taking twenty years off his face in an instant.

'Perfect,' he said. 'Print number three it is, then.'

At the Bethesda Fountain in Central Park the tourists were lounging on the stone balustrade, dabbling their hands in the water and chatting in the sunshine. A street musician sauntered on the terrace, playing Paganini's 'Caprices' on his violin and making a good fist of it. A sign on the nut vendor's wheeled booth urged customers to *Keep the Park Clean*. A police officer astride a large bay horse leaned from the saddle, making conversation with a young female secretary on a break from her Fifth Avenue office.

Anna was just one of several women pushing a pram through the park that lunchtime, three days after her reunion with Rex. That the pram was serviceable was a miracle in itself. It had been Marion's; Grandma Freda had retrieved it from the basement, where it had spent over forty years gathering dust. In preparation for their granddaughter's arrival in New York, Grandpa Wolfgang had oiled the wheels and tightened the brake, while Freda had conjured suitable blankets from only God knew where, because the original padding was falling to pieces.

Reluctantly, Anna had been forced to enlist her grandparents in the subterfuge needed for the day's mission. And that had involved lying to them too, which made her feel dreadful. She had told them that while on her way to visit the fictitious Mr Howell Bell, she had bumped into an old school friend who had insisted on seeing Bär. While they gave her no sign of it, Anna suspected they knew exactly what she had planned, because an hour later Wolfgang offered to take Ivo to the Empire State Building, and Freda insisted that she and Marion visited Bloomingdale's. It would teach her another important lesson in the clandestine arts: no operation can succeed with proper support and effective misdirection.

Anna was beaming like a crazy woman as she stopped the pram at the spot where Rex was waiting. Pulling back the hood, she said, 'Look, *Liebling*, this is your Grandpa Rex. When you grow up, you're going to be as handsome as he is.'

Rex bent over the pram and gently touched Bär's cheek. Bär looked at him and giggled.

For one horrible moment, Anna thought her father was about to burst into tears.

'If I did nothing else in my life right—' he said, looking at the infant and then at Anna. He seemed unable to complete the sentence. Or, perhaps, unwilling.

The time they spent together then was even more precious to Anna than their meeting two days before. This time, she had brought her camera, because she knew it might be years before she would see Rex again. She only took two pictures – both showing Rex holding his grandson – feeling that firing off more would only highlight the inevitable passing of one minute into the next.

Rex bought ice creams and they sat on the grass beside the lake swapping memories of Uncle László and those mad days in Hollywood. When it was time to part, Rex took his final look at his grandson. 'Bring him up on Grandpa Cantrell's philosophy,' he said, as though the pram were a font, and this was a christening.

'And what's that, Papa?'

'Take what life throws at you. Use it wisely. Give a fair payment in return. Don't quibble over the bill – and find happiness, however long or how hard the search for it may be. And never listen to people with stunted imaginations that shout.'

It seemed a fine alternative to the comment that Ivo's mother had made to her at Graz: that Anna and Ivo should make fine babies together for the Fatherland.

They held each other in silence. Anna wished the projector would jam, freezing the movie on that one frame, because the thought of it ending and having to leave the theatre alone seemed the most unbearable thing that she could ever experience.

She watched Rex walk away beneath the elm trees towards Broadway. She had to dab her cheeks with her handkerchief for several minutes before she could even think of making her way back to West 76th Street.

Was this how it felt, she wondered, when someone you loved died?

Anna was still in the grip of a profound grief as she approached the Central Park West exit. Which was why she didn't notice the man on the bicycle until she'd stepped out in front of him, and it was almost too late. She heard the rasp of gravel as he swerved to avoid her, missing the pram by inches, and only then because he slung himself sideways, dragging the bike around him like a matador swirling his cape.

And because Anna's mind was elsewhere, she automatically apologized for not looking where she was going in German, the language she'd been using for the past twelve years. '*Es tut mir so leid!*'

He righted the bike, balancing with one leg on the ground. To her surprise, he too spoke in German, assuring her it was all his fault, and wanting to know if she was alright: '*Nein, nein, es war ganz und gar meine Schuld. Geht es Ihnen gut?*'

His English accent was unmistakable, as clear as her own when she was speaking German. 'You're English,' she said.

'Yes. Yes, I'm afraid I am.'

He was a good-looking boy, she thought – entirely objectively. Not as handsome as Ivo, naturally, but full of what she imagined good, solid Englishmen of the upper middle classes should look like, though her view was formed entirely on the English actors she'd met as a child in Hollywood. About her own age, she decided. Certainly no more than two or three years older.

'So am I,' Anna said. 'Well, half, anyway.'

'What a coincidence,' he said with a smile. 'Which half? Top, or bottom? Left, or right?'

'You missed out front or back.'

'So I did,' he said, with a self-deprecating roll of the eyes. He put out his hand to shake hers. 'Taverner,' he said, in that formal way Englishmen could have of introducing themselves, as though they must give their pedigree before they could give the rest. 'Harry Taverner.'

'Anna,' she replied, surprised that the warm, confident grip of a stranger could feel like a handshake from an old friend. His eyes offered the same invitation to trust. 'Anna…' – a pause, while she decided which Anna she preferred to be at that moment – 'Cantrell. And I'm really very sorry for stepping out in front of you like that. It's a bit difficult to explain…'

'I know that name,' he said, interrupting her without noticing that he did so. 'Though I can't for the life of me think where from.'

'I'm a photographer, but I'm afraid it's highly unlikely you'll have seen any of my work. I live in Austria, in Vienna.'

'Another coincidence!' he said, with an easy smile that she missed when it had gone. 'I'll be there in a couple of months – at the British embassy. I'm only here in New York temporarily, making up the numbers at the consulate press office. Probably because the Foreign Office couldn't think what else to do with me.'

She shared his brief laughter, as though the mysterious workings of the British foreign service were a joke they had long shared.

'What are you doing in New York?' he asked. 'Apart from getting mown down by inattentive English cyclists?'

'I'm here with my husband and my mother. We're visiting my grandparents. I've just been with my father. I haven't seen him for a very long time.' Why did he seem so easy to talk to? she wondered – this stranger who had appeared out of nowhere on a warm May afternoon, a stranger who thought he knew her name.

'I don't intend to appear impertinent, Mrs Cantrell,' he said, 'but it's pretty obvious you've been crying. And I think it started before I almost ran you over. There's a soda fountain over there. Please, at least let me buy you a drink to settle you down. There's a lot of traffic on Central Park West today, and American drivers are even more inattentive than Englishmen on bicycles.'

It didn't sound like a pickup line. And he didn't seem the sort of lizard who'd make advances to a young mother pushing a pram. His honest blue eyes convinced Anna he was quite genuine in his concern for her.

She certainly considered saying no. Very nearly did. But in her heart, she was more than happy to have an excuse not to leave Central Park just yet, not to face the stark reality of parting from Rex, not to have to walk back into the Bauer house and her old life.

Just ten minutes' respite. Just a short delay. That's how she saw the proposal.

So she said yes.

The Berlin apartment. 1989

Elly didn't dare look at the clock by the bed: she was afraid that if she did, it would break the spell, and Harry would stop talking. She knew he was frightened that if he did, his memory might betray him, but she wondered how long he could continue. He seemed to have no need of rest, even though dawn couldn't be many more hours away. She tried to put out of her mind the notion that he was consigning a last testament to her care.

'I'd barely passed out from basic training with the Service,' Harry said, laying aside the photo of the *Hindenburg*. 'The New York embassy was a very temporary, makeweight posting. My cover was assistant press officer, in reality little more than a glorified clerk. I was to collate all the articles and cuttings we were gathering on fascist sympathizers in America. Naturally, we trawled for absolutely anything we could find, including articles on life back in Germany and Austria, or the goings-on in German-American communities in the States – anything – just in case a name might crop up that would be worth cross-checking later. The reason I half remembered Anna Cantrell's name was because of a story the *Chicago Tribune* had run on the February War. They'd used one of her photos, the one she'd taken of the shell-damaged library at the Born-Hof. It was so striking I'd looked to see who had taken it, and luckily it had her by-line attached.

'After I left her in Central Park, I went back to the office and looked in the registry files. She had a card all to herself, though there was bugger all on it – just the press cutting attached. It seems my predecessor had sent a query to our head of station in Vienna, Tom Kendrick, asking if Miss Cantrell was a reliable, independent source, or a Dollfuss stooge.'

'I've seen Kendrick's photo, in the Service's museum,' Elly said. 'He was quite a character, wasn't he?'

'One of the best. I learned a lot from Tom,' Harry said. 'He got so far up the Gestapo's nostrils they temporarily arrested him in '38. Managed to escape with his modesty intact, thank God.

'Anyway, Tom had learned about Anna from that bastard traitor Kim Philby – you'll recall Philby visited Anna's exhibition, the day the fighting started in Vienna. Kendrick had got to know her slightly better when she was hanging around the international journalists covering the uprising. So he was able to confirm that in respect of Anna Cantrell, there was nothing known against. And that's all her card said.'

Harry turned his face to the ceiling. He was smiling, as if he could see the past playing itself back to him in the plaster. The white stubble on his jaw made him look like a prisoner enduring an interrogation. Then he said softly, 'It wasn't going to stay that way, though.'

Elly wondered if the story had become something close to a confession for him. And that, like all confessions, once begun it could not be stopped.

'You need to rest, Daddy. You must be exhausted.'

If he was, it wasn't going to stop him – when Harry turned to his daughter, she saw how his eyes gleamed. Elly saw that they were the eyes of a twenty-three-year-old, a neophyte to the secret world, a novice eager to make his mark, a young man with a reputation to make, a young man yet to hear the ticking of the clock.

'By the time Anna finished her soda,' he continued, 'she'd told me about Rex, about Ivo, about the encounter with the Nazi on the *Hindenburg*, about how she feared her husband might be falling under the fascist spell… To be honest, it worried me a little. I thought she might have an injudicious nature. But then I realized I'd provided her with the perfect confidant: a sympathetic stranger. A confession with no priest to pass judgement. If I'd bumped into her even an hour later, it would have been too late. She'd have resigned herself to Rex's departure. The wound would have started to heal. The defences would have gone up.' He rolled a fist against his mouth, whether in contemplation or regret, Elly wasn't sure. 'I said something about how I wouldn't know anyone in Vienna when I got there, except a few boring people in the passport control department of the embassy. That was to be my cover in Vienna: passport control officer. It meant the same thing as spy.'

'And Anna said you were welcome to visit the family on Karolinengasse, when you got there?' Elly suggested.

'"Please, Harry, look us up when you arrive" is what she said. "We'll show you the sights. Cities can be lonely places if you don't know anyone." I told her I would be honoured. Then we said goodbye.'

'What you really mean is, you took advantage of her vulnerability.'

'Of course I did,' Harry told her, with a sad smile. 'Isn't that what we always do with our agents?'

Nine

Vienna. 1936

Ivo's unpaid leave expired at the end of June. For Marion, the day couldn't come soon enough. She was beginning to find the stolid formality of the house on West 76th Street unendurable.

It was the Hamburg-America line that carried them all home, there being no cabins available on the *Hindenburg*. Anna suspected that may not have been true, and that Grandpa Wolfgang was trying to make a point. But the steamship *Hansa* was comfortable enough, and not one of the passengers appeared anywhere near as unpleasant as the odious Herr Eisner.

In early July, Professor Koppitz died. Anna attended the memorial service at Perchtoldsdorf, standing at the back of the church amongst many of his former students. Fifty-two seemed far too young, she thought – certainly for a man who had used his own body as the model for Austrian perfection.

The professor's widow, still a renowned photographer in her own right, was gracious as Anna shook her hand. Although her rustic compositions and landscapes were a little too *Heimat* for Anna's tastes, too much like state propaganda, when Frau Koppitz spoke to her afterwards, saying, 'I remember you well, my dear.

Rudi always believed you were one of his most talented students', it touched her deeply.

It could be said, she supposed, that it had been the professor who'd brought her and Ivo together. The encounter with Frau Koppitz in Perchtoldsdorf made her question whether she was judging Ivo unfairly. She'd known about Ivo's politics when she married him, she told herself. He comes from a traditional family, with traditional notions. He believes in a strong nation and conservative values. There's much to be admired in such views. Just because he made a friend of a Nazi when he went to Berlin doesn't mean to say he's a card-carrying fascist himself.

But there was no denying the indifference towards her that seemed to be spreading over him like hoarfrost across a window-pane. Whatever it was they were now doing in bed, in her mind it certainly wasn't lovemaking. But she was too scared to turn away from him, as that would just make her fear real – fear that the sex was no longer because he loved her, but simply to fulfil Frau Wolff's diktat that they should make babies for the Fatherland.

On the first day of August 1936, the day the Olympic Games opened in Berlin, Anna's doctor informed her she was pregnant again. This time the joy was tempered by a definite murmur of disquiet. In the tram home she waited for it to subside, for the delight to reassert itself. But it did not. Remembering how she'd felt when she learned she was carrying Bär only made the contrast worse.

To her surprise, when she returned to the apartment, Ivo was there.

'Guess what? I'm pregnant again,' she told him, hoping he wouldn't spot the anxiety in her eyes, or the slightly fixed nature of her grin.

'Really?' he replied, as if she'd told him the front-door hinges needed oiling.

'Aren't you pleased?'

'Those bastards at Steyr-Daimler-Puch have laid me off,' he said. 'I'm out of work.' And he stamped across to the drinks cabinet to throw back three shots of schnapps, rapid fire.

Later, as they lay together in bed, Ivo made no sign that he'd even remembered what Anna had said to him earlier. When she'd told him she was pregnant with Bär, he had caressed her belly in wonder. That night, he lay beside her as immobile as a piece of driftwood washed up on the banks of the Danube.

Anna stared at the ceiling, cracks in the plaster thrown into relief by the light on the bedside table, barely able to breathe for the sharp stone that seemed to have lodged in her throat. Silent tears spilled from the corners of her eyes. She yearned for him to at least acknowledge her presence. Yet at the same time she was desperate for him not to notice her pain, because she knew how contemptuous he was of weakness.

Listening to Ivo's slow, mournful breathing, she tried to explore in her mind the wall he'd raised between them – and she did so tentatively, in case she pushed too hard and discovered something she'd wish she hadn't. It was the natural shock and humiliation he was feeling at his abrupt dismissal; he was worrying about how he could support the family now that he had no job and there was a second child on the way; it was just his pride.

But Anna knew she didn't have to be Dr Freud to understand there was something deeper, something far more threatening to her happiness, behind her husband's coldness.

She rolled over to look at him. The perfect symmetry of his face, the sculptured contours that had looked so striking in the photos of Professor Koppitz now looked unpleasingly angular. The angry child was peering through the cracks at her again, and she didn't like it.

Eventually, she mastered herself enough to say, gently: 'It's not the end of the world. You'll get something else soon enough.'

He grunted. 'In Vienna? In times like these?'

'So, it may take a while. That's not a worry. The rent on the apartment is taken care of, thanks to Grandpa Wolfgang.'

Ivo aimed a harsh laugh at the ceiling. 'Don't you understand how demeaning it is for a man to have to subsist on the charity of his wife's grandparents?'

'I don't remember you complaining when we boarded the *Hindenburg*.'

The words were out of Anna's mouth before she'd had time to think. Even as they landed, she wished she'd never uttered them. But it was too late – and she waited for the inevitable blast of anger. She had learned in two years of marriage that questioning Ivo Wolff's sense of manly honour came at a cost. True, he'd never hit her, but the icy silences that could last for days afterwards still had the power to bruise.

To her surprise, all he said was, 'There'd be more opportunity for me in Germany – in Berlin.'

What did he mean – *in Berlin*?

The realization flowed up into her as if she'd stepped barefoot into an icy puddle.

'It's where they're forging the future,' Ivo went on, as if talking to himself. As if she wasn't there. 'It's where we need to be, if we're to be a part of it.'

He'd already made the decision, Anna realized. She could tell by that oh-so-reasonable tone in his voice. And he'd made it without bothering to ask her, as though her fears were irrelevant.

'A future that doesn't seem to include the Jews, by the sound of it,' she said. 'Do you think I don't read the newspapers? Besides, we can't go to Berlin, Ivo: they've passed a law there banning German citizens from marrying Jews. Have you thought of that?'

Apparently, he already had.

'I'm not a German citizen,' he said airily. 'Your father's a gentile and Marion isn't observant. That makes you a *Mischlinge,* a half-blood.'

Anna's mouth gaped in disbelief. 'Oh, that's fine then. I'd be only *half* unacceptable. What an invitation! How could I possibly resist?'

But his plan seemed impervious to her sarcasm. 'I'll go on ahead – get settled,' he said. 'You can join me when I've found something.'

'How are you going to afford a hotel?'

'Manis has invited me to stay with him next week. He's going to introduce me to a few people.'

People like Herr Eisner, the anti-Semite she'd seen him laughing with on the *Hindenburg*, she assumed.

Trying her best to sound calm and reasonable, but realizing she felt more frightened for what the future might hold than at any time since she'd followed her mother aboard the *Deutschland*, she said, 'There's one person you seem not to have considered.'

'Bär's too young to care about a move to Berlin.'

'I was talking about Marion.'

'She can come, too. Or stay in Vienna, if she wants to.'

'She needs me.'

'She's not a child. She's, what, forty-six? Old enough to stand on her own two feet – which is what she seems to be doing perfectly satisfactorily, if you ask me. Nightclubs... escorts young enough to be her sons... hanging around with degenerates and cocaine addicts, people who think puking paint onto a canvas makes it "art"...'

Anna ignored Ivo's tone of contempt. 'Ivo, it's *you* I'm worried about more than anyone.'

'Me? Why are you worried about me?' He looked at her, puzzled. Then a flicker of understanding crossed his face as, for the first time since he'd spoken, he noticed the tears in her eyes. 'Oh, you foolish girl. You think I'm taken in by all the marching and the flag-waving, don't you? You're frightened I'll fall for all that anti-Jewish nonsense. So what if you're a half-blood? I married you with my eyes wide open. I'm not ashamed of you.'

If that was the case, she wondered why he'd asked her to lie about her religion in the wedding register.

'I'm going to Berlin with one aim and one aim only,' he continued, as if her fears meant nothing to him. 'And that's to make something of *myself*.'

After that, there was no more talking. It was done. Fixed. And – if she wanted the marriage to survive – unalterable.

Ivo switched off the bedside light, plunging the room into darkness. For Anna, it felt like the fall of a guillotine blade, severing hope in one brutal slice.

Soon he was asleep, leaving her still staring into space, listening to the rhythm of the rain on the window, unable to escape the conviction that it was the overture to the score of a failing marriage.

The day after Ivo left for Berlin, Anna had just settled Bär down for his nap when the phone rang.

'May I speak to Miss Anna Cantrell, please,' said the English voice on the other end of the line.

'Speaking. Who is this?'

'The careless fellow with the bicycle – from Central Park.'

For a moment, Anna had to think – then she remembered. 'Oh, Mr Tanner—'

'Taverner. Harry Taverner.'

'Yes, of course. I'm sorry. How are you?'

'I'm well. More to the point, I'm in Vienna.'

'Oh, yes. At the British consulate, I seem to recall.'

'That's right – assistant passport officer. I hope I'm not imposing, but you did give me your number, and I've been here for a fortnight now. Thought it was about time to say hello.'

'Well, it's very pleasant to hear from you,' Anna said. She pictured him standing beside his bicycle, a curl of blond hair falling fetchingly over his brow, his handsome face creased in an apologetic smile for almost having run her down. It had been a startlingly handsome smile, she recalled – hurriedly reminding herself that she was a married woman. A newly pregnant married woman.

'I was wondering if you and Herr Wolff would care to be my guests at a little function that we're putting on at the embassy next Thursday?'

'Oh,' said Anna, wrong-footed.

'It's nothing very formal. Just a little get-together.'

'I'm afraid my husband is away,' Anna said. 'He's in Berlin. I'm not too sure when he'll be back.'

Without missing a beat, he said, 'You're more than welcome to come on your own. It's all very respectable. There's an organization called the British Council we set up a couple of years back. It's to help us promote British culture abroad. There'll be a few writers, journalists – that sort of thing. All we're missing is a representative of the photographic arts. I thought you'd be the ideal person to call.'

His voice was so easy-going it seemed churlish to refuse. And if she were being honest, it would be good to get out of the apartment for a while and into new company. She thought of asking if Marion could come, but then realized Marion probably wouldn't go within a city block of a British embassy.

'That's very thoughtful of you, Mr Taverner. I'd be delighted.'

'Please, call me Harry.'

'Will I be safe from your bicycle – Harry?' she replied, laughing.

'Quite safe. The ambassador doesn't approve of us bicycling. Only yesterday, when he caught me with my cycle clips still on, he asked me what I thought Britain's standing in the world would be if Lord Palmerston had arrived each day at the Foreign Office on a penny-farthing.'

The image made Anna laugh even more.

'You're on the Karolinengasse, I believe.'

'Yes, number eleven, apartment six.'

'I'll have a formal invitation sent round,' he said. 'We're on the Metternichgasse. Will you need a taxi?'

Anna knew the street. It was on the other side of the Belvedere gardens – no more than a fifteen-minute walk. 'No, the exercise will do me good.'

'You can't miss us,' he said. 'There's a flag. And a doorman.'

'I should hope there is,' she replied, grinning.

'Starts at six. Carriages at nine. That's if you *have* a carriage, of course. I don't.'

'Where do I park my six white horses?'

'We can borrow the ambassador's garage. He never looks in there.'

'I shall look forward to it. Goodbye, Harry.'

'Goodbye – Anna Cantrell.'

It was some time after he'd rung off, while she was replaying in her mind their meeting in Central Park, that Anna tried to recall whether she'd ever told him that she was a photographer. She couldn't remember doing so: at the time, she'd been too consumed with the unhappiness at bidding farewell to Rex to take in much. She supposed it was entirely possible that she had.

The embassy occupied an imposing corner site in the diplomatic quarter. Carved in stone above the door was the British royal coat of arms. A Union Jack hung limply in the warm early evening air from a flagstaff that jutted from a first-floor balcony, just as Harry Taverner had told her.

Anna entered the black and white tiled lobby, showed her invitation card to a major domo, and was escorted down a series of red-carpeted corridors to a modest but well-appointed room decorated in Hapsburg white and gold but sporting a portrait of the new king, Edward VIII. A vast chandelier with enough crystal in it to light half of Vienna hung from the ornate ceiling.

Anna guessed there were about thirty people in the room, mostly men, some of them journalists she'd encountered during the February War. Of the few women present, Anna recognized only Frau Koppitz.

So much, she thought, for Harry Taverner's statement that he was missing a representative of the photographic arts. She wondered what else he might not be telling the whole truth about. She'd already asked herself how it was that a humble assistant passport officer got to invite people to an embassy function.

He must have been keeping an eye open for her, because within moments of her entering the room, there he was at her side, offering her a glass of champagne. 'I'm so glad you could come,' he said. 'These things always need a little brightening up.'

Double-breasted charcoal-grey suit, Savile Row tailoring, she noted. Smart, but understated, like those English actors in the movies. All he lacked was the pencil-thin moustache. She was glad of that. She didn't care for moustaches.

He led her into the room, introducing her to an Englishman who wrote for the London *Daily Telegraph* and the *New York Times*, and whose name she immediately forgot; a brace of smart-suited men from the chancellor's office; an official from the Museum of Fine Arts; a filmmaker from the state propaganda office; a publisher of art books; a representative of the Federation of Austrian Artists… and, finally, to Frau Koppitz. At which point, Harry – now confident she could swim perfectly well on her own – promised to catch up with her later.

'My dear, how good to see you again,' Frau Koppitz said. 'I'm so sorry we didn't get the opportunity to chat at Rudi's service. Now I've got you to myself, you really must tell me all about your trip to America, and your father's work in Hollywood. Rudi told me he was a cameraman for the movies. Is that so?'

They chatted amiably for a while, and then the conversation turned to Anna's career.

'I've noticed your work is beginning to get the attention it deserves, my dear. Congratulations. Rudolph would be so pleased.'

'Bad timing on my part,' Anna replied, with a roll of her eyes. 'My husband wants to take the family to Berlin.'

'I think that would be an excellent idea,' said Frau Koppitz, patting her on the arm.

'You do?' said Anna, surprised.

'Of course. The market for photography in Germany is much larger than it is in Austria. More forward-thinking, more international. If you have any ambition to be known outside this backwater, I'd suggest packing your bags right now.'

A waiter refilled their empty champagne flutes. As Frau Koppitz lifted hers in a toast to Anna's new life in Berlin, Anna caught a glimpse of Harry Taverner talking to some guests across the room. He looked so at ease, punctuating the conversation with occasional gusts of bright laughter. He had Ivo's confidence, but without the hard edge – an inner surety that whatever the setting, he would fit it smoothly, making everything run better by his presence.

He's the oil in the engine, she thought – he takes the friction out of any room he's in. It was hard for her to imagine anyone who might look less like an assistant passport control officer.

She realized Frau Koppitz was speaking to her again: 'I have contacts in Berlin that you might find useful, my dear – at the Reich Office for Public Enlightenment and Propaganda. Dr Goebbels has a most discerning eye for a good photograph. I could put you in touch with his people.'

'That's very kind, Frau Koppitz. But I don't think I'd be very good at taking direction from a politician.'

'The artist must accept that he, or in our case *she*, has a duty greater than merely to their muse,' Frau Koppitz said, as if addressing a class of her late husband's students.

'You mean, to tell the truth?'

'I mean to the state – to be the mirror that shows the world its cultural health and advancement. Look at Frau Leni Riefenstahl in Germany – she manages to make films that tell the truth, are artistic, *and* serve the nation at the same time.'

Anna nodded politely but said nothing. She remembered Ivo banging on for ages about Riefenstahl's film of the 1933 Nuremberg Rally. Out of the corner of her eye, she saw Harry

Taverner detach himself from the chancellor's men and head in her direction, as if he'd sensed her unspoken cry for help.

'Glad to see you two have become acquainted,' he said, when he reached her side.

'Professor Koppitz was my lecturer, at the Institute for Applied Arts,' Anna told him.

'We were just discussing the work of Leni Riefenstahl,' Frau Koppitz said. 'I was telling Anna that an artist has a duty to the land that nurtured them, a duty to the state as well as to art. Don't you agree, Herr Taverner?'

Harry grinned. 'Oh, that's way over my head, I'm afraid, Frau Koppitz,' he said. 'Charlie Chaplin's about my level.'

And then he rescued Anna by insisting that he really must introduce her to the French cultural attaché.

The Belvedere Park gates were shut when Anna left, and she was forced to walk through Schwarzenbergplatz and up Prinz Eugen Strasse to get home. Vienna was coming alive for the evening: the restaurants were filling up, the trams full of people heading to the inner Ring. Empty taxis passed her, looking for trade until it was time to pick up the smart people in tuxedos and ballgowns from the Staatsoper and the Musikverein. She waved them on whenever they slowed.

As she walked, she wondered if Harry Taverner's attention that evening might have bordered on the flirtatious. And, if she was being honest with herself, she didn't mind. She even felt a little peeved he hadn't suggested a coffee at the Mozart or the Central. But, really, what had she been expecting? He was probably doing no more than his diplomatic duty. After all, she was a married woman with a second child on the way, even if she was only twenty. So why would he be remotely interested in her?

He was, of course. Though not – at least not then – in the way she imagined.

Ivo returned from Berlin three weeks later. He arrived in a sunnier mood than Anna had seen him in for a long while.

'How is son number two?' he enquired pleasantly, laying on the table a parcel wrapped in brown paper.

'Behaving himself – if it is a *he*,' Anna replied, looking down at her stomach.

'Glad to hear it. That must be his Austrian sense of duty to the law, learned from his father. And what of my beautiful wife?'

Surprised, she mumbled something vaguely affable, forgotten even before the words were out of her mouth.

Ivo's apparent good humour did not comfort her – it must mean things had gone well for him in Germany. She had spent much of his absence praying he'd get nowhere. But this Ivo was better than the one who'd left, she decided, so there was no profit in spoiling for a fight.

'Don't you want to see what I've brought you?' he asked, nodding at the parcel.

The present turned out to be a neat little rural landscape, painted in oils. It seemed an unlikely choice of gift for a man she believed to be indifferent to art, except for the sort he didn't like. Anna noted the signature: Albert Arnz.

'Know anything about a painter named Arnz, Mama?' she asked Marion, who was in her bedroom putting on her warpaint in preparation for supper at the Café Landtmann with a Belgian exporter of industrial machinery.

'German. Dusseldorf School. Not top tier, not like Caspar David Friedrich, but good enough,' Marion answered. 'Why'd you ask, honey?'

'Ivo's brought home a painting of his, from Berlin.'

'Good. The boy's learning.'

'How on earth did you afford the painting?' Anna asked. She was washing up, after their supper. Ivo was lounging in a kitchen chair, smoking and reading the paper. Anna couldn't help wondering for an uncharitable moment if Ivo might have somehow charged it to Marion's account at Weiner Bauer Bank.

'I didn't afford it. I was given it.'

'Someone *gave* you a painting?'

'I thought you'd like it.' Ivo looked at her. 'At least it's not the degenerate garbage your mother's friends go in for.'

'*Who* gave it to you?'

'Manis.'

Anna frowned. 'Manis Möller doesn't strike me as the artistic sort.'

'He got it from a Jewish family who were leaving Germany – in exchange for getting them a clean tax clearance certificate. It's one of a pair. He kept one, gave the other to me.'

'I thought Manis Möller was in the Kripo,' Anna said, an alarm bell ringing in the back of her mind. 'He's a policeman, not a tax official.'

'He knows people. He can make things happen.'

Anna pushed the little painting away from her. 'I'm not stupid, Ivo,' she said. 'I've read the newspaper stories about Jews being forced to hand over their valuables if they want to leave the country.'

'Do you want it or don't you?' he said sneeringly.

'No, not if its owner was coerced by Manis Möller. That's disgusting.'

Ivo shrugged. 'Then I'll sell it. Should be worth a schilling or two.' Leaving the painting on the table, he picked up his suitcase and went into the bedroom.

Anna heard him whistling as he unpacked. He seemed oblivious to her discomfort, blind to her objection. She set about putting the painting back in its wrapping. Her fingers felt dirty, as though she was handling stolen goods. She was tying the string when she heard Ivo call out.

'I've got a job in Berlin. I'm joining the Kripo.'

For a moment Anna said nothing, the objections rising in her throat like bile.

'So, you finally get to be a policeman. How wonderful.'

'You don't sound pleased for me. Care to tell me why, Anna?'

She knew he was leading her onto the ice. If she stamped her foot, it might crack. And she didn't want to consider for a moment the depth and the coldness of the water lying beneath.

'I don't know, Ivo. I'm happy here in Vienna. Berlin frightens me—'

'Nonsense,' he said, cutting across her as if her only grievance was the unreliable climate. 'It's the best thing for everyone.'

'Do I get any say in this?'

He gave her a look that was utterly devoid of understanding. 'A say? Why do you need a say? I'm your husband. You're my wife.'

He might as well have said, *You're my shoebox*, or *You're my shaving brush*.

Anna made sure she was standing straight, and that her shoulders were back. If this was going to be a battle, she might as well behave like a soldier. 'I don't want to go,' she said bluntly.

'What do you mean?'

'I'm not one of your *Heimwehr* recruits, Ivo. I don't have to obey orders. I don't want to go to Berlin.'

For a moment he seemed not to know how to answer her. He clearly hadn't been expecting resistance.

'I'm the head of this family,' he said, very coldly. 'If I say we go, then we go.'

'And if I say no? What then, Ivo?'

'I'll go without you.'

Anna felt the confrontation spiralling out of control. His indifference seemed impenetrable. 'What about Bär?' she said, her voice in danger of cracking. 'What about the child I'm carrying? Are you going to abandon them?'

Anna couldn't believe it: he was *actually* laughing.

'Of course I'm not going to abandon them, you foolish girl. They'll come with me.'

Anger stopped the tears even as they began to well in Anna's eyes. It gave her voice a vehemence that startled her. 'You can forget all about *that*, Ivo. I'm their mother. If you're going to walk out on us, the children will stay with me.'

'You're not even an Austrian citizen,' he sneered. 'Do you seriously think any court in the Republic will grant *you* custody – a woman whose own mother is a drug user and a degenerate? A *Jew*?'

The next few moments seemed to pass in one great heaving wave of misery, as if Anna were trapped in a sinking ship sliding beneath the water. She turned and fled for the safety of the bedroom. To her relief Ivo didn't follow.

Anna was still lying face down on the bed, her ribs aching from the sobbing, when she heard him shout from the hallway that he was going out to see his friends.

'Maybe you'll have seen sense by the time I get back!'

Then the door slammed, and Anna was alone.

Sinking. Drowning. Wondering how long the pain would last before she reached the seabed.

It was a warm August day and in the Karlsplatz women were wearing cotton dresses, the men in shirtsleeves. A band was playing from somewhere behind the trees.

The park was precious to Anna, the safe place where she read her father's letters. In normal times she would never have brought Marion here. But these were not normal times.

'I've thought about taking Bär and going back to America,' she said, 'but Ivo would alert the police the moment he came home and found we'd gone. They'd put a watch on all the train stations and the ports. They'd be bound to catch us.' She swallowed hard. 'And if I just leave him, he keeps Bär and—' she touched her belly, 'he'll take this little one from me. So, I have no alternative but to stay with him.'

'Do you still love him?' Marion asked.

Anna took a moment to answer. 'I don't *like* him. Not at this moment. I've seen a side of him that scares me. But he loves Bär, so maybe he was over-reacting. Maybe I shouldn't have pushed him. Maybe Berlin won't be so bad.'

She shook her head, realizing she had gone from defiance to acceptance, acceptance to defiance, and then back again in less time than it had taken for a *Buchtein* vendor pushing his cart to pass where they were sitting. But it had been like that for days now.

'We'll sub-let the apartment,' Marion said, putting her arm around her daughter's shoulder. 'We'll go to Berlin together.'

'That's a crazy idea, Mama.'

'You're my little girl, aren't you? I'm not going to let you go alone.'

Anna laid a hand on her mother's wrist. 'Mama, even you must have heard how they're behaving towards Jews in Germany. Going there would be like walking through a gate and ignoring the sign that says: "Beware of the dog".'

Marion let out a snort of derision. 'Honey, where have you been? It's not exactly the Promised Land here in Austria either, is it? But do you think I give a flying fuck what a bunch of overgrown rejects from the Boy Scouts in *lederhosen* think? Besides, *American passports* – remember? Herr Hitler cares too much how he's seen in American newspapers to let his thugs go around insulting folks like us. Only yesterday I saw in the *Herald Tribune* that he's behaving himself, what with the Olympics and all. We'll be fine.'

'If you say so, Mama.'

Marion patted Anna's knee. 'Everything okay now?' she asked.

Even in her distress, Anna had to admit she found her mother's spirit uplifting.

Marion took her to the Landtmann to cheer her up. She ordered champagne. Anna wondered if her mother had any cocaine in her handbag but resisted asking. When the champagne arrived, Marion offered a toast.

'Here's to inadequate men everywhere,' she said. 'And if that bastard of a husband of yours lays so much as a finger on you, I swear to God I'll break this champagne flute in half and use the broken stem to carve *Moët* on one of his balls and *Chandon* on the other. Then I'll tie a knot in his goddamn dick to make an ampersand in the middle.'

If the scales had not yet fallen completely from Anna's eyes, they were at least flaking away. In the days that followed, she often replayed in her mind Ivo's threat to take away the children, as though she were considering the symptoms of a suspected illness. Was he serious? Or had he let his temper get the better of him? Was the illness a minor malaise, or an incurable and fatal malady?

For Ivo's part, he seemed almost to have forgotten the incident. He said little about what his new job would entail, and when Anna pressed him, he became evasive.

'Won't you have to do basic training?' she asked one evening, over supper. 'No one just becomes a detective overnight.'

'It's a special department,' he replied, sounding almost bored. 'I'll be learning on the job. They're taking my experience in the *Heimwehr* into account.'

In early November, Ivo returned to Berlin for what he would only describe as 'meetings'. It was while he was away that Anna received another telephone call from Harry Taverner.

'I was wondering if you might care to pop into the embassy for a brief chat, over tea and biscuits,' Taverner said, without preamble.

'Tea and biscuits?'

'Oh, we couldn't run the empire if it weren't for tea and biscuits.'

'I usually drink coffee.'

'I'm sure we'll have some stashed away in the basement for special occasions. The truth is, we'd rather like to pick your brains if that's alright with you.'

They met in a room that might have been an office but could equally have been a comfortable holding pen where a visitor might wait while someone decided upon what level of diplomatic interest they merited. At one end was a desk that looked unused; at the other a sofa and three armchairs were grouped around an occasional table. There was a window with drawn net curtains, so that she couldn't quite see what was outside, and the obligatory portrait of King Edward over the fireplace. The room was nowhere near as grand as the one she'd been in on her first visit to Metternichgasse, but instead workmanlike. The coffee, however, came in a silver pot and the Scottish shortbreads on monogrammed porcelain.

'Anna, this is Major Warwick,' Harry said, both men standing as she was shown in. Harry's colleague was an older, dapper man in his middle-fifties with a military bearing – his boss, Anna assumed. He had a smooth, competent face, and an air that told her he'd be just the chap you needed if your motor car broke down in a blizzard.

'I'm very pleased to make your acquaintance, Frau Wolff,' Warwick said. 'Is "Wolff" appropriate? Or would you prefer Bauer, or perhaps Cantrell? We wouldn't want to get it wrong.'

'Anna is fine,' she said.

'Then Anna it shall be,' said Warwick, as if bestowing a title on her. He invited her to sit in one of the armchairs. He and Harry Taverner settled themselves on the sofa opposite, directly beneath the picture of the king.

Anna had read the stories in the international press, about Edward and his affair with an American divorcée. She half expected the two men smiling at her so pleasantly to ask if she knew who was spreading the rumours.

'I hope I'm not in trouble,' she said, jokingly, 'only Mr Taverner didn't say what this was about. I mean, I'm not even really an English citizen.'

'But you could be,' Warwick said, 'if you wanted.'

'Why would I want that?' Anna asked, surprised.

'That would depend on how English you feel yourself to be. *Do* you consider yourself to be an Englishwoman?'

'Not really. I've never been there.'

'But your father is a British citizen, yes?'

'Yes.'

'And he's not become a naturalized American – so far as we know?'

'If he has, he hasn't told me about it.'

'And you? You haven't taken Austrian citizenship, following your marriage?'

'No. My husband wants me to. My mother doesn't. I'm on her side, to be honest.'

If either man detected the present state of her marriage from her answer, they were too professional to mention it.

'So, you're residing here on your marriage certificate and an American passport,' Major Warwick surmised. 'With a visa, I presume.'

'That's right.'

Harry Taverner leaned towards her, his elbows resting on his knees. Anna noticed that the creases in his trousers were as crisp as those of the major's. His jacket fell open and she could see he was wearing braces. She had a rebellious desire to reach out and twang the elastic.

'An American passport could be more useful than a British one, I suppose,' Harry said, addressing the plate of shortbreads. 'Fewer objections, from *some* quarters.'

'What is this all about?' Anna asked, a sense of disquiet growing inside her.

'How would you describe your husband's politics, Anna?' Taverner asked, looking up at her.

'I'm not sure that's got anything to do with you, has it, Mr Taverner?'

'Please, call me Harry.'

'I shan't call you anything at all, unless you tell me why you've asked me here.'

Taverner gave her a warm smile, as if to reward a correct answer. 'Herr Wolff, your husband, was in the *Heimwehr*, wasn't he? Before Chancellor Dollfuss was assassinated.'

'I wasn't aware that belonging to a government organization was a crime in Austria,' Anna said, surprised at herself for defending Ivo.

'We weren't suggesting for a moment that it was,' Harry assured her.

'Ivo resigned his commission. He told me he was tired of commanding a gang of ill-disciplined incompetents.'

'And now he's teamed up with a fellow named Möller, from Berlin, who's done him the favour of landing him a job with the Reich criminal police.'

Anna stared at Taverner, then at Warwick. 'How do you know about that? Is this some sort of interrogation?'

Taverner looked appalled. 'Good heavens, no, Anna. Whatever gave you that impression?'

Warwick said, 'The late Professor Koppitz thought very highly of you, Anna, or so I am led to believe. His widow, also.'

Anna wondered if she should simply get up and leave. She didn't care much for where this conversation was going.

'Are you going to ask me about *her* politics, too?'

Warwick smiled. 'I believe we already know about those.'

Harry Taverner picked up the thread the moment Warwick stopped speaking, as if they had rehearsed lines for a play they were performing.

'Frau Koppitz seemed to think it would be a good idea if you went to Berlin. Didn't she say it might help your career?'

'It might, if I *had* a career,' Anna said, wondering how Taverner knew what she and Koppitz's widow had been talking about. To her recollection he'd been on the far side of the room when they'd talked about this. And how did he know about Ivo's trips to Berlin – or Möller, for that matter?

'The point is, Anna, we rather tend to agree with her,'

Warwick said. He took a crocodile-skin cigarette case from the inner pocket of his suit jacket, popped the lid and offered her one. She accepted. He picked one for himself, tapping it on the case before putting it between his lips. Harry Taverner conjured a lighter as if from nowhere.

'What has my future career got to do with Frau Koppitz? Or you, for that matter?'

Warwick drew deeply on his cigarette, then waved it in her direction like a lecturer indicating something he had chalked on a blackboard. 'You're beginning to get your photographs published in all sorts of places,' he said. 'And very fine photographs they are too, if I may say so. Berlin is the perfect place from which to progress, I'd have thought.'

With the lighting of the cigarettes, Taverner seemed to have transferred responsibility for what came next to his superior, lying back in the sofa as though he intended to take a snooze.

'Did Frau Koppitz tell you she has friends in the German propaganda ministry?' Warwick continued. 'Including, as I understand it, Dr Joseph Goebbels.'

'Yes. She said she'd mention me to him.'

'That's splendid.' Another languid draw on his cigarette.

'I told her I wasn't interested.'

'Why on earth not? Every journalist and photographer worth his salt – worth *her* salt – would stab their mother to be admitted to circles like that.'

'I don't like the politics there.'

'Gracious me! Who does?' Warwick said, smiling. He looked at Taverner for confirmation, then back at Anna. 'Certainly not us. Not the League of Nations. I dare say not even the devil himself. But sometimes one has to hold one's nose when doing the right thing.'

Now Anna was beginning to understand. 'Let me guess, Major Warwick: doing the right thing, as in going to Berlin to worm my way into Dr Goebbels' good books, with the assistance of Frau Koppitz – that sort of good thing?'

Warwick held her gaze for a long time without answering. The smoke from his cigarette gave him a distinctly Machiavellian air.

'You really would be doing your country a great service,' he said at length.

'I thought we agreed I was an *American* citizen.'

'But you're also half English,' Harry Taverner observed, from the depths of his relaxation beneath the portrait of his king. 'You told us just now. You told *me* in Central Park. I think we get the idea.'

'Did you somehow arrange that near collision, Mr Taverner?' Anna asked.

Taverner shook his head slowly, as if he rather enjoyed the suggestion. 'That, I can assure you, was a coincidence. A very pleasant coincidence, I'll admit. But happenstance all the same.'

'You're asking me to spy for you, aren't you?' Anna said. 'That's what this charade is about. After Dr Goebbels – what next? Would you like me to break into the Reichstag and take photographs of what Herr Hitler keeps in his desk drawer?'

'Very imaginative,' said Warwick with a growling laugh. 'Very droll.' He took another long pull on his cigarette, then blew the exhaled smoke away. 'Let us imagine, Anna, that Dr Goebbels had in his pocket an Anglo-American photographer taking pictures of Herr Hitler's wonderful new Germany. He would be able to say to the world, to all his critics, "How can this possibly be propaganda when the lens is objective, not German, not controlled by my ministry?" He would find such an arrangement entirely to his advantage. And, to be honest, so would we – though obviously for different reasons. You would have his trust. And very possibly the trust of certain other highly placed diners at the fascist table. Perhaps even the host of the feast himself.'

For a moment Anna said nothing. Then she burst out laughing. 'It's the most preposterous suggestion I've ever heard! I'm Anna Cantrell, not Mata Hari. I'm not a spy. I don't have a cloak. I don't have a dagger. Oh, and by the way, I'm pregnant!'

Even this news didn't appear to dent Major Warwick's studied *sang-froid*.

'Oh. Are you?' he said, with barely a lift of an eyebrow. 'Well, never mind. That's not a permanent condition, is it? I don't think Herr Hitler's going anywhere in the immediate future.'

'English, American or somewhere in between, you'd be doing this for your country,' Harry Taverner said.

Anna put as much derision into her voice as she could muster. 'Which bit of me? Top… bottom… front… back?'

'The heart bit,' Harry said. 'The bit that makes you want to fight against the bully.'

'You *do* know that my father went to America in 1914 expressly to avoid doing that?'

Warwick laughed again, the same rich gurgle. 'Bloody sensible of him, if you ask me. Wish I had. No, we don't hold that against you in the slightest. Do we, Harry?'

'No, sir, not in the least.'

Anna stood up. 'Well, all I can say, gentlemen, is I hope you didn't expend too much effort over this little meeting. I'd make an utterly useless spy.'

'Would you allow us to make that judgement, Anna?' Warwick said, smiling serenely. 'If it's the danger that concerns you, the worst that could happen is that they'd expel you. In that event, we'd look after any ramifications. We'd take good care of you.'

Anna pretended to study the king's portrait. The two men were regarding her expectantly and she didn't want them to see her mind working. But the suggestion certainly intrigued her. Her nascent career could certainly do with a boost. And even Dr Joseph Goebbels couldn't force her to shoot photos she didn't want to shoot.

At length, she said, 'Let me see what happens when I get to Berlin.'

'Perhaps, then, you wouldn't object if Mr Taverner here was to occasionally… shall we say, bump into you there?' Warwick said. 'Just to get a feel for how you're settling in, as it were.'

'Bumping into people seems to be a habit of Mr Taverner's, doesn't it?'

'It would be a very gentle, very innocent bump,' Harry assured her with a grin. 'You really would be doing us a great favour. And in return, I'm sure we might be able to open a few doors for you with the picture editors at friendly newspapers.'

'That's pretty much what Frau Koppitz said she could do for me.'

'Yes, but we play for a different team, Anna,' Taverner said. 'And we rather think you do, too.'

'Major Warwick' was but one of the many work names used by Thomas Kendrick, MI6 station chief, Vienna. Now he waited until the door had closed behind Anna and the sound of her footsteps had faded away down the corridor before speaking.

'You were right, Taverner,' he said, stubbing out his cigarette in the ashtray on the desk. 'The student I remember from the

February War has grown into a very smart and self-assured young woman. Ideal material.'

'I had hoped she might say yes immediately, sir.'

Kendrick gave Harry a reassuring smile. 'Look on the bright side. She didn't say no.'

'I'll keep at it,' Taverner said. 'When she gets to Berlin and sees what's going on there, I'm pretty sure she'll come around to our way of thinking.'

'Let's hope so,' Kendrick said. 'If Möller is as close to Goebbels as we think, she's really the perfect choice.'

Taverner opened the door for his boss. As Kendrick passed him Harry said, to himself as much as to his station chief, 'I wonder if Anna Cantrell is aware that her husband has joined the Nazi Party?'

PART TWO

Dancing at the Adlon

Ten

The Berlin Tiergarten in Spring
Mixed media on canvas. Marion Bauer. 1937

The swastika banners were a brilliant, blazing red. From the Brandenburg Gate, from the Reichstag, the Interior Ministry, the Foreign Ministry, from every civic building, in every public park – even from the elegant façade of the Hotel Adlon on Unter den Linden – they hung like unfurled sails waiting for the next gust of Nazi bluster to make them billow.

Anna hated those banners as she had hated nothing else before in her life.

Almost everyone she encountered in Berlin seemed so certain of a stellar future under the firm but wise hand of Chancellor Hitler.

'He's giving us back our culture,' the local baker told her, when she picked up her *knüppel* rolls.

'He's all that stands between civilization and the plague of bolshevism,' said the fellow at the dairy, who'd taken a shine to her and gave her more cream than she paid for.

'He's got lovely eyes,' said the woman at the market stall, where Anna bought her vegetables. 'And he'll put the Jews in their place.'

Anna had heard more of that sort of talk than she cared for. In her second week in the city, pushing Bär in his pram through the Tiergarten, she saw three men screaming insults at an elderly man with a *kippah* skullcap on his head.

She had the Leica camera with her, on a strap around her neck, because the park had been proving to be a rich seam of great shots. Now, she raised the viewfinder to her eye, assuming the risk of being caught on film would bring the bullies to their senses. But all she got for her trouble was a face full of sweaty, angry Berliner.

The apartment Ivo had found for them was larger than the one in Vienna. It was near the Jannowitz U-Bahn station, not too far from Ivo's office on the Alexanderplatz.

Anna saw little of her husband during the later months of her pregnancy. Whatever his role in the *Kriminalpolizei*, the Kripo – he had told her he couldn't discuss it with her because of state security – it was important enough to make him a martyr to his desk. Anna wondered if he was having an affair.

The sudden and momentous changes in her life so far – New York for Hollywood; Hollywood for Vienna; Vienna for Berlin – had left Anna without a sense of truly belonging anywhere. Although she wouldn't admit it, even to herself – she was lonely. Sometimes, when Bär was asleep and there was no one else in the apartment, she would pause in whatever she was doing, wrap her arms around her body, and gift herself the solitary comfort of a hug.

In April, Antje was born. She was named Antje because that's what Ivo wanted. Was there an Antje anywhere else in his family, or its history? Anna never found out. In any case, she'd learned not to ask questions – even small ones. Questioning Ivo was about as productive as flicking gravel at concrete. She no longer trusted what was in his heart – could she even tell any more? She was sure of one thing: he was pushing her away, and she wasn't sure she had the strength to resist.

Caring for a boy of two and a newborn daughter left her little time or energy for photography. When she did manage to shoot a few pictures and develop them in the temporary darkroom she'd set up in one corner of the basement boiler room of the apartment block, it was like catching a fragment of a favourite tune she remembered from long ago.

Berlin was proving worse than Anna could have imagined. She found the bombastic posturing of the Nazis unbearable: the banners, the parades, the rallies – the implicit violence of the state barely concealed. She witnessed with her own eyes men and women being chased down and beaten up on the street, to the studied disregard of an indifferent or even compliant population. She saw the graffiti scrawled across shop fronts bearing Jewish names, and the smashed windows. She read the reports of mass arrests and the sending to specially constructed camps of those who objected to the regime. And she knew both Ivo and Möller had lied to her: *It's not as bad as the international press make it out to be... Just a few people getting rightly upset over profiteering...*

In August, Harry Taverner contrived a brush-past encounter in the Tiergarten. Anna reckoned he must have been observing her routine, choosing the park as the perfect place for what would seem like a random meeting. To her surprise, the notion of him covertly watching her didn't feel at all voyeuristic. Rather, it gave her a sense of reassurance – though she did find herself wishing she'd paid more attention to her hair before she'd set out.

'Have you been hiding in the bushes all this time?' she asked, as they shared a bench beneath the Goethe monument.

'Night and day.' He laughed. 'I've become quite the expert on German shrubbery. I'm seriously thinking of setting up a horticultural club at the embassy.'

When she told him that Ivo had yet to introduce her to anyone in the Nazi hierarchy, he simply replied, 'Give it time. We're in this for the long game. You've got a brand-new baby. We're not unreasonable. We're not expecting you to dash off between nappy changes to photograph the next Party rally.'

Marion, too, found Berlin oppressive. Her friends amongst the artistic community in Vienna had given her the names of comrades in the city, but most of these were now either in hiding or planning to flee the country. The Reich Chamber of Fine Arts had decreed that only German citizens could wield a paintbrush or a sculptor's chisel. Artistic expression by Jews was forbidden. But that didn't stop Marion painting. Her American passport, renewed at the embassy on the Bendlerstrasse at the same time as Anna's, got her out of trouble on more than one occasion when confronted by a policeman with the words, '*Ihre Papiere, bitte!*'

And it didn't take Marion long to find male companionship. She was soon spending frequent nights with a doctor she'd met while sketching the lime trees in Unter den Linden. Anna suspected it was not his physical attributes that had attracted her: he was short, bald and had a nervous twitch under his left eye. She reckoned it was his ability to supply her mother with the same recreational stimuli she'd noticed on the table that night at the Red Panther.

By September, Ivo had begun to take an interest in Anna again. For a week or two she couldn't fathom his motive, because it certainly wasn't sexual: he made that clear enough to her. Then he started inviting her to office *soirées* after work, and the truth dawned on her: he needed an adornment on his arm to make an impression with his superiors. Anna accompanied him to a succession of awful engagements at which her only function appeared to be to nod approvingly when some uniformed or sharp-suited Party official with a grandiloquent title espoused his admiration for the Führer.

Standing in line to shake a leather-gloved hand, or to make small talk, was a struggle. Anna found it hard to resist what she would have called 'Doing a Marion'. But while she briefly toyed with the notion of ruining Ivo's standing with these strange, robotic men, she suspected his revenge would be merciless. She amused herself by imagining them wearing Vanity Fair lingerie under their uniforms.

In reward for this outward restraint, Ivo hired a nanny to help with the children. Anna loathed her from the start.

Hannelore Lange was a plump Saxon of eighteen who had come from the country, where her father was a farmer and local party functionary. She had a ponderous, forgetful way of speaking and treated Bär and Antje with rustic detachment, as if she were herding calves. She appeared to have no interest in anything beyond the sycophantic editorials in the *Völkischer Beobachter*, the Nazi Party's newspaper. Anna wondered if Ivo had installed her as an informer, but at least her arrival allowed Anna to get out of the apartment more often. Which was why she happened to be passing the Academy of Arts at the Palais Arnim on an icy November afternoon beneath a dazzlingly clear polar sky.

'Anna! I don't believe it – it *is* you.'

'Luka!' she cried, hugging him even before she had a chance to consider if that was the appropriate response when a married woman with two children met a male friend in the street.

'What are you doing here in Berlin?' he asked, when she broke the embrace.

'My husband has a job here. Don't ask me what it is, I couldn't tell you.'

'Do I detect not all is well?' he asked astutely.

Her silence told him everything.

'Well, it's good to see you, anyway,' he said.

'And you, too. Are you still a student here?'

'My studies are complete,' he said proudly. 'Now I'm in the publications department of the Academy. Booklets, brochures, exhibition programmes, that sort of thing. And you? How's the photography going?'

All Anna could do was blow through her closed lips to tell him, *Don't ask me.*

'We have a great café here,' he said, nodding back over his shoulder. 'Not as good as the Ludwig or the Central, of course, but they do great *Eierkuchen.* The apple sauce is to die for. Are you in a hurry?'

'Not really,' she said. 'And it is very cold.' She thought about apple sauce for a moment. 'To die for, you say?'

He grinned. 'Unquestionably. Has to be on the menu for my last meal.'

'Then let's die together.'

She took his arm. She did it without thinking – a friendly gesture, nothing more. But then she felt the warmth of him, his uncomplicated decency, flowing into her like an antidote to her troubles.

Anna's affair with Luka Vogel began for the same reason a lot of affairs begin: she was lonely. He was a friend. His eyes didn't drift away from hers mid-sentence. He laughed at her jokes. And he didn't threaten to take away her children if she had the temerity to object to his relentless ambition. If she'd had the slightest inkling of where it would lead, she would have turned on her heel and sought her consolation elsewhere.

It snowed that winter. The whitened streets and the frosted tramlines added a romantic intensity to the affair that it didn't really warrant, at least not for Anna. But when she walked to Luka's untidy little room between Hermannplatz and Tempelhof aerodrome, she could imagine herself making the journey wrapped in furs in a sleigh. Tucked beneath the eiderdown of his bed, sleepy in the fug from the iron stove in the corner, the soft grey afternoon light penetrating the silvery rime on the window, Anna could see herself as the heroine in a novel by Pushkin or Turgenev.

She thought of how easily Marion embarked upon her affairs, so joyously reckless. But she, Anna, wasn't like that. When she'd taken her marriage vows at the Antoniuskirche in Graz she'd meant every word. Breaking them didn't sit comfortably with her. But she was sure she felt nothing for Ivo – nothing but an underlying fear of how he might respond if she tried to leave. Had *he* changed during their marriage, or had she simply been too young, too naïve, to see the real Ivo for what he truly was? How ironic, she told herself, to have been fooled by an image.

Freed a little from the children, thanks to Hannelore, Anna could indulge her passion for photography again. It also gave her ample excuse to leave the apartment. And with Harry Taverner making good on his promise, she began to see more of her pictures published in the international press.

'Leave him,' Luka said to her earnestly on a damp January day beside the Wannsee. Anna had wanted to record the dramatic winter landscape in sharp chiaroscuro. The conditions were perfect for what she wanted: roiling grey clouds, leafless trees reflecting sharply in the dark water – a landscape loaded with Wagnerian intensity. 'We'll get somewhere together.'

His suggestion made her feel as if she'd just been caught kicking a puppy. She knew the affair was little more than an opiate, a diversion to numb the grief she felt at the dying of her love for Ivo. Yet all it had done was to endanger the heart of an innocent young man.

'Oh, Luka – don't be silly,' she said as gently as she could. 'You're not going to take on a married woman with a two-year-old and an infant. You've got your whole life ahead of you. Be realistic. It would be dangerous for both of us. Ivo has friends in the Party. Haven't you heard how they're treating people in Dachau?'

'I don't care. I love you. I've always loved you – from the moment I first saw you at the Academy in Vienna.'

Anna took his hand and kissed it. Then she laid it against her cheek. His skin was icy cold because he'd forgotten his gloves. 'It's just a dream, Luka. That's all. Best to enjoy what we have. Don't spoil it by wishing too hard.'

On the S-Bahn home, he barely said a word. It was if the cold landscape she'd photographed had somehow seeped inside him.

It was an important after-work function, Ivo had said. Anna must attend because everyone would be there. Hannelore was to look after Bär and Antje alone, because Marion was 'at the doctor's'.

Anna was sitting at her dressing table, putting the finishing touches to her make-up. In the mirror she could see the door to the bathroom across the hall was open. Ivo was standing before his shaving mirror, buttoning the collar of his shirt.

'So who exactly is *everyone*?' she called out, imagining the same god-awful ghouls in uniform that peopled the other events he'd taken her to.

'Everyone who matters,' Ivo shouted in reply.

He came back into the bedroom, pulling on his jacket. And that was when she saw the pin on his lapel, glinting in the reflection in the mirror.

For a moment she said nothing. She told herself that the cold sensation in her limbs was disappointment. But she knew it wasn't. It was disgust. And fear.

'You've joined the Party, then,' she said icily. 'Was I not worth consulting?'

He touched the little swastika badge as if it were a talisman and he needed protecting from evil. 'Why would I do that – consult you?'

'Because I'm your wife.'

'Why would you have objected?'

'I can't begin to imagine,' Anna said, tilting her face upwards as she ran a brush through her hair, so he wouldn't see her expression.

'It means nothing,' said his reflection. 'But no one gets a decent job here without being a Party member. They wouldn't have let me apply to clean the city dog pound if I hadn't joined. So what if I have to wear a badge?'

'How long have you been a member?'

'Since I left the *Heimwehr*. First Austria, now here.'

'Jesus! That's years.' She stared at herself in the mirror. I'm looking into the face of a fool, she thought. 'I suppose I should be grateful you eventually found the guts to tell me. What took you so long?'

Ivo seemed puzzled. 'Why are you so upset?'

'Ivo, the Party was banned in Austria,' Anna said, letting the hairbrush fall. 'All the time we were there, you could have been arrested.'

'But I wasn't.'

'Is that why you wanted to come here, to Berlin?'

'I told you: this is the future.'

'Well, I don't much like the idea of a future in which the person I married keeps secrets from me, Ivo,' she said, glancing at the reflection of the metal blemish on his lapel. 'Is there anything else you haven't told me?'

He came close to her seat. Standing behind her, he rested his palms on her shoulders. Against her skin, they felt like the hands of someone making an arrest. He leaned forwards so that his face was above hers in the mirror. 'I could ask you the same question,' he said. 'I don't know what you get up to when you go out with your camera, do I? Now, put on your coat. The car will be here any minute.'

The headquarters of the Reichskulturkammer, the Reich Chamber of Fine Arts, occupied a floor of the main building of the Ministry of Public Enlightenment and Propaganda on the Alexanderplatz.

An official Daimler-Benz dropped Ivo and Anna outside the main entrance at exactly 7 p.m. A fine drizzle that seemed to have drifted in from the cold Helgoland shore made the stone facia and the rows of identical windows gleam in the light from the streetlamps. It glistened on the uniform of the SS guard who stepped forward to open the Daimler's passenger door. It left icy droplets on the door's frame that Anna could feel through her gloves as she climbed out.

Another uniformed SS man checked their names against a list on a clipboard. Then they were escorted by a flunky in a suit up the carpeted stairs and into a brightly lit chamber with others leading off it – offices, Anna guessed. Offices where you laboured at whatever the business of Public Enlightenment and Propaganda required of you.

The grand chamber was already half-full. Many of the male guests were in uniform, trying to hold themselves with Prussian bearing despite a distinct absence of martial physique. The women, most of them much older than Anna, had almost all made the hideous mistake of trying to outdo each other by wearing more make-up, tighter dresses, and showing injudicious amounts of cleavage. The only one she recognized was the more soberly dressed Frau Koppitz. The professor's widow smiled, gave her a brief wave, and went on talking to the men she was with. Unlike the function Anna had attended at the British embassy in Vienna, this once had a forced, officious air to it, the laughter sounding contrived.

There was a table against one wall, stacked with bottles and glasses. Waiters in white jackets and gloves hovered attentively. Arranged around the chamber was a collection of paintings on easels. None of the guests seemed to be particularly interested in them, and a cursory glance gave Anna no clue as to a theme or style. The collection appeared to be uncollated, random, thrown together without any discernible thought. But Anna had learned enough from Marion and her studies at the Academy in Vienna to appreciate that more than a few of the works were worth serious money.

'You've brought me to an art exhibition?'

Ivo was searching for faces he recognized. 'In a manner of speaking,' he said absently.

'I didn't think you were interested in art.'

'Aesthetically, no. But—' His eyes alighted on Manis Möller.

Anna's heart sank. He was in conversation with another man, a languorous character in an expensively tailored lounge suite, a bowtie at his throat.

'That's Adolf Ziegler,' Ivo told her. 'He's the president of the Reich Chamber of Fine Arts. He's my ultimate boss.'

Anna gave Ivo a hard stare. 'You said you'd joined the Kripo.'

'I have. Keep your voice down.'

'What do the police have to do with fine art?'

'Paintings get stolen, don't they? Just like anything else.'

Anna cast her eyes around the pieces of art assembled in the chamber. 'Were *these* stolen?'

'You could say that. They certainly ended up in the wrong hands.'

'And now they're in the right hands?'

'They're back where they should be.'

'But this isn't an art gallery.' Anna remembered what Ivo had told her the day he returned from Berlin with the Albert Arnz landscape that Möller had given him: *He got it from a Jewish family who were leaving Germany – in exchange for getting them a clean tax clearance certificate…*

How many of the paintings in this room, she wondered, had been procured by threats and coercion? Some of them must be worth thousands of Reichsmarks.

Looking around at these ordinary little men and their blowsy wives and mistresses, she was reminded of a gangster movie Rex had worked on, called *Little Caesar*. Is that what these people were – small-time crooks who'd somehow got their hands on a whole country?

Ivo's voice broke into her thoughts. He was looking in the direction of a short, stocky man in his fifties with receding, wavy hair. 'Look, that's Hoffmann, he's Hitler's photographer. I could introduce you, if you'd like.'

Anna was about to tell him she very much *wouldn't* like when an imperious rapping silenced conversation in an instant, as if a judge had called a court to order with his gavel. Everyone's eyes turned to the entrance. Beside the open door stood a tall SS officer, a gloved hand gripping a silver-tipped baton.

'Attention!' he shouted. 'The Reichsminister for Public Enlightenment and Propaganda – His Excellency, Herr Doktor Goebbels.'

The officer stood aside. A small man in a brown uniform, a swastika armband around the left upper sleeve, stepped into the room to a chorus of *Heil Hitler!*

Anna had only ever seen the Reichsminister in newsreels and newspaper photographs. He struck her now as entirely unprepossessing. He was shorter than she had imagined, with a high, sloping forehead. His hair was oiled and worn brushed tightly back over the crown of his head. The gaunt face, with its sunken, blemished cheeks and mouth that was too wide for the little jaw, made her think of a malnourished stoat.

Adolf Ziegler stepped forward to welcome him. There followed a scrum of guests eager to shake the Reichsminister's little hand, a lot of fawning from the men and curtseying from the women.

Zeigler showed him the paintings and then Goebbels spent a while speaking with Frau Koppitz before making a brief speech.

'I must congratulate Kriminalinspektor Möller and all in his department for their hard work,' he announced in his flat Bavarian drone. 'It is entirely due to them that these works of art have been recovered for Germany. Had you not seized them, they would have been spirited out of the Reich. We would have lost them. They would have languished out of public sight, not to be admired or appreciated, but kept for purely speculative reasons, by grubby hoarders, by greedy Jews who squat like toads in their cellars and their private vaults counting their money and their ill-gotten possessions. Well done! Now, please enjoy your champagne before the Reichsminister for Economics asks who paid for it.' He laughed, and it sounded to Anna like a schoolboy laughing at a dirty joke.

After the address, Ivo announced he was going to speak to Möller. 'Come with me,' he said, holding out his hand. Anna didn't take it.

'I'll stay here if you don't mind.'

Ivo coughed into his fist to control his anger. 'I know you don't like him. But just for tonight, make the effort. For me.'

'Best if I don't,' Anna told him, speaking quietly but standing her ground. 'I might be tempted to ask him how many Jews he's robbed in return for allowing them the privilege of leaving Germany. And you wouldn't want me to show you up, would you? Not when you're surrounded by such a fine collection of moral paragons.'

Ivo grabbed her wrist. He squeezed so hard Anna thought the blood flow to her fingers would stop. 'Shut up,' he growled. 'Remember where you are.'

Anna held his gaze defiantly. Her eyes blazed. She knew the very last thing he'd risk in this place was a scene. 'Let go of me!' she hissed, trying to keep her face passive. 'I want to stay here. Maybe I'll talk to Frau Koppitz – if that's *allowed*.'

Ivo relented. He shrugged and let go of her wrist. 'Please yourself. Just don't get drunk and make a show of yourself – like your mother.'

As he stalked off in Möller's direction, Anna hailed a waiter and got her champagne flute recharged. It was all she could do to keep it from spilling over, her hands were trembling so much.

As she looked up, she saw Frau Koppitz approaching. To her consternation, Reichsminister Goebbels was at her side. Like a hare caught out in the open by a hawk, Anna could do nothing but freeze and wait for the talons to strike.

'Anna, my dear! How lovely to see you in Berlin,' Frau Koppitz said, beaming. 'So, you took my advice. I'm so pleased. Let me introduce you to His Excellency, Herr Doktor Goebbels. I'm sure you've been dying to meet him.'

Up close, the Reichsminister looked even less appealing than at a distance. His eyes were beady, and the flesh on his cheeks had the texture of a baked rice pudding. Anna wondered if she was supposed to curtsey, or at the very least shake his hand. In the event, she found herself unable to do anything but give him a sickly smile.

'Your Excellency, this is Frau Wolff – the American girl I was telling you about,' Frau Koppitz said proudly.

When he smiled at her, it reminded Anna of the lizards she'd seen in the California desert when Rex had taken her on a day's location filming – except lizards didn't have bad teeth.

'Enchanted, young lady,' he said. 'I am led to believe you are a photographer. Is that correct?'

Anna wondered how she was meant to address him. Calling such a mediocre little man 'your excellency' would be like labelling one of Bär's childish scribbles a masterpiece. She just about managed, 'Yes. Yes, I am.'

'Frau Koppitz tells me your father is a cameraman in Hollywood?'

'Yes, he is. I learned a lot from him.'

Goebbels nodded sagely. 'Photography is the magic eye through which our people may get a glimpse of the great future we are in the process of making for them,' he told her sententiously. His voice reminded Anna of a Vienna tram conductor, high-pitched and monotonous as he called out the next stop. 'And who is your husband? Is he here tonight?'

'That's him, over there – Ivo.'

Goebbels turned his head to where Ivo was in conversation with Manis Möller.

'What a handsome fellow! You married well, Frau Wolff. A fine figure.'

For an awful moment Anna thought he was going to echo what Ivo's mother had once told her, about making babies for the Fatherland. She wondered what the penalty would be for calling a Reichsminister a creep.

'We could make use of a handsome fellow like that in our work,' Goebbels continued, as if he were admiring a racehorse. 'He looks as though he was born to have his image on a poster. Is he one of Möller's fellows?'

'Yes, Herr Doktor,' Anna said, arriving at a title she could live with. 'But please don't ask me what he does. I've really no idea. He prefers not to share his work with me.'

'Laudable, very laudable, Frau Wolff,' Goebbels said, waving a finger to indicate his approval. 'It is best for both parties in a marriage that the husband draws a distinct line between his professional life and his family one. That way both may serve the Reich to the best of their abilities. But you may rest assured that he is a valued member of the Nazi Party. He has helped make tonight possible.'

Dr Goebbels was about to move on to the next waiting sycophant when he paused. 'You must send my office a sample of your work, Frau Wolff,' he said. 'I will order them to await it. We have need of people with a good eye for a striking image. Old Hoffmann over there' – he pointed a weak chin in the direction of the photographer – 'while he can take a decent picture of the Führer, in truth is just a glorified taker-of-snaps. Baby portraits, pets and paddling about in the Wansee – that's about his limit. I need people who can inspire.'

After the Reichsminister had turned his back on her, Anna glanced over at Ivo. He was staring at her, his mouth open. He didn't look astonished, surprised or even jealous.

He looked greedy.

In the car home, Ivo was a changed man. He sat very close to Anna, his hand resting on her thigh.

'What did he say to you? Did he know who I was? What did you tell him?'

Anna looked straight ahead at the back of the driver's cap. She knew for sure now that her husband was a thief – a man who preyed on the frightened and the vulnerable. What she found surreal was the fact that he could earn the admiration of the highest in the state for it.

Did her silence make her an accomplice?

'We only spoke for a few moments,' she said.

'But you *spoke*. Do you have any idea how privileged that makes you?'

'He wants to see some of my photographs.'

'That's wonderful.'

In the darkness of the car's interior, Ivo kissed her neck. It was the first intimacy he'd shown towards her in months. It repelled her. She knew it wasn't done through love, or even out of lust. He was trying to take ownership of something he'd just realized might actually be valuable to him.

'I'm so proud of you,' he said. 'I told you it was right for us to come here to Berlin. And now we're really on our way.'

But precisely where to, Ivo didn't say, preferring to keep the destination to his cold, quiet self.

Eleven

'Look at this. Isn't it wonderful?' Ivo pushed that day's copy of the *Berliner Tageblatt* across the breakfast table for Anna to read.

It was one week after the gathering at the Chamber for Fine Arts, and Ivo was behaving as if their relationship was the strongest, most tranquil marriage ever consummated. He had made love to her last night, as if celebrating a victory. It had revolted her.

Anna studied the front page. It was a report of the visit by the Chancellor of Austria to the Führer at Berchtesgaden. Herr Schuschnigg had come to plead with Hitler for his nation's continuing independence. He had left like a man walking home with empty pockets and a bloodied nose after being comprehensively mugged. The headline screamed *Unification – Only a Matter of Time!*

From the lounge came the sound of giggling as Hannelore played with Bär. Antje was in her cot beside Anna. Marion was sleeping off the effects of a night at the Resizenz-Kasino.

'Wonderful in what way?' Anna asked, over her coffee, *brötchen* and ham.

'Didn't I tell you it would happen? It's only a matter of time.'

'Before *what* happens?'

'Before Austria becomes what it is meant to be: part of the Reich.'

Anna stared into her coffee. She imagined she heard a door slamming, and pictured herself on the wrong side of it, cut off from escape. She pictured in her mind an anxious father surrounded by his frightened family, standing before a faceless man in a uniform while he handed over an heirloom – a painting – in return for a tax certificate that would allow them all to leave a homeland that had turned against them, that hated them. Then the drone of Reichsminister Goebbels barged its way into her head: *Photography is the magic eye through which our people may get a glimpse of the great future we are in the process of making for them...*

'Where does it stop, Ivo?' she asked, looking up at her husband. 'Only with Austria? Will that give your friends enough space for all their flags, for their rallies, for all that marching up and down? Where are you going to find a big enough building to put all the works of art Manis Möller is going to be able to steal?'

Perhaps she'd only said it in her head, because Ivo just wiped his fingers on his handkerchief and rose from the table. The only thing he said as he put on his jacket, ready for the day ahead, was: 'Have you sent those pictures to Dr Goebbels yet? I don't want him thinking I have an ungrateful wife.'

Luka had promised to take her to see a matinee of *The Marriage Swindler* with Viktoria von Ballasko at the Wintergarten. Her explanation to Hannelore would be that she was visiting Berlin photo editors with a view to selling her work. Anna knew what would follow. After the movie, they would take the U-Bahn back to Luka's room and make love. She had come to think of sex with Luka as putting a cooling balm on a burn – it wouldn't heal the wound, but it would temporarily soften the pain. The only question was how much of a scar would be left afterwards.

He arrived outside the cinema with an attractive young woman on his arm. It suddenly struck Anna that perhaps he'd never really forgiven her for standing him up when they'd been teenagers, and that this was to be her long-delayed punishment: public humiliation in front of his new lover. It didn't seem the sort of thing Luka would do, but it surprised Anna to realize that if it was, she could live with it.

'You remember my little sister, Louisa,' Luka said, as they drew close.

Anna clapped her hand over her mouth to stifle a laugh at her own foolishness. 'Yes, of course I do. I'm so sorry, I didn't recognize you.'

It wasn't surprising, Anna thought. The last time she'd seen Louisa Vogel was in the Karlsplatz in Vienna, shortly after Bär had been born. That had been almost three years ago. Louisa had been a young student then. Now she was a poised and confident young woman.

'My, you've changed,' Anna said, shaking Louisa's hand.

In reply, she was offered little more than a polite smile. Anna remembered the hostility Louisa had shown her for missing the date with her brother, the night Ivo had taken her to the Rathauskeller. She wondered if Luka had told her about their affair.

'I positively insisted Lulu come and meet you,' Luka said. 'She's only been here a week.'

'You're working in Berlin?' Anna said.

'I've just started as an assistant at the Galerie Brensinger, the antiques showroom on Oranienburger Strasse,' Louisa told her, her expression still barely rising above coolly civil. She glanced at Luka. 'Someone has to keep an eye on this scallywag – to make sure he doesn't get himself into trouble. I've been doing that since we were little.'

'Well, that's wonderful,' Anna said. 'Have you come to see the movie with us?'

She half hoped Louisa would say yes, realizing that it would make spending a couple of hours in Luka's bed out of the question. To her surprise, the prospect of escape gave her a sense of relief. When Luka had suggested they get a place together, she had felt cruel. Now, for the first time since they started the affair, she just felt grubby.

'No, I'm on my lunch break,' Louisa said. 'But Luka was insistent I should meet you again. I'm sure he had his reasons. How is your husband, Frau Wolff? Well, I trust.'

Louisa Vogel couldn't have made herself clearer, Anna thought, as she and Luka took their seats in the crowded cinema.

'I'm sorry about Lulu,' he said. 'She's always been highly protective of me, even though I'm the eldest. It can sometimes come across as her being a bit chilly.'

'So, she knows about us?'

'I haven't told her in so many words. But she's not stupid.'

'I don't want to cause a rift in your family, Luka.'

'You won't. I'm not a child, whatever Lulu might think. I can make my own decisions.'

Oh, Luka, thought Anna as the lights dimmed, a child is exactly what you are, and I should never have let you convince me otherwise.

Before the main feature started, there were the newsreels to endure: a barrage of bombastic Party propaganda, narrated by a hectoring man shouting in a shrill and strident voice. Anna watched von Ribbentrop striding up the steps of the Foreign Ministry, his new domain… Germans in the Sudetenland persecuted by the Czechs… and the item that really sent an icy chill through her limbs: a march by cheering, uniformed stormtroopers through the Austrian city of Linz. The camera caught every detail: their swagger, their grinning faces, the swastika flags waving, the local civilian population seemingly roaring their approval… all filmed in a dramatic style that even Rex would have found hard to fault.

Later, in his room at Tempelhof, she clung to Luka more fiercely than usual. She feared everything that had once seemed certain was about to be washed away in a torrent that she could do nothing to withstand.

And because Luka was the innocent she had always suspected him to be, he – in return – mistook her fear for love.

On the morning of the last day in February 1938, beneath a dull grey sky, Anna Cantrell and Harry Taverner sat together on a bench in the Berlin Zoologischer Garten. It was another of their carefully contrived accidental encounters.

Anna had come to look forward to these brief meetings. Caught between a husband who cared too little for her and a lover who cared too much, she saw them as little islands of solid ground poking above the swirling, dangerous currents of her life.

On this particular day, the chill wind blowing meant there were few visitors to observe them, while an agitated screaming from the monkey house added an extra layer of security to their conversation.

'Well, it's happened,' Anna said. 'Last week I came face to face with Dr Joseph Goebbels. He asked to see a sample of my work.'

'That's wonderful news.'

'Not really. He's a loathsome creep. Besides, he may just have been stringing me a line.'

'Let's wait and see – hope for the best.'

Anna shook her head. 'I'm not sure I can do it.'

'It's early days. You're bound to feel a little anxious as this stage.'

'You don't understand. Getting close to people like that, it's... it's...' – she searched for the right word – 'it's *contaminating*. Just being in the same room as them makes my skin crawl.'

'Ignore them,' Harry said. 'Just point your camera where they ask you to – for a better cause.'

'Look, Harry, if I have *any* pretensions to being a decent photographer, I can't risk getting a reputation for taking publicity snaps for a corrupt regime. It'll ruin any hope I have of being taken seriously. Don't you see that? I have to remain independent. Otherwise, I might as well just resign myself to a career taking wedding photos.'

'We understand perfectly,' Harry said. 'We're not asking you to compromise your artistic integrity. It's the doors they open to you that we're really interested in, and the unguarded conversations they might let slip when they invite you in. We're not asking you to become another Hoffmann, or a Leni Riefenstahl.' He gave her a sympathetic smile. 'And we're not asking you to be Mata Hari, either.'

'I'm pleased to hear it. She was executed, wasn't she? Besides, I've had two children – it would take some effort to turn me into a belly dancer.'

Harry chuckled. Glancing at a nearby stall selling hot drinks, he stood up. 'Wait here a moment.'

He returned bearing two cups of hot chocolate and cherry brandy.

'Is this a bribe?' Anna asked, half laughing. 'If an appeal to her better nature doesn't work, offer her stomach something irresistible?'

'That's my modus operandi blown,' Harry said, looking suitably guilty.

Anna sipped her drink and felt a sweet, luxurious warmth spreading through her. 'Are spies any good at giving advice on relationships?' she asked.

'Taking care over an agent's emotional state is as crucial as taking care over her cover,' he replied, amused by her question as he looked directly at her. Though he was about Ivo's age, Anna noticed there was a maturity in his gaze that her husband lacked.

'Only mine seem to be rather a mess at the minute,' she said, returning her gaze to the steaming cup.

'Problems with Ivo?'

'And my lover.'

Taverner took a moment to reply. 'Ah, I didn't know about him.'

'Not much of a spy, are you?'

He gave her a sheepish grin. 'Rubbish, to be honest.'

'Well, at least I know you've not got me under surveillance.'

From the monkey house came a sudden shriek. It seemed the perfect punctuation to the exchange. They held each other's gaze for a moment, before letting out the laughter. Anna decided that either Harry Taverner was the sort of man she could entrust her innermost thoughts to – or the most skilful manipulator she'd ever met. She couldn't tell which.

'I don't know how much longer I can stay with Ivo,' she said. 'It's not working.'

'So… you took a lover.'

Was that a trace of discomfort she thought she heard in his voice? She tilted her head as she looked at him. 'Why, Harry Taverner, don't tell me you're jealous.'

'Not my place to be,' he said, just a fraction too late to hide his embarrassment. But the look he gave her – inquiring, but at the same time deeply solicitous – seemed to invite her to go further. Anna fortified herself with another sip of the hot chocolate and brandy and took a deep breath.

'I feel nothing for Ivo any more, except disappointment,' she said. 'And embarrassment, I suppose – at letting my heart rule my head. I should have learned that from my parents' marriage.' She gave Harry an apologetic smile. 'Sorry, and all that, but I may not have access to Ivo's circle for much longer.'

'And this lover of yours: not the antidote you thought he'd be?'

'No. Luka's a decent enough boy, but I shouldn't have used him. It's wrong. And if I end it, I'm not sure he's going to take it very well.'

'Could he cause trouble for you?'

'Luka? No, I don't think so. He's not the vindictive sort.'

Harry pondered her words for a while. Then he gave her a reassuring smile. 'I'm sure you'll make the right decision,' he said, though whether he was talking about her entangled private life or her professional one, she couldn't be sure.

When they stood up to go their separate ways, Harry suggested they kiss each other on the cheek to preserve the fiction that they were just two friends meeting by chance.

'Sometimes,' he said softly into her ear, 'events have a habit of throwing something at us that makes us take stock of who we are, forces us to acknowledge where our true convictions lie. Then the choice becomes easy.'

He took the empty cups back to the stall, then waved goodbye, walking away at a calm, unhurried pace in the direction of the U-Bahn station.

It was only when he disappeared from her view that Anna discovered he'd taken a chunk of her sense of security with him, as if it was his to bestow by his presence.

The following morning, German troops swept unopposed across the Austrian border, welcomed by crowds of people cheering and waving swastika flags. The land that had been Anna's home since she was eight years old no longer existed as an independent nation. She woke to discover that she was now married to a citizen of Hitler's Third Reich.

It was Hannelore, not Ivo, who left the Party newspaper, the *Völkischer Beobachter*, lying on the coffee table in the lounge later that week.

Anna only picked it up to see what was showing at the cinema. On the front page was a photograph of frightened-looking Jews kneeling on a Vienna pavement. Uniformed men stood over them while they scrubbed graffiti opposing *Anschluss*, the conjoining of Austria and Germany, off the concrete. A jeering crowd, including children, looked on.

The very next morning, Anna sent a parcel of her photographs to the private office of the Reichsminister for Public Enlightenment and Propaganda. In the accompanying letter, she wrote:

Dear Dr Goebbels,

I hope you remember me from the function at the Chamber of Fine Arts. I enclose a sample of my work. If your ministry would consider me a suitable recorder of the new Germany, I would be honoured to assist in any way I can.

Yours sincerely,

Frau Wolff (Anna Cantrell)

A fortnight later, Anna had yet to receive a reply. She had long ago learned to overcome the feeling of rejection when a prospective publisher turned down one of her photos, but this was different. Her immediate fear was that the offer made by Herr Doktor Goebbels that evening at the Alexanderplatz had been nothing but polite conversation. In her head was the image of a minor functionary stuffing her photographs into a waste bin deep in the bowels of the Ministry for Public Enlightenment and Propaganda.

Anna was beginning to give up hope when an invitation arrived by Ministry courier for her to join the official press party attending a tour of the futuristic new passenger terminal at Tempelhof airfield.

Less than ten minutes later, after calling the telephone number on the card, Anna walked to the mailbox at the end of the street and posted a letter. It was addressed to Mr H Taverner, Passport Control Office, British Embassy, Vienna.

Dear Harry,

Sorry about the short notice. I've decided my interest in photography should take a new course. If you are able to come to Berlin again soon, I would be grateful for your guidance. My turn for the hot chocolate and brandy.

Yours sincerely,

Anna Cantrell

Perhaps unsurprisingly, Anna Cantrell began her career as an agent for British intelligence with trepidation. She knew the risks involved in defying the regime. But if Hitler's screeching rage issuing from the radio wasn't enough to convince her, the growing sense of menace on the streets would have done the job amply.

Harry assured her the worst that could happen, if they discovered who she was really working for, would be expulsion from Germany. In that event, he would find a way of getting the children out with her. It took not the slightest effort on Anna's part to believe he was the sort of man who could make it happen.

At Tempelhof airfield, Anna shot some fine pictures of the vast, curved concourse topped with a pair of concrete eagles. One appeared in that week's *Völkischer Beobachter* and was used later picked up by *Le Figaro* in France, Italy's *La Stampa*, and several publications in America, Brazil and Argentina. Further invitations followed, increasingly for Anna alone. True to his word, Harry Taverner contacted some tame photo editors. Assignments and commissions followed. Soon Anna had a burgeoning career on her hands.

Whenever the Reichsminister for Propaganda noticed her amongst the photographers he would come over and talk to her. It made her stomach churn. But it delighted Ivo, who was soon appointed Manis Möller's successor when the odious Möller moved on to higher things – though once again, quite what those *things* were, Ivo never disclosed.

To distance her from suspicion, Harry arranged that they would communicate through a cut-out. Instead of writing to him directly in Vienna, she was directed to a man named Pfeiffer, who ran a photographic shop close to the Moritzplatz U-Bahn station. Herr Pfeiffer was a genial, bald, utterly unremarkable Saxon, whose internment as a prisoner of war in 1916 had turned him into an Anglophile. The new Germany had made him a vehement anti-Nazi. Thomas Kendrick – alias Major Warwick – had recruited him, and his store was now the emergency switchboard through which Anna could reach Harry in Vienna.

'You'd be surprised what we can learn from photographs and the faces who appear in them,' Harry told her at their next meeting, at the Natural History Museum. He opened the copy of *Berliner Illustrirte Zeitung* he'd brought with him. 'Who's this bold-looking fellow at Goering's right – the one in uniform? We haven't seen him before. Do you know who he is? Seen him at any of the ministry parties, for instance?'

To protect her credibility, and her self-respect, Anna took just as many photos of events that could legitimately fall under the banner of news. She captured the moment when Gottfried von Cramm, the world number one tennis player, was led away from court after being sentenced to a year in prison for homosexual relations with a Jew. Her photo of the Führer's train departing for his state visit to Prime Minister Mussolini of Italy was widely used. And when May's Czechoslovakia crisis brought a flurry of international diplomats to Berlin, Anna was there with her camera to record the comings and goings.

It was no easy matter to juggle her role as a professional photographer with that of a loving and dutiful mother. She would never have managed it without the help of Marion and Hannelore, and it was not achieved without a significant measure of guilt on Anna's part.

'You're a marvel,' Harry told her one sunny afternoon in the shadow of the Brandenburg Gate as Berliners in their summer finery flowed by.

'I don't *feel* like a marvel. You're really the only one I'm being honest with.'

'Have you broken it off with Luka?'

'Not yet.'

'Don't confide in him too much. It could be dangerous.'

'As long as he doesn't get too intense, he's the only oasis in my life.'

'That's fine. But don't get complacent.'

Anna laughed. 'Luka isn't even a Party member. He loathes all that nonsense as much as I do.'

'That's as maybe. But this place is breeding a nasty habit of denunciation. And you don't know who he talks to when he's not with you.'

They drew back to let a truck full of brownshirts pass by. Anna turned away from the barrage of wolf-whistles.

'They've asked me to be part of the press team for the next Party rally, in Nuremberg,' she said. Then she glanced at the disappearing truck. 'You can imagine how much I'm going to enjoy *that*.'

At Nuremberg, Anna took some of her best photographs yet, but when she developed them, she seriously considered burning every print *and* the rolls of film they were taken from. The propaganda ministry had made it so easy for her, staging an event whose scale and power were designed specifically to overawe. Where was the skill in recording that? The vast, roaring crowd; the torchlight parades; the manic, rageful speeches; the faux victimhood; the contempt for anything and anyone unprepared to bow before *Ein Volk, Ein Reich, Ein Führer*, chilled her to the marrow. When Herr Hitler railed against the nation's Jews, calling them parasites in the German bloodstream, she knew she could no longer work in the interests of the regime, even if she *was* doing so for a better cause. She had embarked on this journey because of the photograph she'd seen of Jews being forced to scrub a pavement in Vienna. She had thought she was making a stand. She had imagined she could separate her art from her conscience. After Nuremberg, she felt tainted, compromised, complicit.

How long would it be before Joseph Goebbels asked her to take similar pictures in Berlin?

On the train back from Munich, Anna accepted the truth: her marriage to Ivo was a marriage in name only, and she loathed everything he stood for. It was time to get herself, her children and Marion out of Germany.

'You must make your own choices, Anna,' Harry said, when she arranged a meeting through Herr Pfeiffer. 'I'd be the last person to stand in your way.'

For a moment, Anna found herself wishing he'd put up more of a fight. 'I didn't think you'd be so amenable. I thought you'd insist I stay.'

'I didn't buy your soul, Anna; I just asked if you'd do something useful for us. If you think getting out is the right thing to do, that's good enough for me.' His calm, proficient manner cracked just a little. 'Of course, that doesn't mean I shan't miss our little meetings.'

'Oh. Yes – me, too.'

'They've moved me to Berlin, you know – what with the way things seem to being heading.'

For a moment neither spoke. Then Anna said, 'The problem is, if I leave him, Ivo will try to stop me taking the children. He's threatened that once already, and I don't think he was bluffing. You said you might be able to help.'

'We could probably work something out – a little subterfuge. What about this lover of yours?'

'Luka? I'll feel like the worst bitch in the world. But the time has come, I'm afraid.'

Was that a flicker of relief she saw in his eyes? She couldn't be sure, because he hurriedly brushed away the ribbon of fair hair that always seemed to fall across one side of his brow.

'Where will you go?' he asked.

'I don't know. That would rather depend upon my mother.'

'The possibility of a British passport remains on the cards,' Harry said. 'Your father is still a citizen.'

Anna pulled a face. 'Marion would go to the South Pole before she went to England. It will have to be somewhere else.'

'Well, no point in making a decision immediately,' Harry said confidently. 'Who knows where any of us will be in a year or two from now?'

'Why do you say that?'

'Don't you read the papers?'

'Of course.'

'Then you'll know that Herr Hitler has been making threats to Czechoslovakia. There could well be war in Europe soon. Then all bets are off.'

'Do you think it will come to that?'

'Some of us do. Some of us don't.'

'And which side of the debate is Harry Taverner on? If I may ask.'

Harry smiled. 'The winning side, I hope. And I think that's where you want to be too.'

Luka had invited her to spend two days with him at the spa resort of Bad Saarow, while Ivo was in Munich for the Party conference. Anna thought of cancelling, but decided the tranquil lakeside resort would give her the best opportunity to let him down gently.

An honest talk, she thought, would be kinder than a letter.

The guest house was called Die Weiden – The Willows. It looked like something out of a children's fairy tale, with round dormer windows poking out like the eyes of elves peering through a thicket of thatch. The clientele was mostly Berlin bourgeoisie. Luka had booked separate rooms, because Anna would have to show her passport and papers to the host and a tryst between a married woman and a single man would set tongues wagging. As an extra precaution, Anna had told Marion and Hannelore that she was shooting scenic pictures for the propaganda ministry's tourism department. If Ivo found out where she was staying, a room booked under her name would hopefully make her alibi convincing.

Luka arrived an hour after Anna. He wanted them to go straight to his room to make love, but she said she wasn't feeling well and that a walk along the shore might help perk her up. Sensing that something was amiss, he went with her like a man being led to the gallows. Anna felt like the worst person on earth.

'I'm so sorry, Luka – it's over,' she said, when they sat together on a bench beneath the trees, looking out at the pleasure boats gliding on the water. 'There's really no easier way to say it, I'm afraid.'

'But I love you. I always have.'

Seeing the misery in his eyes, Anna felt like the spawn of Ivan the Terrible and Lady Macbeth. She prayed he wasn't going to weep – the guilt would overwhelm her.

'It can't work,' she said, wanting to lay her hand on his to comfort him, but knowing it would only make things worse. 'I'm a married woman with two children. It's best if we break it now. I know it hurts, but we're both only twenty-two. I've already chosen my path. You have yours ahead of you, and it's open. Take it.'

'I don't *want* to take it,' he said, as if he were a child and she was trying to give him unpleasant medicine. 'I have to be with *you*.'

'But you can't. I don't want that.'

Luka stood up. 'You lied to me,' he said bitterly. His face was twisted, wounded.

'That's something I never did. You'll come to see that soon enough.'

Luka turned his back on her and walked away in the direction of the nearby boathouse and jetty. For an awful moment Anna feared he might keep on walking, right into the lake. But he didn't. There was nothing left for her to say, nothing that wouldn't make things worse. She got up and set off back to the guest house.

Luka wasn't around for dinner. Anna ate alone, but her appetite faded before the food was served and she left most of her *frikadellen*. She downed a glass of wine while she browsed through the magazine on the terrace overlooking the lake. At eleven, she went to Luka's room to check on him. She received no answer to her knock.

If the host disbelieved her explanation for wanting to borrow a torch so that she could stroll along the lakeshore footpath at midnight, he passed no judgement. Anna spent the next hour and a half in the moonlight, ranging the torch beam over the black water and expecting in the very next second to see Luka's body floating there.

Back in her room, she considered her options. They hadn't checked in together; the rooms were booked under different names; any connection with Luka was deniable, save for the fact that several people had seen them together. She could pass that off as simply two strangers happening to fall into conversation.

Her fear of a scandal was as nothing in comparison to her worry that Luka had done something foolish.

Next morning, a Saturday, Anna woke at five. There was still no sign of Luka. She paid to use the guest house phone and called the number of his apartment in Berlin on the chance he'd made his way home. Louisa answered. Unless she was prepared to lie through her teeth like a criminal, there seemed to Anna no alternative but to enlist her help.

Louisa Vogel arrived two hours later, having caught the first train from Berlin. As they set off to resume the search, Anna explained what had happened.

'You really are a bitch, aren't you?' Louisa said icily. 'Didn't you see how vulnerable he was to your so-called charms?'

Was. Did Louisa also think her brother was dead?

'I was always honest with him, I promise you,' Anna said. 'I made it clear to him on several occasions that he shouldn't let his feelings run away. I've never hidden my situation from him.'

The recrimination in Louisa's voice was razor-sharp. 'He was just a toy to you, wasn't he? There you were, the sophisticated woman from America, standing in our apartment at the Born-Hof, with my mother fussing about with the best china, while you took your photographs as though we were all just creatures in the zoo. You should be disgusted with yourself.'

And Anna was. Which was why she said nothing as they combed Bad Saarow for either a body or a wounded boy.

In the end, they found the latter: Luka, sitting under a willow tree where he'd been most of the night. He was wet with dew and pale from the cold, exhaustion and the pain of a sick heart. Louisa would have none of the help Anna offered, snarling her away as she helped her brother back to the guest house. Anna could only watch them go, too full of guilt to speak.

That night, back in Berlin, Marion was out as usual. Anna asked Hannelore to clean the dishes while she put Bär and Antje to bed. She calmed herself with a hefty slug of Ivo's schnapps, feeling drained and exhausted, and like the worst woman in the world.

Just before she climbed into bed, she went to close the curtains in the window that gave a view down into the street. Right on the edge of a pool of light from a streetlamp she saw a figure in a raincoat and homburg hat looking up at her. For a moment she wondered if, in his rejection, Luka Vogel had decided to follow her. But it wasn't Luka – the man was too short, too stocky.

When he caught sight of her staring at him he paused, before stepping away into the cover of darkness.

A deliberate pause.

A pause just long enough to let her know he wanted her to see him.

Twelve

Early the next morning, Anna went to Herr Pfeiffer's shop to arrange an emergency meeting with Harry Taverner. The rendezvous was arranged for the following day at twenty past eleven, outside the Philharmonie concert hall. If Anna was confident that she wasn't being followed, she would carry her camera case slung across her left shoulder. If it was hanging from her right hand, Harry would walk away. The fallback was to meet outside the Anhalter station thirty minutes later.

'Everyone's under observation now,' he said with a reassuring laugh, when she told him about the man she'd observed from her apartment window. 'It's positively a badge of honour.'

'I'm scared, Harry. He wanted me to know he was there.'

'Good.'

Anna scowled. '*Good?* How can it be good?'

'If they were going to arrest you, they'd have done it without warning.'

'That's not exactly reassuring, Harry.'

'Do you think Ivo might have found out about your affair? Perhaps he's sent one of his department's goons to keep watch on you.'

'I don't think so; I was careful. And anyway, my relationship with Luka Vogel is now officially over.'

Harry said nothing, but his eyes held hers a beat longer than she'd been expecting.

'I *know*. I'm a cold, heartless bitch. You don't have to remind me.'

'Are you alright?' he asked, with the merest hint of a consolatory smile.

The question surprised her. '*Me?* Yes, of course. I'm bombproof.'

He didn't seem convinced by that. 'I suppose it could be the Foreign Ministry, trying to intimidate.'

'But Goebbels' people think I'm the bee's knees.'

Harry seemed to find this amusing. 'They're like rats in a sack, Anna,' he said. 'And jealous rats at that. Don't worry. You haven't passed over state secrets. You haven't photographed classified documents. You haven't plotted to overthrow Herr Hitler. You're guilty of nothing but taking photographs. Photos *they* commissioned. I wouldn't worry. They just like making people nervous. It's all part of the strong-man approach.'

They walked down to the Landwehr canal and strolled along the tree-lined bank until they found an empty bench. The people they passed in the cool September sunshine seemed untroubled to live in a city that was fast becoming the centre of a political maelstrom.

'Is Hitler really going to invade Czechoslovakia?' Anna asked, looking along the canal to where Nazi banners hung from an iron bridge.

'It's on the cards,' Harry admitted. 'He's been clear enough that if the Czechs don't give him the Sudetenland, he'll send his troops in and take the whole country.'

'Surely Britain and France will stop him?'

'Probably not.'

'So then what? Poland?'

'That rather depends on Herr Hitler,' Harry answered.

Anna grimaced. For Berliners, the subject of war had become much like the weather: would it rain, or would it shine? Whatever the outcome, there was nothing one could do about it.

'Well, whatever happens, it's time for me to hang up my Mata Hari outfit. Sorry to let you down, Harry…'

He pulled a pack of *Neue Front* cigarettes from the inside pocket of his suit. He offered her one and lit it, cupping his hand around his lighter, which allowed him to whisper, 'They taste like smoking old socks, but they're Party cigarettes, so we'll fit in.' Then he took one for himself. 'Have you decided where?'

'Not yet. I have to talk to Marion.' Anna took a long pull on her cigarette. She coughed; Harry was right. When she exhaled, grey smoke drifted on the gentle breeze out over the water. 'I shall miss you, Harry Taverner,' she said.

'Oh, I don't doubt we'll meet up again, somewhere,' he replied confidently, with a soft smile that seemed just ever so slightly knowing. 'If you need me, you know how to get in touch.'

'May I take your photo – for my scrapbook?' Even as the words left her mouth, Anna knew it was a foolish request.

'I'd rather you didn't.'

She realized then how little she knew about him. He'd never mentioned lovers, a home, a family. But then she supposed it was meant it to be that way. And there was every chance that if he did choose to pull aside the curtain, everything he might reveal to her would likely be a fiction.

Embarrassed, Anna looked at her feet. 'Silly me. Of course you don't want your photo taken. Anyway, if Ivo saw it, he might ask me who you were. Then I'd have to tell him about the handsome Englishman who picked me up in Central Park. And if Marion got to hear about *that*—' She raised her open palms to the heavens to indicate the impending flood of retribution.

When they stood up, they shook hands and went their separate ways.

Two down, only one to go, Anna thought, as she walked back to the apartment.

But escaping Ivo, she knew, would be the hardest evasion of all.

For the next few days, despite Harry Taverner's reassurance, Anna found herself compelled to search the street from her bedroom window each night before sleep. The watcher did not return. She was forced to conclude that Harry had been right to dismiss her fears. And she forgot about the man in the raincoat and homburg entirely when, at very short notice, she got a phone call from the propaganda ministry.

'Frau Wolff,' said the voice at the other end of the line, 'if you have no commitments, the Reichsminister would like you to go back to Munich.'

If they'd wanted her to shoot the construction of the new train station, or a Party ceremony, she'd have politely refused. But this invitation was to join the official German press contingent attending the Munich Conference, an opportunity she couldn't turn down. And so, Anna Cantrell was there with her camera when the British prime minster, Neville Chamberlain, and his French counterpart, Édouard Daladier, arrived to negotiate with Adolf Hitler for a peaceful resolution to the Czech crisis.

It was the first event after which she had no doubts about calling herself a photojournalist.

One night, in the hotel bar, she caught a glimpse of Harry. Tall and lithe, his suit nevertheless fitted him perfectly. He looked a different kind of creature entirely to the stout, balding civil servants and functionaries around him. His fair hair was for once neat and oiled, swept back the way Luka had worn his when he'd tried – and failed – to impress her. On Harry Taverner, it worked. He was talking to the man she remembered from the embassy in Vienna, Major Warwick. When their eyes met, Harry waved.

One of the journalists she was with – a dreadful bore from the Swiss *Neue Zürcher Zeitung* – suggested she might care to continue their conversation in his room. Anna refused of course, surprised to find herself wishing it had been Harry doing the asking.

She went up to her room and changed out of her work dress into the amber chiffon cocktail dress she'd brought in case she found herself in any official soirée, doing her best to force her chestnut hair in an approximation of the way Katharine Hepburn wore hers. But when she came back down again, Harry had gone.

Back in Berlin, Anna's relationship with Ivo was deteriorating rapidly. Now she could see no difference between her husband and all the other strutting, overbearing Party members she encountered. Every moment she spent with Bär and Antje served only to convince her that she had to free them from their father's influence. It was the night Marion went hunting at the *Kranzler*, and Hannelore had gone to visit her sick father in Gatow, that she discovered he was one step ahead of her.

'We must regularize your position,' he announced after Anna had put the children to bed.

'What do you mean – regularize my position? I'm not a book-keeping error.'

'I mean your nationality. You should be a German citizen.'

'I'm perfectly happy as I am, thank you.'

He grabbed her by the arm, sinking his fingers into her flesh. 'This present arrangement is not proper. A Party member's wife should be a citizen of the Reich. We will go to the interior ministry and have the situation corrected.'

Wincing from his grip, Anna pulled herself free. She could feel the fear spreading like poison. He was hell-bent, she realized, on turning her into something she wasn't, cutting off any chance she might have of escaping him. 'I don't need regularizing *or* correcting, thank you,' she said, trying sound calm, rational. 'There are more important things going on in the world, if you hadn't noticed.'

Ivo put his fists on his hips and glared at her. It surprised her how easily handsome could become ugly. It all depended on what was behind the eyes.

'I know what you're up to,' he said harshly.

At first, Anna thought, Dear God! He's found out about Harry. The colour drained from her face. But when he spoke again, she realized it was the petulant child lashing out in irrational anger, not the cold, calculating Kripo officer.

'You're scheming with your bitch of a mother to steal my children and bring them up amongst Jews and homosexuals,' he shouted. 'I won't have it!' His expression had become so twisted with rage that he could have been a villain in one of Rex's silent movies, overacting to make up for the lack of soundtrack. He stepped forward, like a bare-knuckle fighter about to throw a punch.

Anna took a pace backwards, raising a hand to deter him. 'Ivo, calm down. You're talking nonsense. You're the one who threatened to take the children, not me.'

That seemed to check him somewhat.

'Marion has done nothing but offer you kindness,' she continued, as evenly as she could, although inside she was shaking. 'It's her money that pays for this apartment. Are you going to steal it from her, in return for an exit stamp in her passport?'

At the last moment, Ivo gained control of his temper. 'You'll do as you're told,' he snarled. 'If not, I'll have them cancel your visa and you'll be deported. *Without* the children.'

Later, Anna would look back and marvel at where the courage came from. Perhaps she was more like Marion that she'd thought. Or maybe she was just learning how to deal with bullies. Either way, when she spoke, she barely recognized her own voice.

'No, Ivo, you won't,' she said calmly, 'because you're not the one with the phone number of Joseph Goebbels' private office.'

In the first week of October came an event that made even Marion accept that Berlin was no longer safe for any of them. In an official proclamation, the Reich Interior Ministry announced that the passports of all Jewish citizens were invalid. They would only be reissued when they had been handed in and the letter *J* stamped on them.

'How long before they do the same to the passports of foreign citizens living here?' Anna asked her mother on one of Marion's rare appearances at the apartment. 'It's time to leave.'

Marion demurred only until an officer of the *Ordnungspolizei* stopped her in the street two days later and demanded to see her papers. On noticing her passport bore the gold engraving of a bald eagle, wings outstretched, and the legend *United States of America* on the cover, he let it drop to the pavement and, with the most courteous of smiles, ground it under the heel of his boot.

———

'The question is, where do we go?' Anna said, as she and Marion sat together over coffees at the Café Kranzler. Outside, a stiff breeze blew the leaves off the trees along Unter den Linden.

'Not back to America,' Marion said. 'I've got the Bauer blood that prefers Europe. I always have had. I couldn't stand the disapproving looks.'

'A friend of mine is sure there'll be war in Europe before long,' Anna said. 'And he's not the only one who thinks that.' She took a steadying breath and then said the unsayable. 'Why not England?'

Marion gave her the eyes of death but said nothing.

Anna took a bite of her *Herrentorte*, licked her lips and said, 'Oh, well. Then I suppose Paris might be fun.'

Anna planned their escape with all the diligence that Uncle László planned his movies, and with the same paucity of resources. Whether it would be a box office hit or an almighty flop would depend upon keeping the details from the ever-present Hannelore Lange. She had begun to ask questions whenever Anna said she was going out, noting the answers with a ponderous look in her eye, as if to ensure she had the details right for passing on to Ivo later. She was too dim – or too sure of herself – to hide it.

First there was the timing. They would have to make a break for it when Ivo's attention was elsewhere. When he announced that he was being sent to Munich on business for ten days, Anna struggled to hide her relief from him. He would leave Berlin in early November. That was four weeks away – too far for comfort, too close for procrastination.

Anna wondered if he'd found himself a mistress there. It would please her if he had. She needed him distracted.

In a surprising display of application and efficiency, Marion went to the US embassy near the Tiergarten to confirm that her passport hadn't been damaged beyond acceptance beneath the Orpo officer's boot. To make it to the French border only to have her papers rejected would be a disaster. After an uncomfortable wait, the news came that it hadn't.

Funds were an issue. In Germany and Austria, the Nazis had taken over the Weiner Bauer Bank and dismissed all its Jewish directors and staff. Marion wasn't sure how long her account would be accessible because it was in the Bauer name. A telegram was sent to Grandpa Wolfgang, asking him to send her monthly stipend to Banque Mercier-Bauer in Paris.

With a three-year-old and an infant to marshal, they could take little with them: only what they could carry in two suitcases. Everything else would have to be left behind. In that regard, they were no different from any of the thousands of frightened people trying to leave Hitler's Germany that year, before the prison gates slammed shut. They considered selling their clothes and jewellery to raise cash but abandoned the idea: Hannelore would quickly notice the diminishing contents of wardrobes and dressing table drawers.

The day that Ivo left for Munich, his demeanour was colder than ever. When the department car arrived to pick him up, he didn't even bother with the pretence of kissing Anna's cheek.

An icy knot in Anna's stomach told her he was suspicious.

She waited until the car had gone before running to her bedroom. Opening the dressing table drawer, she pulled out the tortoiseshell keepsake box that held her bracelets, rings, necklaces and passport.

Ivo hadn't touched her jewellery. He had no need to. But he had taken her passport.

Thirteen

Harry Taverner let his pen run over the paper as he reread the words of the report he was compiling. London insisted on despatches that were erudite, concise and, above all, factual. No waffling. Certainly, no personal speculation. Not that there was cause to speculate. The facts were well-known, and in the public domain. Earlier that morning, a young Jew named Herschel Grynszpan had walked into the German embassy in Paris and shot one of its diplomats, Ernst von Rath. The would-be assassin had claimed it was in retribution for the expulsion of Polish Jews living in Germany. Rath still clung to life – just. London was eager for details of Berlin's reaction.

Satisfied with his report, Harry was about to summon an appropriately cleared typist when the phone on his desk rang.

'Passport Control Office,' he said, laying his cigarette in the ashtray.

That wasn't what it said on the office door. In fact, the door had no sign on it at all, because the office was not listed on any floor plan.

'Mr Taverner, there's a woman here asking for you,' said the desk clerk. 'She's most insistent. I think she's an American.'

He knew of only one American woman in Berlin who might bother him at work.

'Does she go by the name "Cantrell", by any chance?'

'Yes, Mr Taverner. That's the name.'

Harry tipped back his head and let out a soft whistle of disbelief at the ceiling. His first thought was: What's the point of having dead-letter boxes, brush contacts, dead drops and safe houses if your agent is crazy enough to simply walk through your front door and ask for you by name?

His second was that Anna must be in serious trouble. If there was really no time for her to arrange a meeting through Herr Pfeiffer, then she needed his help. And she needed it now.

'Tell her there's no one of that name at the embassy,' he said. 'And that she should go across the street to the Tiergarten and wait by the Goethe monument.'

'Yes, Mr Taverner,' the clerk said.

Just before he replaced the handset in its cradle, Harry heard Anna's voice call out, 'Thank you, Mr No One. You're a lifesaver.'

As he tidied the pages of his report, Harry wondered if the Gestapo had the same problem with staff not taking security seriously.

In the Tiergarten, a few hardy souls clustered around the chestnut sellers' stalls, or walked, heads down, along the paths. The bare trees looked as though a forest fire had swept over them. The area around the Goethe statue was deserted. In the grey November light, the stone figures of the poet and his attendant muses had the spectral appearance of characters from a Wagner opera performed in some ghostly Valhalla.

Anna was waiting by the railings, gloved, scarfed and pale. When she saw him approaching, she couldn't mask her relief.

'What in God's name possessed you to come to the embassy? The Gestapo have people watching us,' Harry said in a low voice.

'I didn't know what else to do. I had to see you, and quickly.'

'What's wrong?'

Her breath misted in the cold air. 'I'm leaving Ivo. I'm taking Marion and the children to Paris.'

'With the greatest of respect, Anna, I can't in all good conscience tell you that your domestic arrangements figure particularly highly on the list of our problems at present. Sorry, and all that, but we've got other things to worry about.'

Anna shook her head. 'You don't understand. The bastard's stolen my passport.'

'Ah. That puts a different complexion on things.'

'I'm desperate, Harry. You're the only person I could think of who might help. You're supposed to be a passport control officer, aren't you? I was hoping you might be able to "control" one up for me. All I need is something that will get me across the French border with Bär and Antje. Marion's still got her US passport, though some Nazi bastard tried to grind it into the pavement. That's the other reason we're going. The writing on the wall has got so large even Marion can't ignore it. Please, Harry – if we can't get out of Berlin before Ivo returns from Munich, we're trapped. He's demanding I take German citizenship.'

She watched him as he considered her words. Why did he have to look so bloody inscrutable? What was it about Englishmen and their inability to show emotion? Was he trying to punish her for throwing in the towel with the Ministry for Propaganda?

Then he gave her a smile that seemed to raise the temperature several degrees. 'How long have we got?'

'Before Ivo returns? Ten days.'

'Then we'd best get to work.'

The plan that Harry came up with as they walked together through the Tiergarten was simple but effective, as all good plans should be. He would purchase the tickets himself, in advance, from the ticket desk at the Lehrter Bahnhof. To the clerk, he'd be just another young father buying seats for his wife and his two children – second class, upholstered, because it would be a long journey. Nine hours at least. While his English accent might stick in the clerk's memory, the man would have no reason to connect him to a female American passenger and her family travelling a day later. The day before their departure, Anna would send Hannelore out on an errand. In her absence, she would take the suitcases to the station and deposit them in a left-luggage locker. On the day itself, Harry would telephone the apartment pretending to be a representative of a photo agency, wanting to know why he hadn't received the pictures Anna had sent him. She would then dispatch Hannelore to the local post office with a pre-prepared envelope. When the coast was clear, Anna, Marion and the children would flee the apartment. Anna would leave two notes for Hannelore. The first, which would be left plainly visible on the kitchen table, would suggest they had gone to Tempelhof aerodrome because Bär had said he wanted to see the aeroplanes. A second note, which would be found only later, when the police searched Ivo and Anna's bedroom, would list details of that day's Imperial Airways flight from Tempelhof to Croydon Aerodrome, London. Together, the two notes should tie up the police for a few hours while they checked the passenger manifest.

In reality, the family would cross the Tiergarten, pass through the Brandenburg Gate and wait by the Hotel Adlon. Harry would arrive in a car borrowed from the embassy garage. He would pull up briefly to the kerb, they would climb in and be away inside a minute. They'd be on the train to Paris before Hannelore even began to suspect they weren't coming home.

When they got back to the Goethe monument, she asked, 'Do your girlfriends know you can be this devious, Harry?' Something about him – she couldn't quite say what – made her assume he wasn't married.

'Work and pleasure. Always keep them apart – that's my advice,' he said with a self-conscious laugh that made her think she might have embarrassed him.

'That's exactly what Dr Goebbels told me.'

Harry took her jibe with good grace. 'Even professional liars and fantasists can tell the truth sometimes.'

'And what am I?' she asked, before she'd considered if the question might not be a little reckless.

'Are you asking me if you're a liar or a fantasist?'

'Am I work or pleasure?'

'I'll tell you what you are, Anna Cantrell,' Harry said, recovering his composure. 'You are making me late for a meeting.'

He went through the details of the plan once more to make sure she'd got everything in her head. When he was sure she had the script right, he said, 'I'll give you an emergency passport when I pick you up at the Hotel Adlon.'

'You're our saviour, Harry. You're a good man.'

'I'm just doing what any agent runner is meant to do: looking after his investment.'

On the spur of the moment, Anna kissed him on the cheek. 'I've never thought of myself as an investment.'

Turning to go, Taverner stopped. 'Second thoughts—' he announced.

For an awful moment, Anna feared he was going to change his mind. But that was at odds with the faint smile on his lips.

'What is it?' she asked.

'I'm being frightfully ungallant. You've been a conscientious, diligent source, Anna Cantrell. We should mark your retirement in a fitting manner. I'll need a day to sort out the passport. But let me present it to you with our thanks for what you've done for us so far.'

She wondered if he meant some sort of ceremony at the embassy. 'That's very kind, Harry, but we really do have to—'

Catching the quizzical look on her face he cut in, laughing. 'What I meant was – allow me to book a table at the Hotel Adlon. Just the two of us. Best bib and tucker and all that. You do cut the rug, don't you?'

Anna stared at him. The Adlon was the best hotel in Berlin. 'Are you asking me out on a date, Harry Taverner?'

He gave her a look of imperishable innocence. 'Dancing at the Adlon – work or pleasure? You decide. Tomorrow evening at nine alright with you? I'll sort out the reservation – perks of being a diplomat and all that.'

'I suppose so,' she said, unable to stifle a grin. 'Or rather: yes. *Definitely*. That would be lovely.'

And with that, he turned and walked away in the direction of the embassy.

It was like an order to abandon ship, only stretched out over forty-eight hours. Man the lifeboats! We're sinking! – but not quite yet.

Saying goodbye to friends was out of the question. All her photography equipment would have to remain – save for the Leica that Rex's money had bought her. She couldn't leave that. Caching away the essentials for the journey without Hannelore noticing required the skills of a master pickpocket. Most of Bär's and Antje's toys would have to stay, though that was bound to lead to tears later. But toys could be replaced.

Not once did Anna question the morality of separating the children from their father. Saving Bär from growing into one of the blond-haired, juvenile automatons that marched about with their swastika armbands, or Antje into a dead-eyed ice maiden in white vest and dark shorts from the *Bund Deutscher Mädel*, the League of German Girls, was a cause whose morality was beyond doubt.

As the hours passed, her nervousness worsened. She had to check herself from biting Hannelore's head off at the least provocation, in case the girl cottoned on to the fact that something was afoot. To Anna's surprise – and relief – Marion discovered in herself a measure of maternal efficiency that her daughter had thought long forgotten.

On the morning of her assignation at the Adlon, a formal invitation card arrived at the apartment. It was dropped through the letterbox by someone other than the local postman: the morning post had already arrived. The card purported to invite her to a soirée arranged by the Associated Press, at the Adlon, starting at eight that evening. She knew it was a clever ploy by Harry to cover their meeting, because the last line read: *Enjoy mixing work with pleasure.*

'I'll have to go,' she told Hannelore. 'If I don't turn up, they'll think I'm being rude. I won't get my pictures published. Then I'll be in trouble with Dr Goebbels, too.'

That evening, as she did most evenings, she helped Hannelore put the children to bed. She took a bath and started to get herself ready. It felt strange, putting her make-up on, doing her hair, choosing what dress to wear, all for a man who was neither Luka nor her husband. But it was undeniably exciting. To calm her nerves, she went into the lounge to put some music on the gramophone: Billie Holiday's 'If Dreams Come True'. It was the only record of hers left in the apartment. She kept it hidden beneath a sheet of brown paper in her underwear drawer. Ivo had smashed the rest.

The taxi dropped Harry Taverner at the canopied entrance of the Hotel Adlon on Unter den Linden at a quarter to nine. On the ride from his apartment, he'd listened impassively while the driver railed against the young Jew who'd shot the German diplomat in Paris two days before. 'If the Führer wants my advice, I'd bury the lot of 'em,' he said as Harry paid the fare and stepped out onto the pavement.

Harry slammed the passenger door, cutting off the driver's parting: 'Heil Hitler!'

The Adlon's handsome façade glowed in the floodlights. The hotel was one of the most imposing buildings on a street where grand was commonplace, thought Harry, though the enormous swastika banners draped across its Prussian-neoclassical face did little to impress him.

He fished in his overcoat pocket for the reservation card he'd picked up earlier when he'd made the booking, and read it again in the yellow glare spilling from the hotel entrance:

THE HOTEL ADLON IS PLEASED TO WELCOME

Captain H Taverner

TABLE 12, 21.00 HRS

Dress: white tie
Dancing to the music of the Joe Bund Orchestra
9th November 1938

Below the date, the maître d' had written: *And guest.*

Harry knew the evening would cost him more than he cared to think about. There was no way to claim it back on expenses. It would have to be potato noodles for the rest of the month. But it was worth it; he was sure of that. There was something about Anna Cantrell that had already begun to captivate him. It wasn't her beauty – though there was no denying *that.* He had done everything he could to remain detached and professional, but he couldn't deny that whenever they met, he found himself more pleasantly unsettled than the last time. Whether she felt the same, he couldn't tell. She was part American, and Americans didn't do flirtation the way the English did. They were too open, too confident. It might just be friendliness.

But she was just so damned fascinating. Take her upbringing. It was so utterly unlike the closed, genteel world of the Devon market town he'd grown up in, with its tweedy certainties that the country was going to the dogs and probably had been for two hundred years, that Labour would ruin everything if given half a chance, that abroad was a dangerous place – save for the empire, which was best kept in check by brave fellows in khaki with rifles, a squadron of fighter planes, and the occasional stiffening visit by the Royal Navy… It was almost beyond his imagination to picture a childhood spent in Hollywood. But most of all, he admired Anna Cantrell's determination and strength of character. He couldn't think of more important qualities for an agent.

The doorman greeted him with a courteous *'Guten Abend, mein Herr.'* Harry pushed through the revolving doors and into a glittering cavern of honey-gold marble pillars, Turkish rugs and polished glass on which no thumbprint would survive ten seconds before someone rubbed it off with a chamois leather cloth. In the centre of the vast lobby was a fountain that wore an extraordinary collar of tusked elephant heads in black stone halfway up its central stem. Around it swam a shoal of young bellboys dressed like grooms from a Ruritanian royal court, complete with white gloves and peaked hats.

Harry checked in his coat and hat at the cloakroom and waited for Anna to arrive. Beneath the chandeliers Berlin's great, good, not so good and positively downright unpleasant milled. Most of the men were in tails, save for those in crisp military uniforms. The women looked as though they'd climb over each other's backs to get near the *prominenten*. Harry observed a deal of back-slapping, hand-kissing, even heel-clicking. Despite enduring more embassy functions than he cared to remember, he still felt an idiot, standing there in tie and tails like a stage magician preparing to pluck a bunch of tulips out of nowhere.

Flowers! Damn it – I should have brought flowers.

Harry looked around. To his relief, no one was brandishing anything more floral than a boutonnière in the lapel. Panic over.

Anyway, she'd think I was trying to play the lounge lizard.

When Anna walked through the door, for an instant Harry didn't recognize her. She was wearing a crêpe-de-chine, halter-neck ballgown the colour of fine claret. Bare shoulders. Slender arms. With her hair worn up, the lobby lighting gave her long neck a sinuous grace as she turned her head, seeking him out. She wore her coat over her arm, and Harry guessed she'd taken it off under the awning to make an entrance. He half expected the lobby to blaze with the firing of camera flashlights.

She could have been a movie star, he thought. Anna Cantrell might have left Hollywood when she was eight, but Hollywood hadn't left her. It had simply waited for her to grow up.

'Are you sure it's secure here, Harry?' she teased, as she gave him a chaste kiss on each cheek in the German style. 'There seems to be a lot of men all dressed in the same disguise. Do you think they're watching us?'

'They're undoubtedly watching *you*,' he replied into her ear.

They drank daiquiris in the bar and talked of New York, as if that night was simply the follow-on from their first meeting in Central Park, and the two and a half years in between had never happened.

In the restaurant, Harry had chosen a table with security in mind. Table twelve was set discreetly beside a marble pillar, its back to one of the arched, mirrored panels on the wall. No one could approach unobserved. The nearest table was just far away enough for the diners sitting there not to be able to eavesdrop. Not that Harry expected interruption, but he had learned to consider such things when out in public. Besides, the table's position offered a measure of intimacy he found pleasing.

The Adlon's kitchens were renowned, yet, as he ate, Harry barely remembered what he'd ordered. He was falling under a spell, and he knew it. And Anna, too, was soon forgetting – for the first time since only God knew when – the tribulations that assailed her. The orchestra struck up 'They Can't Take That Away From Me', and before they knew it, they were together on the dance floor.

'Fancy that,' she said into his lapel. 'They're playing music written by a Jew. Let's hope Goebbels hasn't booked a table tonight. It would put him off his soup.'

'I love this song,' Harry said, as he took her in his arms and tried to pretend her perfume and the heat of her weren't affecting his judgement.

'It's from *Shall We Dance*. Have you seen it?'

'Three times,' Harry admitted. 'Fred Astaire's a bit of a hero.' He looked down at his polished black Oxfords. 'Me, I'm just a clodhopper, I'm afraid.'

'You're doing fine,' she said, laughing.

'The song seems rather appropriate, don't you think?'

'How so?'

He quoted one of Astaire's lines. '"Well, tomorrow we'll all be straightened out. You'll be on your way, and I'll be on my way..."'

Anna smiled into his shoulder and gave Ginger Rogers' response: '"Where?"'

'"Oh, I've got to get back to being a bachelor again..."'

Taking her cue, Anna responded, '"I hope you enjoy your gaiety..."'

'You know it, too,' Harry said admiringly.

'I should do. I saw it *four* times. Rex was one of David Abel's cameramen. Do you know the next line?'

Harry lifted his head and grinned as he delivered Astaire's words: '"Thanks. I hope you enjoy your divorce."'

Anna laid her head against his neck. 'Like you said, seems rather apposite, doesn't it?'

The band swung into 'Begin the Beguine.' They danced on in silence for a while before Harry said, 'Why didn't we do this at the start, instead of at the end?'

'Because in real life they don't give you the script before you start shooting.'

When they had danced their fill and returned to the bar for more daiquiris, Harry reached into his jacket pocket and drew out a small pamphlet of German poetry. He handed it to Anna. She could feel the outline of the emergency passport through the cheap paper.

'I can't thank you enough, Harry,' she said, transferring it to her clutch bag. 'You're a lifesaver. Literally.'

It was two o'clock when they stepped out of the hotel, arm in arm. Despite Harry's attempt at professional detachment, he was dangerously close to suggesting they take a taxi to his apartment. And Anna would have accepted; she was feeling exactly as she had that night at the hotel bar in Munich, when she'd wished it was Harry inviting her to his room and not that dreadful bore from the *Neue Zürcher Zeitung.*

But the Adlon's elegant interior had provided luxurious insulation from what had been happening elsewhere in Berlin that night.

They walked out beneath the hotel canopy and into mayhem.

A small crowd of the Adlon's customers had gathered outside the hotel. They were peering and pointing down Unter den Linden. A truck raced past packed with men wearing swastika armbands, their faces twisted in a mix of excitement and rage. Harry and Anna heard the cry '*Juden raus!*' – 'Jews out!' – as they swept by. From somewhere not far away came the crash of breaking glass. A distant plume of fire backlit the bare lime trees.

'What's happening?' Harry asked the doorman.

'Ernst von Rath died of his wounds,' the man said. 'I heard it on the radio. Dr Goebbels made a speech – if we want to take our revenge on the Jews, the police have been told not to stand in our way. I'm off shift in ten minutes – I hope there'll still be a few windows left to smash, and a few of the bastards left for a good kicking.'

The Berlin apartment. 1989

Elly Taverner studied her father's face. His eyes were fixed on something far away, and she guessed he was seeing his younger self, standing beneath the Adlon's awning, Anna Cantrell on his arm. Or perhaps he was imagining raw hatred as a tangible, menacing entity stalking the streets of the city he loved. The clarity of his memory was extraordinary, which only made the knowledge that he was slowly losing it more devastating for her. She leaned across the bed and brushed a wave of white hair from over his ear.

'*Kristallnacht*, the night of broken glass,' he said, as if to someone she couldn't see. 'After that night there was no question of what lay in the future for the Jews in Germany. All those shops looted, the schools and the synagogues burned... The death toll was relatively low, but of course it was just the beginning.'

Elly swung herself off the bed. 'You really should sleep, Daddy. You must be exhausted.'

But he looked more vigorous than she'd seen him in a long while.

'Just make me a coffee, Puffin – the Dallmayr,' he said. 'The tin's in the first cupboard on the right, bottom shelf.' As Elly headed for the kitchen, she heard Harry call after her: 'And you'd best make it strong, please, Puffin. There's a lot more to tell you. Dancing at the Adlon was only the start of it.'

Fourteen

'Did Frau Wolff enjoy her evening?' Hannelore asked, when Anna surfaced at half-past ten the next morning.

'Yes, thank you,' Anna said, taking the proffered cup of coffee. 'It was just a business function, all very ordinary, really.'

As she drank, she wondered if Hannelore would scuttle away to write down her reply in a notebook. Evidence for the prosecution's opening address: *The accused claimed she was at a work engagement, when in fact she was dancing with a handsome English spy and is therefore a traitor to the Reich. Regarding the aforesaid foreign agent, the accused admits to feeling emotionally conflicted.*

Putting on her best face, Anna prepared herself for the escape. As planned, she dispatched Hannelore on an errand to Wildau, where Marion's doctor friend lived, to collect medicine for a sudden fictitious attack of sciatica. The journey would take a good two or more hours to complete.

'Be careful, Hannelore,' Anna said as the maid left. 'It was pretty dreadful on the way home in the taxi. Don't get caught up in the riots.'

'Serves those swine right,' said Hannelore from the doorway. 'They've been sucking our blood for far too long.'

'I think the stupid girl means swine like me,' Marion said from her bedroom, loudly enough for Hannelore to hear. 'How's this goddamn country going to function when it's got rid of all the bright people?'

They packed hurriedly, taking turns to keep Bär and Antje occupied. When they'd finished, Anna lugged the cases downstairs and bore them to the corner of Stausberger and Palisaden, where she waited for a taxi.

Across the street was a ransacked shop, the frontage smashed in, the pavement littered with debris. A sign hung by one corner over the empty window; Anna had to tilt her head to read it: *Issur Feigenbaum & Sons, Fashionable Footwear*. Beneath it stood a respectable-looking man in a smart raincoat, his back to her, his legs slightly apart. She realized with revulsion that he was relieving himself over the wreckage. When he'd finished, he turned to walk away, saw her, shrugged and gave her a thumbs-up sign on the assumption she approved.

It took a while for a taxi to arrive, but eventually a black sedan with a narrow chequerboard stripe beneath the windows pulled over to her wave. The driver helped her with the cases. 'Not a good day for a young lady to be out and about,' he said, giving her a hand onto the running board. 'I don't know what's got into this place, I really don't. It shames us.'

Despite the driver's apparent disgust at what had happened to his city, Anna couldn't bring herself to speak during the drive to the Lehrter Bahnhof. She felt as though she was tiptoeing through a pack of wild animals, trying not to look as if she might be tempting to eat. They passed a synagogue that was still billowing smoke through the front door. A fire engine was parked nearby, but the hoses were trained on the adjacent buildings, cooling the brickwork while the fire burned itself out inside. She saw a crowd of people – no different from any she'd met in Berlin during her life there – looting a clothes store with the word *Jude* and a crude Star of David painted on the glass. Knowing there was nothing she could do, she had to turn her head away when they passed an elderly man being beaten up while uniformed Orpo officers stood by laughing.

All the way to the station – where she checked the suitcases into the left-luggage office – and back again, Anna cursed herself for not having brought the Leica with her. She knew that she was watching the unfolding of a world-changing event, and that not to record it would be a betrayal of everything she aspired to. Which was why, when she arrived back at the apartment, she did what any photojournalist worthy of the name would have done: she went back out into the Berlin streets with her camera.

Anna reasoned she was safe enough. There were dozens of international journalists in Berlin that day; the propaganda ministry hadn't managed to expel them all. She imagined there was safety in numbers. And, anyway, taking pictures wasn't against the law – not yet. If she was stopped, she'd invoke the name of Joseph Goebbels. The Orpo weren't to know she was no longer taking commissions from the propaganda ministry.

As she went in search of subjects, Anna felt much as she had in Vienna during the February War: the thrill of being present while history was made or changed, of bearing witness, of being the lens through which others would see the extraordinary and the momentous.

Seen close up, the aftermath of *Kristallnacht* was terrifying. Anna could almost taste the hatred and the violence on the cold November air. She could smell the carbonized exhalation of burned-out buildings; there was dried blood and broken glass to avoid wherever she walked. There were faces flushed with brutality, into whose eyes she could not bear to look. There were no victims to be seen – they'd all gone into hiding. Or if they weren't hiding, they were being arrested, carted off to the new internment camps at Buchenwald, Dachau and Sachsenhausen.

Anna fired off two rolls of film. By the time she'd finished, she no longer considered it a mere record, but a testament.

She was standing by a ransacked gallery on the Friedrichstrasse, reloading the Leica, when a black Mercedes Benz pulled up next to her. She never even noticed it approaching – the thoughts in her head were too loud for her to hear its engine. And the slamming shut of its doors only registered as she found herself face down on the cold leather of the back seat.

Fifteen

Anna knew they'd arrived at the headquarters of the Reich Security Main Office because she'd once photographed the outside of the building for a propaganda ministry puff-piece. She also knew it housed some of the most unsavoury and downright dangerous departments in the Nazi orbit, including the Gestapo.

The stony-faced, trench-coated goons who'd snatched her off the street had refused to answer her questions, though save for bundling her into the car they hadn't hurt her. Now, they frogmarched her through the front entrance, one on either side and one behind, in case she tried to struggle free and bolt.

The lobby was vast, cold and echoing, peopled by unsmiling men in grey suits and women with expressions that could chisel granite. Anna's greatest fear was that they would take her below ground. Everyone knew the Gestapo had cells there where they practised their skills at amateur orthodontics. The thought of upstairs wasn't much more comforting – windows could be fallen out of.

A sallow young man with oiled hair and a central parting escorted them up several flights of stairs and along a linoleum-tiled corridor, depositing her at last in a plain, dingy room on the fourth floor that smelt of stale cigarette smoke and disinfectant. She knew there was no point in asking why they'd brought her there, or demanding they release her. The conventions and rules of her world did not apply there.

'Give me your wristwatch,' the young man said. It was the first time anyone had spoken to her since she was abducted, other than to demand to see her papers.

'Do I get it back?' she asked.

'What do you take us for, Frau Wolff? Common thieves?' He held out his hand and waited.

She knew the goons would take it by force if she resisted, so Anna unclipped the watch and handed it over. He put it his pocket and took her camera bag from one of the thugs who'd thrown her into the car.

'That's an expensive Leica camera,' Anna objected. 'And it's precious to me.'

With supreme indifference, he said, 'Please wait here,' as if she had a choice. Then he followed the goons out of the room, locking her in.

Their footsteps faded away down the corridor, leaving a silence that she knew was designed to intimidate. She understood the way the game was to be played; by now, there could be no one left in Berlin who didn't. First, there would be a long period of solitude and silence, the perfect conditions for fear to grow in the imagination. Then would come the questioning, not necessarily violent at first, but relentless, persistent, designed to wear you down. She might be there for days. At some point they'd put her in a cell with no mattress and a ceiling light that never went out.

In her mind she pictured Marion and the children fretting in the apartment, and the Paris train pulling out of the Lehrter Bahnhof without them. By the time she was released, Ivo would be back from Munich.

She remembered what Harry had said to her at the Goethe monument: *What in God's name possessed you to come to the embassy?… The Gestapo have people watching us…*

Was that why she was there? Had they seen her go in? Had they guessed she'd been working for the British Secret Intelligence Service? They wouldn't need evidence to prove it; they could just beat a confession out of her. That's how they worked. Everyone knew the score.

Then she remembered something else Harry had said, when she'd had her interview with him and Major Warwick in Vienna: *If it's the danger that concerns you, the worst that could happen is that they'd expel you…*

But what could be worse than expulsion? She'd lose Bär and Antje. She cursed herself for the undeniable stupidity of what she'd done. In thrall to her selfish desire to be a photojournalist, she had put everything at risk.

The room was designed to make waiting an ordeal, a time in which the germ of fear could multiply. There were no notices on the walls, no pictures – not even one of the Führer. The only furniture was a metal desk with three tubular-metal chairs set around it. The desk was bare: no telephone, no blotter, no pen case, not even a lamp for shining in your eyes while they screamed their questions at you.

Anna looked around at the walls painted a sickly dun colour. At the door with its chipped varnish, a glass panel above letting in an insipid light. At the scratched lino floor. Nothing to interest the senses. Nothing to stimulate. A tired, nondescript box, designed to send you mad after half an hour. She sat down on one of the hard metal chairs and braced herself for the ordeal.

Anna had glanced at her watch when she'd taken it off her wrist – it had read 3.20 p.m. After what she reckoned was about forty-five minutes, though it could well have been only ten, she caught herself picking at the skin on her fingertips.

It's working, she thought. I shouldn't be surprised; it probably works with everyone – even the brave, eventually.

When, at last, she heard footsteps approaching, the noise scared the life out of her. It sounded like an army on the march, a harsh, rhythmic drumbeat on the lino. Anna hurriedly returned to her seat. She didn't want whoever was coming in to see that she'd been unnerved.

The door opened. In the corridor she could see the young man with the oiled hair. He was carrying her Leica camera.

Thank God, she thought, it's all been a mistake. He's going to apologize and send me on my way.

But then he stood deferentially aside. Anna saw someone else standing behind him. Someone she recognized.

'Well, this is a surprise, Anna,' said Manis Möller.

Anna was on her feet before Ivo's friend had taken more than two paces into the room. A cold, hard claw seemed to have gripped her windpipe, stopping off her breath. Why was he here? Had Ivo sent him? Had Hannelore Lange worked out what she was up to? Was her husband even now striding down the corridor? Was this hateful little room, this chillingly nondescript corridor, where her dreams were destined to die, choked out on the scuffed linoleum?

'I hear you've been abusing our renowned German hospitality,' Möller said. 'Tut, tut. How ungrateful of you.'

If he thought he was being menacing, he was way off the mark. To Anna, he looked more like a seller of dirty post-cards.

'I don't know what you mean.'

Möller raised her Leica camera, as if it might be evidence for the prosecution. 'Taking photographs to make us look bad.'

Anna couldn't stop a bitter laugh from escaping her mouth. '*Look bad?* Have you been out on the streets, Herr Möller? Me shooting a few snapshots isn't going to make things look worse than they already are, you can take my word for that. Is my husband here?'

'Ivo is in Munich. I thought you knew that.'

A flicker of hope stirred inside her. If she could talk her way out of this, maybe all was not yet lost. 'And I thought you knew he was on important Party business,' she said. 'I'm sure he's got enough on his plate without learning you've taken it into your head to have me arrested.'

Möller gave a weaselly little laugh. 'We don't arrest people on a whim, Anna. Only if they're suspected of committing a crime. *Have* you committed a crime, Anna?'

'Alright, I confess,' she said, trying to sound brave. 'This morning I put on grey shoes with a brown skirt.'

'Very droll,' Möller said. 'Must be that American chutzpah we all admire so much.'

'Why are you here, asking me questions, Herr Möller? I thought you were something to do with the Reich Chamber of Culture. What are you doing in the Reich Security Main Office, where the Gestapo is based?'

His answering smile had a nasty chill to it.

'That's the wonderful thing about art, Anna,' he said. 'It's universal. It crosses borders.'

Oh God, she thought. Borders. Trains to Paris. He knows.

Möller gestured for her to sit. He walked around to the other side of the desk and laid the Leica on the metal top. He remained standing. He looked as cadaverous as Goebbels himself, only taller, and without the charm.

'I've always thought Ivo was a little unwise to propose marriage to you,' he said. 'And by what he tells me now, I was right.'

'The state of my marriage has nothing to do with you, Herr Möller.'

'It does if you're working against the interests of the state.'

She held his gaze, refusing to let him see how frightened she was. 'I don't know what you mean.'

'You came with such a good recommendation from Frau Koppitz,' he said wearily. 'Reichsminister Goebbels was most taken with you. I, however, was never quite so sure. I've been keeping my eye on you, Anna Cantrell.'

She remembered the man she'd seen from her bedroom window, the way he'd lingered. Confident. Arrogant. Making a point. It dawned on her now that he must have been Möller's man.

'I imagine that would have been a trifle tedious for you, Herr Möller. I live a very ordinary life.'

'Ordinary?' he echoed, with a lift of one thin eyebrow. 'I didn't appreciate that dancing the night away at the Hotel Adlon with an English diplomat was so commonplace.'

Anna knew her shock must be clearly visible to him in her eyes, even if she'd managed to keep the muscles in her face still.

'Oh, yes,' he continued. 'Herr Taverner – listed with the Foreign Ministry as a passport control officer. You were seen entering the British embassy. Then, later, entering the Adlon Hotel with this Englishman. Can you explain that – as an American?'

It was Rex who saved her. Rex, who'd spent his younger life thinking on his feet to stay one step ahead of trouble. Rex, who'd passed the skill to his daughter.

A little bit of this... for a little bit of the other. Don't tell the rozzers... and don't tell your mother...

'My father's English,' she said. 'Ask Ivo, if you want. Harry Taverner is a cousin. We hadn't seen each other in years. I heard he was in Berlin. We decided to celebrate the reunion in style. Anything wrong with that?'

Möller considered this with his cheeks sucked in, which made his face look even more skeletal. But he seemed convinced. He pointed to the Leica on the desk. 'To whom were you planning to send the photographs you took with this camera?'

'I hadn't thought about it.'

'The international press?'

'I'm a photojournalist. That's what I do: try to have my pictures published.'

'In publications that bear hostility towards the Reich.'

'In publications that tell the world what's going on.'

'And what exactly do you think is "going on"?'

Anna let out a cynical laugh. 'I'm sorry. I must have got it wrong. All those smashed-up buildings and burned-out synagogues... I hadn't realized it was all part of Herr Speer's plan to construct a shiny new Berlin for the Führer. I've seen the photos of the models in the newspapers. It'll look wonderful when it's finished.'

Möller stared at her for a while. Then he reached down and picked up the camera. He opened the back, letting it hang down, and snatched out the film. The roll curled around his fingers like an amorous, celluloid snake and then slipped to the floor. Anna imagined the images it contained – each one a record of the wanton destruction of someone's life, their business, their faith, their future – extinguished in the light of this squalid little room. And although she'd only been an observer to the destruction, she felt – yes – grief.

Möller put the Leica back on the desk, lens upwards. He reached inside his jacket and from a belt holster withdrew a small, black semi-automatic pistol.

Dear God, he's going to shoot me, Anna thought, feeling the strength flood out of her and the fear surge in. If they break people's bones in the basement and boast about it in public, why shouldn't they shoot people in broad daylight in pokey little rooms? Maybe that's why this one stinks of disinfectant.

'You have other rolls of film?' Möller said, pointing the pistol directly at her face. 'Give them to me.'

Faced with the indifferent, soulless eye of the pistol's barrel, Anna complied. She reached into the pocket of her coat and handed over the other roll she'd shot.

She felt like a coward.

A long time later, she would look back on this moment and understand why so many went to their deaths without resistance. Fear, she learned that day, could paralyse a person as efficiently as curare poison on the tip of a blowpipe dart.

Möller snapped off the top of the container, pulled out the film and waved it like a banner to destroy what was on it. Then he let it drop to the floor, where it wrapped itself around the other roll, as if for comfort.

Flipping a catch on the Sauer pistol, Möller let the magazine slide into his cupped hand. He shoved the magazine into the back pocket of his trousers and checked that the chamber of the pistol had no round in it. When he was sure there was no danger of accidental discharge, he took the pistol by its barrel and, with a powerful swing from the shoulder that seemed impossible for such a gaunt frame, brought the butt down onto the camera.

The blow sounded like artillery fire landing close by. The table bounced. Anna jumped with the shock. Then Möller swung again. Blow after blow. Until Anna, her eyes tightly shut, had lost count. Smashing the Leica that Rex had bought her to smithereens.

No one came to see what the noise was. No one even peered around the door. When the appalling racket stopped, Anna could hear the faint clatter of typing coming from a nearby office. She assumed that in this place the staff took the sound of violence as part of the soundtrack to their everyday life.

'Get out of here,' Möller said, pointing to the door. 'Think yourself fortunate that Reichsminister Goebbels has ordered that Jews with foreign passports shouldn't be molested. *For the time being*. If it were up to me—'

But he couldn't be bothered to finish the sentence. And Anna wasn't going to wait around for him to find the energy.

The strength in Anna's legs seemed to have deserted her. She wobbled like a drunk – the first taxi driver she hailed had been wary of letting her into his cab. On the drive back to the apartment she went through all the possibilities, none of them encouraging.

Hannelore had known about her plan from the start and had betrayed her. She'd been picked up because the man she had seen that night from her bedroom window had been sent to report on her every move, and therefore knew about her visit to Harry at the embassy. And her trip to the station, carrying the packed bags.

But then, she reasoned, Möller would never have let her go. She'd still be in that awful room – or somewhere even worse.

In the end she concluded that she'd been picked up simply because she'd been spotted taking embarrassing pictures in the wonderful new Germany that Ivo had so longed to help create.

To her relief, Hannelore seemed to take Anna's explanation for her late return – that she'd been caught up in the rioting – at face value. Even so, Anna slept barely an hour that night.

The next morning, Harry's call came through exactly on time.

'I'm so sorry you didn't get the photos,' Anna said, just as his plan required her to. Then, before he could reply, she added, 'I had a bit of a problem yesterday.'

'Should I be concerned? About the consignment, that is.'

'I don't think so. I just got caught up in the disturbances.'

'Do we need to talk? My publishers are on a tight deadline. Will it require changing?'

'I don't think so,' Anna assured him. 'Remind me to tell you all about it some time.' She rang off, confident that he had understood her.

Hannelore was despatched to the post office with the envelope. She went without raising a single objection, which told Anna she was probably right in her judgement that Hannelore was innocent of all accusations – except for the one about being as dumb as a washing mangle.

'We're going to the train station, to see the locomotives. We may even get to ride on one,' Anna told Bär, who jumped at the news. Antje was too young to care where they were going, as long as getting there required her to spend a significant proportion of the journey in her mother's arms.

Harry had warned them not to take a taxi right up to the Adlon, because the doorman might recall them getting out. Anna asked to be dropped off in the Pariser Platz. As they walked towards the hotel, she could see, in the distance, columns of smoke rising into the overcast skies from Jewish properties that still smouldered. The taxi driver had told them the Jewish community in Germany was to be fined a billion Reichsmarks for the privilege of having their homes, business and synagogues destroyed. He seemed to think they should be made to pay more.

They waited at the agreed pickup point beneath one of the streetlamps, trying to look inconspicuous amongst the crowd, until Harry arrived in a borrowed embassy car. Anna had half expected him to still be wearing tails from the night before last.

'Is everything alright?' he asked as they climbed in. 'You sounded worried on the phone.' He was speaking German, just as Anna had asked him to, because she hadn't told Marion that an Englishman had arranged their escape for fear of her mother blowing a gasket. She'd have to tell Marion the truth when the train stopped at the French frontier and she would have to hand over a British passport. But that would be hours away.

'I think it's all fine,' she told him. 'When we reach the station, just keep an eye out for goons in leather coats.'

He grinned. 'You're with me, and I have' – he dropped from German into French – '*protection diplomatique*.'

At the Lehrter Bahnhof, to Anna's immense relief, there were no goons in leather coats. Harry carried their suitcases to the Deutsche Reichsbahn train. Bär was transfixed by the huge black locomotive that seemed to be exhaling steam like a bull preparing to charge. Antje began to cry. Anna asked Marion to take them aboard while she said farewell to the nice German friend named Heinrich who'd so helpfully got the tickets in advance and driven the family to the station, purely out of the goodness of his heart.

Marion gave her a look heavy with suspicion. 'There's an accent there somewhere I can't place. And he said "*protection diplomatique*".'

'He's from Alsace, Mama,' Anna explained, in a moment of inspiration.

When Marion and the children had disappeared into the carriage, Harry asked, 'Will you stay in Paris?'

'I guess so.'

A cloud of stream rose, spilling out on either side of her. Harry thought she looked like a Russian princess about to board the Trans-Siberian Express on a misty winter's night in tsarist Moscow.

'Keep in touch.'

'I might,' she said teasingly. Then, relenting, 'You've been an angel, Harry Taverner. You really have. I'll have to come up with some idea of how to repay you.'

Anna gripped the handlebar beside the door, about to step inside the carriage. Then she paused, let go, stepped up to Harry and kissed him at the edge of his mouth.

It was fleeting enough so that for a long time afterwards, it was hard for either of them to decide whether it was work or pleasure.

By the time Anna reached a conclusion the train was speeding through the Saarland on its way to the French border.

Sixteen

Paris. 1938–1940

Marion took to Paris with such gusto that within days of their renting a pleasant apartment on the Left Bank, close to the Musée Rodin, she was lamenting, 'To hell with Vienna, honey, we should have come straight here from New York!' Several of her old friends had ended up in the city, having fled the Nazis' purge of artists they considered degenerate.

To Anna, it was as if someone had turned the lights on again. On offer were all the vibrant colours in which Berlin and Vienna had been painted before totalitarianism's monochrome palette covered over their souls. There was real American jazz played by black musicians at Le Hot Club. There was cabaret at the Carrousel on the Rue Pierre Fontaine, where Josephine Baker had arrived like a prairie tornado at the start of her career. There was dancing at Bullier's. Whenever Anna took in a Hollywood movie at the Grand Rex or the Marignan on the Champs-Élysées, the accompanying newsreels were a revelation: not a rabidly anti-Jewish scene to be found anywhere.

Anna felt like someone released after a long prison sentence for a crime they hadn't committed. The world seemed familiar yet refreshingly different.

My dear Harry,

I lack the words with which to thank you for all you've done for us. Without you, I dread to think how things would have turned out. I worry about you remaining in that awful city, amongst those dreadful, strutting bullies. I know it's your job, but please don't take any foolish chances – I couldn't bear to think of anything bad happening to you.

I'm sorry I gave up on the work you wanted me to do in Berlin. I know it was in a good cause, but like they say, if you lie down with dogs you wake up with fleas. Besides, it's clear that my husband and his awful friends had started to see through me.

I think often about the evening we spent together dancing at the Adlon. I was happier that night than I had been for a long time, and it was all down to you. If you're ever in Paris, I'd love to see you again. If you can contrive a convincing Irish accent, I'll tell Marion you're an acquaintance from Tipperary.

With my deepest gratitude,

Anna

She sent the letter to Herr Pfeiffer's photography shop in Berlin for onward delivery, fearing an envelope addressed to the British embassy might attract the attention of the Gestapo.

Ten days later, to her surprise, she received a reply.

My dearest Anna,

No need for thanks. All I did was drive you to the station. Glad to hear you're settling in.

Can't think of anything nicer than a few days in Paris,

but rather busy here at present. If and when I can make it, I'll be sure to wear my leprechaun costume.

Yours,

Seamus O'Taverner

Shortly after their arrival, Anna and Marion visited the American embassy and began the process of getting Anna's passport replaced. The staff were sympathetic. 'We've issued hundreds of emergency documents to Jewish refugees fleeing Germany and Austria,' the counter clerk told them. Until that moment, Anna had never considered herself a refugee.

When she wrote 'Cantrell' in the field for the applicant's surname, Marion went into a sulk that took days to dissipate. But Anna was adamant. If she was ever going to recover her career as a photojournalist, it would be under her father's name.

Bär, now almost four, and Antje, not yet two, took separation from their father in their stride. Ivo had never been a particularly demonstrative father. In Berlin, any tenderness he showed them had decreased with each passing month, his attention consumed by his work. Slowly, Anna's fear that Ivo would track them down began to fade.

Anna had not yet given much thought to divorce. She thought it likely that Ivo would be only too happy to grab the opportunity of ending his marriage to a *Mischlinge,* a half-blood. When things had settled down, she'd move to have the union dissolved, if she could find a lawyer prepared to keep her whereabouts secret.

One day, in late December 1938, in the apartment block's chilly lobby, Anna bumped into a young girl she'd noticed when they'd moved in. They started talking. The girl's name was Violette. She worked for several families in the block who couldn't afford, or didn't have the space, for a full-time maid or nanny. Hiring her gave Anna the chance to continue her photojournalism and make her own contribution to Marion's stipend. Scraping together enough to buy a battered, second-hand Rolleiflex Standard from a photography shop on the Boulevard Garibaldi, she wrote to Dorothy Thompson, who sent her the names of a few newspaper bureau chiefs who might be amenable to taking her work.

Violette, the antithesis of the bovine Hannelore, came with an unexpected benefit – for Marion, at least. Her uncle, one Claude Braudel, a physician, was an amateur artist of the avant-garde style. He was a terrible painter but a useful doctor, especially in the field of easing the maladies – real or imagined – of sensitive artists. To Marion, he was perfect: a cross between Matisse and a society dope dealer. She fell for him immediately.

Not that Paris was an island of peace and tranquillity. But in 1939, as spring approached, it would have been hard to find anywhere in Europe that was. In the apartment on the Rue Vaneau, Anna listened to the radio to keep herself informed. Mostly she tuned into the BBC from London, which annoyed Marion no end. But occasionally she let the knob settle on the Grossdeutscher Rundfunk in Berlin, where she inevitably caught excerpts of Hitler's manic speeches. When she did, it was like receiving an electric shock, and she would hurriedly spin the dial for something less alarming.

The looming threat of war was temporarily forgotten in July and August, when the family escaped the heat of Paris for the Languedoc, where Dr Braudel owned property near the coast above Perpignan.

'I know the sort of prescriptions you arrange for my mother, Doctor,' Anna said in a private moment, once Braudel's Delahaye sedan was safely parked and everyone else had got out, 'but if I see any hint of it during our vacation, or if my children should inadvertently come across anything that might endanger them, not even Dr Frankenstein will be able to reassemble what's left over of your corpse. Do I make myself clear?'

'You speak very much like your mother, Mademoiselle,' Braudel replied defensively. But he was true to his promise.

The vacation at the village house made Anna forget what was happening elsewhere in the world. Treks into the *garrigue* reminded her a little of the places Rex and Uncle László had taken her to on shooting days, when she'd been small. Sometimes Dr Braudel would take them down to Leucate where they would dine on mussels, langoustine or octopus fresh from the lagoon.

They had been back in Paris barely a week when, at the end of August, on her way back to the apartment from photographing the Luxembourg Garden in the sultry Parisienne dawn, Anna stopped at a news stand. Looking at the international press shelf, she noticed the previous day's British *Daily Telegraph*, flown in on the mail flight from London.

1000 TANKS MASSED ON POLISH BORDER screamed the headline. Anna bought the paper and read the report while she took her coffee at a nearby pavement café. The by-line told her it had been filed by an intrepid reporter named Clare Hollingworth, who had stopped her car on the German side of the frontier and spotted, hidden amongst the trees, row upon row of Panzers.

Anna imagined how Miss Hollingworth must have felt when she realized she'd stumbled on the scoop of the century. I'm going to feel like that one day, she told herself, as she drained the last drops of bitter espresso.

Any thoughts Anna had of leaving Europe and returning to America ended the very day war was declared. On 3 September, a German submarine torpedoed the passenger liner *Athenia* in the Western Approaches, with the loss of over one hundred passengers and crew. Some of them were European Jews, believing they were on their way to safety in Canada. Some of them were children. Anna slept not a wink that night, for fear of dreaming of Bär and Antje floating face down in the cold Atlantic.

In Paris, life seemed to go on just as before. The anglers still fished from the ivy-draped embankment opposite Notre Dame; the lights stayed on in the Pigalle; the girls still high-kicked at the Moulin Rouge. Only the occasion wail of an air raid siren – quickly followed by the 'all-clear' – and the clusters of men around the *Ordre de Mobilisation Générale* posters and outside the temporary *Bureaux Militaire* booths suggested there was a war on.

The children thrived. Dr Braudel appeared to be well on his way to becoming a permanent fixture in Marion's life. Anna began to relax.

This happy reprieve lasted all of nine months.

*

Refugees loading their possessions onto trucks on the Champs-Élysées, Paris.
Picture taken by Anna Cantrell. Rolleiflex Standard 621 camera. June 1940

There were about thirty of them and the terror showed in their faces. And they have reason to be terrified, Anna thought, as she framed the shot. She understood what it was like to have to escape the place you thought was your home, even if, when she'd left Ivo, it hadn't been under the threat of imminent bombing. The adults were trying their best to appear calm in front of their children as they hoisted their precious belongings over the tailgates of the trucks. A little girl of about Bär's age began to scream and was only comforted when the family dog was safely in her arms. Anna managed to take the shot of the child reaching out to embrace the pet even as her face was still contorted with despair. One human life amongst millions, about to find a temporary comfort when there was little of it to be had anywhere.

Anna knew it was millions, even if no one could truly capture the enormity of the catastrophe that had overtaken the country in just a few weeks. The roads of northern France were the proof, jammed with fleeing civilians and dispirited, defeated soldiery. She'd heard the stories – everyone had – of German aeroplanes strafing without mercy.

Anna was on her way back from the American embassy, where she'd gone to register the family's intention of moving to Dr Braudel's property in the Languedoc, when she'd come across the scene that demanded photographing. She was in a hurry, but it had been too dramatic to resist. Putting aside her natural reluctance to take pictures of other people's misfortune, she fired off a few more shots, telling herself she'd be in the same situation inside the hour, loading what would fit into Claude Braudel's green Delahaye.

Anna was putting the camera back in its case when she heard the screech of tyres. She turned and saw a drab green open-top car slide to a halt barely ten metres from her. The memory of how she'd been snatched from a Berlin street the day after *Kristallnacht* tore the strength out of her legs and sent an icy dagger plunging into her stomach.

Then she saw the driver and the passenger: the man at the wheel wore a civilian suit and looked as if he was melting in the summer heat, while his passenger, already halfway out of the car, was wearing khaki British army battledress. And because of that, it took Anna a moment to recognize him. But only a moment.

'Anna! Anna Cantrell! So, lady luck hasn't deserted Paris entirely,' Harry Taverner called as he loped towards her, his begrimed face breaking into a smile. He gave her a brotherly kiss on the cheek. 'Excuse the stink. It's a cheeky little scent called *parfum de guerre*. I haven't seen clean water and soap in days.'

Even the exhaustion clearly visible in his eyes couldn't put a dent in Harry Taverner's open face. The twist of fair hair that habitually fell over one temple was now plastered to his sweat-streaked forehead and the collar of his tunic was open – the tie missing in action, she presumed – but he still looked as cool and collected as an intrepid explorer in search of headwaters or a lost temple.

'Why, if it isn't Seamus O'Taverner,' Anna said, surprised by the comfort his sudden appearance gave her. 'I see the king's made you a general. No wonder the war's going so well.'

Harry laughed and touched the three pips on his shoulder. 'Just a lowly captain, I'm afraid. I'm hoping if I get out of here with my modesty still intact, they might make me a field marshal.'

'What are you doing in Paris?'

He looked hurt. 'I recall a letter – something about if I was ever in town, you'd like to meet up.'

Anna laughed. It was refreshing to meet someone who wasn't close to panic, someone who could lift you up even in dire circumstances. 'I didn't mean bring the whole German army with you,' she said. 'Seriously, I'd imagined you'd gone back to England when war was declared.'

'I did. But they sent me to France. Now I'm just trying to outrun the Boche like everyone else. What about you?'

'I've just been to the American embassy,' Anna explained. 'They're all staying put. They reckon the Nazis will abide by diplomatic convention. But, honestly, after what we witnessed in Berlin, we're heading south. Marion's doctor friend has a place near Perpignan, down by the border. It's very quiet. Back of beyond, really. But at least if the Germans come that far we can slip across into Spain.'

'Wise move,' he said. 'They seem unstoppable at the moment.'

'How long have we got?' Anna asked, glad to at last be speaking to someone who might know what was going on.

'Three or four days at most. The French government is leaving Paris today, for Tours. You'll be pleased to know that the Italians have decided to kick us when we're down. Mussolini wants the leftovers after Adolf's had his fill.'

'Will it be like Warsaw?'

'Hopefully not. They're declaring Paris an open city. It won't be defended.'

'Nice of them to give you a chauffeur,' Anna said, nodding at the driver who was still sitting behind the wheel. He was a good-looking fellow about Harry's age, with a full, feminine mouth and swept-back hair.

'Oh, that's just a friend from the embassy,' Harry said. He turned towards the car. 'Donald, meet Anna Cantrell.'

The driver gave her a languid wave. 'Hello, Anna,' he said, clearly eager to be on his way.

'Anna, meet Mr Donald Maclean.'

Anna waved back. 'Hello, Donald.'

Noticing his friend's impatience, Harry said, 'Can we give you a lift anywhere?'

'If the Rue Vaneau isn't out of your way…'

As they drove towards the apartment they passed almost every form of wheeled transport piled high with everything from quilted mattresses to live chickens.

To lighten the mood, Anna said, 'So, it's back home for Harry, then.'

'My orders are to head for Le Havre and jump aboard the first Royal Navy ship I see – if they haven't already scuttled back to Portsmouth.'

'Will I see you again?'

'I should bloody well hope so. If you make it to Spain, send me a postcard through the embassy in Madrid. Send it to "Clifford", post office box 371, London. That's Clifford with two *F*s.'

'And who the hell is Clifford?'

'I am. Well, I am when I'm at box 371.'

Anna began to search in her bag for the pencil stub she habitually carried for jotting down notes about photos she'd taken.

'Rather you didn't write it down, if it's all the same to you.'

'Ah,' Anna said. 'Of course. Silly me.'

When they pulled up outside the apartment, Anna noticed Marion was out on the balcony.

'Well, goodbye again, Anna Cantrell,' Harry said. 'And good luck.'

'Goodbye again to you, too, Harry Taverner.' Anna gave him a chaste kiss on the cheek, and waved at the departing car as Maclean whisked him away into the fleeing traffic.

'I recognized that fellow in uniform,' Marion said, when Anna entered the apartment. 'He's the guy who drove us to the railroad station in Berlin.'

Anna cringed. 'Yes, Mama,' she admitted.

Marion looked at her in confusion. 'Last time, he was a German from Alsace. Now he's a goddamned Limey. What's going on?'

Damn, thought Anna. I should have got out of the car and walked the last hundred metres.

Seventeen

11 November 1942
Languedoc-Roussillon, Vichy France

It was an unusually clear day for late autumn. From her bedroom window in the house they rented from Dr Braudel, Anna could see the sunlight and shadows lying like garlands across the drab green Corbières. It reminded her of childhood mornings with Rex, her father setting up his camera on a spot Uncle László had chosen for the day's filming in the Hollywood hills.

Going downstairs, she found Bär and Antje with Marion in the parlour. Her mother was teaching them how to paint elephants. Although only five, Antje's attempt was surprisingly good. Bär, who was now seven, was having more trouble. His looked more like an octopus.

It was four years since they had last seen Ivo. They no longer asked after him. Anna had begun to believe that the separation had caused them no lasting harm.

'Granny Mari is going to look after you for a while,' she told them, 'because Mama is going out to take some photos.'

They barely looked up from their painting, her goodbyes to them little more than a kiss bestowed to the crown of the head. Farewells always troubled her. Tempting fate, she thought. She was about to ask the children for a proper kiss, when Marion interrupted her.

'Be careful, honey,' her mother said. 'The Tramontane will be blowing like crazy up there.'

Tramontane, she thought. Harry will ask me about the weather – his all-clear signal. 'I'll be fine, Mama,' she said distractedly. 'I'll be back before you know it.'

Going to her photo cupboard, Anna loaded the Rolleiflex she had bought in Narbonne with a fresh roll of film and slipped the camera into her bag with a spare roll and the lenses she thought best for the conditions. Then she tied the belt of her blue woollen reefer coat and slung the camera bag over her shoulder.

She gave her mother a hug. Marion had been a little down this past week – Dr Braudel, whose holiday house they rented, had announced that Madame Braudel was proving intractable in the matter of a divorce. Then she went to the door with that purposeful stride she always adopted when going out on an assignment.

Marion watched her daughter go with a mixture of pride and infuriation. She admired Anna's strong streak of independence, which she liked to believe came directly from her – because to think it was anything to do with Rex Cantrell was something she still couldn't stomach. She admired her skill with a camera, which, again, she attributed to her own artistic abilities – Rex Cantrell had only ever filmed what the director told him to film.

It didn't occur to Marion Bauer that two decades hating a man who probably seldom gave her so much as a single thought was a terrible waste of years.

When Anna had gone, Marion spent a while playing with the children, because today was a public holiday – Armistice

Day – and their school was closed. Just as she had done with Rex, she had managed to expunge all thoughts of Ivo Wolff from any consideration of her grandchildren. Given all that had happened to them, they seemed happy and resilient. Bär was now seven and a half, Antje a few months shy of six. But the village was an unrewarding place for them. It was a backwater. When the war was over – whenever that might be – she would convince Anna to take them back to Paris.

Marion found some paper and a box of crayons and set the children to drawing. It pleased her that although Antje was two years younger than her brother, she drew with more confidence, more control. Bär soon got bored. 'I want to go to Marcel's house to play. His brother lets us sit on his motorcycle.'

'A little later, sweetie, when the wind dies down.'

Marion silenced the inevitable wail of protest before it began with a cautionary finger to her lips. 'Granny Mari needs to work,' she said.

Marion went to her bedroom and threw on the brightly stained smock she used for painting. Then, fetching her palette, paints and brushes from the top shelf in the kitchen, where they were stored safe from little hands, she sat herself down before the easel she had erected in the small conservatory at the back of the house. Her view of the back wall of the adjacent property was hardly inspiring, but today was not the day for hiking up into the hills to paint *en plein air*.

Marion didn't hear the two cars pull up outside because the house was a thick-walled *petit mas.* But the sudden hammering on the street door echoed clearly through to where she sat at the easel. So, too, did the shouted, *'Ouvrez-vous, c'est la police!'*

Marion's first thought was that they'd found out about Dr Claude's extra-curricular activities with his prescription pad. On her way to the front door she made a mental sweep of the house, but could think of nothing incriminating.

The two gendarmes were in dark blue uniforms and peaked, pillbox hats. That comforted her. *Les poulets*, the locals called them derisively. If it was anything serious, they sent detectives. And then Marion saw the two men in the field grey uniforms of German officers standing behind them.

Ivo Wolff pushed past into the house, leaving the other man to follow.

'Where is she, Bauer?' he snarled. 'Where's the half-blood bitch who took my children from me?'

For a moment, Marion was too shaken to speak. She turned her head, looking back into the house, as if the expression on her face might warn Bär and Antje. But it was already too late. The children were standing just three paces behind her, staring in frightened bewilderment at a father they barely recognized.

'She's not here,' Marion said. She turned back to Ivo, her mouth suddenly parched with fear. 'What do you want, Ivo? You're not welcome in this house. Leave us alone.'

'Where *is* she?'

'Up in the hills with her camera.' Marion looked at the gendarmes standing deferentially behind Ivo and Möller. 'And you'll need more than Abbott and Costello there to find her.'

Ivo pushed her out of the way. He knelt before Bär, who stared at him in bewilderment, not knowing how he should react. There was no pleasure in his eyes at seeing his father again.

'You've grown to be a fine, strong man, eh, Bernhardt?' Ivo said, reverting to German. 'A good Aryan, like your father and your grandfather.'

'Yes, sir,' said Bär doubtfully.

Marion's heart ached for the boy. He looked petrified by Ivo's immaculate iciness.

'And my little Antje!'

Antje stared at her shoes.

Ivo stood up. He towered over the two children. 'Bernhardt, take your sister and go with these policemen. There's a car waiting outside.'

'Where are we going… Papa?' Bär asked tremulously.

The smile Ivo gave him would have frozen a bushfire. 'To find Mama. Then we're all going to the seaside together for a special holiday.'

The two children gazed at their father with utter incomprehension. Marion guessed that the uniform had transformed Ivo in their eyes into a monstrous caricature of the man they had known. It had robbed him of any remnant of fatherly benevolence they might have remembered.

Ivo's leather-gloved palms smacked together loudly. The two children flinched.

'Do as I say. Hurry!'

'Yes, sir,' said Bär, swallowing to hide his terror. Then, with what Marion considered to be a bravery beyond his years, he took his sister by the hand and followed the gendarmes and Manis Möller out to the waiting cars.

'You can't take them, Ivo,' Marion said, almost pleadingly. 'It will break Anna; you know it will.'

'She should have thought about that before she abducted them.'

'She wanted a better life for them. What's wrong with that? I did the same for her when she was Bär's age.'

'A better life? Amongst deviants and drug addicts?'

For once, the bravado that had always masked Marion's insecurity deserted her. 'For pity's sake, Ivo, don't steal them.

Leave them with their mother. What can you possibly offer them?'

'The hope of a cure,' he said contemptuously. 'I was a fool to allow my family's blood to be tainted by marrying your daughter. I'm going to ensure that stain will be bred out of the line. They'll marry honest Aryans, have honest Aryan offspring. I'm saving them – not stealing them.'

'If it's money you want, you can have it. Give me just a few days.'

Ivo Wolff seemed to find the offer amusing. He jabbed one gloved finger at her.

'You may have been skulking away in this godforsaken backwater, but I'm assuming that even here you've heard about the round-ups in Paris. We're sending your kind to the east, Marion Bauer, for resettlement. I hear the Vichy authorities have a transit camp for Jews down the road at Rivesaltes. One more word from you and I'll make sure you're on the next train out. Understand?'

Marion thought for a moment he was going to hit her. She braced herself for the blow. But he simply turned on his heel to leave.

Ivo Wolff was out in the street when Marion's courage returned. Running to the door, she played the only card she had left.

'If you drive off with those children, Ivo Wolff, I'll make sure your bosses in Berlin learn how you spent years living off the generosity of the Bauer banking family – the *Jewish* Bauer banking family,' she called out. 'Do they know your mother-in-law is a Jew? Do they know your own children have a Jewish grandparent? How many of your precious German race laws have you broken, Ivo Wolff?'

The children were already in the car. Möller was holding the driver's door open. Ivo Wolff was barely a metre away from sliding in.

He paused. He seemed to spend a moment considering what Marion had said.

And then he turned and walked back towards the house.

Marion watched him approach. His face wore the expression of a man disappointed by some minor inconvenience.

As she stepped back, her son-in-law quickened his pace. And at the same time, the fingers of his right hand began to unfasten the cover strap of the leather holster he wore on his hip. Marion couldn't take her eyes off the leather skin of his glove moving over the knuckles. It lent his hand a life independent of the rest of him, as though it was a separate creature, quite apart from the man himself. There was a reptilian ease in the way it flexed and twisted.

And, in that instant, Marion Bauer knew the creature was going to kill her.

Three weeks later, a little after seven thirty on an overcast December morning, a Douglas Dakota aircraft of the British Overseas Airways Corporation lifted off the runway at Portela aerodrome to the north-east of neutral Lisbon. The scheduled service to Bristol was heading well out into the Bay of Biscay to avoid German fighters operating out of Bordeaux and Lorient. Aboard flight 777 that morning was the usual mix of military and civilian passengers: liaison officers, diplomats, businessmen and spies.

Harry Taverner and Anna Cantrell sat together at the rear of the aircraft. Harry was wearing a civilian suit. Anna was dressed in the same blue reefer coat in which she'd met him at the *capitelle* above the village. To the other passengers, they could have been a married diplomatic couple returning to England after a foreign posting – a couple going through a difficult passage in their marriage, because, as the aircraft climbed into the bumpy cloud cover, they barely spoke. After their hurried crossing into Spain and the subsequent journey into Portugal, there was little to say.

Anna stared out of the window into the grey void. She couldn't even see the plane's wingtip. Nothing but water droplets streaming past her eyes. It was as if all the colour, all the vivid brightness of Marion, of Bär, of Antje, had been washed away, leaving only the bare canvas behind.

Eventually the plane broke free of the clouds and sunlight flowed into the cabin. It brought Anna no cheer. She turned away, looking up at the mesh stowage above her head where a second-hand leather suitcase lay. It was filled with the few possessions she'd snatched from Dr Braudel's house before fleeing. And beside it lay the bag containing her battered, second-hand Rolleiflex camera.

I'm lost, she thought. I don't know where to go. I've become the subject of my own photographs: I'm a refugee once more.

The Berlin apartment. 1989

Harry Taverner stared at the flimsy, faded BOAC ticket he had taken from the portfolio case on the bed. Elly could see it still had a little blue sticker with the seat numbers attached, which bore the invitation: *Please present this to the steward upon boarding the aeroplane*. She waited for him to speak again. When he did, it was as if he was recounting something that had happened only yesterday.

'All the way from the Spanish border until we boarded the flight to England, I half expected her to make a bolt for it, to run back into France, go searching for Ivo and the children,' he said.

'I must confess I found her deep silence unnerving. I believed at first that it was her way of expressing her rage at me for forcing her to leave. But I was wrong. She was silent because with every cell of her body she was planning her revenge on Ivo Wolff. She'd accepted she couldn't alter what had happened, and that going after Ivo would probably only result in either her arrest or her death. But she was wise enough even then – courageous enough, I suppose – to know that she must wait, even if it might take years. I didn't appreciate until later that a mother's animalistic instinct to protect her offspring isn't always expressed with visible ferocity.'

'How do you know what happened inside the house?' Elly asked. 'The children and Möller were already outside, in the car. And you were up in the hills.'

'That's the one part of the story that Anna and I could only speculate upon. We went down into the village later, but at that moment I had my hands full up by the old stone *capitelle*, trying to stop Anna from giving us away. We both heard the shot, though faintly, because of the wind. But remember, Ivo once told Anna that he didn't buy into the Nazis' hatred of the Jews. He wasn't a natural killer, not like so many of the others. Therefore, I assume Marion had given him a reason to pull the trigger.'

'What happened after that?'

'After he shot her? Once the two cars had gone, I knew I had to let Anna return to the house, even if only for a few minutes. I don't mind telling you I was scared stiff there might be more Germans on the way. It took me a while to convince her that we had to get away across the border pronto. Anna was close to hysteria, and I can't say I blamed her. In the end, I managed to convince her that she'd have even less chance of getting Bär and Antje back if she was languishing in a Gestapo cell, or on a resettlement train to the east – and we all know now what *that* meant.'

Elly stifled a yawn. She felt dog-tired. She tried to imagine what it must have been like for Anna Cantrell to have her mother murdered and her children taken away, utterly unable to avert the catastrophe she was witnessing as it unfolded before her eyes. Even at this distance – almost fifty years – and having never known the woman whose life Harry was describing, she still felt a measure of emotional pain that brought her to the point of tears.

'You haven't shown me a picture of her yet,' she said. She pointed to the portfolio case. 'Have you got one in there?'

A tired laugh crawled out of the back of Harry's throat. 'Like a lot of photographers, she hated having her own picture taken. She never thought herself interesting enough to be the proper subject for a camera. But there's one in there somewhere. I'll dig it out in a minute.'

'What happened next? Do you feel up to telling me, or do you want to sleep?'

But Harry seemed to have no need of sleep. 'First there was a war to win,' he said. 'I helped Anna find a place with the Ministry of Information in London. Then she managed to get herself accredited as a war correspondent for some American newspapers. Of course, she wrote letters to the Red Cross in Paris and Berlin, seeking word of Ivo and the children, but they had to go via neutral countries, and she never received a reply. After the Normandy landings she went with the press corps to France. Her intention was to try to make it down to the village. She wanted to see if Dr Braudel had made a proper grave for Marion – she planned to buy a decent headstone if he hadn't. Instead, she was assigned to General Devers' US Sixth Army Group. And so she followed the front line down into Bavaria.'

Harry reached into the case and pulled out another photograph. He handed it to Elly. For the first time since he began his story, he was giving her a colour print. It showed a sea of people, as if the photographer had captured from the elevated stage an image of the audience at a rock concert. But on closer inspection, Elly saw they were dressed as if they'd hurriedly escaped a fire. Their grinning faces couldn't hide a crushing weariness.

She turned the picture over and read the typewritten label glued to the back: `Kimpelbeuren Displaced Persons Camp. Bavaria. July 1945.`

'There were eleven million displaced people in Germany and the formerly occupied countries of Europe that summer,' Harry said. 'Most of them trying to make their way home – if their homes still existed. Then there was the matter of almost eight hundred thousand deceased German civilians. How was Anna to know if Bär and Antje were amongst the living or the dead? And if they *were* alive, how was she to find them amongst so many other lost souls?'

Elly stared at the faces in the photograph. In the quiet of the apartment, she began to imagine the sleeping city around her losing its hard edges, the church spires and the apartment blocks, the offices and the museums, the shops and factories all crumbling into blackened ruins, the roads for miles around filling with ghostly columns of weary men, women and children – all searching for the surviving fragments of lives torn apart by war. Out of the silence she began to hear the tramp of tired feet, and the grinding of wheels on shattered roads.

PART THREE

Someone else's memories

Eighteen

Southern Germany, June 1945

The war had come late to Bavaria.

Sitting with her knees up in the back of the open-topped truck, Anna Cantrell could see in the distance pine-clad slopes and mountains with snow on their tops. She could almost imagine the countryside beyond the shimmering concrete ribbon of the autobahn as part of an innocent, untouched world.

But even here, in the ditch that ran alongside the road, nettles sprouted around the remains of strafed trucks and staff cars. A rusting German tank lay askew like a harpooned whale, its barrel angled towards the clear blue sky.

The workers Anna saw toiling in the fields beneath the blazing sun were mostly women. They wore the sleeves of their blouses rolled shoulder-high and scarves on their heads. There were few men to be seen, other than the old or the maimed. Three and a half million of them had not returned from the war; millions more languished in prisoner of war cages. The legions of slave labourers who'd replaced those called up to fight were slaves no longer – they were on their way home. From the speeding truck, she watched the endless columns of trudging, dusty refugees, pulling or pushing almost every conceivable means of transporting one's belongings – from horses, to children's perambulators and wooden sledges.

She resisted her eyes' desire to dissolve them into an amorphous mass, as the best shots came at you unexpectedly, like sniper fire.

Take the camel, for instance. Until she developed the film, Anna couldn't really be sure if she'd managed to capture the moment. Released – or liberated – from a zoo, the beast bore the possessions of its new owners in makeshift canvas panniers slung between its humps. It plodded obediently towards Nuremberg, led by a man in a dust-stained, double-breasted suit. The rest of a large family walked beside the animal, chatting away as if they were taking a maiden aunt out for a stroll. The camel's head had turned towards Anna as she flew past, regarding her with imperious disdain. In the twelve months since she had landed in France, Anna had become accustomed to sights that defied belief, but she reckoned the camel came close to beating them all.

But it was the children in this endless straggling column that drew her attention the most. For two and a half years, whether in London, France, or here in Bavaria, any child even remotely resembling Bär or Antje had the power to draw her attention the way clear, fresh water draws the thirsty. She couldn't stop herself. And when it happened, the grief that stabbed her in the heart was no less painful than it had been that day above the village, when she'd watched through Harry Taverner's binoculars as her precious little boy had led his sister so trustingly into that vile black Citroën.

The image had become a photograph pasted into the album of her memory. One that could never be removed or destroyed. The worst she'd ever taken.

The ride north from Munich had been tough, made bearable only by the good humour of their driver, a skinny black corporal from Columbus, Ohio, named Jerrell Spreece. The US army had loaned Jerrell and the truck to the United Nations Relief and Rehabilitation Administration. Its cargo, including the journalists, was bound for one of the many displaced persons' camps set up by UNRRA around Bavaria.

They seemed to have been driving forever. Maybe a little preparation would help speed their arrival, Anna thought. She pulled a small travelling mirror from her breast pocket, wincing at the reflection of the travel-stained stranger looking back at her.

She was wearing US Army-issue olive-green slacks rolled up at the ankle and a uniform blouse in the same drab colour. It did nothing for her femininity, she decided, but then she'd said farewell to *that* the day she landed in France with only her camera, the clothes she could fit in her pack and orders to join the press corps attached to Sixth Army Group. Marion would be appalled, she thought, as she studied herself in the glass. Marion would have said her daughter looked like a Brooklyn auto-mechanic.

For a start, she'd had her chestnut hair cut into a short bob for the sake of comfort and hygiene. More than once she'd been forced to wash it in a river. And she hadn't worn anything she could call proper make-up since before D-Day, over a year before. Even then it had been the ersatz, war-time austerity stuff. She'd written to Rex in America, begging him to send her some real Elizabeth Arden, reckoning that if decent warpaint was still to be found anywhere in this ruined world, it would be in Hollywood. But she'd been on the move so long that the parcel had yet to catch up with her. Or more likely it had been stolen.

Taking a stub of waxy 'Victory Red' lipstick – provided, or so it was claimed, to improve the morale of women in uniform – she did the best she could as the truck sped on. At least you've got a suntan, she thought.

Anna looked around at the other reporters dozing in the back of the truck. She'd got to know them well and liked them: the easy-going Canadian from *The Toronto Star*… the balding, bespectacled Englishman from the *Daily Mail*… even the intense Frenchman from *Le Monde*, who had a habit of shouting insults at any German who got within ten feet of him.

Eventually, even Anna began to find the soporific swaying of the truck overpowering. She, too, began to doze. It wasn't sleep and she didn't dream. It was more a strange, unsettling limbo, in which time folded back on itself.

She was back in Graz again – all of two weeks ago, now – standing in the doorway of Ivo's parents' house. 'I told Ivo he should never have married a half-blood,' Frau Wolff was saying to her face, quite unabashed. Remembering the pleasant, motherly woman who'd told her she and Ivo would make fine babies for the Fatherland, Anna wondered if she'd gone to the wrong address.

'We've heard nothing from him since he was posted to the east,' Herr Wolff confirmed. 'Nothing at all.'

'When was that?' Anna asked.

'September '43,' said Frau Wolff.

Anna then asked the question that had dominated her thoughts almost every waking moment since she had watched Ivo take Bär and Antje from Dr Braudel's house.

'Do you know where the children are?'

It was Herr Wolff who answered her, his tone surprisingly casual. 'Last heard of, they were in Berlin. Ivo had a girlfriend there. A proper girlfriend: one of us. They moved in together when he was on leave.'

Anna wondered briefly how long it had taken the Wolffs to decide she wasn't a 'proper' partner for their son. They'd been so welcoming in 1934. Now it seemed that even the destruction of Hitler's Third Reich hadn't managed to burn the bigotry out of them.

'Do you have the address?' she asked coldly.

'It was your old apartment, the one you lived in before you walked out on our son,' Frau Wolff told her.

Hope and despair hit Anna simultaneously, a giant wave that seemed to lift her up and then hurl her back down again. She had to hold on to the doorframe to steady herself. She couldn't stop herself imagining Bär and Antje playing together in the apartment near the Jannowitz U-Bahn station while Marion prepared herself for her next assignation, and Hannelore scoured the *Völkischer Beobachter* for stories about her favourite Party luminaries. Fixing them in a place that was secure in her memory was almost as good as seeing them standing before her. But what hope was there that the apartment was still there? She had spoken to enough people to know that Berlin was now mostly rubble.

'Why in God's name didn't you take them in?' she asked. 'You could have protected them.'

Frau Wolff's plump face turned towards her. The little eyes that had beamed with maternalistic affection during the wedding at the Antoniuskirche nearly eleven years ago regarded her now with dumb resentment. 'Why would we do that?' she asked. 'We got rid of your kind after *Anschluss* – all but a few. And they went up the chimney later. Having cleansed this place of Jews, why would we import more?'

And then she slammed the door in Anna's face.

Hearing the noise of it now in her head brought Anna out of her daydream. She felt the truck brakes come on. As the other journalists came awake around her, easing limbs and backs bruised by the hard boards of the cargo floor and fifty miles of autobahn, Anna looked over the side at a large painted sign beside the road.

UNRRA/Red Cross. Displaced Persons Camp, Kimpelbeuren.
All visitors report to Hut 3.

The next moment, Corporal Spreece stuck his head out of the cab window and shouted, 'Franklin Park Conservatory! This is where we's a' stoppin', folks! If you're sick, change here for Mount Carmel East Hospital.'

Anna had fought hard to get herself assigned to cover UNRRA. She'd called in every favour, flirted with every officer in Sixth Army Group's Civil Affairs who could open a door for her. And now she was here, at her first DP camp. She knew the odds of finding Bär and Antje at Kimpelbeuren were infinitesimally small: there were countless camps like this one. But if the children were still alive, a place like this was where the search for them could truly begin; the first footfall on a journey that might end tomorrow, next week, next year... or – and this prospect was the one she dared not contemplate – never.

In a former life, Kimpelbeuren camp had been a factory turning out greatcoats for the Luftwaffe. A cluster of wooden huts stretched back from the road, surrounded by fields. To the north lay Nuremberg; to the south, Munich. The land to the east rose gently in wooded hillsides towards the Czechoslovak border. To the west – all across Europe and back to England – lay Anna Cantrell's recent past, a harsh and rocky terrain sown with loss, anger, bitterness and self-recrimination.

There was nothing that you could call a fence, just a single strand of wire hanging slackly between iron rods rammed into the earth. Its population changed by the hour; the refugees could come and go as they pleased. For most of them, that was a freedom all of its own.

The camp's director was a Dutchman who'd recently arrived from Amsterdam. He was forty, bald and harassed-looking. His experience in Dutch town planning was supposed to give him the skills to look after four thousand displaced persons with a team of twelve other volunteers and three US soldiers seconded from Nuremberg for security. He had the resigned look of a man who knew he was fighting a battle he could never win, but who understood that surrender would bring something immeasurably worse than defeat.

'Have you brought the sulfa drugs we asked for?' he called out, even before the truck had come to a stop.

Corporal Spreece handed him a list of the cargo while the journalists climbed down from the tailgate. The director studied it before sighing. 'Thank God,' Anna heard him say. 'The last thing we need here is an outbreak of typhus.'

Jerrell took back the manifest. He jumped up into the truck and began unloading the boxes, handing them down to the UNRRA staff.

'Oh, that's just great,' said the director wearily, as the first box came down. 'They've sent us more foot powder.' He turned to the journalists. 'The labels are always in English. Some of the mothers here think it's baby powder, but it's way too fierce for infant skin. So we end up with serious cases of inflammation.'

The journalists scribbled in their notebooks while the director made what Anna reckoned was a rehearsed speech. He talked up the camp's successes: over eight thousand DPs already processed and sent on their way… classes established for the children of each constituent nationality, staffed by volunteer teachers recruited from amongst the refugees… a choir formed from those who had the energy to sing… national folk dancing groups…

'Are the DPs here mostly Jews?' asked the reporter from the *Toronto Star*.

'No, in this part of Bavaria the Jewish camps are at Feldafing and the monastery at St Ottilien. We do have some, but mostly we're French, Italian, Serbo-Croats, a decent contingent of Balts, and a smattering of Hungarians. Babel doesn't even come close.'

'So who exactly are all these people?' asked the Canadian, gesturing at the crowd gathering around the truck.

'These are the ones the Nazis failed to work to death,' the director explained. 'They've known nothing but hard labour with starvation rations for months if not years. If they didn't meet their work quotas they were beaten, sometimes even hanged. They've forgotten what normal life is like. We're trying to help them remember.'

'Do you have any German children here?' Anna asked, knowing she would have to ask the same question over and over again at any number of places like this.

The director shook his head. 'We're not permitted to accept native Germans here. They're on their own, I'm afraid.'

Even though Anna had tried to prepare herself, the disappointment hit her hard.

'Do I detect a little sympathy for the enemy?' asked the English reporter. 'After all, they voted for Adolf Hitler. Maybe they should accept the outcome.'

The director took a handkerchief from his pocket and mopped his sweating pate. 'Well,' he said, 'they weren't the first people to vote for a politician with a loud voice and the wrong answers.

And they won't be the last. In the meantime, we've got our hands full coping with the mess that's left over.'

'Why can't these people just go home?' the Englishman asked. 'My readers won't like the notion of them sponging off their charity.'

The director gave him a look of practised forbearance. 'Some of them are too exhausted to make the journey,' he said. 'Some of them have no home to return to, or family alive to welcome them back. Some don't dare to go home because of who now runs the country they fled from. Slowly but surely we're documenting them, getting them papers, helping them find relatives or places to settle. Perhaps you'd prefer the alternative: a mountain of exhausted, broken individuals slowly rotting away, but all in one convenient place, out of sight. Would that please your readers?'

Chastened, the reporter made a play of writing in his notebook. Anna made a mental note for the furtherance of her journalistic career: don't ask foolish questions of harassed men trying their best under difficult circumstances.

The director left them in the care of the welfare officer, a young law student from Boston with wide, expressive eyes, round glasses and thin blond hair that fidgeted even in the faint breeze.

He led them deeper into the camp. 'You can speak to anyone you want,' he said, 'though I can't guarantee you'll find someone to translate. There are very few here who speak English. And don't be surprised by the reactions you get from the children. If you ask a question, some of them will answer you by shouting; others will stay silent and try to hide behind the others. They learned that in the camps.'

'What do you mean?' asked a man from Reuters.

'You know the Nazis – all that shouting when giving orders. They expected a shout of obedience in return. Less than a shout was regarded as defiance.'

'And the silent ones?' asked Anna.

'They'll be our Jews, the ones who learned how not to draw attention to themselves when the selections were being made.'

Walking through the camp, Anna was offered more extraordinary sights than she could possibly capture, even if she'd had twice the rolls of film in her bag. Often, she had to crouch to avoid giving the shot she was taking a fringe of drying laundry: the pathways between the huts were festooned with it. She saw an Orthodox priest in full cassock leading a group of shawled Serbian women in prayer. There were canvas and wood cubicles where whole families sat together, just grateful to have stopped walking. She saw a man in a dirt-stained pinstripe suit whose feet were bound in rags, and children who looked half-feral rolling empty petrol drums around for amusement. She saw sunburned Italian men with faces lined from too much work and too little food singing drinking songs as they sawed timber to repair their hut. There were Frenchmen and women barely out of their teens, sitting squat-legged on the dusty earth singing '*Le Chant des Partisans*', a song that was the bastard child of a march and a lament, full of suffering but determination. There was music all over the camp, in fact: an accompaniment of accordions, flutes, harmonicas – even a cello; each one in competition with another: all battling, lusty human voices singing their national songs, or just celebrating the fact that their owners were alive and free.

Then there were the inmates who wore what looked like striped pyjamas, the ones with numbers tattooed in purple ink on the inside of their forearms. They had different faces to the others. Although the day was bright and the sun hot, theirs seemed to dwell in permanent shadow. Anna had seen their like before – in Dachau. She reckoned it would be a long while before the light found its way back into those eyes.

Entering a space between two huts, she saw a dozen of these lost souls, all women, standing beside a sign nailed to a post. The sign read, in several languages including Hebrew, *De-lousing Station*.

'New arrivals,' the welfare officer said.

The oldest woman in the group was around seventy, Anna guessed, though hard labour and a diet of coarse bread and watery soup had made it hard to be sure. She might have been forty. She wore a tattered pullover across her concentration-camp garb. The pullover had a yellow patch with a black P on it, the mark of a Polish forced labourer. Whether it was hers, or whether it had been given to her, or stolen from its dead owner, there was no way of knowing. She looked like a weathered concrete statue that had seen off enough frosts not to care how cold it got.

The youngest was in her early teens. She might once have had a round, cheerful face beneath a mop of chestnut hair, rosy cheeks and happy grey eyes. Now her face looked like a pale grey balloon out of which the air was slowly leaking, her hair a sparse lichen on a windswept cliff. Freedom had so far failed to clear away the terror that had ingrained itself in the pores of her skin like dirt.

Anna guessed they were Jewish slave labourers from one of the Dachau satellite camps, survivors only because they'd still been able to summon up enough of their dwindling strength to keep working in the local armaments factories until the Nazis fled.

All these women stood hunched, their arms wrapped around their bodies, as if they were plucking up the courage to jump into icy water. In front of them stood two of the American soldiers assigned to the camp. One held a pump that looked like a huge syringe the size of a vacuum cleaner. Its long, thin tin nozzle was coated white with what Anna knew to be DDT powder.

Anna fired off a shot of the soldier with the pump. To her mind, he looked about sixteen. He had the thin bravado of someone only recently arrived in theatre, and the accompanying lack of understanding of just what he was seeing before him.

'For Christ's sake, come over here and get deloused, ya stoopid bitch,' he shouted at the youngest of the women. 'What's the matter wid ya? I'm tryin' to stop you catchin' typhus!'

The young girl tried to bury herself in the chest of the old woman with the pullover. Her whole body shivered with fright.

Anna considered trying to comfort her, but she was wearing her khaki battledress with 'war correspondent' shoulder patches – she'd look just like another camp guard. So she swung her camera behind her back and marched boldly up to the young soldier with the DDT pump.

'Say, where're you from, general?' she asked, painting her face with a friendly smile.

The soldier looked her up and down and gave her a goofy grin, the way young men often do when startled by a good-looking woman. 'Cedar Rapids, Iowa, ma'am.'

'You got a name?'

'Private First Class, Nathan Glover, ma'am. Quartermaster Company, 42nd Infantry Division, US Seventh Army – ma'am.'

'Well, that's all very impressive. May I call you Nathan?'

The soldier blushed. 'I… I… guess so.'

'How long have you been in theatre, Nathan?'

'Since February, ma'am.'

'You can call me Anna.'

'Yes, ma'am.'

'Have you been in any other camps while you've been here, Nathan? Camps like the one at Dachau?'

'Can't rightly say I have, Miss Anna. But I sure heard about them. Nazi bastards… we should put them all up against a wall.'

'Well, I've come up from there,' Anna explained. She glanced at the cowering girl. 'And I can tell you these ladies have had a really bad time of it. They're still frightened of any man wearing a uniform.'

Nathan Glover looked horrified. 'I don't mean to scare them, ma'am,' he protested. 'Truly, I don't.'

Anna smiled to reassure him. 'You and I know that, Nathan. But as far as they're concerned, DDT and Zyklon B could be children of the same strain of murder. So what I suggest is that you and I play a little game – to put their minds at ease as best we can. Can you do that?'

Nathan Glover nodded. 'Yes, ma'am – I mean, yes, Miss Anna.'

Anna clapped him on the shoulder. 'Good boy. It's going to take a little familiarity on both our parts, but it'll be worth it in the end. Trust me. Do you have a girl back in Cedar Rapids, Nathan?'

Nathan's blush deepened. 'I sure do. Ruby-Mae. Prettiest girl in all of Iowa. We's gittin' married just as soon as I get back home.'

'I guess you must miss her, eh, Nathan?'

'Aches like a bad tooth.'

'Have they told you how to delouse properly, Nathan?'

'Yes, Miss Anna. Down the back of the neck, up through the sleeves—' He brandished the pump as if he were at bayonet practice.

'Great. Well, what I'm going to do, Nathan, is this,' Anna said in a matter-of-fact voice. 'I'm going to pull the waistband of my slacks out as far as I can. Then I want you to stick the nozzle of that thing down inside my drawers and pump away as if you were on your first night back home in Cedar Rapids with Ruby-Mae. Can you do that for me?'

The soldier stared at her, his jaw as loose as if he'd been coshed. 'Are you *serious*, ma'am?'

'Deadly serious, Nathan. And while we're doing it, we're both going to laugh our heads off, okay?'

The soldier still hesitated. 'Do I have to, ma'am?'

'It's an order, Private.'

Anna undid her belt and pulled out her slacks as far as she could. Nathan upended the pump and slid the long nozzle in. His face had turned a fetching crimson. 'I guess I'm ready,' he gulped.

'You've been away a long time, Nathan, honey,' Anna said, as she looked into his eyes, the laughter in her bubbling up like water from a spring. 'And I've been so lonesome…'

As Nathan Glover began to pump the handle vigorously, clouds of white DDT spilled out around Anna's waist and from the turn-ups of her slacks. She looked like a leaky stove belching smoke. Overcoming his embarrassment, Nathan began to laugh.

Glad that her horseplay was working on him, Anna looked over at the women. Almost as one, they all stood a little taller, their shoulders straightening as they watched the crazy scene, looks of disbelief and yes – laughter – on their faces. Anna decided to ramp it up a bit.

'Come on, honey,' Anna urged. 'You can do better than that. Ain't you pleased to see me?'

Nathan set to with a will. Soon the DDT was billowing, and Nathan, Anna, the other journalists and the welfare officer were laughing uncontrollably. If Bob Hope had dropped by with a USO troupe, he couldn't have asked for a better reception.

'I think we're done, Nathan, honey,' Anna said, stepping back. Her khaki slacks were stained with patches of white. 'Was it worth the wait?'

'Yes, ma'am,' the private said. 'But now I ain't gonna be able to sleep for a week.'

'I'll ask General Patch at Seventh Army headquarters to give you a Purple Heart. You deserve it.'

Looking at the women, Anna saw they were all now grinning, even the young girl. Brushing herself down, she asked in German if anyone spoke the language.

'I do,' said the old woman with the pullover.

'And your young friend?'

'She's Polish. But I can speak that too.'

'Then can you tell her this from me?' Anna said, beating her slacks with her hands. 'Doesn't matter how big the guy is, or how large the cannon, at the end of the day it all ends up the same: they promise you an avalanche, but all you get is a light dusting of snow.'

She lingered long enough to take a couple of shots of the women, now happily submitting to the delousing. Then she blew a bright farewell kiss to Private Nathan Glover and went off in search of the UNRRA director.

Anna found the director in what he jokingly called 'his office' – a corner of the reception hut that boasted nothing more directorial than a decorator's trestle table for a desk and a requisitioned filing cabinet. She introduced herself.

'I'm pleased to meet you, Miss Cantrell,' he said, shaking her hand. 'I'm Verhoef – Hannie Verhoef. Please, call me Hannie. I hope you will forgive the circumstances. The factory does have an office block, but the DPs' need of solid walls is somewhat greater than mine. How can I help you?' He looked at her slacks. 'Has there been an accident?'

Anna laughed. 'I was helping out with the delousing. It got a little out of hand.'

'If you're seeking an in-depth interview, I can't really tell you anything more than you'd get from the regional administrator in Munich. Don't want to step on any toes, I guess.'

Anna assured him that was not why she had come to see him. 'I need your advice,' she said. 'When we arrived, you said UNRRA doesn't look after native Germans. But if I wanted to find out what had happened to a couple of German children, where would I start?'

The puff of breath that came out of the side of the director's mouth was laden with bafflement. 'Now you're asking, Miss—?'

'Cantrell. Anna Cantrell.'

'Where to start, Miss Cantrell? UNRRA has over fifty thousand unaccompanied children in its care, so the Lord alone knows how many German children there are in the same boat. Whereabouts were they known of last?'

'Berlin. That's where I'm heading.'

The look of doubt on Hannie Verhoef's face told Anna all she needed to know. 'The Russians only let us into Berlin last month,' he said. 'The Yalta Conference was supposed to sort all that out, but the Reds are playing hardball. The city's a mess, but I guess you know that already.' He leaned back in his chair and put his hands behind his head. 'Not that the other major cities are much better; worse, in some cases – like Dresden.'

'Surely there must be records.'

The director gave her a kindly smile, the sort that grandsons keep for dotty grandparents. There was no cruelty in it, only sadness. 'The only thing that rained down on Berlin more than bombs was paper – and that was in cinders,' he said. 'Most official records were either destroyed in the bombing, or burned by the Nazis when they realized the game was up – at least, those that weren't used as fuel to keep them warm. There's no central point collecting names yet, and there are more organizations trying to help than you can count.'

'Can you at least suggest where I might start?'

'Take your pick,' he said. 'You could start with the Red Cross. Then there's the Quakers; the International Volunteers for Peace; the YMCA and YWCA… the Catholic War Relief Services… the Hebrew Immigrant Aid Society…'

'I see what you mean,' said Anna despondently.

'They're all trying to do the best they can. But none of us has been able to do much in Berlin yet. We've got to wait for the Allied Control Council to get up and running. It'll be months before we have a real idea of how this whole upturned ants' nest is to be put back together again.' He paused. 'May I ask… these children – are they relatives of yours?'

'Yes,' Anna said. 'My son and my daughter.'

'Oh.' Verhoef gave her a puzzled look. 'And you're looking for them in… Berlin?'

'It's a long and rather messy story.'

'And none of my business – I quite understand.'

'I didn't mean to be rude,' Anna said. 'It's just that I don't know where to start.'

'My advice would be: go to the last place they were known and ask around,' the director said. 'But you're going to need a lot of luck – and that's if they've survived the Allied bombs and the Red Army. I wish you success. I really do.'

And with that, he lowered his head and went back to his paperwork.

Anna had heard General Eisenhower tell the press he thought it likely Berlin would never be rebuilt, that her ruins might stand forever as a warning to generations to come of just where blind obedience to totalitarianism can lead. Driving through the city in the August heat, she suspected Ike might well be right. No photo she'd taken required a caption. What could you possibly say about fifty-five million cubic metres of rubble lying upon the corpses of around one hundred thousand Berliners that would add anything useful by way of explanation?

Ever since she had entered the city, she had deliberately blanked her mind to what she would find when she reached her old apartment near the Jannowitz U-Bahn station. In England, she'd been unable to listen to the BBC News or read a newspaper whenever a bombing raid on Berlin was mentioned. She'd always understood that there was a strong possibility Ivo had taken the children back to the city. To think of them huddling in a cellar somewhere while the earth around them shook, wondering why their mother hadn't come after them, was more than her imagination could bear. When the V1 flying bombs began to hit London, she'd once unthinkingly thrown herself under the bed and screamed, 'Bär, Antje, under here – with Mama!' In the eerie silence that followed, her sobbing had sounded to her almost as loud as the nearby explosion.

And yet despite almost half a million tons of Allied bombs and uncountable rounds of Soviet artillery, Anna found that Berlin was still a city. Her ruins were not deserted. Far from it. Now, more than three months after her surrender, Berlin – while still on life support – was showing the first signs of recovery. She was going to prove General Dwight D Eisenhower wrong.

For a start, the main streets were mostly now clear, the rubble moved aside by an army of *Trümmerfrauen* – rubble women. As Anna sped past in the jeep she'd wheedled as an official member of the press corps, she could see lines of them ranged up the slopes of smashed masonry in their bright summer dresses as if they were going for a hike in the Grunewald. They appeared to be marching while standing still, arms swinging as they passed buckets of debris down to the person next in line below them.

It's like looking at a landscape of giant, upended slices of very dusty or very blackened Swiss cheese, Anna thought. Those façades that still stood had gaping holes through which you could see other slices with other holes, and through them, more slices and more holes. In the spaces between these vast slices of concrete Emmental were high dunes of pulverized brick and cement, and Gordian knots of tangled girders.

The Karstadt department store was where she and Marion had shopped for furnishings when they'd moved to Berlin with Ivo. Reaching the site now, Anna wondered if she'd taken a wrong turn and got herself lost. The huge building with its twin towers had gone. All that remained were three portions of the back wall. Regaining her bearings, she pressed on. She drove as fast as she could, though in some places the trams were running again and there were more people on the streets than she'd expected, walking about in the summer heat as if nothing had happened.

Once again she noticed the absence of men. Several of those she did see walked with a limp, or used a crutch because a leg was missing. One had no legs at all and was propelling himself along in a wheeled soapbox.

It took Anna several detours to find a bridge across the Spree that hadn't been smashed up, but eventually she reached the Alexanderplatz, where Ivo's office had been before the war, and where she had first been introduced to Joseph Goebbels on that dank February night in 1938. Now, instead of black-uniformed SS men opening the doors of official cars, a single Soviet woman soldier was directing traffic with a flag. She moved like a cross between a ballet dancer and a robot, her broad Slavic face regarding the drivers and their passenger with total contempt.

As Anna waited for the woman to let her go, she looked around.

The department store here had fared better than the Karstadt. The shell of the building still stood, though all the windows had been blown out. Remarkably the huge letters spelling the name *Jonass & Co* still stood precariously along the top, eight storeys above the square. Beyond it, Anna could make out the skeletal curved roof of the Alexanderplatz station. But instead of Nazi banners, there were signs showing the communist hammer and sickle, and the portraits of the top Soviet officers in the governing *Kommandatura* – the headquarters from which the four occupying Allied powers controlled Berlin in a strained and fractious union.

With a brisk wave of her flag, the Soviet traffic cop waved Anna on. Leaving the Alexanderplatz behind, she was soon pulling into the little square where the family had lived before the escape to Paris.

Immediately, Anna's worst fears were realized. The apartment block was no more. Only a portion of the façade remained, a mosaic of differing wallpaper styles where the bombs had scooped away the interior and deposited it in a mountain of rubble, smashed furniture – and crushed residents. She had no idea when the building had been destroyed but she reasoned it must have been shortly before the end, because a faint but ripe smell of death still lingered.

If Bär and Antje had been there when the bomb hit, they would be gone forever. The thought of them lying together beneath the immense weight of debris, like two young Egyptians entombed beneath a pyramid, forced her jaw to gape and tears to well in her eyes.

Anna yanked on the handbrake and stepped out of the jeep. A little way off, rubble women were hauling away buckets of debris for other women to load into a line of trucks parked nearby. Anna could taste the hot summer air as she walked towards them. It was harsh and dusty. Full of grit.

'Does anyone here live in this neighbourhood?' Anna called out, feeling the dry rasp in her throat.

The women went on passing the buckets of rubble. Anna tried again.

'Hello! Can you help me? Is there anyone here from this district?'

The woman nearest to her turned her face in Anna's direction. She was Anna's age, well set, with short arms and muscular legs. She wore a cotton bandanna over her head, tied in a knot at the back. She looked Anna up and down, taking in her military tunic. 'No, we're all Zehlendorf girls,' she said. 'They bus us in because the local bitches are too lazy to get out of bed in the morning.'

Without breaking the rhythm of her work, the next woman above in the file said, 'Wasn't that Odelinda from around here, the one who joined us for a few days when Gisela broke her leg?'

'Oh, yeah, you're right,' said the first.

'Is she still here?' Anna asked.

'Not any more,' said the second woman.

'Do you know where I might find her?'

The woman shrugged. 'Heaven or hell, take your pick, darling. A Russki raped her. She hanged herself.'

The stocky one grunted as she handed her loaded bucket to the gang filling the trucks. 'If every woman in Berlin who was raped by a Russki did that, there'd be no one left to clean away all this shit.'

One of the loading gang called out: 'It's not always so very bad. I hung on to my Russki. He's a nice young lieutenant of artillery. Looks after me, brings me real coffee. It's worth having one flea if it keeps all the other fleas away. I call him DDT. He doesn't understand, of course.'

'Think yourself lucky you've still got something left to sell, darling,' shouted back the oldest woman in the line. 'My man was sixty-three. He had arthritis. But at the end they forced him to join the *Volkssturm*. When he tried to run away, the SS hanged him from a tree for desertion. I would have given myself to the whole fucking Red Army back in '41, every single one of them, if it could have stopped the madness. I hope the coffee's worth it.'

Anna decided it was time to leave. These people were the enemy she, in her own way, had fought against. And now here they were, ravished, widowed, half-starving, clinging to a fragile existence, shovelling the wreckage of the path they had followed into little buckets to be borne away and dumped, buried and forgotten.

'Thanks, anyway,' she said, and turned back to the jeep.

She had left it in the middle of a cleared street, adjacent to the shell of another building whose façade, with its gaping empty windows, reminded her of a Hollywood set made of painted canvas. Scrawled across the lower masonry, executed in chalk, were lines of writing. Anna walked around the jeep and began to read.

The first item she saw was a circle with *37 Tote* written inside – *thirty-seven dead*. Perhaps some were still under the rubble, she thought, yet to be recovered.

Was this the only memorial Bär and Antje were likely to have – just a chalk mark scrawled on a burned wall that would probably soon be demolished?

Anna stared at the roughly drawn sign, struggling to halt the tears that welled in her eyes.

I should have defied Harry Taverner, she thought. I should have stayed in Vichy France and searched for my children.

But Anna knew in her heart that would not have been the answer, though it didn't hold back the tide of guilt that now threatened to sink her to her knees in the hot dust of the street. She read on.

The messages were all forlorn attempts at reuniting families or seeking news of the missing: *Family Putkammer – Elsa is with Cousin Karl in Wustermark… Seeking news of Dieter Eisenach. Send to Magda Eisenach, Church of St Sabastian, Magdeburg… Gabriella is with Uncle Felix…*

The messages covered almost the entire section of wall. Reading them was like hearing the fading cries of survivors from the sinking of a great liner as they trod water and waited for exhaustion and the sea to take them under.

And soon there would be nothing left but the silence.

Anna was about to give up and walk away when a name caught her eye: *H. Lange. Gone home to Gatow.*

She read the brief message again, feeling the excitement turn from an ember into a bright flame. She looked more closely, to make sure it really was an *H* and not an *M*, because the chalk strokes were unsubtle and imprecise.

Just like the woman who had made them.

Nineteen

The village of Gatow, on the western edge of the city by Lake Havel, lay in the zone now controlled by the British. It hadn't suffered nearly as badly as the city centre. Anna reached it late in the afternoon. She knew she was taking a chance. All she had to go on was a brief message chalked on a bomb-damaged wall, a call from the past scrawled on a dusty sepulchre. She had no idea if she would find Hannelore Lange in Gatow: her former maid might have fallen prey to the bombing or a Red Army shell long before she ever had the chance to escape Berlin.

The village church was a trim little building with a square wooden tower and a tiled roof. Surrounded by trees, it stood only a short distance from the water's edge. The priest was friendly enough. It hadn't been that long since the only people in uniform to go there were Russian.

'Herr Lange is the local postman,' he said in answer to Anna's enquiry. 'The family used to live in a house off the Potsdam Road. But when the Russians came, they turfed everyone out and ransacked the place. They're all living on the municipal allotments now. A lot of Berliners are doing that these days.' He gave Anna the directions.

Only a few minutes later she was approaching a row of wooden shelters set in a large communal plot that had been dug up by the Soviets, everything green and edible removed. Now a dozen families were living in plywood and tar-paper shacks, waiting for the replanted earth to produce enough of a harvest to nourish bodies making do on the paltry official ration.

The women of the Lange family were sitting on the earth outside one of the shelters, darning clothes. They watched her arrival with mute suspicion. Anna guessed that because of her khaki battledress blouse, they assumed she was just the latest in a procession of Allied occupiers who'd come to tell them to pack up their belongings and move on.

Hannelore was squatting beside a smoky fire, stirring the contents of a small, cut-down oil drum suspended over the flames. The passing of seven years had not been kind to her, Anna could see. The children's former nanny looked twice as sullen as when Anna had last seen her, and she'd lost a lot of weight. Her eyes had sunk into her face. Where once they had been merely dull, now they looked as mean and wary as those of a hungry vixen.

'Hello, Hannelore,' Anna said pleasantly. 'Long time no see.'

The woman looked up. At first there was no recognition. Then it came. Not so much in a flood as in a slow, greasy trickle.

'Frau Wolff – so you decided to come back. Left it a bit late, haven't you?'

Anna smiled. She didn't want a fight. 'How are you, Hannelore, dear?'

'Oh, can't you see? We're all just wonderful. Things have been great since you ran away.'

'What are you cooking?'

'Supper. Cabbage soup. These days we eat better than we ever did at Café Kranzler. Didn't they tell you?'

Anna glanced at the watery contents of the drum. A few clumps of mushy leaves floated in what looked like a sample drawn from the Landwehr canal. 'I'm sorry we have to meet again under such terrible circumstances,' she said. 'I promise, I bear you no animosity.'

'What's done is done,' Hannelore said, using her wooden spoon to push one of the mats of cabbage deeper into the drum, grimacing as if she were trying to drown kittens in a sack. In a voice heavy with resentment, she added, 'They lied to us, every last one of them. Worst of all, they lied to the Führer. If he'd known earlier what was really going on, he'd have hanged them all from meat-hooks. Instead, they sold us to the Reds and the Jews. *Now* look at us. Slaves in our own land.'

Anna didn't bother to ask who *they* were. The generals… Hitler's inner circle… she'd heard the complaint of betrayal more than once since entering Germany. 'I need your help, Hannelore,' she said. 'I'm trying to find Bär and Antje. I hoped you might be able to help me.'

Hannelore looked up at her, her face wreathed in the steam from the drum. 'Why would I help you? What have you ever done for me?'

'You cared for the children, once.'

'Because Herr Wolff paid me to.'

'I mean *care* as in affection, Hannelore.'

The woman shrugged. 'They were sweet enough, I suppose – for quarter-bloods.'

Anna heard her own sharp intake of breath. For a moment she considered reaching out and shoving Hannelore's head into the boiling cabbage broth. 'That's all over now,' she said coldly. 'And thank God, too. Even the blindest of you must know where it led.'

Hannelore's mouth took on an ugly twist of scepticism. 'Who really knows the truth? The Jews were sent east for resettlement. It was probably the Russians who did it. It could all be lies, anyway.'

Anna felt her hands clench, seemingly of their own accord. 'Sachsenhausen is barely thirty-five kilometres from here,' she said, trying to keep her voice steady. 'I've watched the newsreels from Bergen-Belsen. And I've seen Dachau with my own eyes. You can't pretend you didn't know what was going on.'

That didn't seem to count for much if Hannelore's expression was to be believed. 'If you say so,' she said with a shrug, addressing the cabbage water.

It seemed pointless to pick a fight. What could she possibly expect to achieve? What was the point in making this not overly bright woman admit the guilt of a whole nation? Besides, she needed her help.

'Herr Wolff's parents told me that the children were staying in our old apartment, before it was bombed,' she said. 'I want to know where they are now – if they're still alive.'

Hannelore studied her for what seemed like an age. Then she rubbed her eyes with the back of her hand and yawned. 'Hard work, all this stirring. Lousy rate of pay, too.'

Anna nodded in understanding. She turned and walked back to the jeep, conscious that all the women were watching her. Leaning over the sill, she pulled a half-full carton of Camel cigarettes from beneath the front passenger seat, part of what she had come to call her 'chatty fund'. On the black market, they were prime currency. A single pack was worth two kilos of bread. Most Berliners were happy to do a lot of chatting in return for that sort of inducement.

Returning to Hannelore, she let the carton swing freely in her right hand. The women watching her stared covetously. 'Let's take a little walk, Hannelore,' Anna said. 'See if we can't jog your memory a little.'

Handing her spoon to the nearest of the women, Hannelore Lange stood up and, with Anna beside her, walked a little way off.

When they were out of hearing, Anna waved the carton of Camels as if she were a stage hypnotist.

'I think all those bombs you Amis dropped on us has started to jog my memory,' Hannelore said slyly.

'What can you tell me?'

'Depends on what you want to know, Frau Wolff.'

'I've told you. I want to know if my children are alive. And if so, where they are now.'

'There's a lot of people around here who'd like to have answers to questions like those. What makes you so special, Frau Wolff?'

Anna wondered if pleading might help. She suspected not.

'I'm their mother, Hannelore. They're my babies. Surely you, as a woman, can understand that.'

Hannelore let out a savage bark of derision. 'You think this city has any compassion left for an American? If you want your children so desperately, why don't you go dig in the rubble for them like German mothers have to do? One of my sisters lived in Dresden. She had a child, too. A little girl just like Antje. All she got to bury was a few sticks of charcoal in a shoebox.'

There seemed to Anna no point in speaking of responsibility, of complicity or blind obedience. She let her eyes wander across the skyline for a moment to settle herself, but the trees looked too much like the shadows of weeping mothers, and she found no relief in them.

'What happened after I left with the children?' she asked. 'Did you keep in touch with my husband?'

'Not really,' Hannelore said breezily. 'He dismissed me. Said I should have known what you were planning.'

'I'm sorry. I hope he gave you a decent severance.'

'Quite a lot, actually. I think it was to stop me talking to anyone about how you'd duped him.'

'I didn't dupe him, Hannelore. I needed to save the children from what he had become. I needed to save myself.'

'Looks like it worked out well,' Hannelore said tartly.

'Did you see him again after that?'

'Not until he returned from Paris in '43, with the children. He'd been letting out the apartment to a friend of his.'

How typical of him, Anna thought. It wouldn't surprise her to learn that Ivo had appropriated Marion's account at the Bauer bank to pay the rent.

'Would that friend be Manis Möller, by any chance?'

Hannelore nodded. 'Yes. Creepy sort of fellow. High up in the Ministry for Propaganda. Something to do with fine art.'

'How do you know this?'

'Because Herr Wolff took me on as the children's nanny again.'

'After he'd fired you the first time?'

'He didn't have much of a choice. It was hard to find staff by then, what with the demands of war work. As well as the children, Herr Wolff brought a lady friend back from France, a German woman who'd been living in Paris. Gertrude Steigler, her name was. Very much a party girl. And I don't mean dancing.'

The image of Bär and Antje being mothered by some blonde ice maiden from the National Socialist Party Women's League sprang into Anna's mind, forcing her fingers to tighten on the carton of Camels.

'What happened then?'

'What do you think? We spent most of the time in the bloody basement. Terror bombers by day, terror bombers by night. Murdering bastards.' Hannelore gave Anna a hard stare. '*Your* murdering bastards.'

Anna took the jab on the chin and didn't flinch. She remembered the photos she'd taken in London in the aftermath of the Luftwaffe bomb that had hit a school in Catford, killing thirty-eight children and teachers, and the photos she'd seen of the V2 rocket strike on a busy branch of Woolworths in New Cross that had killed 168.

Dear God, she thought – what have we made of this world we were given?

'And then Ivo was sent east, I understand. Is that right?'

'Yes. That was in September '43.'

'What happened after that?'

Hannelore shrugged. 'When the bombing got worse, a lot of people left for the country. Thousands, in fact. Fräulein Steigler had relations out at Briesen. I believe that's where she took the children. That would have been in April '44.'

The wave of relief almost rocked Anna on her feet. But she kept it from showing on her face. This wasn't the time or place for displays of joy. It would be like rubbing salt into Hannelore's wounds.

'Herr Wolff didn't pay you to go with them?'

'I was no longer needed. I stayed on in the apartment because that's where Herr Möller was. He had important work at the ministry. I cooked for him, ironed his uniform. Generally wiped his arse.'

'Was Herr Möller there when the bomb hit?'

'No. He'd gone to Munich. The apartment was empty.'

'Do you know what happened to him?' Anna asked. If anyone could tell her what had become of Ivo, it would be Manis Möller.

'Oh, yes,' Hannelore said brightly. 'The little weasel came out of the shit smelling of roses. Everyone in the black market knows Manis Möller. Best tightrope walker in the business. The Russians don't touch him because he finds them the artworks he and Herr Wolff stole from the Jews. The Americans don't touch him because, well, what do Americans know about culture? And the British leave him alone because they're too busy wagging their tails for you Amis.'

'Do you know where this Steigler woman is now?'

Hannelore shrugged. 'She might still be in Briesen. It's about a hundred kilometres from here, on the other side of Berlin, out to the east. The Russkies got there at the start of February. If she had any sense, she'd have left well before they got there. I wish to God I had.'

Hannelore looked down at her stomach. Her eyes had suddenly become moist. As Anna followed her gaze, she saw the woman's belly was the only part of her that seemed not to have shrunk.

'Oh, Hannelore, I'm so sorry—' Anna took a step forward, instinctively reaching out to take Hannelore's hand.

The woman retreated, unwilling to accept her pity. 'Funny, I always wanted a baby,' she said, a bitter smile tugging at her lips. It made her skin crease, which only served to emphasize how badly the long months of hunger and the final, awful outrage had scarred her. 'Just not a Russian one.'

Anna held out the carton of Camels. It seemed a crass consolation, but Hannelore snatched it out of her hand as if it were a bar of gold.

'The British are bound to have a doctor at the aerodrome. Go and speak to them,' Anna said. 'If they want money, well, those will get you a decent sum on the black market.'

'Thanks,' Hannelore said. 'But I might keep it. We'll need all the babies we can get, what with so many of our young men no longer around to father more.'

'Good luck, Hannelore, dear,' Anna said, putting out her hand again. To her surprise, Hannelore took it.

'I hope you find Bär and Antje, Frau Wolff. They were good kids.'

As Anna turned to go, she said, 'I don't suppose Fräulein Steigler left you an address in Briesen, when she left?'

'As a matter of fact, she did,' Hannelore said. 'She'd written to Ivo's unit to tell him where she was going. She gave me a copy of the letter in case hers failed to reach him. By then, sending a letter to the east was about as useful as shouting into a hurricane.'

Anna felt jubilation surge in her heart. 'Can you remember the address?'

'I didn't open it. The children were no longer my concern.'

'Do you still have it?' Anna asked. 'Can I see it?'

Hannelore tilted her head back and let out a dry, cynical laugh. 'You might – if you joined the rubble women and started digging. I left it on the kitchen table when I moved out, in case Herr Wolff came home. I'd imagine right now it's under three storeys of brick and concrete.'

Twenty

If Berlin had fallen to the Americans and the British rather than the Russians, Anna would have driven the jeep straight to Briesen the very next morning. But it hadn't. Berlin lay deep within territory occupied by the Soviet army. Nothing signed at Yalta or Potsdam could alter the uncomfortable truth: no one moved in or out of Berlin without Russian permission. After meeting Hannelore Lange and the rubble women, Anna realized that a woman travelling on her own, even one wearing American army fatigues, was shooting craps with her safety, if not her life.

And there was work for her to do. She had secured a reputation as a good photographer. Several of the correspondents attached to the Supreme Allied Headquarters Europe turned to her to illustrate their stories. Martha Gellhorn and Marguerite Higgins had shared a bottle of Jack Daniels with her in Munich, to steady their nerves after they'd all returned from Dachau. The civil affairs and press relations officers of the American Mission in Berlin knew her face. More than a few had tried to impress her with their war stories. Anna had listened politely, and then told them of the time Joseph Goebbels had poured a glass of champagne for her.

It meant that a journey to Briesen was not to be undertaken lightly. Besides, if Hannelore was right, the odds were that the

Steigler woman had fled with the children before the Russians arrived in the town. They could be anywhere now.

Before Anna could contemplate the journey, there was first a regular bed to organize. After months of snatching sleep in barns and in the back of trucks before the inevitable dawn call to buckle up and follow the army forward, she needed somewhere permanent to sleep.

For her first few days in Berlin, Anna dossed down in a tent with other journalists attached to the US 2nd Armored Division, finding the controlled silence after the bugle notes of taps had faded rather unsettling – since landing on the continent almost exactly a year before, the accompaniment to most of her nights had been the rumble of artillery fire just over the horizon.

The tent was soon exchanged for a neat little house in Zehlendorf, in the American zone, provided by a harassed and overworked billeting officer at the *Kommandatura*. 'It's relatively untouched,' he assured her, as he signed the docket.

When she got there, she discovered that 'relatively untouched' meant that the Russians had thoughtfully left the walls standing, the roof on, and most of the floorboards in place. Everything else, even some of the doors, had been carried away. Where the owners of the house were, she had no idea. Probably living on an allotment, like the Lange family, she supposed.

Anna was to share the house with several other members of the press. She was the first to arrive, wandering around the empty, echoing house for ten minutes. Then she heard the growl of an engine. Stepping outside, she saw a truck pull up. In the back were several camp beds and bedding rolls, courtesy of the 2nd Armored Division's quartermaster company. Having long since learned that where the military was concerned, possession was ten-tenths of the law, Anna bagged a bedroom with a door before the others arrived. She needed the privacy because, ever since arriving on German soil, she had started waking in the middle of the night, calling out for Bär and Antje. She suspected it was because there, in Berlin, their presence seemed tantalizingly close.

There was a little summer house at the back of the ruined garden, and Anna looked inside for anything that might make her stay more comfortable. There was nothing. All the Russkies had left was a dead rat, a bicycle tyre with a large nail in it, a pile of rags and a few pots of paint. On a whim, Anna picked one up, went to the front of the house, prised open the lid of the pot with her penknife, and, with a finger wrapped in rag, daubed the words *The Hearst Building* on the wall, naming her new abode after the New York headquarters of the newspaper mogul, Randolph Hearst. At least now its new occupants would be able to readily identify their temporary Berlin home from all the other, similarly ransacked houses in the street.

The lazy ones amongst Anna's new companions sat on their backsides in the nearest army chow-house and relied on official press releases for stories. The good ones went in search of their own. Which was why Anna found herself returning to the Alexanderplatz two days later.

Once home to important Party ministries and the adjacent train station, the ruined square had acquired a new function: it now hosted one of the most thriving black markets in Berlin. In the blown-out interior of the station, and in the nearby canyons of scorched masonry, Berliners traded items they had managed to salvage, save or steal in exchange for food, cigarettes, phoney ration stamps or anything that might improve their lot or stave off hunger and keep despair at bay for just a little longer.

Looking into the faces of the people there, Anna saw herself for an instant back in Vienna, standing in the snow before the down-and-out she'd photographed at the Schwarzenbergplatz tram stop. She could hear the voice of Professor Koppitz in her head: … *One cannot photograph suffering without there being an exchange… you must give a little something of yourself in return…*

Well, I've certainly done that, she thought. I've given my mother and my children. You didn't warn me the cost would be *that* high.

This time, though, Anna was wise enough not to take photos until she'd garnered a little trust. To help, she'd put on a summer dress rather than her khaki fatigues. Even so, it was like turning up to a party to which you had deliberately not been invited. Groups of people huddled conspiratorially together. They held whatever it was they were seeking to exchange close to their bodies, as if they were playing cards and didn't want to show their hand. At first, whenever she approached anyone and explained why she'd come, they would quickly turn away. But eventually she found a few people prepared to talk to her.

'Look what we have to do to feed ourselves,' said one surprisingly well-dressed woman, waving a ration card in her face. 'Meantime, the Amis give all the food to the DPs in the camps.'

Anna's instinct was to remind the woman just why the displaced persons, many of them freed slave labourers, were so hungry in the first place. But she knew she wouldn't get the woman's story that way, so she kept silent and let her continue with her tale of self-pity.

Eventually she was able to shoot some pictures. The first was of an elderly woman sitting on a wall, a pair of crutches near her leaning against the masonry. She was trying to sell the last of her family's spare clothing in return for some margarine. 'You have to be on your guard,' she told Anna bitterly. 'There are bastards who'll mix it with cement powder or grease to make it go further. You don't just get robbed; you get sick into the bargain.'

Then there was the shot she took of three men who looked like bottom-tier Chicago mobsters, with fedora hats on their heads and Oxford brogues with white leather quarters and vamps on their feet.

Anna had just about got what she wanted when she turned a corner and almost ran into a thin figure in frayed trousers and a stained cotton shirt leaning next to one of the smashed-out windows. On the empty sill beside him was a wooden box stuffed with cutlery, not one piece of which appeared to come from the same set as any other.

'Hey, I'm real sorry—' Anna began, and then stopped.

The man looked vaguely familiar. His youthful face wore a patina of weariness that belonged to someone much older, but that wasn't unusual in today's Berlin. A damp fringe of fair hair hung down over his left eye.

'Anna?' he said, staring at her. 'Is it really you?'

Anna put her hand to her mouth in disbelief. 'Luka! Luka Vogel!' she cried.

He grinned. Anna threw her arms around him. The scent of stale sweat didn't bother her: she'd smelled far worse human odours in recent months. But the brittle feel of his body caused her to ease her grip. A long time ago, she had enjoyed that body for a while. It had brought her comfort and a temporary escape from Ivo. She had felt guilty about rejecting it. Now, as she held it once more, she feared she might actually do it harm. She released her grip and stood back to inspect him.

'Thank God you're alive, Luka.'

He held up his left arm. It ended where the cuff of his shirt hung loosely in the dusty air. 'Most of me,' he said.

Anna put her hand to her mouth. 'Oh, Luka, you poor darling—'

He pursed his lips. 'Best thing that could have happened to me. Catching this meant I was in hospital at the end. Well, it wasn't really a hospital, just a basement. With no morphine.'

There was a café-bar Anna knew that had reopened nearby. When she suggested going there, Luka looked uncomfortable. 'I've only just got my Persil ticket,' he said.

She knew what he meant – a clean report from the Allied powers stating he had never been a Nazi and was thus whiter than white. It was a prerequisite to employment.

'I've got a job with the US Information Control Division,' Luka went on. 'They're launching a new newspaper for people in the American zone. They needed a graphic artist. The ones with two hands who applied had all been Party members. That's another reason I should be grateful to the Russkies.' He looked suddenly embarrassed. 'But I don't start until next week.'

'I'm paying,' Anna said.

Luka closed the lid of the cutlery box, scooped it off the windowsill and tucked it under his damaged arm. 'We're done with fascism,' he said proudly, 'and hopefully we've escaped communism. Now we all aspire to becoming good capitalists.' He tapped the box with his remaining hand. 'And capitalists with table manners need knives and forks. I'm doing my bit to restore German etiquette.'

As they left the Alexanderplatz together, Anna spotted a group of children on a nearby hill of rubble. In patched shorts and dresses, undernourished, running wild, they laughed as they chased one another across their playground of ruined masonry.

Anna searched their faces, praying for two she might recognize. But they were all strangers to her.

Surely, she thought, if Bär and Antje are still alive, if they were somewhere in this graveyard of a city, they *must* be able to hear the howling of my heart. Even the dead can't be that deaf.

The café-bar was called Meckler's. Like most other places around it, the windows were gone. The fascia was pockmarked with the white dimples of shrapnel hits. But the pavement was cleared of rubble and there were tables and chairs outside. It catered for Allied military personnel, because they had the money and the owner could claim he was an essential business, so he had access to real coffee and spirits that weren't mostly antifreeze. The chairs and tables on the pavement were wrought iron, like garden furniture. But there were no gardens in the centre of Berlin these days, just vegetable patches, waterlogged bomb shelters and little graveyards.

Two off-duty American GIs in fatigues and forage caps were drinking at the adjacent table when Anna and Luka took their places. Hearing a couple in civilian clothes speaking German, one of them called out, 'Hey! Skedaddle, ya goddamn krauts.'

Anna turned her head towards the man and gave him a serene smile. '*Bitte?*' she said.

The soldier pushed his forage cap back over his forehead. He looked directly at Luka. 'The broad can stay. But you – crawl back under the rubble where ya came from, ya goddamned Nazi. This here place is for victors, not losers.'

Anna put her hand over her mouth as she gave a discrete cough. Then she looked the soldier straight in the eye. 'In that case, Private, I'll be sure to recommend it to Major-General Parks at the *Kommandatura* next time I see him. He likes to hear of new places opening up.'

The soldier stared at her with bulging eyes, as though he'd just been slugged from behind with a rubber truncheon. 'Say, I'm sorry, ma'am. I meant no disrespect. I didn't realize you were an American.'

'I'm also half-British, so I guess I could tell Major-General Lyne, too. Don't know the French or the Russians that well, but then we don't want everyone to know about this place, do we?'

'I guess not,' said the soldier miserably. 'Sorry, ma'am. May I buy you and the gentleman with you a drink, ma'am?'

'That would be very agreeable, Private. Thank you.'

The soldier called over a waiter while his companion stared at his fingernails.

'What do you care for, ma'am? Sir?' asked the soldier.

'Oh, on a lovely day like today, I think champagne is in order, if they have it,' Anna said.

The soldier swallowed hard. 'Two glasses of champagne, please, waiter.'

Anna gave him a smooth smile. She said, 'Oh, I think victors should be ordering champagne by the bottle, don't you, Private?'

The soldier swallowed even harder. 'Yes, ma'am.' He looked at the waiter, with a sickly smile that made his face look like a cracked windowpane. 'A bottle, please.'

'Of your very finest,' Anna added sweetly.

The ruined buildings opposite cast blades of shadow across the sunlit street as Anna and Luka drank their champagne. Luka told her how he'd been conscripted into the Luftwaffe as a clerk and sent on garrison duties to France until three months before D-Day. Then he'd been transferred back to Berlin to serve with a flak battery, until the Russians arrived. He was convinced that if he hadn't lost his left hand when a shell exploded nearby, he'd either have fallen in the final battle for the city or been hanged by the SS, because he would have surely lost his nerve and tried to run away.

'I wish I'd stayed in Vienna,' he said. 'But we all thought Berlin was where the action was. I suppose we were right about that. Just not the way we thought.'

'Is Louisa alright? Is she here?'

'She will be in the next few days – now that I have a job. Right now, she's living with a friend in the countryside outside Hamburg, in the British zone.'

'Is she well?'

'As well as any of us. She had a romantic attachment to a Luftwaffe pilot. But he died. We haven't seen each other for a year. She doesn't know about my hand – I told her I was in hospital with pneumonia. I just didn't want her coming back to Berlin, what with the air raids. And thank God she didn't. You must have heard what the Russians did to our women when they arrived.'

He listened without comment while she told him of her time in France, her sojourn in England and her return to Germany. She didn't mention Marion's murder. There seemed no point.

'If Bär and Antje are still alive, I have to find them, Luka,' she said. 'I don't sleep very well. Most nights I wake up thinking about them, and what they must have gone through. I blame myself. I can't help it.'

He put his hand on hers. She wondered if he still had feelings for her, but when she looked into his eyes, all she could see was the compassion of a good friend.

'You did the right thing, escaping like that,' he said. 'You can't blame yourself if he came after you and took the children. All he achieved was to put them in more danger.'

'I'm going to drive out to Briesen in the next few days to see if I can track down Ivo's mistress – this Steigler woman. It's a remote hope, but right now it's the only one I've got.'

'I'll come with you,' he said. 'Even now, it's not wise for a woman to drive around in the Soviet zone on her own.'

'I'll wear my US Army fatigues,' she promised. 'And I have my American passport and my press accreditation from the *Kommandatura*. I'll be fine.'

'We're friends, right?' he said, smiling. 'I know I was a bit of a gauche kid when we were together. But I've grown up a lot since then. Let me come with you – as a friend. Otherwise, I'll worry endlessly about you getting lost and ending up in Moscow.'

Anna lent across the table and kissed him on the cheek. 'You're a good man, Luka. You always were. I was the unkind one.'

Embarrassed, he shook his head.

'I don't suppose you heard anything of my husband, after I left?' Anna asked. 'Not that I want to see him again. But if he's alive, he might have news of the children.'

'I'm afraid I did my best to keep away from Party functionaries,' Luka said.

'I'm told he was sent east and didn't come back.'

'Then he'd be one amongst millions,' Luka said. 'Wives will be asking after their husbands long after you and I have gone grey.'

'I guess so,' Anna said wearily. She drained her glass. 'Come on, then. I've got things to do. And you've got cutlery to sell.' Then a thought struck her. 'How long have you been dealing on the black market, Luka?' she asked.

'Since the war ended. Three months.'

'I don't suppose you've come across my husband's old friend, Manis Möller? I understand from our former nanny that he's a player in that field.'

Luka's face hardened. 'Yes, I've heard of him. He's one of the king rats in this new sewer we've made for ourselves.'

'Do you think you could ask around, try to arrange a meeting?'

'Do you really want to start wading in that sort of water, Anna? It's not exactly clean.'

'I'll wade through anything if it gets me more news about what might have happened to my children.'

Luka took a deep, resigned breath. 'I'll ask around.'

'Thank you, Luka,' she said soberly. 'I owe you.' She told him the address of the Hearst Building in Zehlendorf. 'And where are you staying, so I can find you again?'

Luka gave her a bright laugh. He looked like the boy she remembered. 'Oh, it's very salubrious. I'm on Hertzallee, down by the zoo.'

'The number?'

He laughed. 'You don't need a number. You can't miss it. It's on the third floor. Green wallpaper and a large potted plant in one corner.'

Anna tilted her head in curiosity. 'How am I supposed to see that from the ground if you're on the third floor?'

'Easy,' he said. 'It doesn't have a front wall any more. It's like living permanently on a balcony. It's fine if the weather's okay, and it'll do till I start earning a wage. But if I need to get up in the middle of the night for a pee, I have to take care not to fall out and land on my head in the street.'

Hearing their laughter, the two soldiers at the adjacent table looked in their direction, gave them pained smiles, and raised their beer glasses in grudging salute.

It was four days before Luka Vogel contacted Anna again. He cycled to Zehlendorf to deliver his message in person because the Reichspost had shut down before the city's surrender, and the only working telephones were under the control of the Allied occupation forces.

'Pick me up at 9 p.m. tomorrow,' he told her. 'We're going to a nightclub.'

'Don't be silly, Luka. I don't have the clothes for a nightclub.'

'We're not going there to dance.'

When she drove the jeep into Hertzallee ten minutes early, he was already waiting for her. The sun was below the horizon, its dying glow painting the ruins a soft purple. In the light from the jeep's headlamps, she saw the yawning hole in the façade of the building behind him. He'd been telling her the truth: the whole front wall was out. She could make out the floors rising like shelves in a bookcase.

'You need to talk to your landlord about that,' she said laughingly, as he climbed in beside her.

'Best not to,' Luka said. 'He might ask for rent.'

'Where are we going?'

'The Zylinder – the Top Hat. It's in Kreuzberg, down by the Mariannenplatz. I'll give you directions as you drive.'

A US Army jeep with its headlamps blazing was assured of an unmolested passage through the city. Anna drove as fast as she dared.

She knew that nightclubs were like cockroaches: almost indestructible; they thrived even in the most inhospitable environments. Places like the Embassy and Rio Rita's had reopened almost in time to greet the first US soldier to arrive with a wad of Allied Occupation marks in his pocket. Where better to find a true cockroach like Manis Möller than in a cellar nightclub?

Three months earlier, the Top Hat had been almost unlit, save for the few lamps that still had paraffin in them. It had also been ankle-deep in water and crammed with civilians sheltering from the fighting in the streets above. Now it was dry, patched up and packed with customers. It had the same dangerous atmosphere Anna remembered from the Red Panther in Vienna. She half expected to see Marion and her artist friends sitting in one of the booths, off their heads on champagne and cocaine.

A jazz band was belting out ersatz Duke Ellington for a cigarette per musician per set. Most of the men on the dance floor were in uniform: American, British, French and Russian. At first glance, the civilians seemed well dressed, but Anna reckoned that if the lights went up they'd look as threadbare as a South Bronx bread line. The women had a brittle surface glamour about them, but their eyes seemed focussed elsewhere – they were the eyes of women who'd accepted that the cost of their next meal wasn't just the price in pfennigs shown on a market stall or a shop counter.

There was no doorman. If a fight started, someone would shout for the military police. Luka announced their arrival to the manager, a wizened roué in a gaudy suit of green and yellow tartan. He escorted them around the tables and into a private room at the back.

Manis Möller was lounging on a battered chesterfield, his heels up on a table. His shoes were off, his mismatched stockinged feet splayed outwards like those of a corpse on a slab. All he lacked was a tag tied to one big toe. His jacket was unbuttoned and gaped open. Anna could see the grip of a Walther *Polizeipistole* tucked into his waistband. If he needed it for protection, it certainly wasn't from the dangerously thin-looking woman whose head lay on his shoulder. Anna reckoned she'd have been better off in Kimpelbeuren DP camp, if only for the regular food.

On the table stood an ice bucket with a champagne bottle in it. Nearby were two empty glasses, one with a lipstick smudge on the rim. Möller nudged the bucket with a stockinged foot. The man in the gaudy suit refilled the glasses and returned the bottle to the ice.

'Well, well. If it isn't the lovely Frau Wolff,' Möller said, favouring her with a weak smile of recognition. He raised his glass. 'We all thought you'd run away for good.'

'It's Cantrell now. Anna Cantrell.'

The man in the check suit glanced questioningly at the champagne, then at Möller. Möller shook his head. Whatever else he was trading in, it wasn't hospitality.

The man nodded and left. Anna looked around for somewhere to sit. But the little room was made for two, and no audience.

'Get rid of the boy,' Möller said, glancing at Luka. He prised his companion's head off his shoulder and gestured towards the door. 'You too, baby.'

The woman went sourly, but Luka hesitated.

'Maybe I should stay with you,' he said to Anna.

Möller flapped one hand at him and laughed derisively. 'You don't want to lose another of these, boy. Get out of here.'

Anna bristled. She flicked a thumb over her shoulder. 'What say I go back there and tell those GIs you've made a pass at me and I didn't like it? They'd come in here and beat you into a real mess – gun or no gun.'

Möller looked hurt. 'Hey, why the bad attitude? We're all old friends, aren't we?'

'We never were.'

'Look, when doing business, I just prefer the talking gets done between the principals. It's easier that way. Just you and me. No one around to misinterpret what was said.'

Anna turned to Luka. 'It's alright. I'll be fine,' she said.

When they were alone, Möller patted the indentation in the sofa where his companion had sat.

'No, thank you,' Anna said. 'I'd prefer to stand.'

Möller laughed. 'I thought from the very first day Ivo brought me to your apartment in Vienna that you were going to be too unmanageable for him. I told him he should never have married a foreigner – and a Jew.'

'No one listens to you any more, Herr Möller. Except maybe in a very small part of a dust pile that used to be a city, in a country that used to be Germany. In the Reich that was supposed to last a thousand years, you can't be sure you'll not be in prison this time next week. But maybe I can help you. Did Luka Vogel tell you why I wanted to see you?'

'He didn't have to.'

'Well, just so there's no misunderstanding: I want my children back.'

Möller looked her up and down. Slowly. Deliberately. His eyes were enjoying the only power he had left over her. 'Oh, the thief wants the spoils of her crime returned to her, does she?' he said at length.

Anna held his gaze without flinching. 'I was never a thief, Herr Möller. I didn't steal my children away from Ivo Wolff. I took them to keep them safe. And, quite frankly, I think you're the very last person who should be accusing someone of criminality.'

He looked affronted. 'I'm just an honest man, trying to make a living in difficult times.'

Anna remembered the last time she had seen him: framed in Harry's binoculars, standing outside Dr Braudel's house. He'd been in uniform then, not that that had made him appear any less disreputable.

'You're an accomplice to my mother's murder,' she said calmly.

His scrawny face darkened. 'I think you should be careful what you say, Frau Anna.'

'My mother was an American citizen. If the Allied Control Council learn about that, they'll hang you at Spandau, long before they get around to the Nazi bigwigs they've caught. Now think again, Herr Möller. You were amongst the last people to see Bär and Antje. What happened to them?'

Like any good black marketeer, Möller took a while to consider the value of the deal on offer. Anna watched his larcenous little eyes while he did so. They disgusted her now no less than they had the day Ivo first brought him home.

'The last I heard, they were getting out of the city, into the countryside. To escape the bombs. Bombs dropped by your people, Frau Anna.'

'To Briesen? I already know that.'

'That's all I have. I don't recall Ivo saying anything else.'

'When did you last speak to him?'

'Shortly before he left for the Eastern Front.'

'Do you know if he's still alive?'

'There are several million women in Germany asking that same question about their men right now, Frau Anna.'

'But only one of them is asking *you*.'

'I wish I could help. I really do.'

'Is it money you want?'

Möller sat up straight in the chesterfield and made a formal bow. 'Welcome to the new Berlin, Frau Anna.'

'I'm not paying you a single mark without some kind of proof.'

'Frau Anna!' he objected, placing a hand over his heart as if she'd mortally offended him. 'I only take money if I have something of value to give. And, right now, I have nothing.'

'Will you ask around? Keep your eyes and ears open? Maybe talk to any of Ivo's friends, if they're still here?'

The sly smile he gave her made her feel as if she'd asked him to pimp for her.

'I'll do what I can,' he said. 'But I can't promise anything. You must have seen how it is here. You need to face the fact they may be under the rubble somewhere.'

Anna took the champagne bottle from the ice bucket, swung it to her lips. Until that moment, she hadn't realized her mouth was as dry and as dusty as that of a rubble woman's. She drained what was left in the bottle and stood it back on the table. 'Where do I ask for you?' she said, licking her lips.

'Here will be fine. If I'm not around, Herr Zuberlein can reach me.'

'The guy in the natty green suit?'

'Indeed.'

As she turned to go, Möller called after her, 'Take care, Anna Cantrell.'

'I intend to,' she said, looking back.

Möller had pulled the Walther out of his waistband and was studying it as if it were a favourite family heirloom. 'I'm pleased to hear it,' he said. 'Because you were always a stranger in this city.'

'Don't I know it?' Anna replied, opening the door to see Luka waiting just outside. She felt a sudden pang of guilt for bringing him into the orbit of a man like Manis Möller.

'It's still a dangerous place to get lost in, you know,' Möller called after her. 'The Gestapo might be gone, but people can still disappear, if they ask too many questions.'

Just before she shut the door on him, Anna gave him a sardonic smile. 'The new Berlin,' she said. 'Just like the old one. Only flatter.'

Twenty-One

They drove south out of the city past Tempelhof aerodrome, close to where Luka had had his apartment before the war. Anna remembered the solace she had gained then, warm in his bed. Looking at him now in the passenger seat, made thin through hunger and pain, maimed by the war, she felt complicit in his suffering.

She had stowed the jeep's canvas top. The deep, chugging rumble of aero engines on the tarmac was audible even above the sound of their own little motor. She pictured herself in the passenger terminal, holding Bär and Antje by the hand, about to board a plane back to Hollywood and Rex.

The image faded, and then all that was left was the hissing of the jeep's tyres on the concrete and the wind blowing over the windscreen as they sped through Schönefeld and onto the autobahn heading east. Anna kept her foot hard on the accelerator. They were deep into the Soviet zone now, and she didn't intend to stop for anyone.

At Ketschendorf they had to pull out to overtake a long convoy of trucks piled high with industrial loot on its way to the Soviet Union. The Russians were taking people too, or so Anna had heard: chemists, physicists, rocket engineers… human reparations they weren't afraid to snatch off the street or out of bed. To make Luka look less like a civilian, she'd filched a khaki windbreaker from a male friend at the Berlin UNRRA office.

Beyond the concrete ribbon of the autobahn, the baked fields lay waiting for the scythe. Anna saw the skeletal remains of horses, long since butchered at the roadside for meat.

Two hours after leaving the city she saw the sign for Briesen and pulled off the autobahn. Even then, she didn't let her hopes run completely out of control. During the drive she had often put herself in the mind of Gertrude Steigler. She felt nothing for the woman, besides a vague feeling that she couldn't possibly have had the visceral determination to protect Bär and Antje the way their mother would have. But self-preservation alone would have made Gertrude stay well clear of the Red Army's advance – Hannelore Lange had said Ivo's mistress had been a card-carrying Party member. The question was, had she kept Bär and Antje with her?

Before the war, Briesen had been a pretty little town with a couple of churches and a market square. Now it was a forlorn collection of battered houses, some with their roofs still missing, and the spires of the churches had been shelled into stumps by the Russians to deter fascist snipers.

Anna stopped the jeep in the centre of the square and pulled on the handbrake. She told Luka to stay in the vehicle, in case anyone took a fancy to it, or slashed the tyres.

A gang of village men was repairing the pockmarked walls of the main church. Anna walked over and asked them if Fräulein Gertrude Steigler or any of her relatives still lived in the town.

'Who wants to know?' grunted a man she assumed was the foreman. He seemed made up of a hard-faced slab of pasty skin that seemed unnourished by either sunlight or generosity, with ears that stuck out like spinnakers. He looked her up and down, his brows lifting ponderously as he took in her US army fatigues. 'Come to liberate us from the Bolsheviks, have you? All by yourself?'

'I understand a Fräulein Steigler came here from Berlin in April last year, to stay with relatives,' Anna said, ignoring the contempt in his voice. 'She came to escape the bombing. She brought two children with her – a boy and a girl. I'm trying to find them.'

'I know where you can find Fräulein Steigler,' said a youth of about fifteen with a sweat-streaked mop of hair. 'Come with me.'

He led Anna around the side of the church and into the shade.

That was when she saw the graves.

They'd been dug before the earth had hardened. Three low mounds with white wooden crosses, unmarked.

Anna felt the strength leave her legs as if she'd been shot. She reached out to steady herself against the stone wall of the church.

'That's Fräulein Steigler,' the boy said, pointing to the middle grave. 'The Reds had their fun with her. She was too stupid to burn her Party card, so they found it and then they shot her. It was a few days after they got here.'

Anna covered her gaping mouth with her hands. Three graves. One identified. Two still to name.

If I scream now, she thought, they'll hear me back in Berlin.

But before she could ask the question, the boy wiped his brow and said, 'The far one's Kurt Wegener. He was daft enough to pick up his dad's shotgun when they arrived. The other's old Herr Kuhlmann. He tried to stop them taking his tractor.'

I'll pray for forgiveness later, Anna told herself, for being so thankful that it's two people I never knew who lie buried here.

'Do you know where the two children she came here with are now?' she asked, her heart flailing against her ribcage.

Before the boy could answer, a coarse voice came from behind her. 'Go and ask Herr Schardt if he wants to talk to an American about his niece, Gertrude.'

Anna turned and saw the foreman, his big hands tucked under his braces, his stained shirt unbuttoned to reveal a sweaty tangle of chest hair.

As the boy hurried away, Anna said, 'I'll go with him. I just want a word, that's all.'

'You'll stay here, until Herr Schardt tells me otherwise. We don't take kindly to occupiers strolling around asking questions. It's bad enough with the Russkies taking whatever suits their fancy.'

Anna thought of simply ignoring him and running after the boy but decided against it. It would be unwise to make enemies in a place like this, so far away from help. She walked back to the jeep.

'Any luck?' Luka asked.

'I don't know yet,' Anna said, and settled down to wait.

Anna checked her wristwatch. Fifteen minutes had passed. Then, from around the church, the boy reappeared. He called to the foreman, who was back with his work gang. 'They'll talk to her, if she's on her own.'

The foreman shrugged. The boy gestured to Anna to follow him.

He led her down a rutted track to a small house on the other side of the village. Behind the house stood a small copse. Crows shrieked from the treetops at her approach. They didn't seem to enjoy being under Soviet occupation any more than the humans in Briesen.

Standing in the porch was a woman in her mid-fifties, in a threadbare summer dress. She wore a scarf over her head and on her feet a pair of battered shoes – men's, several sizes too large. She looked as though she had been grown out of the soil, her skin as parched and cracked as the earth plot beside the house.

'I'm looking for Herr Schardt,' Anna said pleasantly. 'I'm very sorry about his niece, truly sorry.'

'He's out trapping for food. I don't know when he'll be back. Anyway, I'm the Steigler in the family. Gertrude was my sister's child.'

'Then you have my deepest condolences,' Anna assured her. 'But maybe you can help me.'

'I doubt it,' the woman said, giving Anna a hard look. 'We're all out of charity around here.'

Anna dipped into her pocket and pulled out a wad of Allied Occupation marks.

The woman laughed. 'They're no use here,' she said. 'The Russkies don't recognize them.'

Feeling foolish, Anna stuffed the notes back into her slacks. 'I just want to know about the children Fräulein Steigler brought with her when she came here from Berlin. Can you help me? Please, do you know where they are? If you have even the slightest idea—'

'You've wasted your time,' the woman said brusquely, shaking her head. 'Gertrude brought no children here. None.'

'But I've been told by someone who knew Gertrude in Berlin, someone who lived with her, that she came here to escape the air raids,' Anna protested.

'Yes, she did. But she brought no children with her. Maybe she dropped them off along the way. Maybe she left them in Fürstenwalde, or Jacobsdorf… Timbuktu? Maybe there never were any children. What would I know?'

'Are you sure?'

The woman gave a cruel laugh. 'Do you think I wouldn't have noticed? We had enough mouths to feed as it was, and precious little to put in them.'

'Their father was the man Fräulein Steigler was having an affair with,' said Anna. 'Surely, she must at least have mentioned them to you.'

The woman waved a hand dismissively. 'If she did, I don't recall it.'

Anna chewed her bottom lip, afraid the hopelessness she felt would make her weep in the presence of this tough woman, a woman who was regarding her with weary impatience, like a teacher waiting for the slowest child in class to catch up.

At length she found her voice again.

'If you should hear news of them, would you please try to contact me through the Allied *Kommandatura* in Berlin? My name is Anna Cantrell. The children are called Bernhardt and Antje. He'd be ten, she's eight. They speak German and English. I promise you I'll make it worth your while.'

'If I hear anything, I'll be sure to call President Truman immediately,' the woman said scathingly, turning back into her porch.

Anna walked back to the jeep. Luka looked at her expectantly. She said nothing. Starting the engine, she wrenched the jeep around in a spray of dust and drove back towards the autobahn. One hundred metres out of Briesen, she abruptly pulled over, put the shift into neutral, pulled on the handbrake, slumped into Luka's shoulder and poured out her pain in a torrent of tears.

Luka put his maimed arm around her, then turned into her so that he could gently stroke her head with his good hand. While the tears flowed, they allowed themselves to remember the Tempelhof apartment, and the fleeting comfort each had found there.

Just short of Wildau they ran into a traffic jam: on the bridge over the Dahme, a Soviet truck had lost a kissing contest to a T34 tank. It took almost three hours to clear. Then they were stopped by a temporary checkpoint the Soviets had thrown across the autobahn. They spent another two hours by the roadside while the NKVD troops did nothing other than make them wait. Eventually, Anna's papers were returned to her and they were free to go. By the time they reached Berlin it was getting dark.

Anna had never entered the city from this direction before, but she knew where the American zone began. All she had to do was find it. Luka knew Berlin better than she did, and she had assumed he'd guide her. But Luka was by now asleep, and she didn't like to wake him.

It was beginning to get worryingly close to curfew time when Anna admitted defeat and pulled up by the kerb next to the shell of what had once been a factory.

'Luka, I think I'm lost,' she said, nudging him awake.

Rubbing his eyes, he looked around. But, just as Anna had found, when a whole city centre is in ruins, one street looks much like another; one shattered slab of masonry all but identical to the next.

It didn't help that the signposts they passed were now in Russian. The streets were eerily empty. There was no one around to ask for directions. Luka suggested they press on until they found a crossroads.

A quarter moon was rising above the jagged skyline, but its weak glow barely penetrated the canyons of ruins. All Anna could see in the light from the jeep's headlights was an unfolding tapestry of fractured grey concrete, sometimes studded with ink-black windows.

They entered a cleared space and Anna saw ahead of them a row of iron pillars holding up what looked like a covered walkway.

'It's the Kottbusser Tor U-Bahn station,' Luka said in a relieved voice. 'We're in the American zone. Take the second exit out of the square and keep going. Eventually we'll hit Lindenstrasse.'

'Thank God for that,' Anna said, putting her foot down.

They sped along, heading north-west. Anna leaned forward over the steering wheel. There were no formal checkpoints to pass. She was searching for one of the signs written in English, Russian and French to tell you were leaving or entering a sector, trying to ensure she didn't stray into the Russian zone. Approaching a junction, she slowed to make the turn.

As she did so, a truck came out of nowhere. Its lights were off, only a torch beam wavering in the cab. Slamming on the brakes, Anna missed it by inches. The jeep's engine stalled. A dangerous silence fell.

Dark figures spilled out of the truck and gathered around its front fender. The torch beam played over the jeep, blooming against the windshield, etching the glass with dark striations and scratches. Anna heard a peremptory voice call out – in Russian.

'Shit,' she said. 'We must have taken a wrong turn leaving Kottbusser Tor.'

She trod on the clutch and started the engine again, thanking her lucky stars the carburettor hadn't flooded.

The grumble of the engine was the cue for further shouting, though the voices sounded more like those of drunks falling out of a bar than soldiers issuing orders. Then she realized that was exactly what they were: these Russian were tanked to the eyeballs.

'*Frau – komm!*'

The command was followed by raucous laughter. Then the cry was taken up, becoming a chant. '*Frau – komm! Frau – komm!*'

Anna had learned enough in her short time in Berlin to know that these two simple words were amongst the first that most Red Army soldiers had learned when they'd stormed into the city. *Woman – come!*

'We have to get out of here, Anna,' Luka hissed.

Anna didn't need persuading. She didn't need to remember the look in Hannelore Lange's eyes, or the little wooden cross on the grave of Gertrude Steigler at Briesen. Or try to imagine the face of the unknown Odelinda, whose last name the rubble women at the site of her old apartment couldn't remember, the one who'd hanged herself after she'd obeyed the command: *Frau – komm.*

All she knew she had to do was floor the accelerator pedal and hope to God that the engine didn't stall again.

The motor bellowed like a water buffalo with constipation. The tyres spun. Anna wrenched at the steering wheel. The night filled with the oily stench of burning rubber. In the wing mirror, she saw the truck's lights snap on. Figures moving in the glare. Dropping to their knees. Taking aim.

It's alright, she thought. Drunk men can't shoot straight.

She drove her foot down on the pedal until she thought her ankle was going to snap. Instinctively she hunched in the seat, making herself a smaller target. She yelled to Luka to do the same, but the roaring of the jeep's engine defeated her. She felt something akin to an electric shock, or a bullwhip being cracked very close to her left ear – a round flying past, far too close for comfort. Then another.

In the passenger seat, Luka ducked.

'Stay down,' she shouted.

Luka stayed down.

This time Anna didn't miss the turn. A roadside poster portrait of Joseph Stalin, the size of a barn door, flew out of the darkness and disappeared behind her without waving. In the glare of the headlamps a sign read: *You Are Now Entering the American Sector.*

Thank fuck for that, she thought, as she saw a second roadblock ahead. A friendly one.

She slowed the jeep. How stupid would it be now to be shot by friends?

When they came to a halt, all Anna could hear was the sound of her own breathing. All she could smell was the gasoline smell of the jeep, like the sweat of a Derby winner. All she could see were American GIs walking towards her with their carbines levelled.

She put out her hand against the windscreen to steady herself. But the glass was wet, and her hand slipped. When she pulled it away, it had something warm, red and grey in it. Like oatmeal and strawberries. It slid between her fingers and dripped down into the footwell of the passenger seat.

'It's alright, Luka,' she said. 'We're safe.'

His head was still slumped forward on the dash.

'Luka, we've made it.'

But the only reply she got was the ticking of the jeep's motor as it cooled.

Twenty-Two

When Anna arrived at the Lehrter Bahnhof, all she could learn was that Louisa Vogel's train had crossed the checkpoint between Allied and Soviet-occupied Germany. Before the war the journey from Hamburg to Berlin took only a couple of hours on the futuristic, high-speed service the Nazis had built. Nowadays, it could take a couple of days. But Anna was prepared to wait. She believed she owed it to Louisa Vogel.

The station had been blackened by bomb blasts. Most of the roof was gone. There was a pile of rusting railroad tracks stacked in what had once been the first-class lounge, and the nearest thing to comfort was to be found on a hard wooden chair in the little café. Anna had brought a book with her to pass the time: *Let The Record Speak*, a collection of writings by Dorothy Thompson, the journalist who'd helped get her photos published in America.

The hours passed like a slow torture. Marion's murder and the children's abduction had happened almost too quickly to comprehend. But this felt as if she were on death row, waiting for the hangman to arrive.

It was dark when the locomotive – belching steam and emitting weary bellows of sound, as if it were a great, mortally wounded beast breathing its last – pulled into the platform. The door at the end of every carriage opened as if to a single command and a flood of exhausted, grim-faced passengers spilled out, flowing around Anna as she stood there in her blue reefer coat.

Even then it was a while before Anna spotted Luka's sister: they hadn't met since before the war – that awful time at Bad Saarow, after she'd told Luka it was all over. Louisa Vogel was carrying a single small cardboard suitcase and dressed in a man's overcoat too large for her slim frame. Anna reckoned she must have either stolen it or got it by bartering. But her pretty face, though pinched from the discomfort of the long journey, was bright with anticipation at the thought of seeing her brother again.

Anna felt her heart tighten in her chest. This was going to be even worse than she'd imagined.

'Oh, it's *you*,' Louisa said, recognizing her. She looked around for her brother. 'Where is he? Where's Luka? Why are *you* here? Don't tell me he's fallen under that cheap spell of yours again.'

Anna ignored the jibe. She knew she couldn't keep the news about Luka from showing on her face for long, and she didn't want Louisa breaking down on a busy platform where everyone would see the poor girl's agony. The only solution was to get back on the train.

'Come with me,' she said, taking Louisa firmly by the arm. 'We have to talk. Somewhere private.'

They were standing by the first-class carriage. Anna almost pushed Louisa up the steps into the corridor and into the nearest empty compartment.

'What's going on?' Luka's sister demanded to know. 'As far as I'm concerned, you and I have nothing to talk about, whatsoever. You already know what I think about you. Let go of my arm. You're hurting me.'

There's no way of softening the blow, Anna thought. You can't ease someone into heart-rending grief one step at a time.

If she was going to sound brutal, it was because what happened to Luka *was* brutal.

'I'm so, so, very sorry, Louisa. Luka is dead. The Russians killed him. Forgive me – I don't know how else to say it.'

Louisa Vogel stared at her for a moment, expressionless. Then she dropped the little cardboard suitcase. The cheap latch failed and the lid flew open, spilling her change of underwear, two spare dresses and her toiletries onto the compartment floor. She slumped down onto a seat, covering her mouth with her hands.

'They were drunk,' Anna said, sitting opposite her and leaning forward across the gap between them. 'It was just a stupid accident. We shouldn't have even been there. We just got lost.'

Maybe the hours on the train had temporarily paralysed the muscles in Louisa's face. Maybe the news had overwhelmed her so much she was too stunned to react. Whatever the cause, the utter stillness in her eyes, her silence, was more than Anna could bear.

And then Louisa said, very quietly, 'We… you said "we".'

'Yes. I was with him. It was over in an instant. He couldn't possibly have suffered.'

'But you were with him. He was taking you somewhere. Or bringing you back. Were you together?'

'Yes, in a jeep. I was driving. He was in the passenger seat. We ran into a bunch of drunk Russians.'

'I meant *together*,' Louisa said pointedly. The paralysis had ended. Her voice, and her face, were close to breaking. 'He wouldn't have been there if you two weren't *together*.'

Anna shook her head. 'It wasn't like that. We'd learned how to love each other as friends. Good friends. That was better for us than the alternative.'

'Better for "us"?' Louisa said. 'Luka had a choice in this, did he?'

Anna sighed. 'I'm not the *femme fatale* you seem to think I am, Louisa. Far from it. I'm a wreck. You're right. He was better off without me.'

To stop herself breaking down completely, Louisa began to recover her belongings from the compartment floor, stuffing them back into the suitcase. Anna moved to help.

'Don't!' Louisa snapped. When she had refilled the case, she tried to lock it, but the catch was broken. Anna took the belt from her coat and offered it as a strap. Louisa received it in silence, returning to the leatherette seat when the case had been secured. She placed it on her knees, folding her hands together primly on the lid, trying to regain control of herself. 'Can I see him, please?'

'I hope so,' said Anna. 'There's an enquiry going on, of course. But when it's over, I'll take care of the funeral. I promise.'

'That won't be necessary.'

'Let me at least help.'

'The Russians shot him, you say?'

'They're denying it, of course. They say it was the Americans. But that isn't true. I should know, after all. I was right next to him.'

The conductor appeared in the corridor. He tapped on the glass, gesturing for them to leave.

'I don't know what to do,' Louisa said desperately. 'I was going to stay in his apartment until I found work. I don't think I could bear that now – not without him.'

'That's out of the question,' Anna said. 'I've seen it – it doesn't even have a front wall.'

'I can't go back to Vienna. The Born-Hof apartment has gone, bombed to pieces. Our parents were inside.'

Anna covered her mouth. She could feel the tears welling in her eyes. But to weep would be an act of gross selfishness.

When Louisa spoke again, it was if she were talking to an invisible occupant of the compartment, because her words weren't addressed to Anna. 'I can just about afford a shared room in a guest house for about a week. After that, I'll have no money left for rent.'

'You can stay at my place,' Anna suggested. 'There's a room free for a while – the journalist who has it is in Frankfurt, on assignment.'

Louisa turned towards her. For a moment Anna couldn't bear to look into the younger woman's eyes.

'Stay with *you*?'

'I could try to show you that I really cared for Luka. We could swap stories about him. It might help us both.'

Louisa shrugged. She stood up and followed Anna off the train.

They left the Lehrter Bahnhof together, Louisa clasping her little battered suitcase to the overcoat that wasn't really hers, Anna holding back the tears for them both.

Did I look that lost, she wondered, when Marion led me up the gangplank of the *Deutschland*, leaving Rex behind, all those years ago?

If I did, it's a miracle I made it this far.

From the desk of Miss Anna Cantrell,
The Hearst Building,
Zehlendorf,
Berlin

19 September 1945

Dearest Harry,

I heard you'd returned to Berlin from the public affairs people at the Kommandatura. *I'm sure you know by now about poor Luka Vogel. It was a dreadful thing, and though we were no longer 'an item', his death has come as a terrible shock.*

All the more terrible, then, for his poor sister, Louisa. She is a charming, intelligent young woman, and any help you might be able to give her in this distressing time would be a personal favour to me. I know it's a bit presumptuous, but I was hoping you might help find her a job at the Komm. I'm sure getting her a Persil ticket would be easy. Anything you can do would be wonderful.

I know you're a good fellow and would want to help if you can,

Yours sincerely,

Anna

PS: On the off-chance that some delicious fräulein hasn't yet managed to manacle you to her bedpost – how about a drink at the Café Leon sometime? They say the comics are the funniest in Berlin.

Capt. H. Taverner,
Deputy C/O, Urban Census Collation Unit,
Room 501/GF,
British Forces Berlin

26 September 1945

My Dear Anna,

How lovely to hear from you again. Yes, I know about Luka Vogel – quite dreadful. Please accept my condolences.

In regard to his sister, yes, we have a regular requirement for clerks and secretaries who can jump the deNazification hurdles. I'll try to do what I can.

On the fräulein front – no, I remain entirely un-manacled at present. The idea of a drink at the Leon sounds perfect. We can all do with a laugh these days.

Yours,

Harry

The Berlin apartment, 1989

Harry reached over to his bedside table and picked up his cigarette case. He offered one to Elly and lit it for her, then pulled out one for himself.

Was it too late to be smoking? Or too early?' Elly wondered, hearing a distant clank from a water pipe as someone in the apartment block turned on a tap – either an early riser or a late returner. The clock on Harry's bedside table showed 04.20.

'So, that's how you met Mummy,' she said. 'When she was at her very lowest. It's good to know that something good came out of poor Luka's death.' She thought for a moment. 'But you didn't get married until ten years later, did you? I've never put you down as a slow worker.'

'I promise you it wasn't because I was playing hard to get.'

'I should hope not,' said Elly. 'Mummy always says she fell in love with you at first sight.'

'I'm the first and only fake she's ever fallen for,' Harry said, with a smile. 'If she hadn't learned better, she'd never have become an antiques dealer.'

'Nonsense. You're an original,' Elly said, kissing her father on the cheek. 'Frame's a bit battered, and the varnish is flaking in places. But I suppose the brushwork's good enough. I'd offer, what – fifty quid at auction?'

'Very funny, darling.'

'From what you've told me, I got the impression that Mummy was thawing just a little towards Anna – when they left the train station together. What went wrong?'

'When the results of the inquiry were released, Louisa learned that Luka was only there that day because Anna had gone into the Soviet zone in search of her children. She convinced herself that Anna had persuaded him, that he'd only accompanied her because of her hold over him.'

'But a lifetime is a long while to keep blaming someone,' Elly said softly. 'Anna obviously never intended it to happen.'

Harry took the ashtray from the bedside table and placed it between them. He tapped his cigarette end into it and took a pull. Then he put his thumb under his chin, his hand and the cigarette sticking out of it in front of his face like a tusk.

You're not an antique after all, Elly thought. You're an old bull elephant who knows the end is coming into view, so you're doing your remembering while you still have time. She felt her heart crack for him.

'So, Manis Möller wouldn't, or couldn't, help,' she said, prompting him to continue the story. 'The woman at Briesen had no knowledge of the children. Poor Anna – all that guilt at losing them, and then Luka's death on top. That would have broken some people. What did she do next?'

'There wasn't much Anna could do. As autumn turned to winter, she tried to juggle her work as a press photographer with her continuing search for Bär and Antje. She put advertisements in the papers when they restarted. She visited other DP camps. But the ads went unanswered, and there were countless camps and countless DPs in them. The chances of her finding the children were receding with every passing day.

'And there was something else causing Anna's hopes to wither, perhaps even to die. This was the time when the Jews were truly learning the monstrous scale of the crime that had been committed against them.'

'As Anna asked her questions in numberless dingy offices, at tented local headquarters set up in open fields, in half-destroyed buildings with blown-out windows, she began to hear the last echoes of Marion's family in Europe. News of Bauer uncles and aunts lost at Sachsenhausen… Buchenwald… Sobibor…. She learned of Bauer nephews and nieces, Bauer cousins, all vanished into the smoke at Auschwitz-Birkenau… Belzec… Treblinka… A veritable Cook's Tour of the worst the human species can inflict upon its own kind.'

'The winter that year was brutal. People froze to death. The thought of the children suffering almost made Anna hope they *had* died. But she wouldn't give up.'

'I think I would have lost my mind,' Elly said.

Harry stared at the glowing tip of his cigarette, as if it might show him the way ahead.

'What she didn't know was that the Schardt woman at Briesen hadn't been exactly honest with her. Not only that, neither had Manis Möller. Because Ivo Wolff was alive. He was in Berlin. And he was working for the Russians.'

Elly stared at him in silence as Harry put his hand into the portfolio case, rummaged around, and pulled out a photo of a man sitting in what looked like a prison cell. A man dressed in a civilian suit. A man in his mid-thirties, lean and urbane, whose weary and slightly dismissive expression couldn't hide the fact that he might once have made a very fetching male photographic model.

'When Ivo Wolff was sent to the Eastern Front,' Harry began, 'he got himself taken prisoner by the Red Army. Normally, that would have meant hard labour and starvation in somewhere like Siberia, with a less than one-in-three chance of ever seeing home again. But the Russians kept their eyes open for Germans they thought might be of more use to them than merely as a beast of burden or a human shovel. By early 1945, they already had a group of pro-communist Germans living in Moscow, ready to be put in place to run a Soviet-backed government when the war ended. Walter Ulbricht, later the leader of East Germany, was flown into Berlin even before the shooting stopped.'

Harry blew a puff of cigarette smoke out of the corner of his mouth. It lingered in the air before drifting away, as if someone had just called for a ceasefire.

'The only question Ivo Wolff asked his captors when they asked if he was interested was, "Where do I sign?"

'Three weeks after V.E. Day, the Russians sent him back to Berlin, where Ulbricht's people put him to work. Something of a survivor, was our Ivo. If the Cold War ever turns hot, the missiles fly and the world turns to ash, you'll find the likes of Ivo Wolff still around, asking the cockroaches if they need anyone to do the dusting.'

'How do you know all this?' Elly asked.

'Because even house cleaners for cockroaches make mistakes. Ivo had always enjoyed nightclubs, women and good spirits. And there weren't much of those to be had in the Soviet sector. You must remember, this was before the Wall went up. If Ivo wanted proper fun, a bit like he'd experienced before the war, he had to go into the Western sectors. And that's what he did while the snow was still on the ground in early '46.'

'What happened?'

'The usual. A bar fight. Only this time, Ivo wasn't the one who ended it, like he had when Anna fell in love with him at the Red Panther in Vienna. This time it was the British military police.'

Harry pinned the photo of Wolff to the quilt with his finger.

'I was working at the *Kommandatura*, with Field Intelligence, which was why I got the telephone call. It was standard practice then – just in case someone nicked a Nazi bigwig in disguise and hadn't realized he was on the wanted list. We've caught you a Wolff, they said. What manner of wolf? I asked. A Wolff with two *F*s. First name, Ivo.

'To which I replied: two *F*s? That's fucking fortunate. And started searching through the files for Anna's last known address.'

Twenty-Three

It was raining when Anna arrived at the Top Hat. *As soon as you can make it*, the message had said. She'd been clutching it all the way from the Hearst Building, somehow unable to transfer it to a pocket because if it were out of her sight, it might not exist. Now it was a cold, soggy mess in her palm.

'Delivered by a guy in a green and yellow checked suit,' a housemate had said when Anna returned from an assignment at the Allied Control Council. 'If it's a date, he looked about thirty years too old and fifty pounds too light on his feet to be one of yours.'

Anna had known at once the messenger was Herr Zuberlein. Möller was too much of a black-market baron to deliver it himself. Nor had he signed it – the only signatures Möller was interested in being the ones to be found tucked away in the corner of an oil painting. But if the call meant what she thought it might mean, the note was more precious to her than a Titian or a Vermeer.

As Zuberlein showed her into the club's private room, Möller's smile turned her stomach. He reminded her of the conger eel she'd once seen when she'd taken Bär and Antje to the Berlin aquarium before the war, waiting in its lair for a passing minnow, its eyes blank and soulless.

He'd ordered champagne again, she saw. And on the table, beside the ice bucket, lay a twist of paper that she assumed contained cocaine.

'It's a bit early for all this, isn't it?' she asked, trying to sound nonchalant. 'It's hours before this place gets going.'

'I thought we might want to spend some time together,' Möller said. 'See if we can make a deal. Take off your coat and sit down.'

Sliding onto the chesterfield beside him felt how she imagined it would be to sink into a bath filled with something ice cold and truly disgusting. But the end of the sofa stopped her putting more space between them. 'Well, do you have news of Bär and Antje?' she asked, trying to keep the loathing from showing on her face.

His reply was brutally to the point. 'No. I'm afraid not.'

She opened her mouth to scream at him. What was he playing at – getting her hopes up? Was this some sort of sick game to him?

But if he hadn't got news of the children, then perhaps… 'It's Ivo, isn't it?' she said. 'Is he alive?'

'That all depends on who's asking.'

'You know damn well who's asking.'

'As long as it's not anyone else but you, Frau Anna.'

'Have you heard from him?'

The smile stayed on Möller's face as he poured Anna a glass of champagne before answering. The black marketeer's trick, she thought. Delay showing the goods. Ramp up the customer's expectation.

'Again, that depends,' he said.

'How much do you want?'

Sitting upright in the chesterfield, he raised his glass to her and said, 'Like I said last time, welcome to the new Berlin, Frau Anna.'

'It will take me a while to arrange a transfer of money,' Anna told him. 'It's not like there's a Cook's or a Western Union on the Ku-Dam I can go to.'

Möller put his hand on her knee. 'I wasn't thinking of money.'

Even the sound of the jazz band rehearsing beyond the door couldn't penetrate the sudden leaden silence. Anna felt her skin slither on her bones, all the way up to her neck.

Reach into his waistband, she told herself, so that he thinks he's won. Then pull out the pistol he carries and shoot him dead between those disgustingly venal eyes. She imagined him slumped in the chesterfield, the blood oozing down his hollow cheeks, unable to look at anyone like that ever again.

Welcome to the new Berlin.

And then she remembered there were countless women in the city who for months had had nothing but themselves to sell in return for the slim hope of surviving another day. Of feeding themselves. Of keeping their children alive. Of buying a little hope. Weren't Bär and Antje worth a few moments of self-loathing? If Möller could put her in touch with Ivo to find out where they were, maybe she could bury the cost of the deal deep in her mind, deep enough so that it could never escape.

Her eyes fell upon the twist of cocaine lying on the table. Möller had even brought the anaesthetic with him.

Anna drained her glass in one slug and held it out for a refill. She remembered that night in the Red Panther in Vienna, sitting with Marion and her friends, champagne and cocaine in full view, while a riot broke out around them. Ivo had marched in and stopped it almost by the sheer strength of his personality.

What wouldn't I give for a knight in shining armour right now?

And then, as if she'd uttered some form of occult incantation, the door flew off its lock, slamming back against the crimson, flock-papered wall.

Her saviour turned out to be a Scots Fusilier corporal with a ginger moustache, a kilt and a chest that a bison might envy. For a moment, Anna assumed he was part of a raid.

Möller did, too. His left hand moved inwards, towards his jacket.

'I wouldn'ae do thart, Jerry,' the corporal said.

Möller had no English, but the slow shake of the Scotsman's head needed no translating. Nor did the revolver he'd drawn from the holster on his gleaming white Blancoed belt. Möller let his hand drop.

'Are you Miss Cantrell bae any chance?' the soldier asked, fixing Anna with a ferocious stare.

'Yes, I am.'

'Then y'd best come along, lassie. I've a jeep ootside.'

'Why? What have I done?'

The soldier's bushy ginger brows lifted wearily, as if he hadn't expected to have to explain things to a two-year-old.

'Captain Taverner says I'm t' tell ye tha' he's got yoor man under lock an' key. An' he does nae know how long he can keep him afore th' Rooskies arrive.'

Grabbing her coat, Anna lifted the champagne bottle out of its ice bucket.

Möller watched her. It was if the fire of his impotent fury had burned through whatever it was that held his features together, so that they sagged as if his skull was in danger of collapsing.

'That's the trouble with dealing on the black market,' Anna told him. 'You have to have something worth buying.'

As she followed the corporal through the door, Anna tried not to imagine what she'd be doing now if she hadn't told the reporter from the *Chicago Tribune*, whose room was next to hers in the Hearst Building, where she was going.

The former *Ordnungspolizei* station was in the British sector, a nondescript slab of dirty grey concrete with three rows of identical windows made even more brutal by the Biedermeier apartment block next door. Both had escaped the worst of the fighting, though over the police station's door was an ugly lesion where the Nazi eagle and swastika emblem had been chiselled away. Number 5, Blaumannstrasse was where detainees – suspected war criminals or merely crooks – were held before they were transferred out to the main British interrogation centre at Bad Nenndorf near Hanover. A board outside read: *84 Field Security Section. British Troops Berlin.*

The cell was tiled like a public lavatory and smelt much the same. The door was as thick as the door to a bank vault and had once been painted gloss blue. Now it was a grubby grey. There was no window. The only light came from a bulb in a dirty Perspex hemisphere on the ceiling, like the storm-light on a ship. Blotches of brown showed through the yellowing cover, where generations of flies had gathered to die.

Whenever he was in the cell, Harry Taverner tried to allow himself a moment of reflection on the fate of those who'd languished here since the place had been built half a century before. He had a hunch that more than a few of them would have been resistors to the Nazi regime. Their futures would have been far bleaker than that of the man sitting on the mattress of the single metal bed bolted to the wall.

Ivo Wolff looked as though he hadn't recovered from his hangover, though he'd been brought in late last night and it was now seven in the evening of the following day. He wore no tie, his suit was crumpled, and there was stubble on his chin. But his eyes were as bright as ice. He was still the matinee idol – even if it was one whose studio had fired him and whose agent wasn't answering his calls.

I can see why she fell for him, Harry thought.

'Really, Ivo – if I may call you Ivo –' Harry said, 'you don't strike me as the type who'd enjoy working for the Soviets. All that spouting Comrade Stalin's guff and arse-licking the commissars to stay out of Siberia. Not your style at all, I'd have thought.'

Wolff's eyes closed. Harry would have assumed he'd fallen asleep were it not for the faint smile that made one corner of Ivo's mouth twitch, as if a tired nerve had fired.

'I mean, what do you do all day?' Harry continued. 'Write out the thoughts of Comrade Chairman Stalin to read to German civilians who wish you weren't there? Not much of a career for a man who flew in the *Hindenburg* to New York, is it?'

Wolff's eyes snapped open. 'How did you know that?' he asked, shifting his back against the tiles.

'Oh, we know a great deal about you, Ivo. You'd be surprised.'

'Let me out of here. I'm an accredited member of the Socialist Unity Party of Germany. You have no right to hold me.'

'Ah, yes, the SED, Walter Ulbricht's new party. Or should I really say, Comrade Stalin's? After all, he's the one pulling the strings, back in Moscow, isn't he? Pity the SED isn't actually up and running yet. So as far as I'm concerned, you're just another citizen of an occupied country.'

'I'm also a member of the Soviet delegation to the Allied Control Council,' Ivo said, as if he found the fact tedious. 'Keeping me here will provoke an international confrontation.'

'If you haven't noticed, we've been dealing with one of those since 1939. And we won,' Harry said pleasantly.

'But you won't win one against the Soviet Union. You're deep inside their zone of occupation. Here in Berlin, you, the Americans and the French have a fraction of the power the Red Army can call upon. They could throw you all out before breakfast tomorrow if they chose – those who were still alive. I'm not the one here at a disadvantage, Herr—?'

Harry didn't supply an answer. Instead, he said casually, 'How's the coffee in the Soviet zone, Ivo? Still making it out of acorns? What do they pay you in? Coal?'

He had Wolff's attention now. Anna was right, he thought: you can see the self-interest burning in his eyes like the eternal flame.

He pushed harder. 'Comrade Stalin might have more men stationed in Germany than we do, but he doesn't have the atomic bomb. We're able to offer you a lot more than acorns, coal and unremitting communist gloom, Ivo. Much more.'

Wolff wasn't ready to answer, but Harry could tell by his expression that he was circling the line, interested in the bait, wondering if he should bite.

'When your friends in Moscow have finished looting their sector there won't be much left over for you to enjoy,' Harry continued. 'You'll be stuck in an empty shop with nothing on the shelves. Meanwhile, the Americans are about to start pumping billions of dollars into the Western sector. Before you know it, our Germany will be thriving again. Yours will be stuck permanently in 1945. You'll have backed the wrong side.'

The very tip of Wolff's tongue popped out of one corner of his mouth and slid along his upper lip, like a snake tasting the air. Fast. Almost too fast for Harry to notice. But not quite fast enough.

'What are you suggesting?' Wolff asked.

Harry gave a casual shrug. 'Only that an ambitious man with his future ahead of him needs to think carefully about choosing his friends. We must be about the same age, I should think. Thirty-three?'

'Thirty-four,' Wolff said.

'Well, there you have it. Both of us still young. The war behind us, thank God. All sorts of opportunities ahead. Only you'll be going home to study the Party manifesto, and I'll going to the Royale, and when I get there, there's going to be *real* Johnnie Walker in my glass.'

'I don't have access to military secrets, if that's what you're after,' Ivo said.

Harry smiled. 'Oh, nothing so mechanical. If you're the man I think you are, Ivo, you'll have a glorious career ahead of you in politics, in the SED. Who knows, you might even take over from Ulbricht one day. You could be running eastern Germany by the time you're forty.'

Wolff seemed to like this proposition. His head swung slowly from side to side, as if he was comparing it to several other enticing futures on offer. 'And if someone like me was to find himself in such a rewarding position—'

Harry finished his sentence for him. '—he would have intimate access to top-level decisions on Soviet policy and strategy.'

Wolff nodded, as if out of nowhere they'd reached the same conclusion together. 'I can imagine there would be certain people eager for a sight of such information,' he said.

'I'm sure there would be,' Harry agreed.

'And how would such people express their gratitude? Hypothetically speaking, of course.'

'Handsomely. Very handsomely.'

'In US dollars, of course.'

'Naturally,' Harry affirmed. 'And into a Swiss bank account, I should imagine.'

Ivo frowned. He seemed to have thought of a distasteful downside to this happy situation. 'There would be risks involved, for this hypothetical leader of the SED,' he pointed out.

'And they would be fully recognized. With the provision of an escape route, were anything to go wrong.'

Wolff allowed himself a sharp, reflective laugh. 'It's treason, of course.'

'We'd prefer to think of it as an investment in the future peaceful prosperity of Europe.'

The heavy metal door slowly opened on silent, oiled hinges. Harry only sensed it by a brief waft of stale air across the back of his neck. He turned to see one of his men, Corporal McBride, standing in the narrow gap.

'Yes, McBride?'

'Ye told me I was tae come straight in, sir,' the soldier said.

'You've got her?'

'Aye, sir.'

'I'll be right out,' Harry said. He turned back to the prisoner. 'Think about it, Herr Wolff. But I recommend haste. The Soviets probably already know you're here.'

Anna was waiting in the section office when Harry entered. The two young clerks in British army khaki serge came to attention, seemingly relieved by the appearance of an officer. Harry guessed they'd found the presence of an attractive young woman disconcerting.

'Is it true?' she asked. 'Have you got him?'

'Come with me,' he said. 'I don't know how long I can keep him.'

He led her out into a corridor and past a young soldier on his knees scrubbing the floor with an energy that would shame an East End charlady.

'Are you sure it's him?'

Harry ignored her question. 'If anyone asks, you're here doing a story on how well we treat our detainees. And I can't let you see him alone, I'm sorry. I know this is personal for you, but I've broken just about every paragraph in King's Regulations even by allowing you in here. Fortunately, the colonel's away at Bad Nenndorf.'

'I'm so very grateful, Harry. You don't know how much.'

'See if you still feel that way once you've spoken to him,' Harry said.

They descended a narrow flight of concrete steps and entered a long, low corridor lit by three naked light bulbs hanging from a cable slung along the arched ceiling. Along one side was a row of identical metal doors, each with a spy hole and a hatch for passing food though. The doors were battered and chipped, the heavy-duty brass locks and handles worn a dull ochre colour by decades of use. The whole passage smelt of urine, sweat and brutality.

'Believe me, we've cleaned it up,' Harry said. 'Dread to think what the bastards did to people down here. Maybe we should ask him. After all, he wore the Kripo uniform, didn't he?'

Anna looked away. The man Harry was talking about had once sold her a dream in which firm but fair-minded men made the world a better place, a world she had once expected to share with him.

The corporal who'd driven her there, and whose name she'd learned was McBride, was standing opposite the third door. On a piece of black-painted board attached to the masonry beside the frame, someone had written Ivo's surname in chalk, spelling it with only one *F*. McBride produced a set of keys from the breast pocket of his battledress, turned the lock and eased the door open.

Harry stepped forward, blocking the gap. 'There's someone here to see you, Herr Wolff,' he said, as if this were a hospital and it was visiting hour. 'I'm afraid you don't get to choose whether you'll accept or not.'

Harry stepped into the cell, then stood aside, allowing Anna to pass.

Ivo was sitting on the under-stuffed prison mattress, whistling a tune to himself like a man waiting for a bus. He looked so familiar to Anna that she could believe she'd escaped from him only yesterday. And yet at the same time, he was a stranger to her; she might never have met him at all. There had been a time when her naked body could hold his astounded gaze as securely as sticky amber holds the moth that has landed upon it. But that was ancient history. Now he observed her with nothing more than mild curiosity.

'Hello, Anna,' he said, his voice flat and devoid of emotion. 'I've been wondering when you'd come back. I knew you would, one day.'

He still has power over me, Anna thought. It's the power bestowed by indifference. In this cell, the real prisoner is me. The one with the key is the man sitting so nonchalantly on the bed.

Seeing the tears well in her eyes, Harry Taverner put his hand gently on her elbow. 'Oh, what the hell,' he sighed. 'I'm probably going to be cashiered anyway for letting you in here. If you need me, thump on the door.'

He stepped into the corridor. McBride swung the heavy door shut. It settled in its frame with a dull, metallic thud.

Anna had thought she was prepared. In McBride's jeep, she had rehearsed her opening lines a hundred times: what she was going to say to him about Bär and Antje, about Marion. But now the words were backed up in her throat like the victims of a fire desperate to escape into clean air. Her tongue wouldn't work. The muscles in her jaw were frozen. Her vocal cords had burned through and no longer functioned. All she could do was stare at Ivo Wolff, not knowing if she should fear him or hate him.

After what seemed to her like an age she managed to speak, though to her ears the voice wasn't hers. It was the voice of an entirely different woman, one of ancient years and close to death; a frail voice reaching her from a great distance.

'Where are they, Ivo? What have you done with my children?'

He made no attempt to answer. Not a muscle in his perfect face moved. He just sat on the thin mattress observing her with mild curiosity, as a child might observe a beetle they'd caught in a matchbox.

The tears were flowing now, and she couldn't stop them. 'I can't go on living like this – not knowing,' she said, wiping her eyes with the back of one hand and smudging the eyeliner over her cheeks. 'If they're dead, for the love of Christ tell me. Let me at least grieve. If they're alive, tell me where they are.' Her face crumpled. 'They're my babies.'

'They're my children, too,' he said at length. 'And you turned them against me with lies. You stole them from me, like a common thief.'

If he was expecting pity, Anna wasn't inclined to offer it. 'Were you in love with Gertrude Steigler? Did you sell her a dream about a future together, too? Or was she just a convenient nanny for the children?'

He seemed surprised she knew the name. 'Who told you about Gertrude?'

'Hannelore Lange.'

'You've been busy.'

'I've been desperate, Ivo. That's what I've been.'

He considered her assertion for a moment, like a lawyer in a cross-examination.

'We met in Paris,' he said. 'When I returned to Berlin, I managed to get her transferred to my department.'

'And you installed her in our old apartment, with Bär and Antje. And your old friend, Manis Möller. With Hannelore Lange to do the chores. Happy families all round.'

'You seem to know a lot.'

'Then best not to lie to me, Ivo.'

'The last letter I received from Gertrude said she was planning to take the children to safety, away from the bombing. Somewhere in the countryside.'

'To Briesen.'

'Yes, that's the place.'

'I've been there. They never arrived.'

'Then they're still with Gertrude. Find Gertrude, and you'll probably find the children.'

'Gertrude Steigler is dead,' Anna said flatly. 'The Russians raped and killed her – the very people you're now assisting.'

He seemed as unmoved by this news as he was about her despair for the children. For an instant, Anna found herself pitying the young woman buried beside the church at Briesen.

All he said was, 'Were the children with her?'

'She came alone, according to Gertrude's aunt.'

'Then they could be anywhere. Or they could be dead.'

Anna glared at him, daring him to deny his responsibility.

'How can you not know? You are their father! They were in your care!'

The accusation appeared to mean little to him. 'Perhaps you were too busy whoring around in London or New York – or wherever it is you've been – to notice, but there was a war going on,' he said. 'I had my orders to follow. I did the best I could for the kids. If you want to know where they are, maybe you should ask your American friends, or that British fellow out in the corridor. After all, they're the ones who turned this city into rubble.'

Anna glared at him. 'Don't you dare try to deny responsibility, Ivo. Even if you don't know where the children are, you murdered an American citizen – *my mother*.'

He very nearly laughed, which was the last thing she expected. 'One dead woman amongst so many millions. And no eyewitnesses. By the time it got to court, you and I would be forgotten, barely a footnote to someone else's memories.'

And then, for the first time, his gaze faltered. His eyes dropped. Whatever spark of compassion remained in him – if he'd ever really had any – flickered briefly.

'Look, I can't help you,' he said, sounding almost regretful. 'I'm sorry about the children, but that's how it is. If there was a grave, I'd put flowers on it. What more can I do? You haven't the slightest idea of what I saw out east. We did a lot of very bad things. So, call it retribution, call it victor's justice… a reckoning… call it whatever the hell you want. But I'm not the only father to lose his children, and you're not the only mother. We've a lot of company: Poles, Czechs, Russians, Jews… millions of us. We'd all better get used to it. We can't rebuild this world on a tide of grief or self-recrimination. So, we just have to put it all behind us. It's what we do from now on that really matters. There's no place for sentiment. It's a luxury we can't afford.'

Anna stayed silent while the faint echo of his words dashed themselves to nothingness against the tiled walls of the cell. She had nothing left to say to him. He had torn her life to pieces as easily as if it were made of spider's silk.

She heard raised voices in the corridor and the heavy door swung open. Harry Taverner stepped into the cell. With him was a very tall man in the crisply pressed uniform of a Soviet army officer. His cap bore a smart crimson band above the gleaming peak and a polished leather strap slanted across his chest from one shoulder to his belt.

'This is an outrage,' he said in good English. 'It is an act of kidnap and aggression. This man is an important member of the civilian administration of those areas of the former fascist state now under the control of the victorious forces of the glorious Union of Soviet Socialist Republics! Release him at once.'

'Aye,' murmured Corporal McBride, 'and my Auntie Nelly's the bishop of Galloway.'

Harry coughed loudly, as a distraction. 'Corporal McBride! Escort the German gentleman upstairs, if you please. He's free to go.'

Ivo got to his feet. He didn't bother to look at Anna or Harry. He didn't need to. He knew that where his survival was concerned, they were an irrelevance. Brushing himself down to smooth the creases out of his crumpled suit, he followed the Soviet officer out into the corridor.

Harry held the cell door open for Anna. 'I'm sorry,' he said. 'My hands are tied. There's nothing I can do.' Then, noting the misery in her eyes, he added gently, 'Come on, I'll drive you home.'

Anna sat in the passenger seat of the jeep as it grumbled through the darkened streets. In the footwell was the bottle of champagne she'd taken from Manis Möller at the Top Hat. She had emptied it on the drive to the detention centre before meeting Ivo. Now she wished she'd taken the cocaine from Möller's table as well. Anything, if only it would stop the thoughts in her head that dripped like molten lead from a burning roof, scorching her where they landed.

Maybe we'll lose our way and get ambushed again, she thought. Maybe it will be me instead of Luka who takes the bullet to the back of the head. At least then the darkness would be permanent. I won't have to wake up tomorrow morning to face more unanswered questions, more dashed hopes.

The streetlights were on in this part of the city, and Harry was using the jeep's horn imperiously, calmly confident in his right to go where he pleased.

'Can we drive around a bit?' Anna asked. 'I don't want to go back to the Hearst Building. Not yet.'

'Of course,' he said, though it was hardly the night for sightseeing. It was cold. There were still patches of snow around. A thin mist blurred the sharp edges of the shattered buildings, turning the bombsites into ghostly glaciers of rubble.

They drove through the Tiergarten. Before Anna had fled Berlin, she'd often taken Marion and the children there, to stroll or listen to the musicians, to eat *bratwurst* when it was chilly, ice cream when it was hot. Now the trees had almost all gone. They'd survived the war, succumbing only to the desperation of freezing Berliners whose need for fuel that winter had achieved what Allied bombers and the Red Army could not. In the darkness, she noticed a few campfires burning, where people lived amongst the tree stumps, guarding what was now 500 acres of vegetable patches.

And then ahead of them was the Brandenburg Gate, scorched a sooty black and pitted with wounds from Soviet gunfire. They passed between its pillars, ignoring the 5 km per hour sign because there was almost no one about. Entering Unter den Linden, the headlamps lit up another large portrait of Stalin, like an advertising hording for a product no one wanted to buy.

Harry stopped the jeep in front of a large building that was only a shell, like a stage set. The windows were all blown out and when she looked up, the roof – if there still was one – was lost in the misty night. But the sign was still there above the gaping tunnel of the main entrance, a dusting of frost over the characters that spelled out the words, *Hotel Adlon*.

They sat a while without speaking. Anna couldn't understand why Harry had chosen this of all places to stop. She remembered the night they'd danced there, a November night in 1938. She thought of what it might have led to if the world hadn't got in the way. And in the moment before he spoke, she understood.

That night, he'd brought her the documents that had allowed her to escape. Now he was bringing her a second chance.

'Corporal McBride told me he had a pretty good idea of what he'd walked into at the Top Hat,' he said, his breath a white smudge against the blackened building beside them.

Anna's laugh was as bitter as the cold night air. 'Rescued from the railroad tracks just in time.' She shook her head in disbelief. 'The great photojournalist Anna Cantrell – who thought she knew the ropes – saved at the last moment from becoming a black marketeer's whore by a Scotsman in a kilt.'

Harry ignored her attempt at self-flagellation. 'I'm guessing Wolff had no news for you.'

'None. He barely seemed to care.'

'Then you need to get out of Berlin again, Anna. It's not good for you here.'

'And where do I go? Back to the States? At least in Berlin I can feel closer to them.'

'If you want to stay in Germany, then base yourself in Frankfurt am Main. It's the headquarters of the US Office of Military Government. You can do your job from there, and still keep looking. But staying here – the not knowing will eat you alive.'

Anna thought about what he'd said. Then, in a voice he could barely hear, she murmured, 'How can I just give up?'

He knew it wasn't him she was asking. She was asking Bär and Antje.

'Give it time,' he counselled, 'time for things to get back to something approaching normality. The churches, the Red Cross, the charities, they're all overwhelmed right now. But as time passes, they'll become more organized. They'll co-ordinate the private tracing services and the surviving district records. People will start writing things down, adding connections, making contacts – remembering. A bit like a brain developing. One day, somewhere, they'll pop up like daffodils in spring. Believe me.'

He hadn't mentioned the alternative, and her heart thanked him for it.

'I can't be alone tonight, Harry,' she said. 'Not if I want to see the morning.'

Harry took Anna to the little villa that was his private billet. When she put her arms around him, he gently prised them away.

'Don't tell me Marion was right about Englishmen,' she said, pouting with disappointment.

'This isn't the black market, Anna,' he told her gently. 'Let's wait for prices to settle before we decide if we want to buy.'

She slept in his bed. Harry took the couch.

The following morning, light snow was falling. They went to the Hearst Building together, where Anna packed her few belongings into a battered suitcase much like the ones she'd seen carried by the DPs at Kimpelbeuren. Like the one Louisa Vogel had carried on the train at the Lehrter station.

Harry drove Anna to Tempelhof airfield, where she caught the next Air Transport Command flight for Frankfurt.

Twenty-Four

Headline International News Agency
Frankfurt Bureau

2 April 1948

Dearest Harry,

How are things in Berlin these days? We hear all sorts of dreadful news about how the Sovs are pushing their weight around up there. Saw a photo yesterday of people stopping trains so they could steal the coal. It's been cold here in Frankfurt, but nowhere near as bad as you've had it these last two winters. Hope you've found that delicious fräulein to help you keep warm. Well, maybe not too delicious and not too warm – I guess I must have inherited that old green-eyed trait of Marion's.

No news of the children, yet. But I live in hope.

Anyway, must rush. Got to interview some crusty general who thinks we should drop the atom bomb on Moscow if they carry on the way they are in your neck of the woods. I'll try to talk him out of it, because it would be good to see you again.

Yours,

Anna

Harry Taverner smiled, refolded Anna's letter, and returned it to its envelope. A pleasing coincidence, he thought – it had arrived on the very morning he'd picked to update the file on Ivo Wolff. He allowed himself a moment of irrationality; that somehow she had sensed him thinking of her.

She was right about the winters – down to minus twenty sometimes. In one way he was glad she hadn't been here in Berlin. He knew she would have insisted on being there to record the event when a train carrying refugees from Poland arrived with fifty-three of its passengers dead from hypothermia. She would have wanted the whole world to know, to take notice, to care. And he remembered the words Professor Koppitz had told her when she'd been his student in Vienna, because she'd recited them to him:

> *...One cannot take a photograph that captures suffering without there being an exchange... there may well come a time when you discover your account is empty...*

He didn't like the thought of that. It made him fear for her.

Placing the envelope in his desk drawer, Harry returned his attention to the official file open before him. He took up his pen and began to write.

What was there to say? Ivo Wolff was doing just fine – climbing up the ranks of Walter Ulbricht's SED, making himself flavour of the month with the Russkies. But he hadn't attempted to make any approach to Harry. If he'd been interested after their conversation in the interrogation cell, he hadn't followed through. Nothing. Not even a brush-pass at the *Kommandatura*, or at any of those excruciating functions where everyone pretended they were allies and smiled at each other over the vodka, while outside, the Soviet strangulation of Berlin continued unchecked. In the meantime, his bosses in Moscow were playing hardball: Berlin's approach roads suddenly closed for no reason, barges on the canals stopped, trains halted and inspected, even civilian aircraft using the three permitted air corridors in from the west were liable to harassment by Soviet fighters.

If real fighting broke out, everyone knew how it would end: the Allies were outnumbered three to one. Having someone like Ivo Wolff as a source could provide a desperately needed tripwire. But as he wrapped up his assessment, all Harry could write in the file was,

> *... still known to be motivated mostly by self-interest rather than political conviction. Remains a 'possible' should conditions become more fertile.*

When he'd signed the entry, Harry put the file with the other papers he intended to return to Registry. Then he turned his attention to the material London had asked for in their usual 'by-yesterday-at-the-latest' style. The morning flight from England was due to arrive soon, and the office courier would need the files in the next ten minutes if they were to catch the return service.

Thinking of aeroplanes made Harry consider taking a ride to Frankfurt. He'd been working hard. Maybe he should take a few days off – go and see Anna. But then she'd probably be off with her camera somewhere, perhaps in the company of some handsome American newspaper correspondent. And, anyway, in the present circumstances the department would never allow him the leave.

Bundling the London material together, Harry pushed back his chair, got up and went in search of the courier.

The Northern Air Corridor into Berlin. 5 April 1948

The British European Airways early flight from London's Northolt airport to Berlin had climbed into an English spring sunrise on schedule. After a brief stop at Hamburg, by late morning it was approaching its destination: Gatow airfield in the British sector of Berlin.

The Viking aircraft was a slow, plump aluminium sausage with two very noisy piston engines. Regular customers on the route joked the experience of travelling in one was like sitting in a tin can while a gang of demented blacksmiths with hammers took out their frustrations on the fuselage. Talking was nigh on impossible, so that on that day's service most passengers were dozing, reading newspapers or peering from the large, square windows at the empty landscape drifting by below.

Flight 777 was half-full that morning. The single steward aboard had had plenty of time to attend to his passengers: two Americans – including a woman from Michigan who was travelling alone – an Australian and six Englishmen. When they'd boarded, even the regular ones had wanted to know about the recent harassment of civilian airliners by Soviet fighter planes. The steward assured them it was just the Reds showing off. Besides, he told them, the captain of the flight and his co-pilot were ex-Royal Air Force officers, amongst the most skilled and experienced on the route.

Just as he'd finished securing the tiny galley for the approach to Berlin, a sudden shadow swept across the Viking's interior and the plane lurched.

'Jeez! Did you see that Russki?' shouted one of the Americans, a sergeant in uniform returning to duty in the city. 'If he'd come a foot closer, I could have asked him to swap his watch for a dollar.'

The captain had just throttled back the engines for the descent, and so most of the cabin heard the sergeant call out. Faces turned to the windows, searching for the Soviet plane.

'He's coming round again,' the sergeant shouted.

'I can see him,' confirmed the Australian.

Now everyone was peering out over the Viking's silver wingtip.

'I hope to God he knows what he's doing,' one of the Englishmen said to the man in the seat in front.

The steward gripped the handle on the cockpit door, about to inform the captain that the cabin was prepared for landing. As he lifted the handle, a second, darker, shadow flashed across the plane's interior – followed by a jolt so violent that it hurled him into the ceiling.

Less than a minute later, four innocent crew, ten innocent passengers – and one reckless Russian fighter pilot – lay dead in the wreckage of two aeroplanes on the hard, cold soil of Spandau.

*

Late that afternoon, at the Frankfurt offices of the Headline news agency, the bureau chief emerged from his smoke-filled office, a smouldering cigar clamped between his teeth. He strode across the newsroom, stopping at Anna's cubicle where a sign proclaimed: *Photodesk – come on in, we don't snap.*

'Plans tonight?' he asked brusquely.

'Thought I might have supper with Cary Grant,' Anna said, looking up from a set of contact prints.

'Tell him to get a sandwich: he's dining alone,' the bureau chief replied with a grunt of laughter that wafted cigar smoke into the cubicle.

Anna flapped it away with the contact sheet, trying not to cough. 'Something afoot?' she asked.

'Sure is. Looks like you're on your way, kid.'

'My *way* – where to?'

'Berlin,' he said. 'Word War Three is about to start. You're my star photographer. Miss it at your peril.'

They let her sit on a little foldaway seat behind the pilots, not because she was a journalist but because they were young American fliers and she was a good-looking woman of thirty-two. They'd joshed with her all the way from Frankfurt, but now they were concentrating on their instruments. The C-54 Skymaster bucked and juddered like Uncle László's Studebaker tourer climbing the Hollywood hills. Outside was nothing but a rushing grey void that hurled its watery shrapnel against the windscreen as if God had set a hosepipe on them. For a disconcerting moment, Anna thought the deafening roar she could hear was coming from that nothingness and not the four engines.

How terrifying it must have been for the poor souls aboard the BEA fight, she thought. She hoped to God they'd been too stunned by the collision to understand what was happening.

She knew the area surrounding Tempelhof airfield well. From the ground, she'd often seen the planes landing, diving down between the tall apartment blocks that stood close to the perimeter. They were somewhere below her now, reaching up towards her like a reef. A fraction off course… a few feet too low… if these boys got it wrong, would she know an instant of horrified realization before the plane smashed into the buildings at 100 miles per hour?

They'd given her a set of headphones so she could listen to the talk-down. From somewhere out of the deafening grey howl she could hear a small, tinny male American voice: 'Baker Easy Four Two, this is the final controller... maintain heading three one five... you're almost on the glide path... commence your descent at five hundred feet per minute...'

The pilot's gloved hands eased the control yoke forward. The flight engineer adjusted the four throttle levers. Anna looked out of the side window again. She had no idea how close they were to the ground, but they seemed to be going down fast.

Anna heard the controller say they were one mile from touchdown. Less than a minute to go, she reckoned, and still there was nothing outside but a flowing grey ocean of emptiness. She tensed herself for the impact, wondering if she'd know anything before the end. And then the cloud vanished like smoke blown on the wind and Anna saw the dull, indifferent face of an apartment block whip past, then another. They were below the tops now and still descending. She faced forwards and stared over the pilot's shoulder – and saw tarmac swaying towards her. She felt her stomach lurch and then they were down and braking hard.

As the propellers slowed and they taxied off the runway, Anna saw a row of identical Skymasters lined up in front of Tempelhof's wide, curving terminal – the one she'd photographed for Goebbels' propaganda ministry before the war.

The young captain turned his head towards her, the peak of his Air Force cap pushed jauntily up over his brow. 'Welcome to Berlin, Miss Cantrell; the front line of democracy,' he said with a grin, utterly unperturbed. 'Been here before?'

The Hotel Splendid near the Tiergarten was one of the few hotels in the city centre to have escaped complete destruction. But that had simply made it more appealing to Red Army looters. Even now, three years after the end of the war, the reception still looked like a building site. But with journalists and billeted officers from the *Kommandatura* in residence, at least the kitchen could rely on better provisions than most other places in Berlin.

The clerk asked Anna how long she intended staying. 'That rather depends on Uncle Joe Stalin,' she replied.

Her room was sparsely furnished and cold. When she went into the bathroom and turned the taps, thinking a hot bath might improve her mood, the water pipes gave a loud *clank* and a yellowish trickle dripped into the stained tub, as if the Splendid was weeping bile on behalf of the city. Anna wondered if this was just another of Berlin's regular tribulations, like the ones she'd suffered when she was last there, or had the Soviets cut off the water supply?

Suddenly, for a reason she couldn't fathom, she remembered the temporary latrines Uncle László had ordered dug on location: Czibor Global Studios wasn't going to be some cowboy outfit of itinerant, fly-by-night moviemakers like Metro Goldwyn Mayer. Then she saw herself holding Marion's hand in the restroom at the Montmartre in Hollywood, before the catastrophe of her eighth birthday, gazing in awe at the shiny brass taps her mother had told her were real gold. From there it was but a small jump to the ladies' toilet in the Café Landtmann in Vienna that had seemed – to the newly arrived young Anna – fit for a princess, all gilt mirrors and marble.

You've seen some shit in your life, my girl, she told herself, but at least it's been in upmarket surroundings.

'I regret that in order to conserve our daily ration of coal, madam, the manager has been obliged to turn off the boiler,' the clerk told her when she went downstairs to enquire. 'The heating will come on again at ten o'clock tonight.'

She went out onto the Kurfürstendamm and hailed a taxi.

All that distinguished the Allied *Kommandatura* from the headquarters of an insurance company were the flags of the four occupying powers that fluttered from the flagpoles outside, and the armed sentries guarding the entrance.

Anna checked in at the Information Control Division office to get herself accredited to the press corps before asking the reception duty sergeant to put a call through to Major Harry Taverner.

'Don't move – I'm on my way down,' he said, when the sergeant handed her the telephone handset.

The pleasure evident in his voice was the warmest thing she'd encountered since arriving.

When she saw him on the first-floor landing, heading for the stairs, she waved. He waved back. He was wearing a well-cut grey flannel suit. She thought it might be the one he'd worn in Vienna, when he was pretending to be a passport control officer. But she could also remember him in the garb of a Channel Island itinerant labourer, pedalling his Motobécane bicycle across the Franco-Spanish border, and as the young warrior in uniform.

How many disguises does he have? she wondered. How many Harry Taverners are there?

But it was so good to see him. The imperturbable, everything-will-be-alright-if-we-just-keep-our-heads smile was just what she needed right then. The kiss of greeting she gave him when he reached the bottom of the stairs and spread his arms to embrace her was brief enough, but it was on the lips.

'This is the *Kommandatura*,' he said as he released her. 'You do realize we've just scandalized the British, the Americans, the Russians and the French, all in one go?'

'Have we?'

'Well, maybe not the French.'

Anna grinned. 'Do we have time for a coffee before the balloon goes up?'

'I've already told General Kotikov his Russkies aren't to start anything until we've had at least two cups. We've a lot to catch up on.'

'Seriously, Harry, my editor says this dreadful plane crash could be the thing that starts World War Three. Is he right?'

'I wouldn't go quite that far,' Harry said. 'We reckon it was a stunt that went wrong. Of course, Kotikov is thumping the table and blaming us, but behind the scenes the Sovs are back-pedalling like billy-oh. I think we may have escaped with this one – unlike the poor souls aboard that Viking. But the next *accident* might well end in gunfire.'

'And if that happens?'

'God only knows. There are three hundred thousand Red Army soldiers around here with little more to occupy their time than singing "*Kalinka*" and drinking vodka—' He paused as he saw the pain in Anna's eyes. 'Oh, I'm so sorry… that's my size fifteen feet again… Luka…'

'It's alright, Harry,' she said. 'If anyone should beat themselves up over Luka, it isn't you.'

He suggested a café he knew. They walked arm in arm down Kaiserswerther Strasse. It was cold, the early spring tentative and uncertain. She leaned into him a little – purely for the warmth, she told herself.

'I need your help,' Harry said, after they'd caught up with each other's lives.

'Ask away. You've done me more favours than I ever had a right to ask for.'

'It involves Ivo.'

Anna stopped and looked down at the pavement. 'Oh.'

'Is that a problem?'

'Depends on what you're asking.'

'I want to set up a meeting with him. I can't make a direct approach.'

She nodded in understanding. 'But his ex-wife could.'

'We don't have much time,' Harry said. 'The Soviets are really pushing at the door. Ivo could mean the difference between annihilation and us buying enough time to reinforce.'

'*If* he was prepared to work for you.'

'I still think he might be – with the right incentives.'

'You know Ivo,' Anna said sourly. 'With him, incentives are all that matter.'

A woman was walking towards them, two children about the ages that Bär and Antje would be in tow. Anna caught a snatch of conversation. Educated voices. Polite. Middle class. But all three wore clothes that were patched and frayed. Even in leafy Dahlem, only the occupiers and the black marketeers had money to spend.

'Is it safe to travel into the Soviet sector?' she asked when the trio had passed. 'You'll understand my reluctance, given what happened the last time.'

'I understand completely,' Harry said. 'We can send you in as a member of the press, doing a story on the SED. You'll be quite safe. They'd throw open the doors for a tame photojournalist.'

The very thought of standing in the same room as Ivo Wolff disgusted her. Harry was asking more of her than she could bear to give. She owed him so much, but surely there could be another way?

And then it came to her: a sudden shock, an almost physical jolt, as if one of the many bombs still buried in this gravely wounded city had just detonated nearby.

Why hadn't she thought of it before?

Anna turned her face to his. 'He'll probably want a down payment – US dollars.'

'That's possible.'

'Then I'll do it,' she said softly.

He looked surprised. Perhaps he hadn't expected it to be that easy. 'You're a star, Anna Cantrell,' he said.

Anna laughed, though her mind was racing. 'That's what Rex used to tell me.'

Harry raised a finger to his lips. 'Only this movie can't have an audience. We can't have your name up in lights. And no Oscar at the end, I'm afraid.'

'I'll be happy with a private screening,' Anna said, with a wry smile. 'Now, where's this café you're taking me to?'

I've landed the part of a lifetime, she thought, as she took his arm again and they resumed their walk. But what you don't know, my dearest Harry, is that I've already written the script, designed the set and hired the director – myself. And the ending won't be at all what you're expecting.

Twenty-Five

As the taxi pulled up to the kerb Anna could see the gaudy neon image of a jauntily tilted top hat pulsing above the entrance to the club. She glanced at her wristwatch. It was two minutes after eleven.

Having paid the fare, she climbed out of the cab into a cold grey mist tinged with cement dust. The driver had said a ruined building a few doors down from the club was being demolished and the workmen had uncovered a cellar. The mist and the stink of bodies entombed since 1945 made a sepulchre of the street.

Anna wondered how long they would go on finding the missing buried beneath the slowly recovering city. Perhaps one day someone might stumble across the remains of Bär and Antje. But how would they even know whose pitiful remains they were?

The pain of that thought convinced her that what she planned to do was right. It helped banish the disgust she felt whenever she imagined coming face to face again with the man who had hurt her so. And it softened the present sickly sensation in her stomach – the nausea that came with the imminent prospect of being in the presence of her ex-husband's familiar, Manis Möller.

In the entrance to the club, a man in an overcoat was paying occupation marks to a woman Anna assumed was a prostitute.

With a muttered 'Excuse me', Anna eased past and descended the stairs. A fug of cigarette smoke and cheap perfume enveloped her, but it was better than the smell of death that lingered in the street.

Möller was waiting for her in the same private room of scarlet flock wallpaper that she remembered from two years ago. But this time when she entered, instead of sprawling expectantly in the battered chesterfield sofa, he got to his feet. He even made a little bow to her. She wondered if manners, like a smarter suit, were supposed to indicate status in the black market – to show you'd progressed a little from being a street hustler.

'I confess, Frau Anna, that I was sorely disappointed when you were snatched away just when I thought we had a deal to celebrate,' Möller said, extending a hand – which she declined to shake. 'Such a pity.'

'I'm not for sale this time, Herr Möller,' she said. 'I already know Ivo Wolff is alive and in the Soviet sector.'

This information didn't seem to surprise him. 'And *I* know you have money to spend,' he countered. 'Otherwise you would never have asked to see me.'

'Some of it can be yours.'

Möller smiled, his lips sagging under the weight of his avarice. 'Then how can I help you, Frau Anna?'

'I'm guessing you're still in touch with him. Or have you both given up the stolen art business?'

'He's a difficult man to get close to,' Möller said cautiously. 'But not so difficult for trusted old friends.'

'Can you reach him by telephone?'

'That would depend on what was on offer.'

'I want you to arrange a meeting between us,' said Anna. 'I have a proposition to put to him. Tell him it involves a down payment in the most sought-after currency currently available in Berlin.'

Möller's eyes lit up. 'Have you got your hands on some of the new Deutschmarks the Americans are planning to introduce?' he asked.

Anna held his stare, hoping he could see the contempt in her eyes. 'Even better than that,' she said. 'I'm talking greenbacks – American dollars.'

The following afternoon, Anna called Harry Taverner from the public telephone booth in the reception of the Hotel Splendid. She wasn't afraid of being overheard: the sawing and hammering of the workmen was relentless. But she confined herself to banalities in case the Soviets had put in one of their people as the hotel's switchboard operator, or if the line was bugged. Harry agreed to meet her in an hour, in the Tiergarten.

Leaving the phone booth, she saw a man she recognized checking in at the front desk. It was Tom Goodhew, one of the journalists with whom she'd shared the Hearst Building, before she left for Frankfurt.

'Hey, Tom!' she called as she walked over.

Goodhew looked up from signing the register and grinned. 'Hey, Cantrell! Things must be getting serious if they flew you back in.'

They embraced and Anna asked, 'What brings you here? Did they run out of Jack Daniels at the old place?'

'Just come back from Munich,' Goodhew said. 'We got stopped by the Reds so often I figured they were sizing me up for the Order of Lenin. What have you heard?'

'Nothing good, that's for sure,' Anna said.

'I hear there's a big rally being staged on Saturday, by the Social Democrats. Are you going?'

'Of course,' Anna said. And then an idea occurred to her. 'Come to think of it, Tom, you might be able to do me a favour.'

When she had explained what she wanted him to do, Goodhew said, 'What's the payoff? Why can't you do it yourself?'

'It's a bit tricky, Tom. I don't want my fingerprints on it.'

'Well, I guess it's no skin off my nose,' Goodhew said, pouting. 'But do you want to let me in on the goods – so that I can deny everything if it blows up in your face?'

'What, and spoil an exclusive?'

Goodhew pretended to be mortally offended. 'And there was me thinking we were colleagues.'

'You know the saying, Tom,' Anna said, laughing. 'All's fair in love, war and the newspaper business.'

Anna arrived at the Goethe statue early. Beneath a sullen sky, the park looked like a churned-up battlefield from the previous century. The statue, and the few others that had escaped the bombing and shelling, dotted the barren landscape like the survivors of a doomed last stand, motionless, dumbstruck, too stunned to flee; here and there, Anna could see figures stooping over their vegetable plots, looking like scavengers looting the bodies of the fallen. To the south, along the Tiergartenstrasse, stood a crater wall of shattered buildings, still unrepaired after three years. Perhaps they would stay that way forever, Anna thought. Perhaps Berlin would always be a city of ruins: ruined buildings; ruined people; ruined hopes for ever finding her children.

She remembered the day in 1938 when she'd waited at this very spot for Harry to bring her escape passport. Then, she'd been desperate to flee a marriage to a man she'd come to realize was a monster, a man who lived happily in the company of other monsters. In the years that had followed, she'd had her children taken from her and her mother murdered, survived a world war, seen horrors she'd never forget. She'd made her way in a tough trade and done things she probably would never have done had she been wiser, more sober or less headstrong at the time.

Professor Koppitz was right, she thought. I've made too many transactions and my account is empty. And now I'm about to go overdrawn.

Now that the trees had gone, she saw Harry coming from a distance. He walked with a calm, unhurried stride, almost the only moving, upright figure in this strange landscape.

It's just us, she thought. They've dropped an atom bomb, and we're all that's left.

'Is he agreeable?' Harry asked when he reached her.

'Manis Möller says yes, for a thousand dollars up front – to prove you're really interested.'

Harry considered this for a moment, his expression doubtful, as if he were being asked to pay from his own wallet. Then he shrugged. 'I think we can do that. Where does he suggest?'

Harry had told her to leave the choice of meeting place to Wolff. The one making the brush-contact needed to have control over the location, to feel he was safe and not walking into some kind of ambush.

'The planned Social Democrat rally, on Saturday – at the Brandenburg Gate.'

'That makes sense,' Harry said, nodding slowly. 'We'll be lost amongst the crowd, just about invisible.'

'Ivo wants me to be there. That's his only condition.'

'Don't tell me he needs someone to hold his hand.'

'He said the Soviets will be bound to have people watching the rally. If anyone spots him, he can say he was meeting me.'

'In the hope of a reconciliation?'

'Exactly.'

'Is that possible – a reconciliation?' Harry asked.

Was that a flicker of jealousy she noticed in his usually inscrutable eyes?

'Harry,' she said gently, 'you'd be safer putting your money on Joe Stalin winning the next Miss America beauty pageant than on me getting back together with Ivo Wolff.'

They fell silent as an elderly man walked past, pushing a child's pram filled with muddy asparagus stems. He didn't acknowledge them. A land where people looked well-fed and wore unpatched clothes was alien to him, beyond the power of his imagination.

Harry waited until he was out of earshot before speaking. He gave her a sheepish smile. 'I'm pleased to hear it. Anyway, you're an accredited member of the press corps – what's more natural than you being on hand?'

'Don't worry, Harry Taverner,' Anna said, 'this is one assignment I have no intention of missing.'

Twenty-Six

The smoke-blackened pillars of the Brandenburg Gate gleamed in the aftermath of a spring shower. Beneath the goddess Victoria in her chariot – pummelled by the end of the war into little more than a concrete excrescence – people were gathering in the afternoon sunshine. They looked as grey and as battered as the ruins that flanked the Tiergarten and Unter den Linden, but there was a fierce light burning in their eyes.

They had come to protest at the tightening Soviet grip on their politics, their stomachs, their hearts and their future. They were sick to death of being cold and hungry. They'd had enough of watching anything left of worth in their city being carted away to the east. They were tired of the seemingly random abductions, the removal from their streets of husbands and fathers whom the Soviets thought might be useful in Moscow, or in some god-awful factory deep in the Urals, or lost forever in the gulags of Siberia. They carried placards that read STALIN GO HOME and FREE ELECTIONS. They wore threadbare suits and patched dresses, raincoats and trilbies, overalls and boiler suits. They were Reichsbahn railway workers, Spree bargemen, clerks from Siemens, accountants from AEG, rubble women, children and the unemployed. Before noon, over ten thousand of them had gathered.

Anna pretended to the other journalists present – including Tom Goodhew – that it was just another news story to cover. But she had chosen her camera and lens with care, aware that the tools must suit the task she had in mind. To that end, she was carrying a Leica IIIc she had purchased in Frankfurt, and a telephoto lens.

Harry had suggested the Adlon as the meeting place before the main event. He was waiting for her when she arrived. He looked at her camera case and frowned. 'I can't stop you taking pictures of the rally, but as for the other – I'm afraid we can't have a record of that,' he said. 'You'll have to lose the camera.'

Anna looked around at the growing crowd. 'This is my job, Harry. I need my camera to do it.'

'Wolff will run a mile if he sees you with that. And, anyway, there can't be a visual record. Sorry.'

Anna sighed like a child being told it was past her bedtime. 'Oh, alright,' she said. 'I saw a journalist I know, over by the Soviet war memorial. He can look after my camera until you've had your little tête-à-tête with Ivo.'

Harry looked at his watch. 'Hurry up. He'll be here soon.'

'It's not even two hundred metres away. I'll be back inside five minutes.'

She kissed Harry on the cheek and set off through the growing crowd towards the monument. The first step of her plan had gone exactly as she had hoped.

Ivo Wolff had chosen the rendezvous well. Once inside the eleven-metre-deep northernmost portal of the great sandstone gate, he and Harry would be all but lost amongst the shadows of the interior and the jostle of protesters, invisible to any observer outside.

As Anna approached, returning from entrusting her camera to Tom Goodhew, who'd been waiting for her at the Soviet war memorial, she couldn't spot Harry, even though she knew he was waiting for her inside the arch.

Ivo had insisted that Anna should stand just outside the first pillar, where she would be easy for him to spot. Harry would position himself just inside. Anna would then lead Ivo into the arch. When the contact was over, Anna and Ivo would leave as they'd entered and go their separate ways. Harry would exit on the Unter den Linden side. To any watcher, it would appear that only Anna and Ivo had met.

When Anna located Harry inside the portal, she held up her arms, as if inviting a pat-down. 'See? Clean,' she said. 'Do you want to check my undies for hidden recording equipment?'

'Very amusing,' Harry said. 'I'll take your word for it that they've been de-bugged.'

Anna threw him a look, and then grew serious. 'I've had a good look around,' she told him. 'There's a couple of Red Army trucks with soldiers in them on the Charlottenburger Chaussee, and a few guys with notebooks on the edge of the crowd, but that's about all. Looks like the Sovs are relaxed about all this.'

'You can't be privy to the actual conversation, Anna,' Harry said. 'You do understand that?'

She had expected as much. And if she was being honest with herself, she didn't much care. She was indifferent to Ivo's relentless pursuit of his own self-interest, except for where it had touched Bär, Antje and Marion. She didn't care a fig who else he betrayed, whose secrets he sold, whose trust he let slip through his fingers like so much dirt. There were no other lives – including her own – that required revenging. Only theirs.

'Where do you want me to wait, while you have your big boys' talk?'

'You don't need to go far. All I plan to do is hand over the down payment and set up a system for contacting him. We won't be raising our voices. A few feet away will be fine. Just mill around with the other protesters.'

'That's me all over,' Anna said. 'Always the wallflower.'

'I can believe a lot of things about you, Anna Cantrell,' Harry replied, 'but not that.' He glanced at his watch. 'You'd better take your position.'

Anna swept her hands through her hair and announced, 'Lights… camera… action!'

Harry shook his head in amused disbelief. 'Just remember your lines, and don't fall over the scenery. Isn't that what you show-business people say?'

She blew him a kiss, the way she'd seen actresses do with Rex when they'd come onto the set. Then she walked out of the arch and waited.

He appeared at her side silently and without warning, like a shadow cast by the parting of dark clouds. He was wearing a raincoat and a homburg hat, and he looked like the casting department's idea of the dangerous lover – brooding, intense, predatory.

When Anna heard his voice, at once familiar and repellently alien, she almost jumped out of her shoes.

'Hello, Anna. What a surprise to find you here.'

Like everything he had ever told her, that too was a lie, though in this instance she was complicit in the deceit. There was nothing she needed or wanted to say to him. It was too late now, anyway. The actors had hit their marks and the camera was rolling.

She led Ivo into the arch. He tilted his head and looked at Harry Taverner as if he recalled him from an agreeable holiday encounter but couldn't quite remember his name.

'Ah, the charming English fellow from the cell on Blaumannstrasse,' he said. 'We never did get to finish our conversation. Pity.'

'Perhaps this is the moment to put that right, Herr Wolff,' Harry said. 'Anna—'

Anna shrugged. 'I'll leave you two boys to catch up with each other,' she said.

She crossed to the far side of the roadway and stood against the wall of the portal. The surface was covered in graffiti, scrawled there three years ago by Red Army soldiers. She couldn't read it because it was in Cyrillic script. But she could sense the triumph, the ecstasy of revenge, in the deeply scored marks made by the tips of knives and bayonets. She tried to summon the same feelings inside herself, but they refused to come. There was, instead, only the cold acceptance of what had to be done if she was to go on living.

Anna let the protesters pass her as they headed towards the Tiergarten and the Soviet war memorial.

She didn't cast a single glance at Ivo, or Harry. She had cut them adrift, as if she were the sole survivor of a sinking ship and they were flotsam threatening to drag her down. Only when she'd reached the shore, exhausted from the swim, but alive, would she have time to pull thoughts for Harry from the wreckage washing up around her.

And then Ivo was beside her again. He said nothing as she walked with him out of the Brandenburg Gate. She stole a final brief look at him before they parted.

Still as handsome as the day you walked into the Red Panther, she thought. Still able to make ordinary mortals step aside simply by the power of your own self-belief. The star of the show. Stealing the scene. The rest of us nothing more to you than minor characters and supporting cast.

She knew she would never see him again. All that was left was to grieve over what he'd taken from her.

She found Tom Goodhew waiting at the war memorial. As he handed back her camera case he said, 'So come on, let me into the scoop. Who were they?'

'A couple of black marketeers,' Anna said.

Goodhew looked disappointed. 'The black market? That's old hat. You won't get a headline from that. Find someone in Berlin who *isn't* on the fiddle – now *that* would be newsworthy.'

Slinging the camera bag over her shoulder, Anna walked back through the Brandenburg Gate. Harry had gone. He'd promised to keep in touch, and that cheered her. Maybe there was a gleam of hope for them – if he didn't find out what she had planned.

But first there were things she had to attend to: there was a news story going on around her.

Without her camera Anna had felt unarmed and vulnerable; now she felt strong again. Unbeatable. From the moment Anna had first looked up from her pram at all those extraordinary characters peering in, from the first time she'd looked through the viewfinder of Rex's movie camera, she had learned how to be the eternal observer, always seeing but somehow always remote. Detached. Alone.

The mood of the rally had changed, Anna noticed. Between the Brandenburg Gate and the Red Army war memorial, a Social Democrat politician was rousing the crowd with a stirring speech about how their once great nation could never hope for rebirth while Soviet hands had its throat in a chokehold. The crowd was chanting to his lead, 'Russkies go home! Russkies go home!'

Banners and placards waved like the colours of an army awaiting the order to advance. Anna could see Russian soldiers jumping down from their trucks. They looked nervous now, their officers even more so. On both sides she spotted men with faces flushed in violent anticipation, spoiling for a fight. She sensed the rally was close to getting out of hand.

Anna worked the camera shutter instinctively, as always. She felt the crowd surge around her, carrying her forward like driftwood on a flood tide. She imagined she could look down deep into the water and see clearly; that her eyelids were a single shutter, and that when she blinked she would capture an image of the teeming life swimming beneath the surface.

Overhead, black clouds had gathered, threatening another downpour.

And that was when the first shots rang out. The sound of a volley – aimed above the protesters' heads – crackled around the Brandenburg Gate, echoing off the shell of the Hotel Adlon.

The crowd broke as if a hurricane had sprung from nowhere and scattered it. Protesters scrambled for the shelter of the Gate, spilling back into Unter den Linden. Red Army soldiers followed, striking out with their rifle butts – savage, indiscriminate attacks upon anyone they could reach. The protesters were mostly men, but Anna could see women and even a few children amongst the panicking crowd. Close by were a mother and her young daughter. As the shots rang out, the woman stumbled, dragging down the child.

Anna lifted her camera to take the shot. But her finger froze on the shutter button. In her mind, the child was Antje, and taking the picture would mean freezing her in the moment of death, fixing her fate in Anna's consciousness forever, so that Antje could never again be imagined as living, waiting to be found.

But then the mother was back on her feet, dragging the now wailing child after her towards the sanctuary of the Gate, both alive, both unharmed save for scraped knees and bruised elbows. Anna began to breathe again. Her soul returned to her body, bringing with it the prospect of a different future to the one she had just envisioned.

She heard a shout from close by. Turning, she saw a man with his arm raised. For an instant she thought he was giving the Nazi salute. But he was pointing at the very top of the Brandenburg Gate. All around her, faces lifted. Even those running for their lives looked up.

High up, beside the mound of battered concrete that had once been the goddess Victoria in her chariot, a boy of about Bär's age was pulling with all his might at the Soviet red flag that flew there. How he'd climbed up there, Anna couldn't begin to imagine. A great cheer went up. The protesters yelled encouragement. He tugged and tugged, determined to bring down the hated banner. Anna aimed the Leica and pressed the shutter button.

In the instant she heard the shutter whirr, the boy dropped to his knees and rolled sideways, a marionette whose strings had been cut. The sound of a single shot forced its way into Anna's brain like a needle. And just as she had with the running mother and daughter, Anna saw that it was her Bär lying motionless beneath the flailing hooves of Victoria's horses.

I've killed him, she thought. I've killed him with my camera. First I killed Marion. Then I killed Antje. And now I've killed Bär. I'm the guilty one. Just as Louisa Vogel said that day on the platform, when I told her about poor Luka: the price of the pictures I take – whether with my mind or my camera – is the death of those I love. And I must carry the guilt of it for the rest of my days.

As Anna stood motionless, staring at the top of the Brandenburg Gate, hoping against hope that the boy would rise and wave to show he was unharmed, it began to rain. She let the heavy drops soak her hair, trickle down inside the collar of her coat, touch her skin with cold wet tears. She barely noticed the shocked anger of the crowd, or the nervous way in which the Soviet soldiers brandished their weapons, fearful the protesters would turn on them. She heard only faintly the sound of more Red Army trucks arriving, and the orders barked in Russian as the men climbed down to disperse what remained of the crowd, putting up a cordon between the Soviet and Western sectors.

Three Red Army soldiers pushed past her, and for a moment she feared they would take her camera, smash it just as Manis Möller had. But they showed no interest in her. Instead, they hurried to the ruins of the buildings on either side of the Gate and began to work their way upwards to recover the body.

Slowly, the rain began to wash away Anna's self-recrimination. She felt the crushing weight of it leaving her body. And then, wet and shivering, she suddenly found herself clear eyed and certain of the truth. She was not the criminal; she was the witness. And she must not give up until retribution had been served.

Anna didn't wait for the soldiers to reach the top of the Brandenburg Gate. She lowered her eyes, feeling the rain and the tears stream down her cheeks. Head down, the camera bag held safely against her wet coat, she walked away at her own determined pace across the emptying Tiergarten. There was nothing she could do for the boy, just as she knew there was nothing she could do for Marion, Bär and Antje.

Nothing at all.

Except to take revenge.

There was no way Anna could risk entrusting the film to a commercial darkroom or to the developers at *Die Neue Zeitung,* the newspaper published by the US Information Control Division. She would have to do it herself.

The day after the rally, she purchased the chemicals and the equipment she required from a photography shop she frequented in Charlottenburg. From the same shop she rented a second-hand Zenith enlarger. At the Hotel Splendid, she sweet-talked the workmen into letting her borrow some red paint and a brush.

It was easy enough to turn her room into a makeshift darkroom – it still had the blackout curtains left over from the war. The hardest part was waiting for the red paint to dry on the light bulb hanging from the ceiling.

In her professional judgement, the photos she'd taken during the demonstration were satisfactory. Good, but not great. Only one had caught the death of the young demonstrator, and that was a little out of focus. His body, already on its knees, was barely visible against the concrete of the statue. She'd wire the better pictures to the bureau when she had a moment to spare.

The shots that mattered to Anna were the ones she hadn't taken.

There were five of these. In two of them, Tom Goodhew had been too far away to get a clear shot. In the third, the shoulder of a passing demonstrator half-obscured the target. On the fourth, the shutter had fired at the very instant the subject turned his head, capturing only a rear quarter shot of collar, hair and ear. *Could be anyone, m'lud.*

But the fifth shot was perfect: in frame, and in focus. And one photo was all Anna Cantrell needed.

The commander of the Soviet sector in Berlin was a congenial fellow whose avuncular face, bouffant silver hair and librarian's glasses made him look older than his forty-six years. The life and soul of every diplomatic party, he could drink the other commandants of the occupying powers under the table. The Berlin press corps loved him. But even they knew that beneath this charming exterior, General Alexander Kotikov was as hard and as ruthless as any granite-faced Red Army officer in the city.

Securing an interview with him had been easy: the Red Army press people were only too happy to agree to Anna's request, and Kotikov remembered her as a regular face at news conferences and functions around the city. Now she sat in a comfortable leather armchair on the other side of the largest desk in the *Kommandatura*, a desk on which sat enough telephones to equip the New York newsroom of Associated Press.

It hadn't been a particularly productive interview. Kotikov, resplendent in his Red Army uniform, had spent the last fifteen minutes berating the West. She knew it was fifteen minutes because she'd been glancing at the clock, set to Moscow time, which hung on the wall opposite the huge portrait of Secretary General Stalin. She had listened calmly to the usual tirade: America and its poodle Great Britain were the aggressors... the Soviet Union desired only peace, tranquillity and the fraternal brotherhood of working men and women everywhere... the USSR wasn't sealing off the city from the outside world... it wasn't interfering in German politics... it wasn't intimidating the other occupying powers. And if it was doing any of these things, that was only because the duplicitous West refused to acknowledge its sacrifices in defeating the fascists. And all this delivered while beaming at her like the Santa Claus at Macy's.

Anna waited patiently until the general had finished. Then Kotikov rose to his feet from behind the vast expanse of desktop and gave her a polite bow.

'Please report my words accurately, Miss Cantrell,' he said pleasantly, 'in the spirit of trust between our two great nations. It will be a first, I know, for a Western journalist to do so. But I live in hope.' He nodded to the smartly uniformed aide-de-camp waiting by the door. 'Captain Zhugansky will escort you out.'

'If I might ask one last question before I go, General,' Anna said, remaining resolutely in her seat.

Kotikov's silvery eyebrows arched, but he was too much a gentleman to look irritated. 'Briefly, please.'

Anna opened the envelope that had been lying on her lap throughout the interview. She drew out a single black and white photograph and laid it on the vast expanse of green leather that topped Kotikov's desk.

'Do you recognize the man on the left?' she asked.

Kotikov adjusted his glasses over his cherubic nose and peered at the print.

'He is familiar to me, yes.'

'I thought he would be. I understand he's a rising star in the Socialist Unity Party, the party Comrade Stalin would like to see running Eastern Germany. Knowing him as I do, I would also guess he's working for you in a less public capacity – either in intelligence, or in acquiring stolen art. Possibly both.'

The friendliness drained out of Kotikov's face. 'Is this some sort of crude attempt at blackmail, Miss Cantrell?' the general asked.

'Not at all. If fact, quite the opposite. I'm here to do you a favour, General.'

Anna reached across and tapped the photograph. 'The man pictured here beside him is an officer in the British intelligence service. His name is Harry Taverner. In this photograph, you can clearly see him handing Herr Wolff an envelope. It contains one thousand US dollars – a down payment on acquiring his services in the betrayal of your secrets to the West. Oh, and by the way – Ivo Wolff also used to be a member of the Nazi Party. He worked for Dr Joseph Goebbels.'

Kotikov sat back slowly in his seat. He lifted the photograph from the desk, studying it intently with moist, pale eyes that had lost every trace of bonhomie.

Anna rose from her chair and held out her hand for Kotikov to shake. But he was too busy studying the photo to notice.

Captain Zhugansky opened the door for her, his face frighteningly immobile.

God save us from handsome men in uniform, she thought. At least those without a heart.

She turned to look back at Kotikov. 'If he asks you why I did it, General,' she said, a sad smile playing on her lips, 'tell him it was for Marion.'

Twenty-Seven

The Berlin apartment. 1989

'After all you'd done for her – to blow your cover to the Russians like that,' Elly Taverner said.

She heard the faint sound of the old Weimar-era elevator cranking into life. It must be someone coming home after a night celebrating the border checkpoints opening, or a worker with a pre-dawn start. Watching Harry gaze at the bedroom ceiling, lost in his memories, she noticed how the white stubble on his chin aged him. It was quite thick now, like a winter hoar frost. If it wasn't for his dress shirt and trousers, she could mistake him for an old man down on his luck. But he was smiling. He'd probably still be smiling even when the cruel disease that had started to work its frightfulness on him finally stole away his memories for ever. She resisted taking him in her arms because she knew there was still more of his story that he wanted to give her.

'Oh, my cover was blown long before Anna Cantrell walked into General Kotikov's office,' he said, turning his face to her. 'If you cast your mind back, you'll remember how I told you that Anna and I bumped into each other in Paris, just before the city fell in June 1940. The fellow driving the jeep that day was

Donald Maclean. When he defected in 1951, the Service had to assume I'd been compromised for years. But even if I'd known then about her visit to the general, I honestly don't believe I'd have blamed her.'

'How did you find out about what she'd done?'

'From a Soviet defector who came across in the late fifties.'

'Dare I ask what happened to Ivo Wolff?'

'I'm sure you won't be surprised to learn that he went missing shortly after Anna handed over the photograph. Knowing the Soviets as we do, back to Moscow for a bullet in the back of the head in the Lubyanka, I imagine. Or, if he was lucky, a gulag. He could be in Siberia at this very moment, breaking rocks.'

Elly shook her head in astonishment. 'Well, you know what they say about a woman scorned.' She thought for a moment, then said, 'But that still leaves Bär and Antje unaccounted for. Did Anna ever find out what had happened to them?'

'As a matter of fact, she did.'

Elly closed her eyes in preparation for the news. 'I hardly dare ask,' she said. 'After all Anna's been through, if they're dead I think it's going to break my heart.'

'She'd certainly resigned herself to that possibility, otherwise I think she might not have acted as she did. She might have just put Ivo behind her and got on with her life.'

'So, what happened next?'

Harry held his hands together, palms open. He peered into them, as if about to read from an ancient book he had believed lost forever. 'In June, the Soviets launched their blockade. They sealed off the city entirely. We were all trapped – one hundred miles inside Soviet-occupied Germany. Only the three air corridors remained open; they didn't close those because they thought we'd take it as an act of war. Stalin was playing the game just as hard as he dared, but no further.

'We had over two million people in the Western sector. But the Soviets wouldn't let in so much as a tin of condensed milk. No food, no heating. Stalin thought we'd cave within a week. But we called his bluff. We began the airlift. Day and night, every couple of minutes, an aeroplane would fly in to unload: Tempelhof… Gatow… at Tagel they built the longest tarmac runway in Europe in just ninety days. Coal, flour, medicines, milk… you name it, we flew it in. The Americans even dropped candy bars on little parachutes made from handkerchiefs for the children who lined the fence by the runways.

'Anna and I rented a house on Lake Havel. We could barely sleep for the noise of aero engines. We were there until the blockade was lifted in '49, and for a while after.'

An understandable mistake, Elly thought. The lack of sleep must be getting to him. But his eyes seemed unwearied, filled with the brightness of youth again. 'Surely you mean *Louisa* and I?'

Harry gave her a direct look. 'No, darling. I meant exactly what I said.'

Elly's eyes widened. 'You old rogue, Daddy. You've never told me about this. I suppose I should have seen it coming. I hope it was before you and Mummy got together.'

'Of course it was, darling. And it can hardly come as a surprise to you – not after all I've told you.'

'Was this just a fling? Or was it serious? Something tells me you're going to say "very".'

'And you'd be right,' Harry said, a wistful gleam in his eyes. 'It was. *Very*. And there's something else you I need to tell you. You may find it a little hard.'

'After all I've heard?'

Harry drew a long, slow breath. 'Before we left the Lake Havel house, Anna fell pregnant.'

'Wait a moment,' Elly said, putting out a hand to brace herself against the quilt. '*Pregnant?* Am I about to discover I've had a half-sibling for nigh on forty years and never knew it?'

Harry's smile seemed to have arrived on his lips after a long journey from a distant place. 'If you put it that way, Puffin, I suppose you are.'

'Suppose? That's disturbingly vague for a distinguished former officer of our Service.'

'Then *yes*. Is that better?'

Elly frowned. The shock of Harry's words had snapped her out of her weariness, leaving her lightheaded and unsettled. 'I'm not sure,' she confessed. 'Does Mummy know about this?'

'I've told you before, Louisa knows everything. All of it. I've never hidden anything from your mother. Apart from work, of course.'

A dark foreboding struck Elly. She shivered, praying it was nothing more ominous than the effect of staying awake all night. 'Please don't tell me Anna and the child died in Berlin,' she said. 'Not after all she'd gone through. I feel as though I've come to know Anna Cantrell so well, I don't think I could bear to hear that.'

Harry patted her knee. He hadn't done that since she was a teenager. She realized how much she missed the reassurance of it. He looked at the portfolio case and Elly could see that it was almost empty. He reached over, pulled out a sheet of drawing paper and handed it to Elly.

The paper was cheap and yellowing. Sketched on it was a simple rural scene: three cows in a meadow beside a brook. It was executed in a child's hand, but a child with a clear artistic talent. Elly thought it might be a drawing Marion had made when she was young, or perhaps it was one of Anna's.

Then she saw the signature in the bottom right corner.

Twenty-Eight

Berlin. Lake Havel. Summer
Photo by Anna Cantrell. Rolleiflex Standard 621 camera.
Kodak 120 film. 1951

In her more poetic moments, Anna imagined her love affair with Harry Taverner as the blooming of a delicate, beautiful flower in an arid wasteland, though there was nothing remotely delicate about either of them. And when it rained – which it did often – Berlin's ruins became anything but arid. Sometimes, when they lay entwined in the bedroom of the neat little house they had taken on the edge of the lake, she would allow her mind to carry her back to her childhood in Hollywood. She would see herself as the heroine in one of Uncle László's silent movies: a princess with her chivalrous lover, imprisoned in a high tower on a mysterious island by a jealous king. Her baby girl, sleeping peacefully in her cot in the nursery, would grow up wise and beautiful, and reclaim the kingdom that was her birthright.

Anna had never thought of herself as a weaver of romantic tales. She put it down to all those times her young eyes had peered through the viewfinder of Rex's camera and seen laid out for her an astonishing, fabulous world – a world the young Anna had much preferred to the real one that existed beyond the lens, where castles were made of painted plywood and heroes lounged around the commissary truck and smoked cigars before getting back to the business of chivalry.

The airlift now seemed to Anna like ancient history. When she opened the nursery window, all she could hear was birdsong. Save for the occasional flight in and out of Gatow across the lake, the only shadows flitting across the surfaces of the Havel were those cast by summer clouds and geese on the wing. The skies were clear. The air smelt of pine resin. The sunlight off the water dazzled her.

Shading her eyes and leaning over the windowsill, she watched the early morning swimmers enjoying their exercise. A sailboat wheeled in the inlet, tilting as its canvas hungrily cupped the wind. If Harry had been there, he would have been giving his opinion of the skipper's boat-handling. But ten minutes before she had watched him depart on his commute in his government issue drab green Volkswagen to the *Kommandatura* at Dahlem, a forty-minute ride away across the Grunwald.

Her gaze dropped to the road that ran in front of the apartment block, and in that moment her heart sank: she had seen the *Deutsche Bundespost* mail boy approaching on his bicycle. The last time she'd received a telegram, it had informed her of Rex's death in Palermo.

The boy saw her at the window and raised his young, sun-browned face towards her, smiling.

Bär would be his age now, she realized. Turning from the window, Anna went down to meet him.

He's smiling, she thought. The telegram must contain good news.

That evening, when Harry returned home, Anna did not prevaricate.

'I have something to tell you, and I'm not sure you're going to like it,' she said, after she'd poured him a whisky and soda.

'Try me.'

'I've had a telegram from Headline.'

'Don't tell me – they want to make you bureau chief in New York.'

'That's a desk job. No, they want me to go to Hanoi.'

Harry didn't immediately respond, and Anna wondered if he'd heard her. He sloshed the whisky around his mouth as if he were in the dentist's chair as he considered what Anna had said. Then he set the tumbler down on the coffee table. He was frowning.

'They're not serious, surely? Don't they know you're a new mother? Besides, you've only just come back from Palermo and Rex's funeral.'

Anna gave him a guilty smile that told him all he needed to know. 'It's a once-in-a-lifetime opportunity, Harry. I could really make my name – get into the top rank alongside people like Marguerite Higgins, Martha Gellhorn, Clare Hollingworth…'

'Is this a permanent posting?' Harry asked.

'Heavens, no. The bureau chief in Hanoi has been called back to New York. He's going to set up some new outfit they're putting together – for television. They need someone temporarily, until a proper replacement can be found…'

'And our daughter? What about her?'

Anna looked as guilty as if she'd committed every misdemeanour and felony on the statute book, save perhaps littering. 'I *know*. I feel dreadful. I'm an awful mother, I get it. But she's only four months old, and it would only be for a few weeks – six, maybe seven at most. She'll hardly know I've gone,' she said, desperate to have his understanding, his acceptance. 'We can rehire Hannelore Lange, like we did when I went to Palermo.'

Harry nodded. He knew if he chose to fight, it would be a battle he could not possibly hope to win. And in his heart, he didn't want to. It was Anna's character that made her want to go. It was Anna's character he had fallen in love with.

'And if I said I didn't much fancy the idea of you going to a theatre of war?' he asked. Then he corrected himself. 'If I said *we* didn't...'

Anna remembered something she had said to him long ago, in the hills above the village where Marion had died, on the day Ivo took the children from her: *You know us Cantrells... No time for borders... We cross every last one we can find, if only for the excitement of what we'll discover on the other side...*

'Harry, I'm a photographer,' she announced in a firm, practical voice. 'It's what I was destined to be, from the moment Rex held me up to look through a viewfinder. It's who I am. I'm never going to become some traditional *haus-frau*, setting out the best cutlery when hubby's boss comes to supper. That's not *me*.'

Harry's smile was admiring and sad at the same time. 'It's good that a part of Marion still lives on.'

She kissed him. 'Just promise me you won't have run off with a handsome Sicilian waiter named Bruno by the time I get back.'

'I promise. It's the sort of thing that has the Service clutching its pearls.'

Relieved, Anna threw her arms around him. 'You're a darling. I couldn't do it without you.'

Harry sighed. 'Modern women, eh,' he said, lifting the whisky tumbler in salute. 'Is there no stopping them?'

Anna laid her head against his neck. 'I'll be back before the little one even knows I've gone,' she said.

The two envelopes arrived at the Havel house in the same mail delivery, two weeks to the day after Anna's departure. Because

Herr Taverner was at work, Hannelore Lange left them on the kitchen table until he returned.

'There's mail for you, Herr Taverner,' she said, when he walked in. 'I think one must be from Frau Anna.'

Noting the Hanoi postmark, Harry took it into the privacy of the bedroom and tore open the envelope. The paper inside was crisp, watermarked and expensive. Printed in copperplate at the top, Harry read:

Hôtel Metropole.

PLACE CHAVASSIEUX,
HANOÏ, INDOCHINE FRANÇAISE

Sinking onto the bed, he began to read the lines written beneath. He forced himself not to rush, savouring every moment as if he were consuming a meal prepared by the greatest chef alive, eager to catch every flavour.

My darling Harry,

Just when I thought my nerves had recovered from the noise of airplane engines in recent times… All the way from Paris to Hanoi in an Armée de l'Air C-47. My ears are ringing, and I can't hear myself think. We stopped at more places than the New York subway! I swear to God I could have gotten here faster by Greyhound bus.

But anyway, here I am, and the Metropole is very fine, though not as grand as the Adlon used to be. If you were here, I'd take you dancing.

I've had the introductory lecture from the press people. They say it's all very safe here. The French reckon they'll soon have the Viet Minh licked for good. The day after tomorrow, I'm going up country with a very pompous capitaine d'artillerie *who thinks he's Beau Geste. He has the most ridiculous moustache – it would make Groucho Marx jealous.*

Anyway, down to the bar now for a martini. After that, well, there's a rickshaw rank in the square and I quite fancy taking a ride and pretending I'm Princess Turandot. It's good to be in a city that still has all its walls and roofs.

I enclose a photo I persuaded the bellboy to take when I arrived: yours truly looking the worst for wear after the journey, and the nice driver they've given me, whose name is Thuan. He's going to look after me.

Kiss our little Sweet Pea for me and tell her Mama will be home before she knows it.

P.S. Marion was wrong about Englishmen.

Harry read the letter three times. Then, reluctantly, he laid it aside, went back to the kitchen and picked up the second envelope.

A stamped logo told him had come from the US Information Control Division office in Dahlem. It was twice the size of Anna's envelope, and thicker. Assuming it contained material related to her professional life – information she might need to know about before her return – Harry tore open the gummed flap.

Holding the envelope over the kitchen table, he shook it. Out fell a typed letter, and another envelope. Picking up the letter, Harry read the brief message.

Dear Miss Cantrell,

I am forwarding this to you, having received it from the picture editor at the Die Neue Zeitung. *It contains personal information I believe you will wish to receive. I am happy to be the bearer of good news, if that is what it turns out to be. Contacts like this are sadly rare.*

Please forgive the fact that the enclosed envelope has been opened. This was not the action of the newspaper, or this department. The blame lies with the GDR postal censors, who open all mail addressed to the Western sector.

Yours sincerely,

Robert S. Kippenbaxter,
Press Control Officer,
US Information Control Division Berlin.

The accompanying envelope contained three items which Harry spread out on the kitchen table. The largest was a half-page torn from the *Die Neue Zeitung*. He instantly recognized one of Anna photographs, a shot of soot-blackened labourers hauling sacks of coal out of an American C-54 Skymaster at Tegel airfield. It was one of the first images of the blockade that Anna had captured. Beneath it was a by-line: Anna Cantrell – Headline News Photos Inc.

Only slightly smaller than the page torn from the newspaper was a sketch, a landscape, of three cows in a meadow beside a stream. It was executed in a young, unpractised hand. Nevertheless, there was talent in the work. Accompanying the sketch was a letter, written, or so Harry assumed, by the same hand that had drawn the landscape. As he read the lines, his heart began to race.

My dearest Mamma,

I am in Briesen. Herr Schardt is my new papa and is very nice. So is Frau Schardt. They looked after us when Papa had us sent away from Berlin. Herr Schardt has a brother who got into trouble with the Russians for reading bad newspapers. But I saw one, and there was a photograph in it with your name underneath. So I wrote to the newspaper. I enclose the picture I saw.

Bär and I are well, and we thought you were in America because that is what Papa said. I don't know where Papa is. We are glad there are no more bombs. I hope you receive this letter safely. I also hope you like my drawing of Gretel. She is the cow on the left. The other two are called Ursula and Ottie. I look after them when I come home from school.

Please reply to Fräulein Antje, at Hof Schardt, Briesen, Deutsche Demokratische Republik.

Bär sends his love. We miss you.

Your loving daughter,

Antje

Harry let the sheet of paper fall to the kitchen table. He was out of his seat before it landed.

'I've got to go out!' he shouted to Hannelore Lange, who was in the nursery. 'I'll phone from the *Kommandatura*.'

He didn't wait for a reply.

The published top speed of Harry Taverner's government Volkswagen was around ninety-seven kilometres per hour. With his foot rammed down hard on the accelerator pedal, he managed to push it to over a hundred. He was spotted by several *Autobahnpolizei* and British Military Police patrols, but with the drab olive paintwork and the official registration plates, they assumed the vehicle was on official business and let it pass. He reached the *Kommandatura* in record time.

'Hanoi?' said the Service's night telephone operator.

'To the Hotel Metropole, please.'

'You realize it's not going to be secure.'

'That doesn't matter.'

'It could take hours to set up the line through the international exchanges.'

'I can wait.'

Harry went to his office and prepared for his vigil. He took off his shoes and socks, sat in his chair and rested his feet on an upturned wastepaper basket that had a label stuck to it demanding: *All staff must ensure empty bins before leaving. Under no circumstances may documents of any grade be left overnight.* However long he had to wait for a connection, it would be faster than sending a telegram. And if Anna had left Hanoi, it might be days before she returned. He didn't care about making use of the Service's phone lines. Head Office would undoubtedly complain; now that there was no war on, every paperclip had to be accounted for in triplicate. He'd happily pay the cost. There again, he might just raise the subject of the head of station's gin supply that somehow never appeared in the monthly returns.

It was almost midnight when the phone on his desk rang; five in the morning Hanoi time. He imagined Anna asleep, her hair, splayed on the pillow, catching the light of the sunrise through a window that looked out onto rickshaws and flame trees.

Even then he had to endure the tease of clicks, howls and static down the line, accompanied by more than one apologetic 'I will attempt the connection again…'

Eventually he heard her voice, so faint that she might as well have been speaking from outer space. 'Hello, room eighteen. Hello?'

'Anna, it's me – the other Englishman.'

For a moment there was silence, and he feared the line had been cut again. But then, almost as if she were in the office next door, he heard her, loud and clear, the thrill in her voice unmistakable, even across the gulf between them. 'Harry! Harry! Oh, Harry!'

The Berlin apartment. 1989

Elly Taverner held up Antje's drawing before her, letting her eyes linger on the simply drawn, confident lines. The pencil work looked light enough, but the emotional weight the sketch carried made the flimsy paper feel as heavy in her hands as a centuries-old, priceless manuscript.

'She has Marion's talent, doesn't she?' she said.

Harry nodded.

Laying the drawing down on the quilt, Elly said, 'I can't understand how Frau Schardt could have lied to Anna like that, the day she and Luka went to Briesen in search of the children.'

'Don't judge the Schardts too harshly,' Harry said with a sad, sympathetic smile. 'As the war drew to a close, and in the months afterwards, many bereaved couples in Germany did exactly what they did: offered shelter to evacuees from the bombing, or orphans whose parents had been killed. Later, when the parents of those children couldn't be found, they adopted them, often unofficially. Sometimes, they hid the children's true identities even from the authorities, because they didn't want to give them up.

And occasionally, the children themselves lied about their own identities, because they wanted to stay with their new guardians. Johann and Elke Schardt were no different. They'd lost a daughter in Dresden and had a son killed in France on D-Day. So, in the absence of either Anna or Ivo, they appointed themselves the children's guardians. Remember, Gertrude Steigler had been Ivo's mistress, so it's hardly surprising they believed their niece when she told them what Ivo had told *her*: that Anna Cantrell was the worst mother in the world. That's why Frau Schardt lied to Anna the day she and Luka Vogel came to the village. As for Bär and Antje, all they knew was that their father had vanished, and their mother was on the other side of the Atlantic. They were simply grateful to have a safe home and loving guardians.'

'Anna must have been so happy to get your phone call,' Elly said. 'When was she finally reunited with them?' She was looking so intently at her father that she couldn't help noticing how suddenly the light in his eyes went out, like a lamp in a power cut.

'Do you remember when you were fourteen?' he asked. 'Mummy and I took you to see *As You Like It* at the Royal Shakespeare Theatre in Stratford.'

Elly didn't much care for Harry's sudden change of direction. She wondered if it heralded one of his bouts of confusion. But what really troubled her, and made her feel like a selfish bitch, was the thought he might not be able to finish his story.

'Remember it?' she said, trying to sound light-hearted. 'It's scorched on my memory. It was the year I decided I looked like a horse and no boy would ever fancy me.'

'When we got home, you learned the Seven Ages of Man speech,' he reminded her. 'We couldn't stop you reciting it. You drove us both mad.'

Elly took up his cue.

'"All the world's a stage, and all the men and women merely players..."'

'Exactly. And I'm sure you won't have forgotten what happens in the seventh age.'

Elly bit her lower lip. She wondered if she could bear to speak the words he was waiting to hear, because something seemed to have lodged in her throat and for a moment she couldn't make her mouth work.

'"Last scene of all, that ends this strange eventual history, is second childishness and mere oblivion. Sans teeth, sans eyes, sans taste, sans everything."'

Harry nodded, and Elly knew he'd understood what it had cost her to recite the words.

'And that's the way I'm heading, Puffin,' he said gently. 'No point in dodging the issue. Not my style. So, it's time for you to know how all this ends.'

Reaching into the portfolio case, he drew out the last sheet, spreading it carefully on the quilt as if it were a piece of the finest silk, an heirloom that had lasted centuries.

It was a yellowing page from an English-language newspaper, though which one wasn't clear. The straight creases told Elly it had been lovingly opened and folded many times since it ran off the press. Much of the page was taken up with a photograph. The headline above burned into Elly's heart like a welding torch:

ANGLO-AMERICAN REPORTER
KILLED IN INDOCHINA

Harry's voice, though he was sitting barely two feet from her, reached Elly's ears like a plaintive requiem, sung from far away and long ago.

'From what I understand, after my call Anna couldn't go back to sleep. She was so happy. Presumably she showered and had breakfast. Maybe she went for that ride in a rickshaw, I don't know. Anyway, her driver, Thuan, picked her up at nine. They were due to visit a French base on the Hanoi-Haphong road. On the way, they ran over a Viet Minh landmine. Anna died instantly; Thuan lost a leg. I feel like the worst bastard on earth when I wish it had been the other way around. But I take comfort in the fact that Anna wouldn't have known a thing. I like to think her last thoughts before it all went dark were about holding Bär and Antje in her arms again.'

Elly heard all this and yet heard none of it. She could not tear her eyes away from the photograph of Anna Cantrell.

'It's the picture she told me about in her letter,' Harry said, his voice now barely louder to her than the sound of waves breaking on an empty beach. 'The one the bellboy took of her and Thuan, when she arrived at the Hotel Metropole.'

Elly let the image flow into her soul: the balcony wall of a smart hotel room, the white louvres of the floor to ceiling window shutters folded aside; the net drapes caught by a sudden cooling breeze from the square beyond; a gap-toothed Thuan grinning self-consciously…

And a woman perhaps three years younger than Elly was now. A tall, slender woman in pale slacks and a white shirt, a conical sunhat recently bought at the airport tucked under one arm. A woman looking into the camera lens as if she were greeting an old friend at the end of a long and arduous journey.

Elly sensed the bed she was sitting on lose its shape and form, its solidity. The room swayed around her. All sense of who she was, all the assumptions of her life so far – from her earliest memories till the moment ago when her father had spread this new life out before her – drained away like water between her fingers. This wasn't a photograph she was looking at – it was a mirror. If she smiled, the woman looking back at her would smile too. If she wept now, as she thought she might, she would see tears flowing from this woman's eyes. If she touched her cheek, it would be this woman's flesh she felt against her fingertips.

Elly Taverner was looking at herself.

Twenty-Nine

There was no space in Elly Taverner's thoughts for anything beyond the implications contained in that single photograph. Berlin no longer existed for her. If her life and everything she had believed about herself could be swept away by a single image, then why not a whole city?

And yet she felt a gratifying surge of pride, a sense of having finally arrived at a place long sought but never thought reachable. As she laid the torn page down on the bed, she saw her hands were trembling.

'It can't be true,' she said, her voice faltering. 'I've seen my birth certificate. Mummy's name is on it – Louisa's name is on it.'

The answer came to her even as she stared accusingly at her father: a Service forger, doing an off-the-books favour for a friend. She began to laugh, a slow, self-accusing hiccup. 'Of course! I see it now. I remember you telling me, years ago, that you and Mummy had me a year or two before you were married. I always thought how rebellious and bohemian that was, given it was the fifties.' She shook her head. 'How could you have kept this from me for so long?'

Harry's eyes were brimming. Elly could see the guilt in them, but also relief, as if he'd woken up pain-free after a long illness. 'I've wanted to. Every day of my life since then, I've wanted you to know,' he said. 'But I stayed silent for Louisa's sake, because of how she still felt about Anna and Luka. I did what she asked of me – never to mention it.' He shrugged. 'I love her. What else was I to do?'

Elly cupped her face in her hands. Even the familiar word she had used since she first learned to speak could no longer be trusted. She let out a brittle laugh. '*Mummy!* Do I even call her that now?'

'I think it would break her heart if you didn't. It would certainly break mine.'

'You've lied to me, both of you, all these years…'

'I know it's little consolation,' Harry said, looking penitent, 'but we're by no means the first couple to keep a family secret hidden for too long.'

Elly tried really hard to be angry. But she couldn't manage it. The spark just wouldn't catch. She kept glancing at the picture of Anna Cantrell, and, when she did, she felt Anna's defiant spirit enter her, bringing with it a pride and a courage that was invigorating, uplifting. It banished her exhaustion and made her heart sing. And there was someone else's spirit she sensed, following on from Anna's – Marion's.

'You can hate me for it, if you want,' Harry was saying. 'But, please, not Louisa. It's a rare soul who can despise their husband's ex-lover but adore the child they had together.'

Elly glanced at the phone on the bedside table. 'I even thought of calling her tonight, in New York, to tell her about your little episode. Does she know what you were planning to do?'

'We discussed it before she left. She agreed it was time.'

Elly slowly shook her head. 'What am I going to say to her when she comes back?'

'You'll know what to do. She's ready. She understands now.'

Elly picked up the sheet of newsprint again. She studied Anna's photo again for a few moments. It felt like looking at a picture of an old friend. 'What I don't understand is, why didn't you just come out with it when we sat down together tonight. Why didn't you say, "Eleanora, I've got something important to tell you. Louisa isn't your mother"? I'm a grown woman, I could have handled it.'

Harry's smile was the sort of smile Elly remembered from her childhood. It was paternal and compassionate. It made her feel safe.

'Because you had to know what manner of woman Anna Cantrell really was,' he said. 'I needed you to know her story without judging her, to understand what she'd gone through, how she'd triumphed. Call it selfish, but I needed you to see her the way I remember her now, so that when my memories of her die – which I fear they will shortly do – at least they will live on in you.'

Harry leaned across and took Elly in his arms. She let herself sink against his chest, as she had done when she was little.

'You're Rex Cantrell's granddaughter,' he said gently into her hair. 'At the moment, you're the last frame on the reel.'

They took the old elevator down to the ground floor and crossed the courtyard. The dawn light had yet to penetrate the towering prison-grey walls of the apartment block. It was only when they stepped out into the street that the new day presented itself, wintery and washed of colour. The windows of Elly's car were misted up, a film of moisture on the coachwork.

'We'll have breakfast at the Café Adler by Checkpoint Charlie,' she said, as she swung the car out into the traffic. 'Then I want you to stay there until I get back from my meeting. I'll phone Bonn and tell them I need to take compassionate leave, at least until Louisa gets home.'

The clock on the dashboard told her she might just have time to return to the hotel and fix her make-up. The night without sleep would still show, and the men around the table at her scheduled meeting with the *Bundesministerium* would doubtless jump to the wrong conclusion.

Let them, she told herself. I couldn't care less.

Harry sat quietly in the car, his head jerking forward occasionally as sleep tried to catch him. He had shaved and swapped his dress trousers and shirt for something more casual. He wore his warm Loden overcoat as defence against the early morning chill. He looked to Elly like a man at peace.

They found an underground car park and walked to the café. It was busy with morning customers, but they found a seat by the window looking out onto Friedrichstrasse. Already a crowd had gathered. Trabant cars were coming through almost nose to tail from the Soviet zone. People were standing on the Wall, just as they had the night before.

'It looks as if it's permanent – the lifting of exit restrictions,' Elly said. A thought struck her. 'Did you ever meet them: Bär and Antje? It's hard to imagine them now, in their fifties – the half-siblings I never knew I had.'

'I couldn't,' Harry said. 'The year Donald Maclean defected was the year you were born, and the year Antje's envelope arrived at the Havel apartment. The Service had to assume he'd blown my cover to the Soviets. They couldn't risk letting me run around in East Germany. That was the end of my field work. But we keep in contact, every now and then.'

Elly gazed into her espresso. 'I could drive you across to the Adlon,' she said. 'I've got diplomatic identity, and you're not employed by Her Majesty's Government any more.'

Harry unwrapped a sugar cube and dropped it into his cup.

There was a note of resignation in his voice. 'No point, I'm afraid,' he said. 'The East Germans pulled the hotel down a few years ago.'

'But that didn't stop you trying to find it again, last night, did it?' Elly said, laying her hand on his. 'And I'm so glad that you did.'

'Maybe they'll rebuild it. Then I can take you dancing there. After all, I still have the reservation card.'

From outside in the street a chorus of car horns sounded. Harry looked up. A bright green Trabant was pulling away from the checkpoint. The windows were down, and the people inside had their heads out, grinning, staring at the well-stocked shop windows, waving at passers-by. The car gave a smoky hiccup and rattled off down Friedrichstrasse.

Before Harry Taverner could return to his coffee, another took its place.

'Unstoppable,' he said quietly.

But whether he was speaking of the traffic coming through the Wall, or the woman from his memory, Elly couldn't tell.

Galerie Louisa Vogel

is proud to welcome you to:

THROUGH THE EYES OF TWO WOMEN

1915 – 1952

A collection of photographs and paintings by

ANNA CANTRELL

&

MARION BAUER

Curated by Eleanora Taverner

Complimentary catalogue

Acknowledgements

The genesis for this story began more than thirty years ago, on 11 November 1989. I was then a pilot, working for the now long-defunct British Island Airways. The Berlin Wall was coming down and ITN hired one of our airliners to carry Trevor McDonald, Jon Snow and their television team to present *News at Ten* from Berlin. I was called out to make up the crew that was to fly them there.

We didn't get airborne until after midnight – the three air corridors into East Germany were still then in operation, and we had to await permission from the Four Powers: the UK, America, France and the Soviet Union. But eventually we landed and went to our hotel. Although we'd been up all night, the flight crew all wanted to take the opportunity of going down to Checkpoint Charlie to be witnesses to history in the making. Changing out of my uniform, I happened to look out of the window and down into the hotel car park. A shiny Mercedes pulled up, and a moment later a drab green Trabant car from the East parked alongside. The occupants of each car got out and embraced. They clearly hadn't seen each other for years, possibly since the Wall went up in 1961. It was that small, so very personal reunification that gave me the idea to one day write what has become *Berlin Duet.*

While I have done my best to stay true to historical facts, the rally at the Brandenburg Gate described in Chapter Twenty-Six is fictitious. Although the rally and the shooting of the young lad by the Russians did happen, both events occurred later that year. I have brought forward my version in the interests of narrative pace.

My deepest thanks are due to Sarah de Souza, Sarah Hodgson and everyone at Corvus; to my agent, Jane Judd; and to Belinda Jones, whose copyediting and sound advice has made it a better book. Any howlers that remain are mine, and mine alone.

I must also thank Marcus Benhaimi of the German Bundesarchiv for his advice on German post-war tracing organizations; Rene Peschke and Georg Sauer of Wiener Linien for their glimpses of taking a tram in 1930s Vienna; Christine Bosch for preventing me murdering the German language; and Rabbi Barry Axler for being able to make a whole room smile simply by his presence, and for his sound counsel and forbearance in answering my often far too crass questions.

Finally, for her support and forbearance, I owe my wife Jane a debt I will never be able to repay in full. At least this time she's only had to wait for me to get back from the 1940s, not the 1590s.